**Praise for #1 *New York Times* and *USA TODAY*
bestselling author**

NORA ROBERTS

"Roberts is indeed a word artist, painting her story
and her characters with vitality and verve."
—*Los Angeles Daily News*

"Roberts' bestselling novels are some of the best in
the romance genre. They are thoughtfully plotted,
well-written stories featuring fascinating characters."
—*USA TODAY*

"With clear-eyed, concise vision
and a sure pen, Roberts nails her characters
and settings with awesome precision, drawing readers
into a vividly rendered world of family-centered
warmth and unquestionable magic."
—*Library Journal*

"Roberts has a warm feel for her characters
and an eye for the evocative detail."
—*Chicago Tribune*

"Nora Roberts is among the best."
—*The Washington Post Book World*

Dear Reader,

What is happiness? Vanessa Sexton thought she knew—it was becoming a renowned and successful pianist. But once she achieved that goal, she realized that her life was lonely and cold. So she decided to take a break and go home. To the house she hadn't lived in since she'd left to start her career at sixteen. To the mother she hadn't spoken to since. And to the man with whom she has some *Unfinished Business*. And along the way, she found that happiness was following her heart.

What is a hero? Nine-year-old Radley Wallace doesn't even have to think—Commander Zark, Defender of the Universe, Leader of Perth and star of Rad's favorite comic book. But when he meets Zark's creator, Mitch Dempsey, Rad comes to understand that a true hero is someone who spends time with him, who loves him...and his mother. If only he can get Hester to see that Mitch is her *Local Hero*.

Don't miss these two classic tales of hope, healing and love. Enjoy.

The Editors,

Silhouette Books

NORA ROBERTS

Perfect Harmony

Silhouette® Books

Published by Silhouette Books

America's Publisher of Contemporary Romance

SILHOUETTE BOOKS

Recycling programs
for this product may
not exist in your area.

PERFECT HARMONY

ISBN-13: 978-0-373-28137-4

Copyright © 2011 by Harlequin Books S.A.

The publisher acknowledges the copyright holder
of the individual works as follows:

UNFINISHED BUSINESS
Copyright © 1992 by Nora Roberts

LOCAL HERO
Copyright © 1988 by Nora Roberts

CONTENTS

UNFINISHED BUSINESS

For Laura Sparrow—
old friends are the best friends.

Chapter 1

What am I doing here?

The question rolled around in Vanessa's mind as she drove down Main Street. The sleepy town of Hyattown had changed very little in twelve years. It was still tucked in the foothills of Maryland's Blue Ridge Mountains, surrounded by rolling farmland and thick woods. Apple orchards and dairy cows encroached as close as the town limits, and here, inside those limits, there were no stoplights, no office buildings, no hum of traffic.

Here there were sturdy old houses and unfenced yards, children playing and laundry flapping on lines. It was, Vanessa thought with both relief and surprise, exactly as she had left it. The sidewalks were still bumpy and cracked, the concrete undermined by the roots of towering oaks that were just beginning to green. Forsythia were spilling their yellow blooms, and azaleas held just the hint of the riotous color to come. Crocuses, those vanguards of spring, had been overshadowed by spears of daffodils and early tulips. People continued, as they had in her childhood, to fuss with their lawns and gardens on a Saturday afternoon.

Some glanced up, perhaps surprised and vaguely interested to see an unfamiliar car drive by. Occasionally someone waved—out of habit, not because they recognized her. Then they bent to their planting or mowing again. Through her open window Vanessa caught the scent of freshly cut grass, of hyacinths and earth newly turned. She could hear the buzzing of power mowers, the barking of a dog, the shouts and laughter of children at play.

Two old men in fielders' caps, checked shirts and work pants stood in front of the town bank gossiping. A pack of young boys puffed up the slope of the road on their bikes. Probably on their way to Lester's Store for cold drinks or candy. She'd strained up that same hill to that same destination countless times. A hundred years ago, she thought, and felt the all-too-familiar clutching in her stomach.

What am I doing here? she thought again, reaching for the roll of antacids in her purse. Unlike the town, she had changed. Sometimes she hardly recognized herself.

She wanted to believe she was doing the right thing. Coming back. Not home, she mused. She had no idea if this was home. Or even if she wanted it to be.

She'd been barely sixteen when she'd left—when her father had taken her from these quiet streets on an odyssey of cities, practice sessions and performances. New York, Chicago, Los Angeles and London, Paris, Bonn,

Madrid. It had been exciting, a roller coaster of sights and sounds. And, most of all, music.

By the age of twenty, through her father's drive and her talent, she had become one of the youngest and most successful concert pianists in the country. She had won the prestigious Van Cliburn Competition at the tender age of eighteen, over competitors ten years her senior. She had played for royalty and dined with presidents. She had, in her single-minded pursuit of her career, earned a reputation as a brilliant and temperamental artist. The coolly sexy, passionately driven Vanessa Sexton.

Now, at twenty-eight, she was coming back to the home of her childhood, and to the mother she hadn't seen in twelve years.

The burning in her stomach as she pulled up to the curb was so familiar she barely noticed it. Like the town that surrounded it, the home of her youth was much the same as when she'd left it. The sturdy brick had weathered well, and the shutters were freshly painted a deep, warm blue. Along the stone wall that rose above the sidewalk were bushy peonies that would wait another month or more to bloom. Azaleas, in bud, were grouped around the foundation.

Vanessa sat, hands clutching the wheel, fighting off a desperate need to drive on. Drive away. She had already done too much on impulse. She'd bought the Mercedes convertible, driven up from her last booking in D.C., refused dozens of offers for engagements. All on impulse. Throughout her adult life, her time had been meticulously scheduled, her actions carefully executed, and only after all consequences had been considered. Though impulsive by nature, she had learned the importance of an ordered life. Coming here, awakening old hurts and old memories, wasn't part of that order.

Yet if she turned away now, ran away now, she would never have the answers to her questions, questions even she didn't understand.

Deliberately not giving herself any more time to think, she got out of the car and went to the trunk for her suitcases. She didn't have to stay if she was uncomfortable, she reminded herself. She was free to go anywhere. She was an adult, a well-traveled one who was financially secure. Her home, if she chose to make one, could be anywhere in the world. Since her father's death six months before, she'd had no ties.

Yet it was here she had come. And it was here she needed to be—at least until her questions were answered.

She crossed the sidewalk and climbed the five concrete steps. Despite the trip-hammer beating of her heart, she held herself straight. Her father had never permitted slumped shoulders. The presentation of self was as important as the presentation of music. Chin up, shoulders straight, she started up the walk.

When the door opened, she stopped, as if her feet were rooted in the ground. She stood frozen as her mother stepped onto the porch.

Images, dozens of them, raced into her mind. Of herself on the first day of school, rushing up those steps full of pride, to see her mother standing at the door. Sniffling as she limped up the walk after falling off her bike, her mother there to clean up the scrapes and kiss away the hurt. All but dancing onto the porch after her first kiss. And her mother, a woman's knowledge in her eyes, struggling not to ask any questions.

Then there had been the very last time she had stood

here. But she had been walking away from the house, not toward it. And her mother hadn't been on the porch waving goodbye.

"Vanessa."

Loretta Sexton stood twisting her hands. There was no gray in her dark chestnut hair. It was shorter than Vanessa remembered, and fluffed around a face that showed very few lines. A rounder face, softer, than Vanessa recalled. She seemed smaller somehow. Not shrunken, but more compact, fitter, younger. Vanessa had a flash of her father. Thin, too thin, pale, old.

Loretta wanted to run to her daughter, but she couldn't. The woman standing on the walk wasn't the girl she had lost and longed for. She looks like me, she thought, battling back tears. Stronger, more sure, but so much like me.

Bracing herself, as she had countless times before stepping onto a stage, Vanessa continued up the walk, up the creaking wooden steps, to stand in front of her mother. They were nearly the same height. That was something that jolted them both. Their eyes, the same misty shade of green, held steady.

They stood, only a foot apart. But there was no embrace.

"I appreciate you letting me come." Vanessa hated the stiffness she heard in her own voice.

"You're always welcome here." Loretta cleared her throat, cleared it of the rush of emotional words. "I was sorry to hear about your father."

"Thank you. I'm glad to see you're looking well."

"I…" What could she say? What could she possibly say that could make up for twelve lost years? "Did you… run into much traffic on the way up?"

"No. Not after I got out of Washington. It was a pleasant ride."

"Still, you must be tired after the drive. Come in and sit down."

She had remodeled, Vanessa thought foolishly as she followed her mother inside. The rooms were lighter, airier, than she remembered. The imposing home she remembered had become cozy. Dark, formal wallpaper had been replaced by warm pastels. Carpeting had been ripped up to reveal buffed pine floors that were accented by colorful area rugs. There were antiques, lovingly restored, and there was the scent of fresh flowers. It was the home of a woman, she realized. A woman of taste and means.

"You'd probably like to go upstairs first and unpack." Loretta stopped at the stairs, clutching the newel. "Unless you're hungry."

"No, I'm not hungry."

With a nod, Loretta started up the stairs. "I thought you'd like your old room." She pressed her lips together as she reached the landing. "I've redecorated a bit."

"So I see." Vanessa's voice was carefully neutral.

"You still have a view of the backyard."

"I'm sure it's fine."

Loretta opened a door, and Vanessa followed her inside.

There were no fussily dressed dolls or grinning stuffed animals. There were no posters tacked on the walls, no carefully framed awards and certificates. Gone was the narrow bed she had once dreamed in, and the desk where she had fretted over French verbs and geometry. It was no longer a room for a girl. It was a room for a guest.

The walls were ivory, trimmed in warm green. Pretty

priscillas hung over the windows. There was a four-poster bed, draped with a watercolor quilt and plumped with pillows. A glass vase of freesias sat on an elegant Queen Anne desk. The scent of potpourri wafted from a bowl on the bureau.

Nervous, Loretta walked through the room, twitching at the quilt, brushing imaginary dust from the dresser. "I hope you're comfortable here. If there's anything you need, you just have to ask."

Vanessa felt as if she were checking into an elegant and exclusive hotel. "It's a lovely room. I'll be fine, thank you."

"Good." Loretta clasped her hands together again. How she longed to touch. To hold. "Would you like me to help you unpack?"

"No." The refusal came too quickly. Vanessa struggled with a smile. "I can manage."

"All right. The bath is just—"

"I remember."

Loretta stopped short, looked helplessly out the window. "Of course. I'll be downstairs if you want anything." Giving in to her need, she cupped Vanessa's face in her hands. "Welcome home." She left quickly, shutting the door behind her.

Alone, Vanessa sat on the bed. Her stomach muscles were like hot, knotted ropes. She pressed a hand against her midsection, studying this room that had once been hers. How could the town have seemed so unchanged, and this room, her room, be so different? Perhaps it was the same with people. They might look familiar on the outside, but inside they were strangers.

As she was.

How different was she from the girl who had once

lived here? Would she recognize herself? Would she want to?

She rose to stand in front of the cheval glass in the corner. The face and form were familiar. She had examined herself carefully before each concert to be certain her appearance was perfect. That was expected. Her hair was to be groomed—swept up or back, never loose—her face made up for the stage, but never heavily, her costume subtle and elegant. That was the image of Vanessa Sexton.

Her hair was a bit windblown now, but there was no one to see or judge. It was the same deep chestnut as her mother's. Longer, though, sweeping her shoulders from a side part, it could catch fire from the sun or gleam deep and rich in moonlight. There was some fatigue around her eyes, but there was nothing unusual in that. She'd been very careful with her makeup that morning, so there was subtle color along her high cheekbones, a hint of it over her full, serious mouth. She wore a suit in icy pink with a short, snug jacket and a full skirt. The waistband was a bit loose, but then, her appetite hadn't been good.

And all this was still just image, she thought. The confident, poised and assured adult. She wished she could turn back the clock so that she could see herself as she'd been at sixteen. Full of hope, despite the strain that had clouded the household. Full of dreams and music.

With a sigh, she turned away to unpack.

When she was a child, it had seemed natural to use her room as a sanctuary. After rearranging her clothes for the third time, Vanessa reminded herself that she was no longer a child. Hadn't she come to find the bond she had lost with her mother? She couldn't find it if she sat alone in her room and brooded.

As she came downstairs, Vanessa heard the low sound of a radio coming from the back of the house. From the kitchen, she remembered. Her mother had always preferred popular music to the classics, and that had always irritated Vanessa's father. It was an old Presley ballad now—rich and lonely. Moving toward the sound, she stopped in the doorway of what had always been the music room.

The old grand piano that had been crowded in there was gone. So was the huge, heavy cabinet that had held reams and reams of sheet music. Now there were small, fragile-looking chairs with needlepoint cushions. A beautiful old tea caddy sat in a corner. On it was a bowl filled with some thriving leafy green plant. There were watercolors in narrow frames on the walls, and there was a curvy Victorian sofa in front of the twin windows.

All had been arranged around a trim, exquisite rosewood spinet. Unable to resist, Vanessa crossed to it. Lightly, quietly, only for herself, she played the first few chords of a Chopin étude. The action was so stiff that she understood the piano was new. Had her mother bought it after she'd received the letter telling her that her daughter was coming back? Was this a gesture, an attempt to reach across the gap of twelve years?

It couldn't be so simple, Vanessa thought, rubbing at the beginnings of a headache behind her eyes. They both had to know that.

She turned her back on the piano and walked to the kitchen.

Loretta was there, putting the finishing touches on a salad she'd arranged in a pale green bowl. Her mother had always liked pretty things, Vanessa remembered. Delicate, fragile things. Those leanings showed now in the lacy place mats on the table, the pale rose sugar bowl, the collection of Depression glass on an open shelf. She had opened the window, and a fragrant spring breeze ruffled the sheer curtains over the sink.

When she turned, Vanessa saw that her eyes were red, but she smiled, and her voice was clear. "I know you said you weren't hungry, but I thought you might like a little salad and some iced tea."

Vanessa managed an answering smile. "Thank you. The house looks lovely. It seems bigger somehow. I'd always heard that things shrunk as you got older."

Loretta turned off the radio. Vanessa regretted the gesture, as it meant they were left with only themselves to fill the silence. "There were too many dark colors before," Loretta told her. "And too much heavy furniture. At times I used to feel as though the furniture was lurking over me, waiting to push me out of a room." She caught herself, uneasy and embarrassed. "I saved some of the pieces, a few that were your grandmother's. They're stored in the attic. I thought someday you might want them."

"Maybe someday," Vanessa said, because it was easier. She sat down as her mother served the colorful salad. "What did you do with the piano?"

"I sold it." Loretta reached for the pitcher of tea. "Years ago. It seemed foolish to keep it when there was no one to play it. And I'd always hated it." She caught herself again, set the pitcher down. "I'm sorry."

"No need. I understand."

"No, I don't think you do." Loretta gave her a long, searching look. "I don't think you can."

Vanessa wasn't ready to dig too deep. She picked up her fork and said nothing.

"I hope the spinet is all right. I don't know very much about instruments."

"It's a beautiful instrument."

"The man who sold it to me told me it was top-of-the-line. I know you need to practice, so I thought... In any case, if it doesn't suit, you've only to—"

"It's fine." They ate in silence until Vanessa fell back on manners. "The town looks very much the same," she began, in a light, polite voice. "Does Mrs. Gaynor still live on the corner?"

"Oh yes." Relieved, Loretta began to chatter. "She's nearly eighty now, and still walks every day, rain or shine, to the post office to get her mail. The Breckenridges moved away, oh, about five years ago. Went south. A nice family bought their house. Three children. The youngest just started school this year. He's a pistol. And the Hawbaker boy, Rick, you remember? You used to baby-sit for him."

"I remember being paid a dollar an hour to be driven crazy by a little monster with buckteeth and a slingshot."

"That's the one." Loretta laughed. It was a sound, Vanessa realized, that she'd remembered all through the years. "He's in college now, on a scholarship."

"Hard to believe."

"He came to see me when he was home last Christmas. Asked about you." She fumbled again, cleared her throat. "Joanie's still here."

"Joanie Tucker?"

"It's Joanie Knight now," Loretta told her. "She married young Jack Knight three years ago. They have a beautiful baby."

"Joanie," Vanessa murmured. Joanie Tucker, who had been her best friend since her earliest memory, her confidante, wailing wall and partner in crime. "She has a child."

"A little girl. Lara. They have a farm outside of town. I know she'd want to see you."

"Yes." For the first time all day, Vanessa felt something click. "Yes, I want to see her. Her parents, are they well?"

"Emily died almost eight years ago."

"Oh." Vanessa reached out instinctively to touch her mother's hand. As Joanie had been her closest friend, so had Emily Tucker been her mother's. "I'm so sorry."

Loretta looked down at their joined hands, and her eyes filled. "I still miss her."

"She was the kindest woman I've ever known. I wish I had—" But it was too late for regrets. "Dr. Tucker, is he all right?"

"Ham is fine." Loretta blinked back tears, and tried not to be hurt when Vanessa removed her hand. "He grieved hard, but his family and his work got him through. He'll be so pleased to see you, Van."

No one had called Vanessa by her nickname in more years than she could count. Hearing it now touched her.

"Does he still have his office in his house?"

"Of course. You're not eating. Would you like something else?"

"No, this is fine." Dutifully she ate a forkful of salad.

"Don't you want to know about Brady?"

"No." Vanessa took another bite. "Not particularly."

There was something of the daughter she remembered in that look. The slight pout, the faint line between the brows. It warmed Loretta's heart, as the polite stranger had not. "Brady Tucker followed in his father's footsteps."

Vanessa almost choked. "He's a doctor?"

"That's right. Had himself a fine, important position with some hospital in New York. Chief resident, I think Ham told me."

"I always thought Brady would end up pitching for the Orioles or going to jail."

Loretta laughed again, warmly. "So did most of us. But he turned into quite a respectable young man. Of course, he was always too handsome for his own good."

"Or anyone else's," Vanessa muttered, and her mother smiled again.

"It's always hard for a woman to resist the tall, dark and handsome kind, especially if he's a rogue, as well."

"I think *hood* was the word."

"He never did anything really bad," Loretta pointed out. "Not that he didn't give Emily and Ham a few headaches. Well, a lot of headaches." She laughed. "But the boy always looked out for his sister. I liked him for that. And he was taken with you."

Vanessa sniffed. "Brady Tucker was taken with anything in skirts."

"He was young." They had all been young once, Loretta thought, looking at the lovely, composed stranger who was her daughter. "Emily told me he mooned around the house for weeks after you...after you and your father went to Europe."

"It was a long time ago." Vanessa rose, dismissing the subject.

"I'll get the dishes." Loretta began stacking them quickly. "It's your first day back. I thought maybe you'd like to try out the piano. I'd like to hear you play in this house again."

"All right." She turned toward the door.

"Van?"

"Yes?"

Would she ever call her "Mom" again? "I want you to know how proud I am of all you've accomplished."

"Are you?"

"Yes." Loretta studied her daughter, wishing she had the courage to open her arms for an embrace. "I just wish you looked happier."

"I'm happy enough."

"Would you tell me if you weren't?"

"I don't know. We don't really know each other anymore."

At least that was honest, Loretta thought. Painful, but honest. "I hope you'll stay until we do."

"I'm here because I need answers. But I'm not ready to ask the questions yet."

"Give it time, Van. Give yourself time. And believe me when I say all I ever wanted was what was best for you."

"My father always said the same thing," she said quietly. "Funny, isn't it, that now that I'm a grown woman I have no idea what that is."

She walked down the hall to the music room. There was a gnawing, aching pain just under her breastbone. Out of habit, she popped a pill out of the roll in her skirt pocket before she sat at the piano.

She started with Beethoven's "Moonlight" sonata, playing from memory and from the heart, letting the music soothe her. She could remember playing this piece, and countless others, in this same room. Hour after hour, day after day. For the love of it, yes, but often—too often—because it was expected, even demanded.

Her feelings for music had always been mixed. There was her strong, passionate love for it, the driving need to create it with the skill she'd been given. But there had always also been the equally desperate need to please her father, to reach that point of perfection he had expected. That unattainable point, she thought now.

He had never understood that music was a love for her, not a vocation. It had been a comfort, a means of expression, but never an ambition. On the few occasions she had tried to explain it, he had become so enraged or impatient that she had silenced herself. She, who was known for her passion and temper, had been a cringing child around one man. In all her life, she had never been able to defy him.

She switched to Bach, closed her eyes and let herself drift. For more than an hour she played, lost in the beauty, the gentleness and the genius, of the compositions. This was what her father had never understood. That she could play for her own pleasure and be content, and that she had hated, always hated, sitting on a stage ringed by a spotlight and playing for thousands.

As her emotions began to flow again, she switched to Mozart, something that required more passion and speed. Vivid, almost furious, the music sang through her. When the last chord echoed, she felt a satisfaction she had nearly forgotten.

The quiet applause behind her had her spinning around. Seated on one of the elegant little chairs was a man. Though the sun was in her eyes and twelve years had passed, she recognized him.

"Incredible." Brady Tucker rose and crossed to her. His long, wiry frame blocked out the sun for an instant, and the light glowed like a nimbus around him. "Absolutely incredible." As she stared at him, he held out a hand and smiled. "Welcome home, Van."

She rose to face him. "Brady," she murmured, then rammed her fist solidly into his stomach. "You creep."

He sat down hard as the air exploded out of his lungs. The sound of it was every bit as sweet to her as the music had been. Wincing, he looked up at her. "Nice to see you, too."

"What the hell are you doing here?"

"Your mother let me in." After a couple of testing breaths, he rose. She had to tilt her head back to keep her eyes on his. Those same fabulous blue eyes, in a face that had aged much too well. "I didn't want to disturb you while you were playing, so I just sat down. I didn't expect to be sucker-punched."

"You should have." She was delighted to have caught him off guard, and to have given him back a small portion of the pain he'd given her. His voice was the same, she thought, deep and seductive. She wanted to hit him again just for that. "She didn't mention that you were in town."

"I live here. Moved back almost a year ago." She had that same sexy pout. He fervently wished that at least that much could have changed. "Can I tell you that you look terrific, or should I put up my guard?"

How to remain composed under stress was something she'd learned very well. She sat, carefully smoothing her skirts. "No, you can tell me."

"Okay. You look terrific. A little thin, maybe."

The pout became more pronounced. "Is that your medical opinion, Dr. Tucker?"

"Actually, yes." He took a chance and sat beside her on the piano stool. Her scent was as subtle and alluring as moonlight. He felt a tug, not so much unexpected as frustrating. Though she sat beside him, he knew she was as distant as she had been when there had been an ocean between them.

"You're looking well," she said, and wished it wasn't so true. He still had the lean, athletic body of his youth. His face wasn't as smooth, and the ruggedness maturity had brought to it only made it more attractive. His hair was still a rich, deep black, and his lashes were just as long and thick as ever. And his hands were as strong and beautiful as they had been the first time they had touched her. A lifetime ago, she reminded herself, and settled her own hands in her lap.

"My mother told me you had a position in New York."

"I did." He was feeling as awkward as a schoolboy. No, he realized, much more awkward. Twelve years before, he'd known exactly how to handle her. Or he'd thought he did. "I came back to help my father with his practice. He'd like to retire in a year or two."

"I can't imagine it. You back here," she elaborated. "Or Doc Tucker retiring."

"Times change."

"Yes, they do." She couldn't sit beside him. Just a residual of those girlish feelings, she thought, but she rose anyway. "It's equally hard to picture you as a doctor."

"I felt the same way when I was slogging through medical school."

She frowned. He was wearing jeans and a sweatshirt and running shoes—exactly the kind of attire he'd worn in high school. "You don't look like a doctor."

"Want to see my stethoscope?"

"No." She stuck her hands in her pockets. "I heard Joanie was married."

"Yeah—to Jack Knight, of all people. Remember him?"

"I don't think so."

"He was a year ahead of me in high school. Football star. Went pro a couple of years, then bunged up his knee."

"Is that the medical term?"

"Close enough." He grinned at her. There was still a little chip in his front tooth that she had always found endearing. "She'll be crazy to see you again, Van."

"I want to see her, too."

"I've got a couple of patients coming in, but I should be done by six. Why don't we have some dinner, and I can drive you out to the farm?"

"I don't think so."

"Why not?"

"Because the last time I was supposed to have dinner with you—dinner and the senior prom—you stood me up."

He tucked his hands in his pockets. "You hold a grudge a long time."

"Yes."

"I was eighteen years old, Van, and there were reasons."

"Reasons that hardly matter now." Her stomach was beginning to burn. "The point is, I don't want to pick up where we left off."

He gave her a considering look. "That wasn't the idea."

"Good." That was just one more thing she could damn him for. "We both have our separate lives, Brady. Let's keep it that way."

He nodded, slowly. "You've changed more than I'd thought."

"Yes, I have." She started out, stopped, then looked over her shoulder. "We both have. But I imagine you still know your way out."

"Yeah," he said to himself when she left him alone. He knew his way out. What he hadn't known was that she could still turn him inside out with one of those pouty looks.

Chapter 2

The Knight farm was rolling hills and patches of brown and green field. The hay was well up, she noted, and the corn was tender green shoots. A gray barn stood behind a trio of square paddocks. Nearby, chickens fussed and pecked at the ground. Plump spotted cows lolled on a hillside, too lazy to glance over at the sound of an approaching car, but geese rushed along the bank of the creek, excited and annoyed by the disturbance.

A bumpy gravel lane led to the farmhouse. At the end of it, Vanessa stopped her car, then slowly alighted. She could hear the distant putting of a tractor and the occasional yip-yipping of a cheerful dog. Closer was the chatter of birds, a musical exchange that always reminded her of neighbors gossiping over a fence.

Perhaps it was foolish to feel nervous, but she couldn't shake it. Here in this rambling three-story house, with its leaning chimneys and swaying porches, lived her oldest and closest friend—someone with whom she had shared every thought, every feeling, every wish and every disappointment.

But those friends had been children—girls on the threshold of womanhood, where everything is at its most intense and emotional. They hadn't been given the chance to grow apart. Their friendship had been severed quickly and completely. Between that moment and this, so much—too much—had happened to both of them. To expect to renew those ties and feelings was both naive and overly optimistic.

Vanessa reminded herself of that, bracing herself for disappointment, as she started up the cracked wooden steps to the front porch.

The door swung open. The woman who stepped out released a flood of stored memories. Unlike the moment when she had started up her own walk and seen her mother, Vanessa felt none of the confusion and grief.

She looks the same, was all Vanessa could think. Joanie was still sturdily built, with the curves Vanessa had envied throughout adolescence. Her hair was still worn short and tousled around a pretty face. Black hair and blue eyes like her brother, but with softer features and a neat Cupid's-bow mouth that had driven the teenage boys wild.

Vanessa started to speak, searched for something to say. Then she heard Joanie let out a yelp. They were hugging, arms clasped hard, bodies swaying. The laughter and tears and broken sentences melted away the years.

"I can't believe—you're here."

"I've missed you. You look… I'm sorry."

"When I heard you—" Shaking her head, Joanie pulled back, then smiled. "Oh, God, it's good to see you, Van."

"I was almost afraid to come." Vanessa wiped her cheek with her knuckles.

"Why?"

"I thought you might be polite and offer me some tea and wonder what we were supposed to talk about."

Joanie took a rumpled tissue out of her pocket and blew her nose. "And I thought you might be wearing a mink and diamonds and stop by out of a sense of duty."

Vanessa gave a watery laugh. "My mink's in storage."

Joanie grabbed her hand and pulled her through the door. "Come in. I might just put that tea on after all."

The entryway was bright and tidy. Joanie led Vanessa into a living room of faded sofas and glossy mahogany, of chintz curtains and rag rugs. Evidence that there was a baby in the house was found in teething rings, rattles and stuffed bears. Unable to resist, Vanessa picked up a pink-and-white rattle.

"You have a little girl."

"Lara." Joanie beamed. "She's wonderful. She'll be up from her morning nap soon. I can't wait for you to see her."

"It's hard to imagine." Vanessa gave the rattle a shake before setting it down again. It made a pretty, musical sound that had her smiling. "You're a mother."

"I'm almost used to it." She took Vanessa's hand again as they sat on the sofa. "I still can't believe you're here. Vanessa Sexton, concert pianist, musical luminary and globe-trotter."

Vanessa winced. "Oh, please, not her. I left her in D.C."

"Just let me gloat a minute." She was still smiling, but her eyes, eyes that were so like her brother's, were searching Vanessa's face. "We're so proud of you. The whole town. There would be something in the paper or a magazine, something on the news—or an event like that PBS special last year. No one would talk about anything else for days. You're Hyattown's link to fame and fortune."

"A weak link," Vanessa murmured, but she smiled. "Your farm, Joanie—it's wonderful."

"Can you believe it? I always thought I'd be living in one of those New York lofts, planning business lunches and fighting for a cab during rush hour."

"This is better." Vanessa settled back against the sofa cushions. "Much better."

Joanie toed off her shoes, then tucked her stockinged feet under her. "It has been for me. Do you remember Jack?"

"I don't think so. I can't remember you ever talking about anyone named Jack."

"I didn't know him in high school. He was a senior when we were just getting started. I remember seeing him in the halls now and then. Those big shoulders, and that awful buzz haircut during the football season." She laughed and settled comfortably. "Then, about four years ago, I was giving Dad a hand in the office. I was doing time as a paralegal in Hagerstown."

"A paralegal?"

"A former life," Joanie said with a wave of her hand. "Anyway, it was during Dad's Saturday office hours, and Millie was sick— You remember Millie?"

"Oh, yes." Vanessa grinned at the memory of Abraham Tucker's no-nonsense nurse.

"Well, I jumped into the breach for the weekend appointments, and in walks Jack Knight, all six foot three, two hundred and fifty pounds of him. He had laryngitis." A self-satisfied sigh escaped her. "There was this big, handsome hulk trying to tell me, in cowboy-and-Indian sign language, that no, he didn't have an appointment, but he wanted to see the doctor. I squeezed him in between a chicken pox and an earache. Dad examined him and gave him a prescription. A couple hours later he was back, with these raggedy-looking violets and a note asking me to the movies. How could I resist?"

Vanessa laughed. "You always were a soft touch."

Joanie rolled her big blue eyes. "Tell me about it. Before I knew it, I was shopping for a wedding dress and learning about fertilizer. It's been the best four years of my life." She shook her head. "But tell me about you. I want to hear everything."

Vanessa shrugged. "Practice, playing, traveling."

"Jetting off to Rome, Madrid, Mozambique—"

"Sitting on runways and in hotel rooms," Vanessa finished for her. "It isn't nearly as glamorous as it might look."

"No, I guess partying with famous actors, giving concerts for the queen of England and sharing midnight schmoozes with millionaires gets pretty boring."

"Schmoozes?" Vanessa had to laugh. "I don't think I ever schmoozed with anyone."

"Don't burst my bubble, Van." Joanie leaned over to brush a hand down Vanessa's arm. All the Tuckers were touchers, Vanessa thought. She'd missed that. "For years I've had this image of you glittering among the glittery. Celebing among the celebrities, hoitying among the toity."

"I guess I've done my share of hoitying. But mostly I've played the piano and caught planes."

"It's kept you in shape," Joanie said, sensing Vanessa's

reluctance to talk about it. "I bet you're still a damn size four."

"Small bones."

"Wait until Brady gets a load of you."

Her chin lifted a fraction. "I saw him yesterday."

"Really? And the rat didn't call me." Joanie tapped a finger against her lips. There was laughter just beneath them. "So, how did it go?"

"I hit him."

"You—" Joanie choked, coughed, recovered. "You hit him? Why?"

"For standing me up for his senior prom."

"For—" Joanie broke off when Vanessa sprang to her feet and began pacing.

"I've never been so angry. I don't care how stupid it sounds. That night was so important to me. I thought it would be the most wonderful, the most romantic night of my life. You know how long we shopped for the perfect dress."

"Yes," Joanie murmured. "I know."

"I'd been looking forward to that night for weeks and weeks." On a roll now, she swirled around the room. "I'd just gotten my license, and I drove all the way into Frederick to get my hair done. I had this little sprig of baby's breath behind my ear." She touched the spot now, but there was no sentiment in the gesture. "Oh, I knew he was unreliable and reckless. I can't count the number of times my father told me. But I never expected him to dump me like that."

"But, Van—"

"I didn't even leave the house for two days after. I was so sick with embarrassment, so hurt. And then, with my parents fighting. It was—oh, it was so ugly. Then my father took me to Europe, and that was that."

Joanie bit her lip as she considered. There were explanations she could offer, but this was something Brady should straighten out himself. "There might be more to it than you think" was all she said.

Recovered now, Vanessa sat again. "It doesn't matter. It was a long time ago." Then she smiled. "Besides, I think I got the venom out when I punched him in the stomach."

Joanie's lips twitched in sisterly glee. "I'd like to have seen that."

"It's hard to believe he's a doctor."

"I don't think anyone was more surprised than Brady."

"It's odd he's never married…" She frowned. "Or anything."

"I won't touch 'anything,' but he's never married. There are a number of women in town who've developed chronic medical problems since he's come back."

"I'll bet," Vanessa muttered.

"Anyway, my father's in heaven. Have you had a chance to see him yet?"

"No, I wanted to see you first." She took Joanie's hands again. "I'm so sorry about your mother. I didn't know until yesterday."

"It was a rough couple of years. Dad was so lost. I guess we all were." Her fingers tightened, taking comfort and giving it. "I know you lost your father. I understand how hard it must have been for you."

"He hadn't been well for a long time. I didn't know how serious it was until, well…until it was almost over." She rubbed a hand over her stomach as it spasmed. "It helped to finish out the engagements. That would have been important to him."

"I know." She was starting to speak again when the

intercom on the table crackled. There was a whimper, a gurgle, followed by a stream of infant jabbering. "She's up and ready to roll." Joanie rose quickly. "I'll just be a minute."

Alone, Vanessa stood and began to wander the room. It was filled with so many little, comforting things. Books on agriculture and child-rearing, wedding pictures and baby pictures. There was an old porcelain vase she remembered seeing in the Tucker household as a child. Through the window she could see the barn, and the cows drowsing in the midday sun.

Like something out of a book, she thought. Her own faded wish book.

"Van?"

She turned to see Joanie in the doorway, a round, dark-haired baby on her hip. The baby swung her feet, setting off the bells tied to her shoelaces.

"Oh, Joanie. She's gorgeous."

"Yeah." Joanie kissed Lara's head. "She is. Would you like to hold her?"

"Are you kidding?" Van came across the room to take the baby. After a long suspicious look, Lara smiled and began to kick her feet again. "Aren't you pretty?" Van murmured. Unable to resist, she lifted the baby over her head and turned in a circle while Lara giggled. "Aren't you just wonderful?"

"She likes you, too." Joanie gave a satisfied nod. "I kept telling her she'd meet her godmother sooner or later."

"Her godmother?" Confused, Vanessa settled the baby on her hip again.

"Sure." Joanie smoothed Lara's hair. "I sent you a note right after she was born. I knew you couldn't make it back for the christening, so we had a proxy. But I wanted you and Brady to be her godparents." Joanie frowned at Vanessa's blank look. "You got the note, didn't you?"

"No." Vanessa rested her cheek against Lara's. "No, I didn't. I had no idea you were even married until my mother told me yesterday."

"But the wedding invitation—" Joanie shrugged. "I guess it could have gotten lost. You were always traveling around so much."

"Yes." She smiled again while Lara tugged at her hair. "If I'd known… I'd have found a way to be here if I'd known."

"You're here now."

"Yes." Vanessa nuzzled Lara's neck. "I'm here now. Oh, God, I envy you, Joanie."

"Me?"

"This beautiful child, this place, the look in your eyes when you talk about Jack. I feel like I've spent twelve years in a daze, while you've made a family and a home and a life."

"We've both made a life," Joanie said. "They're just different ones. You have so much talent, Van. Even as a kid I was awed by it. I wanted so badly to play like you." She laughed and enveloped them both in a hug. "As patient as you were, you could barely get me through 'Chopsticks.'"

"You were hopeless but determined. And I'm so glad you're still my friend."

"You're going to make me cry again." After a sniffle, Joanie shook her head. "Tell you what, you play with Lara for a few minutes and I'll go fix us some lemonade. Then we can be catty and gossip about how fat Julie Newton got."

"Did she?"

"And how Tommy McDonald is losing his hair."
Joanie hooked an arm through Vanessa's. "Better yet,
come in the kitchen with me. I'll fill you in on Betty
Jean Baumgartner's third husband."

"Third?"

"And counting."

There was so much to think about. Not just the funny
stories Joanie had shared with her that day, Vanessa
thought as she strolled around the backyard at dusk. She
needed to think about her life and what she wanted to
do with it. Where she belonged. Where she wanted to
belong.

For over a decade she'd had little or no choice. Or
had lacked the courage to make one, she thought. She
had done what her father wanted. He and her music had
been the only constants. His drive and his needs had
been so much more passionate than hers. And she hadn't
wanted to disappoint him.

Hadn't dared, a small voice echoed, but she blocked
it off.

She owed him everything. He had dedicated his life
to her career. While her mother had shirked the responsibility, he had taken her, he had molded her, he had
taught her. Every hour she had worked, he had worked.
Even when he had become desperately ill, he had pushed
himself, managing her career as meticulously as ever.
No detail had ever escaped his notice—just as no flawed
note had escaped his highly critical ear. He had taken
her to the top of her career, and he had been content to
bask in the reflected glory.

It couldn't have been easy for him, she thought now.
His own career as a concert pianist had stalled before
he'd hit thirty. He had never achieved the pinnacle he'd

so desperately strived for. For him, music had been everything. Finally he'd been able to see those ambitions and needs realized in his only child.

Now she was on the brink of turning her back on everything he had wanted for her, everything he had worked toward. He would never have been able to understand her desire to give up a glowing career. Just as he had never been able to understand, or tolerate, her constant terror of performing.

She could remember it even now, even here in the sheltered quiet of the yard. The gripping sensation in her stomach, the wave of nausea she always battled back, the throbbing behind her eyes as she stood in the wings.

Stage fright, her father had told her. She would outgrow it. It was the one thing she had never been able to accomplish for him.

Yet, despite it, she knew she could go back to the concert stage. She could endure. She could rise even higher if she focused herself. If only she knew it was what she wanted.

Perhaps she just needed to rest. She sat on the lawn glider and sent it gently into motion. A few weeks or a few months of quiet, and then she might yearn for the life she had left behind. But for now she wanted nothing more than to enjoy the purple twilight.

From the glider she could see the lights glowing inside the house, and the neighboring houses. She had shared a meal with her mother in the kitchen—or had tried to. Loretta had seemed hurt when Vanessa only picked at her food. How could she explain that nothing seemed to settle well these days? This empty, gnawing feeling in her stomach simply wouldn't abate.

A little more time, Vanessa thought, and it would ease. It was only because she wasn't busy, as she should be. Certainly she hadn't practiced enough that day, or the day before. Even if she decided to cut back professionally, she had no business neglecting her practice.

Tomorrow, she thought, closing her eyes. Tomorrow was soon enough to start a routine. Lulled by the motion of the glider, she gathered her jacket closer. She'd forgotten how quickly the temperature could dip once the sun had fallen behind the mountains.

She heard the whoosh of a car as it cruised by on the road in front of the house. Then the sound of a door closing. From somewhere nearby, a mother called her child in from play. Another light blinked on in a window. A baby cried. Vanessa smiled, wishing she could dig out the old tent she and Joanie had used and pitch it in the backyard. She could sleep there, just listening to the town.

She turned at the sound of a dog barking, then saw the bright fur of a huge golden retriever. It dashed across the neighboring lawn, over the bed where her mother had already planted her pansies and marigolds. Tongue lolling, it lunged at the glider. Before Vanessa could decide whether to be alarmed or amused, it plopped both front paws in her lap and grinned a dog's grin.

"Well, hello there." She ruffled his ears. "Where did you come from?"

"From two blocks down, at a dead run." Panting, Brady walked out of the shadows. "I made the mistake of taking him to the office today. When I went to put him in the car, he decided to take a hike." He paused in front of the glider. "Are you going to punch me again, or can I sit down?"

Vanessa continued to pet the dog. "I probably won't hit you again."

"That'll have to do." He dropped down on the glider

and stretched out his legs. The dog immediately tried to climb in his lap. "Don't try to make up," Brady said, pushing the dog off again.

"He's a pretty dog."

"Don't flatter him. He's already got an inflated ego."

"They say people and their pets develop similarities," she commented. "What's his name?"

"Kong. He was the biggest in his litter." Hearing his name, Kong barked twice, then raced off to chase the shadows. "I spoiled him when he was a puppy, and now I'm paying the price." Spreading his arms over the back of the glider, he let his fingers toy with the ends of her hair. "Joanie tells me you drove out to the farm today."

"Yes." Vanessa knocked his hand away. "She looks wonderful. And so happy."

"She is happy." Undaunted, he picked up her hand to play with her fingers. It was an old, familiar gesture. "You got to meet our godchild."

"Yes." Vanessa tugged her hand free. "Lara's gorgeous."

"Yeah." He went back to her hair. "She looks like me."

The laugh came too quickly to stop. "You're still conceited. And will you keep your hands off me?"

"I never was able to." He sighed, but shifted away an inch. "We used to sit here a lot, remember?"

"I remember."

"I think the first time I kissed you, we were sitting here, just like this."

"No." She folded her arms across her chest.

"You're right." As he knew very well. "The first time

was up at the park. You came to watch me shoot baskets."

She brushed casually at the knee of her slacks. "I just happened to be walking through."

"You came because I used to shoot without a shirt and you wanted to see my sweaty chest."

She laughed again, because it was absolutely true. She turned to look at him in the shadowy light. He was smiling, relaxed. He'd always been able to relax, she remembered. And he'd always been able to make her laugh.

"It—meaning your sweaty chest—wasn't such a big deal."

"I've filled out some," he said easily. "And I still shoot hoops." This time she didn't seem to notice when he stroked her hair. "I remember that day. It was at the end of the summer, before my senior year. In three months you'd gone from being that pesty little Sexton kid to Sexy Sexton with a yard of the most incredible chestnut hair, and these great-looking legs you used to show off in teeny little shorts. You were such a brat. And you made my mouth water."

"You were always looking at Julie Newton."

"No, I was pretending to look at Julie Newton while I looked at you. Then you just happened to stroll by the court that day. You'd been to Lester's Store, because you had a bottle of soda. Grape soda."

She lifted a brow. "That's quite a memory you've got."

"Hey, these are the turning points in our lives. You said, 'Hi, Brady. You look awful hot. Want a sip?'" He grinned again. "I almost took a bite out of my basketball. Then you flirted with me."

"I did not."

"You batted your eyes."

She struggled with a giggle. "I've never batted my eyes."

"You batted them then." He sighed at the memory. "It was great."

"As I remember it, you were showing off, doing lay-ups and hook shots or whatever. Macho stuff. Then you grabbed me."

"I remember grabbing. You liked it."

"You smelled like a gym locker."

"I guess I did. It was still my most memorable first kiss."

And hers, Vanessa thought. She hadn't realized she was leaning back against his shoulder and smiling. "We were so young. Everything was so intense, and so un-complicated."

"Some things don't have to be complicated." But sitting there with her head feeling just right on his shoulder, he wasn't so sure. "Friends?"

"I guess."

"I haven't had a chance to ask you how long you're staying."

"I haven't had a chance to decide."

"Your schedule must be packed."

"I've taken a few months." She moved restlessly. "I may go to Paris for a few weeks."

He picked up her hand again, turning it over. Her hands had always fascinated him. Those long, tapering fingers, the baby-smooth palms, the short, practical nails. She wore no rings. He had given her one once— spent the money he'd earned mowing grass all summer on a gold ring with an incredibly small emerald. She'd kissed him senseless when he'd given it to her, and she'd sworn never to take it off.

Childhood promises were carelessly broken by adults. It was foolish to wish he could see it on her finger again.

"You know, I managed to see you play at Carnegie Hall a couple of years ago. It was overwhelming. You were overwhelming." He surprised them both by bringing her fingers to his lips. Then hastily dropped them. "I'd hoped to see you while we were both in New York, but I guess you were busy."

The jolt from her fingertips was still vibrating in her toes. "If you had called, I'd have managed it."

"I did call." His eyes remained on hers, searching, even as he shrugged it off. "It was then I fully realized how big you'd become. I never got past the first line of defense."

"I'm sorry. Really."

"It's no big deal."

"No, I would have liked to have seen you. Sometimes the people around me are too protective."

"I think you're right." He put a hand under her chin. She was more beautiful than his memory of her, and more fragile. If he had met her in New York, in less sentimental surroundings, would he have felt so drawn to her? He wasn't sure he wanted to know.

Friends was what he'd asked of her. He struggled to want no more.

"You look very tired, Van. Your color could be better."

"It's been a hectic year."

"Are you sleeping all right?"

Half-amused, she brushed his hand aside. "Don't start playing doctor with me, Brady."

"At the moment I can't think of anything I'd enjoy more, but I'm serious. You're run-down."

"I'm not run-down, just a little tired. Which is why I'm taking a break."

But he wasn't satisfied. "Why don't you come into the office for a physical?"

"Is that your new line? It used to be 'Let's go parking down at Molly's Hole.'"

"I'll get to that. Dad can take a look at you."

"I don't need a doctor." Kong came lumbering back, and she reached down for him. "I'm never sick. In almost ten years of concerts, I've never had to cancel one for health reasons." She buried her face in the dog's fur when her stomach clenched. "I'm not going to say it hasn't been a strain coming back here, but I'm dealing with it."

She'd always been hardheaded, he thought. Maybe it would be best if he simply kept an eye—a medical eye—on her for a few days. "Dad would still like to see you—personally, if not professionally."

"I'm going to drop by." Still bent over the dog, she turned her head. In the growing dark, he caught the familiar gleam in her eye. "Joanie says you've got your hands full with women patients. I imagine the same holds true of your father, if he's as handsome as I remember."

"He's had a few...interesting offers. But they've eased off since he and your mother hooked up."

Dumbfounded, Vanessa sat up straight. "Hooked up? My mother? Your father?"

"It's the hottest romance in town." He flicked her hair behind her shoulder. "So far."

"My mother?" she repeated.

"She's an attractive woman in her prime, Van. Why shouldn't she enjoy herself?"

Pressing a hand against her stomach, she rose. "I'm going in."

"What's the problem?"

"No problem. I'm going in. I'm cold."

He took her by the shoulders. It was another gesture that brought a flood of memories. "Why don't you give her a break?" Brady asked. "God knows she's been punished enough."

"You don't know anything about it."

"More than you think." He gave her a quick, impatient shake. "Let go, Van. These old resentments are going to eat you from the inside out."

"It's easy for you." The bitterness poured out before she could control it. "It's always been easy for you, with your nice happy family. You always knew they loved you, no matter what you did or didn't do. No one ever sent you away."

"She didn't send you away, Van."

"She let me go," she said quietly. "What's the difference?"

"Why don't you ask her?"

With a shake of her head, she pulled away. "I stopped being her little girl twelve years ago. I stopped being a lot of things." She turned and walked into the house.

Chapter 3

Vanessa had slept only in snatches. There had been pain. But she was used to pain. She masked it by coating her stomach with liquid antacids, by downing the pills that had been prescribed for her occasional blinding headaches. But most of all, she masked it by using her will to ignore.

Twice she had nearly walked down the hall to her mother's room. A third time she had gotten as far as her mother's door, with her hand raised to knock, before she had retreated to her own room and her own thoughts.

She had no right to resent the fact that her mother had a relationship with another man. Yet she did. In all the years Vanessa had spent with her father, he had never turned to another woman. Or, if he had, he had been much too discreet for her to notice.

And what did it matter? she asked herself as she dressed the next morning. They had always lived their own lives, separate, despite the fact that they shared a house.

But it did matter. It mattered that her mother had been content all these years to live in this same house without contact with her only child. It mattered that she had been able to start a life, a new life, that had no place for her own daughter.

It was time, Vanessa told herself. It was time to ask why.

She caught the scent of coffee and fragrant bread as she reached the bottom landing. In the kitchen she saw her mother standing by the sink, rinsing a cup. Loretta was dressed in a pretty blue suit, pearls at her ears and around her throat. The radio was on low, and she was humming even as she turned and saw her daughter.

"Oh, you're up." Loretta smiled, hoping it didn't look forced. "I wasn't sure I'd see you this morning before I left."

"Left?"

"I have to go to work. There're some muffins, and the coffee's still hot."

"To work?" Vanessa repeated. "Where?"

"At the shop." To busy her nervous hands, she poured Vanessa a cup of coffee. "The antique shop. I bought it about six years ago. The Hopkinses' place, you might remember. I went to work for them when—some time ago. When they decided to retire, I bought them out."

Vanessa shook her head to clear it of the grogginess. "You run an antique shop?"

"Just a small one." She set the coffee on the table. The moment they were free, her hands began to tug at her pearl necklace. "I call it Loretta's Attic. Silly, I suppose, but it does nicely. I closed it for a couple of days, but… I can keep it closed another day or so if you'd like."

Vanessa studied her mother thoughtfully, trying to imagine her owning a business, worrying about inventory and bookkeeping. Antiques? Had she ever mentioned an interest in them?

"No." It seemed that talk would have to wait. "Go ahead."

"If you like, you can run down later and take a look." Loretta began to fiddle with a button on her jacket. "It's small, but I have a lot of interesting pieces."

"We'll see."

"Are you sure you'll be all right here alone?"

"I've been all right alone for a long time."

Loretta's gaze dropped. Her hands fell to her sides. "Yes, of course you have. I'm usually home by six-thirty."

"All right. I'll see you this evening, then." She walked to the sink to turn on the faucet. She wanted water, cold and clear.

"Van."

"Yes?"

"I know I have years to make up for." Loretta was standing in the doorway when Vanessa turned. "I hope you'll give me a chance."

"I want to." She spread her hands. "I don't know where either of us is supposed to start."

"Neither do I." Loretta's smile was hesitant, but less strained. "Maybe that's its own start. I love you. I'll be happy if I can make you believe that." She turned quickly and left.

"Oh, Mom," Vanessa said to the empty house. "I don't know what to do."

* * *

"Mrs. Driscoll." Brady patted the eighty-three-year-old matron on her knobby knee. "You've got the heart of a twenty-year-old gymnast."

She cackled, as he'd known she would. "It's not my heart I'm worried about, Brady. It's my bones. They ache like the devil."

"Maybe if you'd let one of your great-grandchildren weed that garden of yours."

"I've been doing my own patch for sixty years—"

"And you'll do it another sixty," he finished for her, setting the blood pressure cuff aside. "Nobody in the county grows better tomatoes, but if you don't ease up, your bones are going to ache." He picked up her hands. Her fingers were wiry, not yet touched by arthritis. But it was in her shoulders, in her knees, and there was little he could do to stop its march.

He completed the exam, listening to her tell stories about her family. She'd been his second-grade teacher, and he'd thought then she was the oldest woman alive. After nearly twenty-five years, the gap had closed considerably. Though he knew she still considered him the little troublemaker who had knocked over the goldfish bowl just to see the fish flop on the floor.

"I saw you coming out of the post office a couple of days ago, Mrs. Driscoll." He made a notation on her chart. "You weren't using your cane."

She snorted. "Canes are for old people."

He lowered the chart, lifted a brow. "It's my considered medical opinion, Mrs. Driscoll, that you *are* old."

She cackled and batted a hand at him. "You always had a smart mouth, Brady Tucker."

"Yeah, but now I've got a medical degree to go with

it." He took her hand to help her off the examining table. "And I want you to use that cane—even if it's only to give John Hardesty a good rap when he flirts with you."

"The old goat," she muttered. "And I'd look like an old goat, too, hobbling around on a cane."

"Isn't vanity one of the seven deadly sins?"

"It's not worth sinning if it isn't deadly. Get out of here, boy, so I can dress."

"Yes, ma'am." He left her, shaking his head. He could hound her from here to the moon and she wouldn't use that damn cane. She was one of the few patients he couldn't bully or intimidate.

After two more hours of morning appointments, he spent his lunch hour driving to Washington County Hospital to check on two patients. An apple and a handful of peanut butter crackers got him through the afternoon. More than one of his patients mentioned the fact that Vanessa Sexton was back in town. This information was usually accompanied by smirks, winks and leers. He'd had his stomach gouged several times by teasing elbows.

Small towns, he thought as he took five minutes in his office between appointments. The people in them knew everything about everyone. And they remembered it. Forever. Vanessa and he had been together, briefly, twelve years before, but it might as well have been written in concrete, not just carved in one of the trees in Hyattown Park.

He'd forgotten about her—almost. Except when he'd seen her name or picture in the paper. Or when he'd listened to one of her albums, which he'd bought strictly for old times' sake. Or when he'd seen a woman tilt her head to the side and smile in a way similar to the way Van had smiled.

But when he had remembered, they'd been memories of childhood. Those were the sweetest and most poignant. They had been little more than children, rushing toward adulthood with a reckless and terrifying speed. But what had happened between them had remained beautifully innocent. Long, slow kisses in the shadows, passionate promises, a few forbidden caresses.

Thinking of them now, of her, shouldn't make him ache. And yet he rubbed a hand over his heart.

It had seemed too intense at the time, because they had faced such total opposition from her father. The more Julius Sexton had railed against their blossoming relationship, the closer they had become. That was the way of youth, Brady thought now. And he had played the angry young man to perfection, he remembered with a smirk. Defying her father, giving his own a lifetime of headaches. Making threats and promises as only an eighteen-year-old could.

If the road had run smoothly, they would probably have forgotten each other within weeks.

Liar, he thought with a laugh. He had never been so in love as he had been that year with Vanessa. That heady, frantic year, when he had turned eighteen and anything and everything had seemed possible.

They had never made love. He had bitterly regretted that after she had been swept out of his life. Now, with the gift of hindsight, he realized that it had been for the best. If they had been lovers, how much more difficult it would be for them to be friends as adults.

That was what he wanted, all he wanted, he assured himself. He had no intention of breaking his heart over her a second time.

Maybe for a moment, when he had first seen her at the piano, his breath had backed up in his lungs and his pulse had scrambled. That was a natural enough reaction. She was a beautiful woman, and she had once been his. And if he had felt a yearning the night before, as they had sat on the glider in the growing dusk, well, he was human. But he wasn't stupid.

Vanessa Sexton wasn't his girl anymore. And he didn't want her for his woman.

"Dr. Tucker." One of the nurses poked a head in the door. "Your next patient is here."

"Be right there."

"Oh, and your father said to stop by before you leave for the day."

"Thanks." Brady headed for examining room 2, wondering if Vanessa would be sitting out on the glider that evening.

Vanessa knocked on the door of the Tucker house and waited. She'd always liked the Main Street feeling of the home, with its painted porch and its window boxes. There were geraniums in them now, already blooming hardily. The screens were in the open windows. As a girl, she had often seen Brady and his father removing the storms and putting in the screens—a sure sign that winter was over.

There were two rockers sitting on the porch. She knew Dr. Tucker would often sit there on a summer evening. People strolling by would stop to pass the time or to relay a list of symptoms and complaints.

And every year, over the Memorial Day weekend, the Tuckers would throw a backyard barbecue. Everyone in town came by to eat hamburgers and potato salad, to sit under the shade of the big walnut tree, to play croquet.

He was a generous man, Dr. Tucker, Vanessa remembered. With his time, with his skill. She could still remember his laugh, full and rich, and how gentle his hands were during an examination.

But what could she say to him now? This man who had been such a larger-than-life figure during her childhood? This man who had once comforted her when she'd wept over her parents' crumbling marriage? This man who was now involved with her mother?

He opened the door himself, and stood there studying her. He was tall, as she remembered. Like Brady, he had a wiry, athletic build. Though his dark hair had turned a steely gray, he looked no older to her. There were lines fanning out around his dark blue eyes. They deepened as he smiled.

Unsure of herself, she started to offer him a hand. Before she could speak, she was caught up in a crushing bear hug. He smelled of Old Spice and peppermint, she thought, and nearly wept. Even that hadn't changed.

"Little Vanessa." His powerful voice rolled over her as he squeezed. "It's good to have you home."

"It's good to be home." Held against him, she believed it. "I've missed you." It came with a rush of feeling. "I've really missed you."

"Let me have a look at you." Still standing in the doorway, he held her at arm's length. "My, my, my…" he murmured. "Emily always said you'd be a beauty."

"Oh, Dr. Tucker, I'm so sorry about Mrs. Tucker."

"We all were." He rubbed her hands briskly up and down her arms. "She always kept track of you in the papers and magazines, you know. Had her heart set on you for a daughter-in-law. More than once she said to me, 'Ham, that's the girl for Brady. She'll straighten him out.'"

"It looks like he's straightened himself out."

"Mostly." Draping an arm over her shoulder, he led her inside. "How about a nice cup of tea and a piece of pie?"

"I'd love it."

She sat at the kitchen table while he brewed and served. The house hadn't changed on the inside, either. It was still neat as a pin. It was polished and scrubbed, with Emily's collection of knickknacks on every flat surface.

The sunny kitchen looked out over the backyard, with its big trees leafing and its spring bulbs blooming. To the right was the door that led to the offices. The only change she saw was the addition of a complicated phone and intercom system.

"Mrs. Leary still makes the best pies in town." He cut thick slabs of chocolate meringue.

"And she still pays you in baked goods."

"Worth their weight in gold." With a contented sigh, he sat across from her. "I guess I don't have to tell you how proud we all are of you."

She shook her head. "I wish I could have gotten back sooner. I didn't even know Joanie was married. And the baby." She lifted her teacup, fully comfortable for the first time since her return. "Lara's beautiful."

"Smart, too." He winked. "Of course, I might be a tad prejudiced, but I can't remember a smarter child. And I've seen my share of them."

"I hope to see a lot of her while I'm here. Of all of you."

"We're hoping you'll stay a good long time."

"I don't know." She looked down at her tea. "I haven't thought about it."

"Your mother hasn't been able to talk about anything else for weeks."

Vanessa took a smidgen of the fluffy meringue. "She seems well."

"She is well. Loretta's a strong woman. She's had to be."

Vanessa looked up again. Because her stomach had begun to jump, she spoke carefully. "I know she's running an antique shop. It's hard to imagine her as a businesswoman."

"It was hard for her to imagine, but she's doing a good job of it. I know you lost your father a few months ago."

"Cancer. It was very difficult for him."

"And for you."

She moved her shoulders. "There was little I could do…little he would allow me to do. Basically he refused to admit he was ill. He hated weaknesses."

"I know." He laid a hand on hers. "I hope you've learned to be more tolerant of them."

He didn't have to explain. "I don't hate my mother," she said with a sigh. "I just don't know her."

It was a good answer. One he appreciated. "I do. She's had a hard life, Van. Any mistakes she made, she's paid for more times than any one person should have to. She loves you. She always has."

"Then why did she let me go?"

His heart went out to her, as it always had. "That's a question you'll have to ask her yourself. And one she needs to answer."

With a little sigh, Vanessa sat back. "I always did come to cry on your shoulder."

"That's what shoulders are for. Mostly I was vain enough to think I had two daughters."

"You did." She blinked the tears away and took a soothing drink of tea. "Dr. Tucker, are you in love with my mother?"

"Yes. Does that upset you?"

"It shouldn't."

"But?"

"It's just that it's difficult for me to accept. I've always had such a clear picture of you and Mrs. Tucker as a set. It was one of my constants. My parents…as unhappy as they were together, for as long as I can remember…"

"Were your parents," he said quietly. "Another permanent set."

"Yes." She relaxed a little, grateful that he understood. "I know that's not reasonable. It's not even reality. But…"

"It should be," he finished for her. "My dear child, there is far too much in life that's unfair. I had twenty-eight years with Emily, and had planned for twenty-eight more. It wasn't to be. During the time I had with her, I loved her absolutely. We were lucky enough to grow into people each of us could continue to love. When she died, I thought that a part of my life was over. Your mother was Emily's closest and dearest friend, and that was how I continued to look at Loretta, for several years. Then she became mine—my closest and dearest friend. I think Emily would have been pleased."

"You make me feel like a child."

"You're always a child when it comes to your parents." He glanced down at her plate. "Have you lost your sweet tooth?"

"No." She laughed a little. "My appetite."

"I didn't want to sound like an old fogy and tell you

you're too thin. But you are, a bit. Loretta mentioned you weren't eating well. Or sleeping well."

Vanessa raised a brow. She hadn't realized her mother had noticed. "I suppose I'm keyed up. The last couple of years have been pretty hectic."

"When's the last time you had a physical?"

Now she did laugh. "You sound like Brady. I'm fine, Dr. Tucker. Concert tours makes you tough. It's just nerves."

He nodded, but promised himself that he'd keep an eye on her. "I hope you'll play for me soon."

"I'm already breaking in the new piano. In fact, I should get back. I've been skimping on my practice time lately."

As she rose, Brady came through the connecting door. It annoyed him to see her there. It wasn't bad enough that she'd been in his head all day. Now she was in his kitchen. He nodded to her, then glanced down at the pie.

"The dependable Mrs. Leary." He grinned at his father. "Were you going to leave any for me?"

"She's my patient."

"He always hoards the goodies," Brady said to Vanessa, dipping a finger in the meringue on her plate. "You wanted to see me before I left?"

"You wanted me to look over the Crampton file." Ham tapped a finger on a folder on the counter. "I made some notes."

"Thanks."

"I've got some things to tie up." He took Vanessa by the shoulders and kissed her soundly. "Come back soon."

"I will." She'd never been able to stay away.

"The barbecue's in two weeks. I expect you to be here."

"I wouldn't miss it."

"Brady," he said as he left, "behave yourself with that girl."

Brady grinned as the door closed. "He still figures I'm going to talk you into the back seat of my car."

"You did talk me into the back seat of your car."

"Yeah." The memory made him restless. "Any coffee?"

"Tea," she said. "With lemon verbena."

With a grunt, he turned and took a carton of milk from the refrigerator. "I'm glad you stopped by to see him. He's crazy about you."

"The feeling's mutual."

"You going to eat that pie?"

"No, I was just—" he sat down and dug in "—leaving."

"What's your hurry?" he asked over a forkful.

"I'm not in a hurry, I just—"

"Sit down." He poured an enormous glass of milk.

"Your appetite's as healthy as ever, I see."

"Clean living."

She should go, really. But he looked so relaxed, and relaxing, sitting at the table shoveling in pie. Friends, he'd said. Maybe they *could* be friends. She leaned back against the counter.

"Where's the dog?"

"Left him home. Dad caught him digging in the tulips yesterday, so he's banished."

"You don't live here anymore?"

"No." He looked up and nearly groaned. She was leaning on the counter in front of the window, the light in her hair. There was the faintest of smiles playing on that full, serious mouth of hers. The severe tailoring of her slacks and shirt made her seem that much softer and feminine. "I, ah..." He reached for the milk. "I bought some land outside of town. The house is going up slow, but it's got a roof."

"You're building your own house?"

"I'm not doing that much. I can't get away from here long enough to do much more than stick up a couple of two-by-fours. I've got a couple of guys hammering it together." He looked at her again, considering. "I'll drive you out some time so you can take a look."

"Maybe."

"How about now?" He rose to put his dishes in the sink.

"Oh, well...I really have to get back...."

"For what?"

"To practice."

He turned. Their shoulders brushed. "Practice later."

It was a challenge. They both knew it, both understood it. They were both determined to prove that they could be in each other's company without stirring up old yearnings.

"All right. I'll follow you out, though. That way you won't have to come back into town."

"Fine." He took her arm and led her out the back door.

He'd had a secondhand Chevy sedan when she'd left town. Now he drove a sporty four-wheel drive. Three miles out of town, when they came to the steep, narrow lane, she saw the wisdom of it.

It would be all but impassable in the winter, she thought as her Mercedes jolted up the graveled incline. Though the leaves were little more than tender shoots, the woods were thick. She could see the wild dogwoods blooming white. She narrowly avoided a rut. Gravel spit out from under her wheels as she negotiated the last sweeping turn and came to a halt behind Brady.

The dog came racing, barking, his tail fanning in the breeze.

The shell of the house was up. He wasn't contenting himself with a cabin in the woods, she noted. It was a huge, spreading two-story place. The windows that were in place were tall, with half-moon arches over them. What appeared to be the skeleton of a gable rose up from the second story. It would command a majestic view of the distant Blue Mountains.

The grounds, covered with the rubble of construction, sloped down to a murmuring creek. Rain would turn the site into a mud pit, she thought as she stepped from her car. But, oh, when it was terraced and planted, it would be spectacular.

"It's fabulous." She pushed back her hair as the early evening breeze stirred it. "What a perfect spot."

"I thought so." He caught Kong by the collar before he could leap on her.

"He's all right." She laughed as she bent down to rub him. "Hello, fella. Hello, big boy. You've got plenty of room to run around here, don't you?"

"Twelve acres." He was getting that ache again, just under his heart, watching her play with his dog. "I'm going to leave most of it alone."

"I'm glad." She turned a full circle. "I'd hate to see you manicure the woods. I'd nearly forgotten how wonderful they are. How quiet."

"Come on." He took her hand, held it. "I'll give you the tour."

"How long have you had the land?"

"Almost a year." They walked across a little wooden bridge, over the creek. "Watch your step. The ground's a mess." He looked down at her elegant Italian flats. "Here." He hoisted her up and over the rubble. She felt the bunching of his arm muscles, he the firm length of her legs.

"You don't have to—" He set her down, hastily, in front of a pair of atrium doors. "Still Mr. Smooth, aren't you?"

"You bet."

Inside there was subflooring and drywall. She saw power tools, sawhorses and piles of lumber. A huge stone fireplace was already built into the north wall. Temporary stairs led to the second level. The scent of sawdust was everywhere.

"The living room," he explained. "I wanted plenty of light. The kitchen's over there."

He indicated a generous space that curved off the main room. There was a bay window over the sink that looked out into the woods. A stove and refrigerator were nestled between unfinished counters.

"We'll have an archway to keep in tune with the windows," he went on. "Then another will lead around to the dining room."

She looked up at the sky through a trio of skylights. "It seems very ambitious."

"I only intend to do it once." Taking her hand again, he led her around the first floor. "Powder room. Your mother found me this great pedestal sink. The porcelain's in perfect shape. And this is a kind of a den, I guess. Stereo equipment, books." When he narrowed his eyes, he could see the finished product perfectly. And oddly, so could she. "Do you remember Josh McKenna?"

"Yes. He was your partner in crime."

"Now he's a partner in a construction firm. He's doing all these built-ins himself."

"Josh?" She ran a hand over a shelf. The workmanship was beautiful.

"He designed the kitchen cabinets, too. They're going to be something. Let's go up. The stairs are narrow, but they're sturdy."

Despite his assurances, she kept one hand pressed against the wall as they climbed. There were more skylights, more arches. The eyebrow windows, as he called them, would go over the bed in the master suite, which included an oversize bathroom with a tiled sunken tub. Though there were a mattress and a dresser in the bedroom, the bath was the only finished room. Vanessa stepped off subflooring onto ceramic.

He'd chosen cool pastels with an occasional vivid slash of navy. The huge tub was encircled by a tiled ledge that sat flush against another trio of windows. Vanessa imagined soaking there with a view of the screening woods.

"You've pulled out all the stops," she commented.

"When I decided to move back, I decided to do it right." They continued down the hall, between the studded walls. "There are two more bedrooms on this floor, and another bath. I'm going to use glass brick in that one. The deck will run all around, then drop down to the second level on the west side for sunset." He took her up another flight of splattered steps into the gable. "I'm thinking about putting my office up here."

It was like a fairy tale, Vanessa thought, circular in shape, with more arching windows. Everywhere you stood there was a lofty view of the woods and the mountains beyond.

"I could live right here," she said, "and feel like Rapunzel."

"Your hair's the wrong color." He lifted a handful. "I'm glad you never cut it. I used to dream about this hair." His gaze shifted to hers. "About you. For years after you left, I used to dream about you. I could never figure it out."

She turned away quickly and walked to one of the windows. "When do you think you'll have it finished?"

"We're shooting for September." He frowned at her back. He hadn't thought of her when he'd designed the house, when he'd chosen the wood, the tiles, the colors. Why was it that now that she was here it was as if the house had been waiting for her? As if he'd been waiting for her? "Van?"

"Yes," she answered, keeping her back to him. Her stomach was in knots, her fingers were twisted. When he said nothing else, she forced herself to turn, made her lips curve. "It's a fabulous place, Brady. I'm glad you showed it to me. I hope I get the chance to see it when it's done."

He wasn't going to ask her if she was going to stay. He didn't want to know. He couldn't let it matter. But he knew that there was unfinished business between them, and he had to settle it, at least in his own mind.

He crossed to her slowly. He saw the awareness come into her eyes with his first step. She would have backed away if there had been anywhere to go.

"Don't," she said when he took her arms.

"This is going to hurt me as much as it does you."

He touched his lips to hers, testing. And felt her shudder. Her taste, just that brief taste, made him burn. Again he kissed her, lingering over it only seconds longer. This time he heard her moan. His hands slid up her arms to cup her face. When his mouth took hers again, the testing was over.

It did hurt. She felt the ache through every bone and muscle. And damn him, she felt the pleasure. A pleasure she had lived without for too long. Greedy for it, she pulled him closer and let the war rage frantically inside her.

She was no longer kissing a boy, however clever and passionate that boy had been. She wasn't kissing a memory, no matter how rich and clear that memory had been. It was a man she held now. A strong, hungry man who knew her much too well.

When her lips parted for his, she knew what he would taste like. As her hands dug into his shoulders, she knew the feel of those muscles. With the scent of sawdust around them, and the light gentle through the glass, she felt herself rocked back and forth between the past and present.

She was all he remembered, and more. He had always been generous, always passionate, but there seemed to be more innocence now than there had been before. It was there, sweet, beneath the simmer of desire. Her body trembled even as it strained against his.

The dreams he thought he had forgotten flooded back. And with them the needs, the frustrations, the hopes, of his youth.

It was her. It had always been her. And yet it had never been.

Shaken, he pulled back and held her at arm's length. The color had risen over her cheekbones. Her eyes had darkened, clouded, in that way that had always made him churn. Her lips were parted, soft, unpainted. His hands were lost, as they had been countless times before, in her hair.

And the feeling was the same. He could have murdered her for it. Twelve years hadn't diluted the emotion she could pull out of him with a look.

"I was afraid of that," he murmured. He needed to keep sane, he told himself. He needed to think. "You always could stop my heart, Vanessa."

"This is stupid." Breathless, she stepped back. "We're not children anymore."

He dipped his hands in his pockets. "Exactly."

She ran an unsteady hand through her hair. "Brady, this was over a long time ago."

"Apparently not. Could be we just have to get it out of our systems."

"My system's just fine," she told him. It was a lie. "You'll have to worry about your own. I'm not interested in climbing into the back seat with you again."

"That might be interesting." He surprised himself by smiling, and meaning it. "But I had more comfortable surroundings in mind."

"Whatever the surroundings, the answer's still no."

She started toward the steps, and he took her by the arm. "You were sixteen the last time you said no." Slowly, though impatience simmered through him, he turned her to face him. "As much as I regret it, I have to say you were right. Times have changed, and we're all grown up now."

Her heart was beating too fast, she thought. His fault. He had always been able to tie her into knots. "Just because we're adults doesn't mean I'll jump in your bed."

"It does mean that I'll take the time and make the effort to change your mind."

"You are still an egotistical idiot, Brady."

"And you still call me names when you know I'm right." He pulled her close for a hard, brief kiss. "I still want you, Van. And this time, by God, I'm going to have you."

She saw the truth of it in his eyes before she jerked away. She felt the truth of it inside herself. "Go to hell."

She turned and rushed down the stairs.

He watched from the window as she raced across the bridge to her car. Even with the distance, he heard her slam the door. It made him grin. She'd always had a devil of a temper. He was glad to see it still held true.

Chapter 4

She pounded the keys. Tchaikovsky. The first piano concerto. The first movement. Hers was a violently passionate interpretation of the romantic theme. She wanted the violence, wanted to let it pour out from inside her and into the music.

He'd had no right. No right to bring everything back. To force her to face feelings she'd wanted to forget. Feelings she'd forgotten. Worse, he'd shown her how much deeper, how much more raw and intense, those feelings could be now that she was a woman.

He meant nothing to her. Could be nothing more to her than an old acquaintance, a friend of her childhood. She would not be hurt by him again. And she would never—never—allow anyone to have the kind of power over her that Brady had once had.

The feelings would pass, because she would make them pass. If there was one thing she had learned through all these years of work and travel, it was that she and she alone was responsible for her emotions.

She stopped playing, letting her fingers rest on the keys. While she might not have been able to claim serenity, she was grateful that she had been able to exorcise most of the anger and frustration through her music.

"Vanessa?"

She turned her head to see her mother standing in the doorway. "I didn't know you were home."

"I came in while you were playing." Loretta took a step forward. She was dressed as she had been that morning, in her sleek suit and pearls, but her face showed a hesitant concern. "Are you all right?"

"Yes, I'm fine." Vanessa lifted a hand to push back her hair. Looking at her mother, she felt flushed, untidy and vulnerable. Automatically, defensively, she straightened her shoulders. "I'm sorry. I guess I lost track of the time."

"It doesn't matter." Loretta blocked off the urge to move closer and smooth her daughter's hair herself. "Mrs. Driscoll stopped by the shop before I closed. She mentioned that she saw you going into Ham Tucker's house."

"She still has an eagle eye, I see."

"And a big nose." Loretta's smile was hesitant. "You saw Ham, then."

"Yes." Vanessa turned on the stool, but didn't rise. "He looks wonderful, almost unchanged. We had some pie and tea in the kitchen."

"I'm glad you had a chance to visit with him. He's always been so fond of you."

"I know." She took a bracing breath. "Why didn't you tell me you were involved with him?"

Loretta lifted a hand to her pearls and twisted the

strand nervously. "I suppose I wasn't sure how to bring it up. To explain. I thought you might be…might feel awkward about seeing him again if you knew we were…" She let her words trail off, certain the word *dating* would be out of place at her age.

Vanessa merely lifted a brow. "Maybe you thought it was none of my business."

"No." Her hand fell to her side. "Oh, Van…"

"Well, it isn't, after all." Slowly, deliberately, Vanessa patched up the cracks in her shield. "You and my father had been divorced for years before he died. You're certainly free to choose your own companions."

The censure in her daughter's voice had Loretta's spine straightening. There were many things, many, that she regretted, that had caused her shame. Her relationship with Abraham Tucker wasn't one of them.

"You're absolutely right," she said, her voice cool. "I'm not embarrassed, and I certainly don't feel guilty, about seeing Ham. We're adults, and both of us are free." The tilt of her chin as she spoke was very like her daughter's. "Perhaps I felt odd about what started between us, because of Emily. She had been my oldest and dearest friend. But Emily was gone, and both Ham and I were alone. And maybe the fact that we both had loved Emily had something to do with our growing closer. I'm very proud that he cares for me," she said, color dotting her cheeks. "In the past few years, he's given me something I've never had from another man. Understanding."

She turned and hurried up the stairs. She was standing in front of her dresser, removing her jewelry, when Vanessa came in.

"I apologize if I seemed too critical."

Loretta slapped the pearls down on the wood. "I don't want you to apologize like some polite stranger,

Vanessa. You're my daughter. I'd rather you shouted at me. I'd rather you slammed doors or stormed into your room the way you used to."

"I nearly did." She walked farther into the room, running a hand over the back of a small, tufted chair. Even that was new, she thought—the little blue lady's chair that so suited the woman who was her mother. Calmer now, and more than a little ashamed, she chose her next words carefully. "I don't resent your relationship with Dr. Tucker. Really. It surprised me, certainly. And what I said before is true. It's none of my business."

"Van—"

"No, please." Vanessa held up a hand. "When I first drove into town, I thought nothing had changed. But I was wrong. It's difficult to accept that. It's difficult to accept that you moved on so easily."

"Moved on, yes," Loretta said. "But not easily."

Vanessa looked up, passion in her eyes. "Why did you let me go?"

"I had no choice," Loretta said simply. "And at the time I tried to believe it was what was best for you. What you wanted."

"What I wanted?" The anger she wanted so badly to control seeped out as bitterness. "Did anyone ever ask me what I wanted?"

"I tried. In every letter I wrote you, I begged you to tell me if you were happy, if you wanted to come home. When you sent them back unopened, I knew I had my answer."

The color ran into and then out of Vanessa's face as she stared at Loretta. "You never wrote me."

"I wrote you for years, hoping that you might find the compassion to open at least one."

"There were no letters," Vanessa said, very deliberately, her hands clenching and unclenching.

Without a word, Loretta went over to an enameled trunk at the foot of her bed. She drew out a deep box and removed the lid. "I kept them," she said.

Vanessa looked in and saw dozens of letters, addressed to her at hotels throughout Europe and the States. Her stomach convulsing, she took careful breaths and sat on the edge of the bed.

"You never saw them, did you?" Loretta murmured. Vanessa could only shake her head. "He would deny me even such a little thing as a letter." With a sigh, Loretta set the box back in the trunk."

"Why?" Vanessa's throat was raw. "Why did he stop me from seeing your letters?"

"Maybe he thought I would interfere with your career." After a moment's hesitation, Loretta touched her shoulder. "He was wrong. I would never have stopped you from reaching for something you wanted and deserved so much. He was, in his way, protecting you and punishing me."

"For what?"

Loretta turned and walked to the window.

"Damn it, I have a right to know." Fury had her on her feet and taking a step forward. Then, with an involuntary gasp, she was clutching her stomach.

"Van?" Loretta took her shoulders, moving her gently back to the bed. "What is it?"

"It's nothing." She gritted her teeth against the grinding pain. It infuriated her that it could incapacitate her, even for a moment, in front of someone else. "Just a spasm."

"I'm going to call Ham."

"No." Vanessa grabbed her arm. Her long musician's

fingers were strong and firm. "I don't need a doctor. It's just stress." She kept one hand balled at her side and struggled to get past the pain. "And I stood up too fast." Very carefully, she relaxed her hand.

"Then it won't hurt to have him look at you." Loretta draped an arm over her shoulders. "Van, you're so thin."

"I've had a lot to deal with in the last year." Vanessa kept her words measured. "A lot of tension. Which is why I've decided to take a few months off."

"Yes, but—"

"I know how I feel. And I'm fine."

Loretta removed her arm when she heard Vanessa's dismissive tone. "All right, then. You're not a child anymore."

"No, I'm not." She folded her hands in her lap as Loretta rose. "I'd like an answer. What was my father punishing you for?"

Loretta seemed to brace herself, but her voice was calm and strong when she spoke. "For betraying him with another man."

For a moment, Vanessa could only stare. Here was her mother, her face pale but set, confessing to adultery. "You had an affair?" Vanessa asked at length.

"Yes." Shame rushed through her. But she knew she could deal with it. She'd lived with shame for years. "There was someone… It hardly matters now who it was. I was involved with him for almost a year before you went to Europe."

"I see."

Loretta gave a short, brittle laugh. "Oh, I'm sure you do. So I won't bother to offer you any excuses or explanations. I broke my vows, and I've been paying for it for twelve years."

Vanessa lifted her head, torn between wanting to understand and wanting to condemn. "Did you love him?"

"I needed him. There's a world of difference."

"You didn't marry again."

"No." Loretta felt no regret at that, just a vague ache, as from an old scar that had been bumped once too often. "Marriage wasn't something either of us wanted at the time."

"Then it was just for sex." Vanessa pressed her fingers against her eyes. "You cheated on your husband just for sex."

A flurry of emotions raced over Loretta's face before she calmed it again. "That's the least common denominator. Maybe, now that you're a woman, you'll understand, even if you can't forgive."

"I don't understand anything." Vanessa stood. It was foolish to want to weep for something that was over and done. "I need to think. I'm going for a drive."

Alone, Loretta sat on the edge of the bed and let her own tears fall.

She drove for hours, aimlessly. She spent most of the time negotiating curving back roads lined with budding wildflowers and arching trees. Some of the old farms had been sold and subdivided since she'd been here last. Houses and yards crisscrossed over what had once been sprawling corn or barley fields. She felt a pang of loss on seeing them. The same kind of pang she felt when she thought of her family.

She wondered if she would have been able to understand the lack of fidelity if it had been some other woman. Would she have been able to give a sophisticated little shrug and agree that the odd affair was just

a part of life? She wasn't sure. She hadn't been raised to
see a sanctified state. And it wasn't some other woman.
It was her mother.

It was late when she found herself turning into Brady's lane. She didn't know why she'd come here, come
to him, of all people. But she needed someone to listen.
Someone who cared.

The lights were on. She could hear the dog barking
from inside the house at the sound of her car. Slowly she
retraced the steps she had taken that evening. When she
had run from him, and from her own feelings. Before
she could knock, Brady was at the door. He took a long
look at her through the glass before pulling it open.

"Hi."

"I was out driving." She felt so completely stupid that
she took a step back. "I'm sorry. It's late."

"Come on in, Van." He took her hand. The dog sniffed
at her slacks, wagging his tail. "Want a drink?"

"No." She had no idea what she wanted. She looked
around, aware that she'd interrupted him. There was a
stepladder against a wall, and a portable stereo set too
loud. Rock echoed to the ceiling. She noted there was a
fine coat of white dust on his hands and forearms, even
in his hair. She fought a ridiculous urge to brush it out
for him. "You're busy."

"Just sanding drywall." He walked over to turn off the
music. The sudden silence made her edgy. "It's amazingly therapeutic." He picked up a sheet of sandpaper.
"Want to try it?"

She managed to smile. "Maybe later."

He stopped by the refrigerator to pull out a beer. He
gestured with it. "Sure?"

"Yes. I'm driving, and I can't stay long."

He popped the top and took a long drink. The cold

beer eased through the dust in his throat—and through the knot that had lodged there when he saw her walking to his door. "I guess you decided not to be mad at me anymore."

"I don't know." Hugging her arms, Vanessa walked to the far window. She wished she could see the moon, but it was hiding behind a bank of clouds. "I don't know what I feel about anything."

He knew that look, that set of her shoulders, that tone of voice. It had been the same years before, when she would escape from one of the miserable arguments between her parents. "Why don't you tell me about it?"

Of course he would say that, she thought. Hadn't she known he would? And he would listen. He always had. "I shouldn't have come here," she said with a sigh. "It's like falling back into an old rut."

"Or slipping into a comfortable pair of shoes." He winced a little at his own words. "I don't think I like that much better. Look, do you want to sit down? I can dust off a sawhorse, or turn over a can of drywall compound."

"No. No, I couldn't sit." She continued to stare out the window. All she could see was her own pale reflection ghosted on the glass. "My mother told me she'd had an affair before my father took me to Europe." When he didn't respond, she turned to study his face. "You knew."

"Not at the time." The hurt and bewilderment on her face had him crossing to her to brush at her hair. "Not long after you were gone, it came out." He shrugged. "Small towns."

"My father knew," Vanessa said carefully. "My mother said as much. That must have been why he took me away the way he did. And why she didn't come with us."

"I can't comment on what went on between your parents, Van. If there are things you need to know, you should hear them from Loretta."

"I don't know what to say to her. I don't know what to ask." She turned away again. "In all those years, my father never said a thing about it."

That didn't surprise him, but he doubted Julius's motives had been altruistic. "What else did she tell you?"

"What else is there to tell?" Vanessa countered.

Brady was silent for a moment. "Did you ask her why?"

"I didn't have to." She rubbed a chill from her arms. "She told me she didn't even love the man. It was just physical. Just sex."

He contemplated his beer. "Well, I guess we should drag her out in the street and shoot her."

"It's not a joke," Vanessa said, whirling around. "She deceived her husband. She cheated on him while they were living together, while she was pretending to be part of a family."

"That's all true. Considering the kind of woman Loretta is, it seems to me she must have had some very strong reasons." His eyes stayed on hers, calm and searching. "I'm surprised it didn't occur to you."

"How can you justify adultery?"

"I'm not. But there are very few situations that are simple black and white. I think once you get over the shock and the anger, you'll ask her about those gray areas."

"How would you feel if it was one of your parents?"

"Lousy." He set the beer aside. "Want a hug?"

She felt the tears rise to burn the backs of her eyes. "Yes," she managed, and went gratefully into his arms.

He held her, his arms gentle, his hands easy as they stroked along her back. She needed him now, he thought. And the need was for friendship. However tangled his emotions were, he could never refuse her that. He brushed his lips over her hair, enchanted by the texture, the scent, the warm, deep color. Her arms were tight around him. Her head was nestled just beneath his.

She still fitted, he thought. She was still a perfect fit.

He seemed so solid. She wondered how such a reckless boy could have become such a solid, dependable man. He was giving her, without her even having asked, exactly what she needed. Nothing more, nothing less.

Her eyes closed, she thought how easy, how terrifyingly easy, it would be to fall in love with him all over again.

"Feeling any better?"

She didn't know about better, but she was definitely feeling. The hypnotic stroke of his hands up and down her spine, the steady rhythm of his heart against hers.

She lifted her head, just enough to see his eyes. There was understanding in them, and a strength that had developed during the time she had been without him.

"I can't make up my mind whether you've changed or whether you're the same."

"Some of both." Her scent was waltzing through his system. "I'm glad you came back."

"I didn't mean to." She sighed again. "I wasn't going to get near you again. When I was here before, I was angry because you made me remember—and what I remembered was that I'd never really forgotten."

If she looked at him that way five more seconds, he knew, he'd forget she'd come looking for a friend. "Van…you should probably try to straighten this out with your mother. Why don't I drive you home?"

"I don't want to go home tonight." Her words echoed in her head. She had to press her lips tightly together before she could form the next words. "Let me stay here with you."

The somewhat pleasant ache that had coursed through him as he'd held her turned sharp and deadly. With his movements slow and deliberate, he put his hands on her shoulders and stepped back.

"That's not a good idea." When her mouth turned into a pout, he nearly groaned.

"A few hours ago, you seemed to think it was a very good idea." She shrugged his hands off her shoulders before she turned. "Apparently you're still a lot of talk and no action."

He spun her around quickly, threats hovering on his tongue. As she watched, the livid fury in his eyes died to a smolder. "You still know what buttons to push."

She tilted her head. "And you don't."

He slipped a hand around her throat. "You're such a brat." When she tossed back her head, he was tempted to give her throat just one quick squeeze. He reminded himself that he was a doctor. "It would serve you right if I dragged you upstairs and made love to you until you were deaf, dumb and blind."

She felt a thrill of excitement mixed with alarm. What would it be like? Hadn't she wondered since the first moment she'd seen him again? Maybe it was time to be reckless.

"I'd like to see you try."

Desire seared through him as he looked at her, her

head thrown back, her eyes hooded, her mouth soft and sulky. He knew what it would be like. Damn her. He'd spent hours trying not to imagine what now came all too clearly to his mind. In defense he took a step backward.

"Don't push it, Van."

"If you don't want me, why—?"

"You know I do," he shouted at her as he spun away. "Damn it, you know I always have. You make me feel like I'm eighteen and itchy again." When she took a step forward, he threw up a hand. "Just stay away from me." He snatched up his beer and took a long, greedy swallow. "You can take the bed," he said more calmly. "I've got a sleeping bag I can use down here."

"Why?"

"The timing stinks." He drained the beer and tossed the empty bottle into a five-gallon drum. It shattered. "By God, if we're going to have another shot at this, we're going to do it right. Tonight you're upset and confused and unhappy. You're angry with your mother, and you're not going to hate me for taking advantage of all of that."

She looked down at her hands and spread them. He was right. That was the hell of it. "The timing's never been right for us, has it?"

"It will be." He put a hand on either side of her face. "You can count on it. You'd better go up." He dropped his hands again. "Being noble makes me cranky."

With a nod, she started toward the stairs. At the base, she stopped and turned. "Brady, I'm really sorry you're such a nice guy."

He rubbed at the tension at the back of his neck. "Me, too."

She smiled a little. "No, not because of tonight. You're

right about tonight. I'm sorry because it reminds me how crazy I was about you. And why."

Pressing a hand to the ache in his gut, he watched her go upstairs. "Thanks a lot," he said to himself. "That's just what I needed to hear to make sure I don't sleep at all tonight."

Vanessa lay in Brady's bed, tangled in Brady's sheets. The dog had deserted him to sleep at her feet. She could hear the soft canine snoring as she stared into the deep, deep country dark.

Would she—could she—have gone through with her invitation to come to this bed with him? A part of her yearned to. A part of her that had waited all these years to feel as only he could make her feel.

Yet, when she had offered herself to him, she had done so recklessly, heedlessly, and in direct opposition to her own instinct for survival.

She had walked away from him just this evening, angry, even insulted, at his cocky insistence that they would become lovers. What kind of sense did it make for her to have come back to him in emotional turmoil and rashly ask to do just that?

It made no sense at all.

He had always confused her, she thought as she turned restlessly in his bed. He had always been able to make her ignore her own common sense. Now that she was sleeping—or trying to—alone, her frustration was tempered by gratitude that he understood her better than she understood herself.

In all the years she had been away, in all the cities where she had traveled, not one of the men who had escorted her had tempted her to open the locks she had so firmly bolted on her emotions.

Only Brady. And what, for God's sake, was she going to do about it?

She was sure—nearly sure—that if things stayed as they were she would be able to leave painlessly when the time came. If she could think of him as a friend, a sometimes maddening friend, she could fly off to pick up her career when she was ready. But if he became her lover, her first and only lover, the memory might haunt her like a restless ghost throughout her life.

And there was more, she admitted with a sigh. She didn't want to hurt him. No matter how angry he could make her, no matter how deeply he had, and could, hurt her, she didn't want to cause him any real pain.

She knew what it was like to live with that kind of pain, the kind that spread and throbbed, the kind that came when you knew someone didn't care enough. Someone didn't want you enough.

She wouldn't do to Brady what had been done to her.

If he had been kind enough to allow her to hide in his home for a few hours, she would be kind enough to repay the favor by making sure they kept a reasonable distance between them.

No, she thought grimly, she would not be his lover. Or any man's. She had her mother's example before her. When her mother had taken a lover, it had ruined three lives. Vanessa knew her father had never been happy. Driven, yes. Obsessed with his daughter's career. And bitter, Vanessa thought now. Oh, so bitter. He had never forgiven his wife for her betrayal. Why else had he blocked the letters she had sent to her daughter? Why else had he never, never spoken her name?

As the gnawing in her stomach grew sharper, she

curled up tight. Somehow she would try to accept what her mother had done, and what she hadn't done.

Closing her eyes, she listened to the call of an owl in the woods, and the distant rumble of thunder on the mountain.

She awoke at first light to the patter of rain on the roof. It sent music playing in her head as she shifted. Though she felt heavy with fatigue, she sat up, hugging her knees as she blinked at the gloom.

The dog was gone, but the sheets at her feet were still warm from him. It was time for her to go, as well.

The big tiled tub was tempting, but she reminded herself to be practical and turned instead to the glassed-in corner shower. In ten minutes she was walking quietly downstairs.

Brady was flat on his stomach in his twisted sleeping bag, his face buried in a ridiculously small pillow. With his dog sitting patiently beside him, he made a picture that turned her heart upside down.

Kong grinned and thumped his tail as she came to the bottom of the steps. She put a warning finger to her lips. Kong obviously wasn't up on sign language, as he let out two sharp, happy barks, then turned to lick Brady's face wherever he could reach.

Swearing, Brady shoved the dog's face away from his. "Let yourself out, damn it. Don't you know a dead man when you see one?"

Undaunted, Kong sat on him.

"Here, boy." Vanessa walked to the door and opened it. Delighted to have his needs understood, Kong bounded outside into the pattering rain. When she looked back,

Brady was sitting up, the sleeping bag pooled around his waist. Bleary-eyed, he scowled at her.

"How come you look so damn good?"

The same could be said about him, she thought. As he'd claimed, he'd filled out a bit. His naked chest looked rock-firm, his shoulders leanly muscled. Because her nerves were beginning to jump, she concentrated on his face.

Why was it he looked all the more attractive with a night's stubble and a surly set to his mouth?

"I used your shower. I hope you don't mind." When he just grunted, she worked up a smile. If she felt this awkward now, she wondered, how would she have felt if he'd joined her in the bed? "I appreciate the night's sanctuary, Brady. Really. Why don't I pay you back by making some coffee?"

"How fast can you make it?"

"Faster than room service." She slipped past him to the adjoining kitchen. "I learned to keep a travel pot with me in hotels." She found a glass pot and a plastic cone filter. "But I think this is a little out of my league."

"Put some water in the kettle. I'll walk you through it."

Grateful for the occupation, she turned on the tap. "I'm sorry about all this," she said. "I know I dumped on you last night, and you were very…" She turned, and her words trailed off. He was standing now, tugging jeans over his hips. Her mouth went bone-dry.

"Stupid," he finished for her. Metal rasped on metal as he pulled up the zipper. "Insane."

"Understanding," she managed. He started toward her. Her feet knocked up against the unfinished counter as she took a hasty step in retreat.

"Don't mention it," he said. "And I do mean don't mention it. I've had an entire sleepless night to regret it."

She lifted a hand to his cheek, then hastily dropped it when she saw his eyes darken. "You should have told me to go home. It was childish of me not to. I'm sure my mother was worried."

"I called her after you went up."

She looked down at the floor. "You're much kinder than I am."

He didn't want her gratitude, he thought. Or her embarrassment. Annoyed, he passed her a paper filter. "You put this in the cone and put the cone on the glass pot. Six scoops of coffee in the filter, then pour the hot water through. Got it?"

"Yes." There was no need for him to be so snotty when she was trying to thank him.

"Terrific. I'll be back in a minute."

She set her hands on her hips as he padded upstairs. An exasperating man, she thought. Sweet and compassionate one minute, surly and rude the next. With a half laugh, she turned back to scowl at the teakettle. And wasn't that just the combination that had always fascinated her? At least she was no longer a naive girl certain he would turn into a prince.

Determined to finish what she had started, she measured out the coffee. She loved the rich morning aroma of it, and wished she hadn't had to stop drinking it. Caffeine, she thought with a wistful sigh. It no longer seemed to agree with her.

She was pouring the boiling water over the coffee when Brady came back. His hair was damp, she noted. And there was the lingering scent of soap around him.

Because her mind was set to be friendly, she smiled at him.

"That had to be the quickest shower on record."

"I learned to be quick when I was an intern." He took a long, deep sniff of the coffee. It was his bad luck that he could also smell his shampoo on her hair. "I'm going to feed Kong," he said abruptly, and left her alone again.

When he returned, she was smiling at the coffee, which had nearly dripped through. "I remember one of these in your kitchen on Main Street."

"My mother always made drip coffee. The best."

"Brady, I haven't told you how sorry I am. I know how close you were."

"She never gave up on me. Probably should have more than once, but she never did." His eyes met Vanessa's. "I guess mothers don't."

Uncomfortable, Vanessa turned away. "I think it's ready." When he reached for two mugs, she shook her head. "No, I don't want any, thanks. I've given it up."

"As a doctor, I can tell you that's commendable." He poured a full mug. "As a human being, I have to ask how you function."

She smiled. "You just start a little slower, that's all. I have to go."

He simply put a hand on the counter and blocked her way. There was rain on his hair now, and his eyes were very clear. "You didn't sleep well."

"I'd say that makes two of us."

He took a casual sip of his coffee as he completed a thorough study of her face. The fatigue he saw was due to more than one restless night. "I want you to do something for me."

"If I can."

"Go home, pull the covers over your head, and tune out until noon."

Her lips curved. "I might just do that."

"If those shadows under your eyes aren't gone in forty-eight hours, I'm going to sic my father on you."

"Big talk."

"Yeah." He set the mug aside and then, leaning his other hand on the counter, effectively caged her. "I seem to remember a comment last night about no action."

Since she couldn't back up, she held her ground. "I was trying to make you mad."

"You did." He leaned closer until their thighs met.

"Brady, I don't have the time or patience for this. I have to go."

"Okay. Kiss me goodbye."

Her chin tilted. "I don't want to."

"Sure you do." His mouth whispered over hers before she could jerk her head back. "You're just afraid to."

"I've never been afraid of you."

"No." He smiled an infuriating smile. "But you've learned to be afraid of yourself."

"That's ridiculous."

"Prove it."

Seething, she leaned forward, intent on giving him a brief, soulless kiss. But her heart was in her throat almost instantly. He used no pressure, only soft, soft persuasion. His lips were warm and mobile against hers, his tongue cleverly tracing the shape of her mouth before dipping inside to tease and tempt.

On a breathless murmur, she took her hands up and over his naked chest to his shoulders. His skin was damp and cool.

He nipped gently at her lips, drowning in the taste of her. Using all his control, he kept his tensed hands on the counter. He knew that if he touched her now, even once, he wouldn't stop.

She would come to him. He had promised himself that as he'd sweated through the night. She would come to him, and not because of a memory, not because of grief. Because of need.

Slowly, while he still had some control, he lifted his head and backed away. "I want to see you tonight, Van."

"I don't know." She put a hand to her spinning head.

"Then you think about it." He picked up his mug again, surprised the handle didn't shatter in his grip. "You can call me when you make up your mind."

Her confusion died away, to be replaced by anger. "I'm not playing games."

"Then what the hell are you doing?"

"I'm just trying to survive." She snatched up her purse and ran out into the rain.

Chapter 5

Bed sounded like a wonderful idea, Vanessa decided as she pulled up in front of the house. Maybe if she drew down the shades, put the music on low and willed herself to relax, she would find the sleep she had lost the night before. When she felt more rested, she might have a clearer idea of what to say to her mother.

She wondered if a few hours' sleep would help her resolve her feelings about Brady.

It was worth a shot.

She stepped out of the car and rounded the hood to the sidewalk. When she heard her name called, she turned. Mrs. Driscoll was lumbering toward her, clutching her purse and a stack of mail. A huge, wood-handled black umbrella was tight in her fist. Vanessa's smile came naturally as she moved forward to greet her.

"Mrs. Driscoll. It's good to see you again."

Only a little winded, Mrs. Driscoll peered out of sharp little eyes. "Heard you were back. Too skinny."

With a laugh, Vanessa bent to kiss her leathery cheek. As always, her former teacher smelled of lavender sachet. "You look wonderful."

"Take care of yourself." She sniffed. "That snippy Brady tells me I need a cane. He thinks he's a doctor. Hold on to this." Bossy by nature, she shoved the umbrella into Vanessa's hand. She opened her purse to stuff her mail inside, stubbornly keeping her balance. The rain made her bones ache all the more, but she had always loved to walk in it. "It's about time you came home. You staying?"

"Well, I haven't—"

"About time you gave your mother some attention," she interrupted, leaving Vanessa with nothing to say. "I heard you playing when I walked to the bank yesterday, but I couldn't stop."

Vanessa struggled with the heavy umbrella, and with her manners. "Would you like to come in, have some tea?"

"Too much to do. You still play real nice, Vanessa."

"Thank you."

When Mrs. Driscoll took the umbrella back, Vanessa thought the little visit was over. She should have known better. "I've got a grandniece. She's been taking piano lessons in Hagerstown. Puts a strain on her ma, having to haul her all that way. Figured now that you're back, you could take over."

"Oh, but I—"

"She's been taking them nigh on a year, an hour once a week. She played 'Jingle Bells' real well at Christmas. Did a fair turn on 'Go Tell Aunt Rhodie,' too."

"That's very nice," Vanessa managed, beginning to feel desperate, as well as wet. "But since she's already got a teacher, I wouldn't want to interfere."

"Lives right across from Lester's. Could walk to your place. Give her ma a breather. Lucy—that's my niece, my younger brother's second girl—she's expecting another next month. Hoping for a boy this time, since they've got the two girls. Girls just seem to run in the family."

"Ah…"

"It's hard on her driving clear up to Hagerstown."

"I'm sure it is, but—"

"You have a free hour once a week, don't you?"

Exasperated, Vanessa dragged a hand through her rapidly dampening hair. "I suppose I do, but—"

Violet Driscoll knew when to spring. "How about today? The school bus drops her off just after three-thirty. She can be here at four."

She had to be firm, Vanessa told herself. "Mrs. Driscoll, I'd love to help you out, but I've never given instruction."

Mrs. Driscoll merely blinked her little black eyes. "You know how to play the thing, don't you?"

"Well, yes, but—"

"Then you ought to be able to show somebody else how. Unless they're like Dory—that's my oldest girl. Never could teach her how to crochet. Clumsy hands. Annie's got good hands. That's my grandniece. Smart, too. You won't have any trouble with her."

"I'm sure I won't—I mean, I'm sure she is. It's just that—"

"Give you ten dollars a lesson." A smug smile creased Mrs. Driscoll's face as Vanessa rattled her brain for excuses. "You were always quick in school, Vanessa. Quick and well behaved. Never gave me any grief like Brady. That boy was trouble from the get-go. Couldn't help but like him for it. I'll see that Annie's here at four."

She trundled off, sheltered under the enormous umbrella, leaving Vanessa with the sensation of having been flattened by an antique but very sturdy steamroller.

Piano lessons, she thought on a little groan. How had it happened? She watched the umbrella disappear around the corner. It had happened the same way she had "volunteered" to clean the blackboard after school.

Dragging a hand through her hair, she walked to the house. It was empty and quiet, but she'd already given up on the idea of going back to bed. If she was going to be stuck running scales with a fledgling virtuoso, then she'd better prepare for it. At least it would keep her mind occupied.

In the music room, she went to the gracefully curved new cabinet. She could only hope that her mother had saved some of her old lesson books. The first drawer contained sheet music she considered too advanced for a first-year student. But her own fingers itched to play as she skimmed the sheets.

She found what she was looking for in the bottom drawer. There they were, a bit dog-eared, but neatly stacked. All of her lesson books, from primer to level six. Struck by nostalgia, she sat cross-legged on the floor and began to pore through them.

How well she remembered those first heady days of lessons. Finger exercises, scales, drills, those first simple melodies. She felt an echo of that rush of emotion that had come when she had learned that she had the power to turn those printed notes into music.

More than twenty years had passed since that first day, that first lesson. Her father had been her teacher then, and though he had been a hard taskmaster, she had been a willing student. How proud she had been the first time he had told her she'd done well. Those small and rare words of praise had driven her to work all the harder.

With a sigh, she dipped into the drawer for more books. If young Annie had been taking lessons for a year, she should have advanced beyond the primary level. It was then that she found the thick scrapbook, the one she knew her mother had started years before. With a smile, she opened the first page.

There were pictures of her at the piano. It made her laugh to see herself in pigtails and neat white ankle socks. Sentimentally she paged through photos of her first recital, her early certificates of accomplishment. And here were the awards that had once hung on her walls, the newspaper clippings from when she had won her first regional competition, her first national.

How terrified she'd been. Sweaty hands, buzzing ears, curdling stomach. She'd begged her father to let her withdraw. He'd refused to listen to her fears. And she'd won, Vanessa mused.

It surprised her that the clippings continued. Here was an article from the London *Times,* written a full year after she had left Hyattown. And here a picture of her in Fort Worth after she'd won the Van Cliburn.

There were dozens—no, hundreds—Vanessa realized. Hundreds of pictures, snippets of news, pieces of gossip, magazine articles—many she had never seen herself. It seemed that everything that had ever been printed about her was here, carefully preserved. Everything, Vanessa thought, down to the last interview she had granted before her concerts in D.C.

First the letters, she thought, the book weighing

heavily on her thighs, and now this. What was she supposed to think? What was she supposed to feel? The
mother she had believed had forgotten her had written
her religiously, even when there had been no answer.
Had followed her every step of her career, though she'd
been allowed no part in it.

And, Vanessa added with a sigh, had opened the door
to her daughter again without question.

But it didn't explain why Loretta had let her go without a murmur. It didn't explain the years away.

I had no choice.

She remembered her mother's words. But what had
she meant? An affair would have destroyed her marriage. There was no doubt of that. Vanessa's father would
never have forgiven her. But why had it severed her relationship with her daughter?

She had to know. She would know. Vanessa rose and
left the books scattered on the rug. She would know
today.

The rain had stopped, and the watery sunlight was
already struggling through the clouds. Birdsong com-
peted with the sound of a children's television show that
chirped through the window of the house next door.
Though it was only a few blocks away, she drove to the
antique shop. Under other circumstances she would have
enjoyed the walk, but she wanted no interruptions from
old friends and acquaintances. The old two-story house
was just on the edge of town. The sign that read Loretta's
Attic was a graceful arch over the front door.

There was an old-fashioned sleigh in the yard, its
metal fittings polished to a gleam. A scarred whiskey
barrel was filled to overflowing with petunias, their
purple-and-white petals drenched with rain. On either
side of the entrance, well-groomed beds spilled over

with spring color. A beribboned grapevine wreath hung on the door. When she pushed it open, bells jingled.

"It's circa 1860," she heard her mother say. "One of my finest sets. I had it refinished locally by a man who does a great deal of work for me. You can see what a wonderful job he does. The finish is like glass."

Vanessa half listened to the exchange coming from the next room. Though she was frustrated to find her mother with a customer, the shop itself was a revelation.

No dusty, cramped antique shop this. Exquisite glass-fronted cabinets displayed china, statuettes, ornate perfume bottles and slender goblets. Wood gleamed on each individual piece. Brass shone. Crystal sparkled. Though every inch of space was utilized, it was more like a cozy family home than a place of business. The scent of rose-and-spice potpourri wafted from a simmer pot.

"You're going to be very happy with that set," Loretta was saying as she walked back into the main room. "If you find it doesn't suit after you get it home, I'll be more than willing to buy it back from you. Oh, Vanessa." After fumbling a moment, she turned to the young executive type beside her. "This is my daughter. Vanessa, this is Mr. Peterson. He's from Montgomery County."

"Damascus," he explained. He looked like a cat who'd been given a whole pitcher of cream. "My wife and I just bought an old farmhouse. We saw that dining room set here a few weeks ago. My wife hasn't been able to talk about anything else. Thought I'd surprise her."

"I'm sure she'll be thrilled."

Vanessa watched as her mother accepted his credit card and went briskly about completing the transaction.

"You've got a terrific place here, Mrs. Sexton," he

went on. "If you came over the county line, you'd have to beat off customers."

"I like it here." She handed him his receipt. "I've lived here all my life."

"Cute town." He pocketed the receipt. "After our first dinner party, I can guarantee you some new customers."

"And I can guarantee I won't beat them off." She smiled at him. "Will you need some help Saturday when you pick it up?"

"No, I'll drag a few friends with me." He shook her hand. "Thanks, Mrs. Sexton."

"Just enjoy it."

"We will." He turned to smile at Vanessa. "Nice meeting you. You've got a terrific mother."

"Thank you."

"Well, I'll be on my way." He stopped halfway to the door. "Vanessa Sexton." He turned back. "The pianist. I'll be damned. I just saw your concert in D.C. last week. You were great."

"I'm glad you enjoyed it."

"I didn't expect to," he admitted. "My wife's the classical nut. I figured I'd catch a nap, but, man, you just blew me away."

She had to laugh. "I'll take that as a compliment."

"No, really. I don't know Mozart from Muzak, but I was—well, I guess enthralled's a good word. My wife'll just about die when I tell her I met you." He pulled out a leather-bound appointment book. "Would you sign this for her? Her name's Melissa."

"I'd be glad to."

"Who'd have expected to find someone like you in a little place like this?" He shook his head as she handed the book back to him.

"I grew up here."

"I can guarantee my wife'll be back." He winked at Loretta. "Thanks again, Mrs. Sexton."

"You're welcome. Drive carefully." She laughed a little after the bells had jingled at his exit. "It's an amazing thing, watching your own child sign an autograph."

"It's the first one I've signed in my hometown." She took a deep breath. "This is a beautiful place. You must work very hard."

"I enjoy it. I'm sorry I wasn't there this morning. I had an early delivery coming."

"It's all right."

Loretta picked up a soft rag, then set it down again. "Would you like to see the rest of the shop?"

"Yes. Yes, I would."

Loretta led the way into the adjoining room. "This is the set your admirer just bought." She ran a fingertip over the top of a gleaming mahogany table. "It has three leaves and will sit twelve comfortably when extended. There's some beautiful carving on the chairs. The buffet and server go with it."

"They're beautiful."

"I bought them at an estate sale a few months ago. They'd been in the same family for over a hundred years. It's sad." She touched one of the glass knobs on the server. "That's why I'm so happy when I can sell something like this to people who will care for it."

She moved to a curved glass china cabinet and opened the door. "I found this cobalt glass at a flea market, buried in a box. Now, the cranberry I got at auction, and paid too much. I couldn't resist it. These saltcellars are French, and I'll have to wait for a collector to take them off my hands."

"How do you know about all of this?" Vanessa asked.

"I learned a lot by working here before I bought it. From reading, from haunting other shops and auctions." She laughed a little as she closed the cabinet door. "And through trial and error. I've made some costly mistakes, but I've also wangled some real bargains."

"You have so many beautiful things. Oh, look at this." Almost reverently, she picked up a Limoges ring box. It was perhaps six inches high and fashioned in the shape of a young girl in a blue bonnet and blue checkered dress. There was a look of smug pleasure on her glossy face. "This is charming."

"I always try to keep in a few Limoges pieces. Whether they're antique or new."

"I have a small collection myself. It's difficult to travel with fragile things, but they always make hotel suites more like home."

"I'd like you to have it."

"I couldn't."

"Please," Loretta said before Vanessa could set it down again. "I've missed a number of birthdays. It would give me a great deal of pleasure if you'd accept it."

Vanessa looked up. They had to turn at least the first corner, she told herself. "Thank you. I'll treasure it."

"I'll get a box for it. Oh, there's the door. I get a lot of browsers on weekday mornings. You can take a look upstairs if you like."

Vanessa kept the little box cupped in her hands. "No, I'll wait for you." Loretta gave her a pleased look before she walked away to greet her customer. When she heard Dr. Tucker's voice join her mother's, Vanessa hesitated, then went in to meet him.

"Well, Van, getting a look at your mother at work?"

"Yes."

He had his arm around her mother's shoulders. Loretta's color had risen. He's just kissed her, Vanessa realized, trying to analyze her feelings. "It's a wonderful place."

"Keeps her off the streets. Of course, I'm going to be doing that myself from now on."

"Ham!"

"Don't tell me you haven't told the child yet." He gave her a quick, impatient squeeze. "Good grief, Loretta, you've had all morning."

"Tell me what?"

With these two, Ham thought, a man had to take the bull by the horns. "It's taken me two years to wear her down, but she finally gave me a yes."

"A yes?" Vanessa repeated.

"Don't tell me you're as thickheaded as your mother?" He kissed the top of Loretta's head and grinned like a boy. "We're getting married."

"Oh." Vanessa stared blankly. "Oh."

"Is that the best you can do?" he demanded. "Why don't you say congratulations and give me a kiss?"

"Congratulations," she said mechanically, and walked over to peck his cheek.

"I said a kiss." He swung his free arm around her and squeezed. Vanessa found herself hugging him back.

"I hope you'll be happy," she managed, and discovered she meant it.

"Of course I will. I'm getting two beauties for the price of one."

"Quite a bargain," Vanessa said with a smile. "When's the big day?"

"As soon as I can pin her down." It hadn't escaped him that Vanessa and Loretta hadn't exchanged a word or an embrace. "Joanie's fixing dinner for all of us tonight," he decided on the spot. "To celebrate."

"I'll be there."

When she stepped back, he grinned wickedly. "After the piano lesson."

Vanessa rolled her eyes. "News travels fast."

"Piano lesson?" Loretta repeated.

"Annie Crampton, Violet Driscoll's grandniece." He gave a hearty laugh as Vanessa wrinkled her nose. "Violet snagged Vanessa this morning."

Loretta smiled. "What time's the lesson?"

"Four. She made me feel like I was the second-grade milk monitor again."

"I can speak to Annie's mother if you'd like," Loretta said.

"No, it's all right. It's only an hour a week while I'm here. But I'd better get back." This was not the time for questions and demands. "I have to put some kind of program together. Thank you again for the box."

"But I haven't wrapped it."

"It's all right. I'll see you at Joanie's, Dr. Tucker."

"Maybe you could call me Ham now. We're family."

"Yes. Yes, I guess we are." It was less effort than she had expected to kiss her mother's cheek. "You're a very lucky woman."

"I know." Loretta's fingers dug into Ham's.

When the bells jingled behind Vanessa, Ham took out a handkerchief.

"I'm sorry," Loretta said as she sniffled into it.

"You're entitled to shed a few. I told you she'd come around."

"She has every reason to hate me."

"You're too hard on yourself, Loretta, and I won't have it."

She merely shook her head as she balled the hand-kerchief in her hand. "Oh, the choices we make in this life, Ham. And the mistakes. I'd give anything in the world to have another chance with her."

"Time's all you need to give." He tilted her chin up and kissed her. "Just give her time."

Vanessa listened to the monotonous plunk of the keys as Annie ground out "Twinkle, Twinkle, Little Star." She might have good hands, but so far Vanessa hadn't seen her put them to good use.

She was a skinny girl with pale flyaway hair, a sulky disposition and knobby knees. But her twelve-year old hands were wide-palmed. Her fingers weren't elegant, but they were as sturdy as little trees.

Potential, Vanessa thought as she tried to smile her encouragement. Surely there was some potential buried there somewhere.

"How many hours a week do you practice, Annie?" Vanessa asked when the child had mercifully finished.

"I don't know."

"Do you do your finger exercises every day?"

"I don't know."

Vanessa gritted her teeth. She had already learned this was Annie's standard answer for all questions. "You've been taking lessons regularly for nearly a year."

"I don't—"

Vanessa put up a hand. "Why don't we make this easy? What do you know?"

Annie just shrugged and swung her feet.

Giving up, Vanessa sat beside her on the stool. "Annie—and give me a real answer—do you want to take piano lessons?"

Annie knocked the heels of her orange sneakers together. "I guess."

"Is it because your mother wants you to?"

"I asked if I could." She stared sulkily down at the keys. "I thought I would like it."

"But you don't."

"I kinda do. Sometimes. But I just get to play baby songs."

"Mmm." Sympathetic, Vanessa stroked her hair. "And what do you want to play?"

"Stuff like Madonna sings. You know, good stuff. Stuff like you hear on the radio." She slanted Vanessa a look. "My other teacher said that's not real music."

"All music is real music. We could make a deal."

Suspicion lighted in Annie's pale eyes. "What kind of deal?"

"You practice an hour every day on your finger exercises and the lesson I give you." She ignored Annie's moan. "And I'll buy some sheet music. One of Madonna's songs. I'll teach you to play it."

Annie's sulky mouth fell open. "For real?"

"For real. But only if you practice every day, so that when you come next week I see an improvement."

"All right!" For the first time in nearly an hour, she grinned, nearly blinding Vanessa with her braces. "Wait till I tell Mary Ellen. She's my best friend."

"You've got another fifteen minutes before you can tell her." Vanessa rose, inordinately pleased with herself. "Now, why don't you try that number again?"

Her face screwed up with concentration, Annie began

to play. A little incentive, Vanessa thought with a lifted brow, went a long way.

An hour later, she was still congratulating herself. Tutoring the girl might be fun after all. And she could indulge her own affection for popular music.

Later in her room, Vanessa ran a finger down the Limoges box her mother had given her. Things were changing for her, faster than she had expected. Her mother wasn't the woman she had thought she would find. She was much more human. Her home was still her home. Her friends still her friends.

And Brady was still Brady.

She wanted to be with him, to have her name linked with his as it once had been. At sixteen she had been so sure. Now, as a woman she was afraid, afraid of making a mistake, of being hurt, of losing.

People couldn't just pick up where they had left off. And she could hardly start a new beginning when she had yet to resolve the past.

She took her time dressing for the family dinner. It was to be a festive occasion, and she was determined to be a part of it. Her deep blue dress was cut slimly, with a splash of multicolored beadwork along one shoulder. She left her hair loose, and added braided earrings studded with sapphires.

Before she closed her jewelry box, she took out a ring with a tiny emerald. Unable to resist, she slipped it on. It still fit, she thought, and smiled at the way it looked on her finger. With a shake of her head, she pulled it off again. That was just the sort of sentiment she had to learn to avoid. Particularly if she was going to get through an evening in Brady's company.

They were going to be friends, she reminded herself.

Just friends. It had been a long time since she had been able to indulge in the luxury of a friendship. And if she was still attracted to him—well, that would just add a touch of spice, a little excitement. She wouldn't risk her heart, or his, on anything more.

She pressed a hand to her stomach, swearing at the discomfort. Out of her drawer she took an extra roll of antacids. Festive the evening might be, she thought as she took a pill. But it would still be stressful.

It was time she learned to deal with stress better, she told herself as she stared at her reflection. It was time she refused to allow her body to revolt every time she had to deal with something uncomfortable or unpleasant. She was a grown woman, after all, and a disciplined one. If she could learn to tolerate emotional distress, she could certainly overcome the physical.

After checking her watch, she started downstairs. Vanessa Sexton was never late for a performance.

"Well, well." Brady was lounging at the base of the steps. "You're still Sexy Sexton."

Just what she needed, she thought, her stomach muscles knotting. Did he have to look so gorgeous? She glanced at the front door that he'd left open behind him, then back at him.

"You're wearing a suit."

He glanced down at the gray tweed. "Looks like."

"I've never seen you in a suit," she said foolishly. She stopped a step above him. Eye-to-eye. "Why aren't you at Joanie's?"

"Because I'm taking you to Joanie's."

"That's silly. I have my own—"

"Shut up." Taking her shoulders, he hauled her against him for a kiss. "Every time I do that, you taste better."

She had to wait for her heart to flutter back into place.

"Look, Brady, we're going to have to set up some ground rules."

"I hate rules." He kissed her again, lingering over it this time. "I'm going to get a real kick out of being related to you." He drew back, grinning. "Sis."

"You're not acting very brotherly," she murmured.

"I'll boss you around later. How do you feel about it?"

"I've always loved your father."

"And?"

"And I hope I'm not hard-hearted enough to begrudge my mother any happiness she might have with him."

"That'll do for now." He narrowed his eyes as she rubbed her temple. "Headache?"

She dropped her hand quickly. "Just a little one."

"Take anything?"

"No, it'll pass. Shouldn't we go?"

"All right." He took her hand to lead her out. "I was thinking…why don't we drop by Molly's Hole on the way home?"

She couldn't help but laugh. "You still have a one-track mind."

He opened the car door for her. "Is that a yes?"

She tilted her head, slanted him a look. "That's an I'll-think-about-it."

"Brat," he muttered as he closed the door.

Ten minutes later, Joanie was bursting through her front door to greet them. "Isn't it great? I can hardly stand it!" She grabbed Vanessa to swing her around. "We're really going to be sisters now. I'm so happy for them, for us!" She gave Vanessa another crushing hug.

"Hey, how about me?" Brady demanded. "Don't I even get a hello?"

"Oh, hi, Brady." At his disgusted look, she laughed and launched herself at him. "Wow! You wore a suit and everything!"

"So I'm told. Dad said we had to dress up."

"And did you ever." She pulled back. "Both of you. Lord, Van, where did you get that dress? Fabulous," she said, before Vanessa could answer. "I'd kill to be able to squeeze my hips into that. Well, don't just stand out here, come on in. We've got a ton of food, champagne, the works."

"Hell of a hostess, isn't she?" Brady commented as Joanie rushed inside, shouting for her husband.

Joanie hadn't exaggerated about the food. There was a huge glazed ham, with a mountain of whipped potatoes, an array of vegetables, fluffy homemade biscuits. The scent of cooling apple pies wafted in from the kitchen. The home's festive air was accented by candles and the glint of crystal wineglasses.

The conversation was loud and disjointed, punctuated by Lara's cheerful banging of her spoon against the tray of her high chair.

Vanessa heard her mother laughing, more freely, more openly, than she could ever remember. And she looked lovely, Vanessa thought, smiling at Ham, leaning over to stroke Lara. It was happiness, she realized. True happiness. In all her memories, she could pull out no picture of her mother's face when it had been truly happy.

As the meal wore on, she nibbled lightly, certain that no one would notice her lack of appetite in the confusion. But when she saw Brady watching her, she forced herself to take another bite, to sip at the iced champagne, to laugh at one of Jack's jokes.

"I think this occasion calls for a toast." Brady rose.

He shot Lara a look as she squealed. "You have to wait your turn," he told her, hefting his glass. "To my father, who turned out to be smarter than I always figured. And to his beautiful bride-to-be, who used to look the other way when I'd sneak into the backyard to neck with her daughter." Over the ensuing laughter, glasses were clinked.

Vanessa drank the bubbly wine and hoped she wouldn't pay for it later.

"Anyone for dessert?" Joanie's question was answered by communal moans. "Okay, we'll hold off on that. Jack, you help me clear the table. Absolutely not," she said when Loretta stood to stack plates. "The guest of honor does not do dishes."

"Don't be silly—"

"I mean it."

"All right, then I'll just clean Lara up."

"Fine, then you and Dad can spoil her until we're done here. Not you, either," she added when Vanessa began to clear the table. "You're not doing dishes on your first dinner in my home."

"She's always been bossy," Brady commented when his sister disappeared into the kitchen. "Would you like to go into the living room? We can put on some music."

"No, actually, I'd like some air."

"Good. There's nothing I like better than walking in the twilight with a beautiful woman." He gave her a cocky grin and held out a hand.

Chapter 6

The evening was soft and smelled of rain. There were lilacs blooming, their scent an elegant whisper on the air. She remembered they had been Joanie's favorite. To the west, the sun was sinking below the mountains in a blaze of red. Cows stood slack-hipped in the fading light. They walked around the side of the house toward a field thick with hay.

"I hear you've taken on a student."

"Mrs. Driscoll gets around."

"Actually, I heard it from John Cory while I was giving him a tetanus shot. He heard it from Bill Crampton—that's Annie's father's brother. He runs a repair shop out of his garage. All the men hang around over there to tell lies and complain about their wives."

Despite her dragging discomfort, Vanessa had to laugh. "At least it's reassuring to know the grapevine still works."

"So how'd the lesson go?"

"She has…possibilities."

"How does it feel to be on the other end?"

"Odd. I promised I'd teach her how to play rock."

"You?"

Vanessa bristled. "Music," she said primly, "is music."

"Right." He put a fingertip behind her earlobe so that he could watch the jewels she wore there catch the last light of the setting sun. And so that he could touch her. "I can see it now, Vanessa Sexton on keyboards with a heavy metal band." He considered a minute. "Do you think you could wear one of those metal corsets, or whatever they're called?"

"No, I couldn't, no matter what they're called. And if you're only along to make fun of me, I can walk by myself."

"Touchy." He draped an arm around her shoulders. He was glad the scent of his shampoo was still in her hair. He wondered if any of the men he'd seen her linked with in magazines and newspapers had felt the same way.

"I like Jack," she said.

"So do I." They walked along a fence thick with honeysuckle.

"Joanie seems so happy here, on the farm, with her family. I often wondered about her."

"Did you ever think about me? After you'd left, after you'd hit it so big, did you ever think about me?"

She looked out over the fields. "I suppose I did."

"I kept thinking you would write."

Too much, she thought. Too often. "Time passed, Brady. And at first I was too angry and hurt. At you and at my mother." Because she wanted to lighten the mood, she smiled. "It took me years to forgive you for dumping me the night of the prom."

"I didn't." He swore and stuck his hands in his pockets. "Look, it's a stupid thing and long over, but I'm tired of taking the rap."

"What are you talking about?"

"I didn't dump you, damn it. I'd rented my first tux, bought my first corsage. Pink and yellow roses." Now that he had brought it up, he felt like a total fool. "I guess I was probably as excited about that night as you were."

"Then why did I sit in my room wearing my new dress for two and a half hours?"

He blew out a long breath. "I got arrested that night."

"What?"

"It was a mistake," he said carefully. "But by the time it was straightened out, it was too late to explain. The charges were pretty thin, to say the least, but I hadn't exactly been a Boy Scout up until then."

"But what were you arrested for?"

"Statutory rape." At her astonished look, he shrugged. "I was over eighteen. You weren't."

It took almost a full minute before it could sink in, before she could find her voice. "But that's ridiculous. We never…"

"Yeah." To his undying regret. "We never."

She pulled both hands through her hair as she tried to reason it out. "Brady, it's almost too ludicrous to believe. Even if we had been intimate, it wouldn't have had anything to do with rape. You were only two years older than I was, and we loved each other."

"That was the problem."

She put a hand on her stomach, kneading a deep ache.

"I'm sorry, so sorry. How miserable you must have been. And your parents. Oh, God. What a horrible thing for anyone to go through. But who in the world would have had you arrested? Who would have—" She saw his face, and her answer. "Oh, no!" she moaned, turning away. "Oh, God!"

"He was dead sure I'd taken advantage of you. And he was dead sure I would ruin your life." And maybe, Brady thought as he stared out over the fields, he wouldn't have been far off. "The way he put it, he was going to see I paid for the first, and he was going to do what needed to be done to prevent the second."

"He could have asked me," she whispered. "For once in my life, he could have asked me." She shivered against a quick chill. "It's my fault."

"That's a stupid response."

"No," she said quietly. "It's my fault, because I could never make him understand how I felt. Not about you, not about anything." She took a long breath before she looked at Brady again. "There's nothing I can say that can make up for what he did."

"There's nothing you have to say." He put his hands on her shoulders, and would have drawn her back against him if she hadn't held herself so stiff. Instead, he massaged her knotted muscles, patiently, with his competent physician's hands. "You were as innocent as I was, Van. We never straightened it out, because for the first few days I was too mad to try and you were too mad to ask. Then you were gone."

Her vision blurred before she blinked back the tears. She could picture him all too easily—young, rebellious, angry. Afraid. "I don't know what to say. You must have been terrified."

"Some," he admitted. "I was never formally charged,

just held for questioning. You remember old Sheriff Grody—he was a hard-edged, potbellied bully. And he didn't like me one little bit. Later I realized he was just taking the opportunity to make me sweat. Someone else might have handled it differently."

There was no use bringing up the way he'd sat in the cell, bone-scared, helplessly angry, waiting to be allowed his phone call, while the sheriff and Sexton consulted in the next room.

"There was something else that happened that night. Maybe it balanced the scales some. My father stood up for me. I'd never known he would stand up for me that way, no questions, no doubts, just total support. I guess it changed my life."

"My father," Vanessa said. "He knew how much that night meant to me. How much you meant to me. All my life I did what he wanted—except for you. He made sure he had his way even there."

"It's a long way behind us, Van."

"I don't think I can—" She broke off on a muffled gasp of pain.

He turned her quickly. "Vanessa?"

"It's nothing. I just—" But the second wave came too sharp, too fast, doubling her over. Moving fast, he scooped her up and headed back for the house. "No, don't. I'm all right. It was just a twinge."

"Breathe slow."

"Damn it, I said it's nothing." Her head fell back as the burning increased. "You're not going to cause a scene," she said between shallow breaths.

"If you've got what I think you've got, you're going to see one hell of a scene."

The kitchen was empty as he came in, so he took the back stairs. At least she'd stopped arguing, Brady thought as he laid her on Joanie's bed. When he switched on the lamp, he could see that her skin was white and clammy.

"I want you to try to relax, Van."

"I'm fine." But the burning hadn't stopped. "It's just stress, maybe a little indigestion."

"That's what we're going to find out." He eased down beside her. "I want you to tell me when I hurt you." Very gently, he pressed on her lower abdomen. "Have you ever had your appendix out?"

"No."

"Any abdominal surgery?"

"No, nothing."

He kept his eyes on her face as he continued the examination. When he pressed just under her breastbone, he saw the flare of pain in her eyes before she cried out. Though his face was grim, he took her hand soothingly.

"Van, how long have you been having pain?"

She was ashamed to have cried out. "Everyone has pain."

"Answer the question."

"I don't know."

He struggled for patience. "How does it feel now?"

"It's fine. I just want—"

"Don't lie to me." He wanted to curse her as pungently as he was cursing himself. He'd known she wasn't well, almost from the moment he'd seen her again. "Is there a burning sensation?"

Because she saw no choice, she relented. "Some."

It had been just about an hour since they'd eaten, he thought. The timing was right. "Have you had this happen before, after you've had alcohol?"

"I don't really drink anymore."

"Because you get this reaction?"

She closed her eyes. Why didn't he just go and leave her alone? "I suppose."

"Do you get gnawing aches, here, under the breastbone?"

"Sometimes."

"And in your stomach?"

"It's more of a grinding, I guess."

"Like acute hunger pangs."

"Yes." The accuracy of his description made her frown. "It passes."

"What are you taking for it?"

"Just over-the-counter stuff." And enough was enough. "Brady, becoming a doctor's obviously gone to your head. You're making a case out of nothing. I'll take a couple of antacids and be fine."

"You don't treat an ulcer with antacids."

"I don't have an ulcer. That's ridiculous. I'm never sick."

"You listen to me." He propped a hand on either side of her head. "You're going into the hospital for tests—X-rays, an upper G.I. And you're going to do what I tell you."

"I'm not going to the hospital." The very idea of it made her remember the horror of her father's last days. "You're not my doctor."

He swore at her richly.

"Nice bedside manner. Now get out of my way."

"You stay right here. And I mean right here."

She obeyed, only because she didn't know if she could manage to stand. Why now? she wondered as she fought against the pain. Why here? She'd had nasty attacks like this before, but she'd always been alone, and she'd always been able to weather them. And she would weather it this time. Just as she was struggling to sit up, Brady came back with his father.

"Now, what's all this?" Ham said.

"Brady overreacting." She managed to smile, and would have swung her legs off the bed if Brady hadn't stopped her.

"She doubled up with pain when we were outside. There's burning in the abdomen, acute tenderness under the breastbone."

Ham sat on the bed and began his own gentle probing. His questions ran along the same lines as Brady's, and his face became more and more sober at her answers. At last he sat back.

"Now what's a young girl like you doing with an ulcer?"

"I don't have an ulcer."

"You've got two doctors telling you different. I assume that's your diagnosis, Brady."

"It is."

"Well, you're both wrong." Vanessa struggled to push herself up. Ham merely shifted the pillows behind her and eased her back. With a nod, he looked back at his son.

"Of course, we'll confirm it with X-rays and tests."

"I'm not going in the hospital." She was desperately hanging on to one small bit of control. "Ulcers are for Wall Street brokers and CEOs. I'm a musician, for God's sake. I'm not a compulsive worrier, or someone who lets tension rule my life."

"I'll tell you what you are," Brady said, anger shimmering in his voice. "You're a woman who hasn't bothered to take care of herself, who's too damn stubborn to sit back and admit when she's taken on too much. And you're going to the hospital if I have to hog-tie you."

"Easy there, Dr. Tucker," Ham said mildly. "Van, have you had any vomiting, any traces of blood?"

"No, of course not. It's just a little stress, maybe a little overwork—"

"A little ulcer," he told her firmly. "But I think we can treat it with medication if you're going to hang tough about the hospital."

"I am. And I don't see that I need medication, or two doctors hovering over me."

"Testy," Ham commented. "You'll have medication or the hospital, young lady. Remember, I'm the one who treated you for damn near everything, starting with diaper rash. I think a cimetidine might clear this up," he said to Brady. "As long as she stays away from spicy food and alcohol for the length of the treatment."

"I'd like it better if she had the tests."

"So would I," he agreed. "But short of dosing her with morphine and dragging her in, I think this is the cleanest way to treat it."

"Let me think about the morphine," Brady grumbled, and made his father chuckle.

"I'm going to write you a prescription," he told Vanessa. "You get it filled tonight. You have twenty minutes before the pharmacy in Boonsboro closes."

"I'm not sick," she said, pouting.

"Just humor your soon-to-be-stepfather. I've got my bag downstairs. Brady, why don't you come along with me?"

Outside the door, Ham took his son's arm and pulled him to the head of the stairs. "If the medication doesn't clear it up within three or four days, we'll put some pressure on her to have the tests. Meanwhile, I think the less stress the better."

"I want to know what caused it." Fury vibrated

through his voice as he stared at the closed bed-room door.

"So do I. She'll talk to you," Ham said quietly. "Just give her some room. I'm going to tell Loretta. Vanessa won't like that, but I'm going to do it. See that she gets the first dose in her tonight."

"I will. Dad, I'm going to take care of her."

"You always meant to." Ham put a hand on Brady's shoulder. "Just don't push too hard too fast. She's like her mother in that way, tends to pull back when you get close." He hesitated, and though he reminded himself that his son was a grown man, he could only think that the grown man was his son. "Are you still in love with her?"

"I don't know. But this time I'm not going to let her get away until I do."

"Just remember, when a man holds on to something too tight, it slips right through his fingers." He gave Brady's shoulder a final squeeze. "I'll go write that prescription."

When Brady walked back into the bedroom, Vanessa was sitting on the edge of the bed, embarrassed, humiliated, furious.

"Come on." His voice was brisk and unsympathetic. "We can just get to the pharmacy before it closes."

"I don't want your damn pills."

Because he was tempted to throttle her, he dipped his hands into his pockets. "Do you want me to carry you out of here, or do you want to walk?"

She wanted to cry. Instead, she rose stiffly. "I'll walk, thank you."

"Fine. We'll take the back stairs."

She didn't want to be grateful that he was sparing her the explanations and sympathy. She walked with her chin up and her shoulders squared. He didn't speak until he slammed the car door.

"Somebody ought to give you a swift right hook." His engine roared into life. Gravel spit from under the tires.

"I wish you'd just leave me alone."

"So do I," he said fervently. He turned off the lane onto asphalt. By the time he'd hit fifth gear, he was calmer. "Are you still having pain?"

"No."

"Don't lie to me, Van. If you can't think of me as a friend, think of me as a doctor."

She turned to stare out the darkened window. "I've never seen your degree."

He wanted to gather her close then, rest her head on his shoulder. "I'll show it to you tomorrow." He slowed as they came to the next town. He said nothing until they pulled up at the pharmacy. "You can wait in the car. It won't take long."

She sat, watching him stride under the lights through the big glass windows of the pharmacy. They were having a special on a popular brand of soft drink. There was a tower of two-liter bottles near the window. There were a few stragglers left inside, most of whom obviously knew Brady, as they stopped to chat while he stood by the drug counter. She hated the feeling of being trapped inside the car with the pain gnawing inside her.

An ulcer, she thought. It wasn't possible. She wasn't a workaholic, a worrier, a power-mad executive. And yet, even as she denied it, the grinding ache dragged through her, mocking her.

She just wanted to go home to lie down, to will the pain away into sleep. Oblivion. It would all be gone tomorrow. Hadn't she been telling herself that for months and months?

When he came back, he set the small white bag in her lap before he started the car. He said nothing as she sat back in the seat with her eyes closed. It gave him time to think.

It didn't do any good to snap at her. It did even less good to be angry with her for being sick. But it hurt and infuriated him that she hadn't trusted him enough to tell him she was in trouble. That she hadn't trusted herself enough to admit it and get help.

He was going to see that she got that help now, whether she wanted it or not. As a doctor, he would do the same for a stranger. How much more would he do for the only woman he had ever loved?

Had loved, he reminded himself. In this case, the past tense was vital. And because he had once loved her with all the passion and purity of youth, he wouldn't see her go through this alone.

At the curb in the front of her house, he parked, then walked around the car to open her door. Vanessa climbed out and began the speech she'd carefully planned on the drive.

"I'm sorry if I acted childishly before. And ungrateful. I know you and your father only want to help. I'll take the medication."

"Damn right you will." He took her arm.

"You don't have to come in."

"I'm coming in," he said as he pulled her up the walk. "I'm watching you take the first dose, and then I'm putting you to bed."

"Brady, I'm not an invalid."

"That's right, and if I have anything to say about it, you won't become one."

He pushed open the door—it was never locked—and hauled her directly upstairs. He filled a glass in the bathroom, handed it to her, then opened the bottle of medication and shook out a pill himself.

"Swallow."

She took a moment to scowl at him before she obeyed. "Are you going to charge me for a house call?"

"The first one's for old times' sake." Gripping her arm again, he pulled her into the bedroom. "Now take off your clothes."

Pain or no pain, she tossed back her head. "Aren't you supposed to be wearing a lab coat and a stethoscope when you say that?"

He didn't even bother to swear. Turning, he yanked open a drawer and searched until he found a nightshirt. She would wear silk to bed, he thought, clenching his teeth. Of course she would. After tossing it on the bed, he pushed her around and dragged down her zipper.

"When I undress you for personal reasons, you'll know it."

"Cut it out." Shocked, she caught the dress as it pooled at her waist. He merely tugged the nightshirt over her head.

"I can control my animal lust by thinking of your stomach lining."

"That's disgusting."

"Exactly." He tugged the dress over her hips. The nightshirt drifted down to replace it. "Stockings?"

Unsure if she should be mortified or infuriated, she unrolled them down the length of her legs. Brady gritted his teeth again. No amount of hours in anatomy class could have prepared him for the sight of Vanessa slowly removing sheer stockings in lamplight.

He was a doctor, he reminded himself, and tried to recite the first line of the Hippocratic oath.

"Now get in bed." He pulled down the quilt, then carefully tucked it up to her chin after she climbed in. Suddenly she looked sixteen again. He clung to his professionalism, setting the bottle of pills on her nightstand. "I want you to follow the directions."

"I can read."

"No drinking." A doctor, he repeated to himself. He was a doctor, and she was a patient. A beautiful patient with sinfully soft skin and big green eyes. "We don't use bland diets so much anymore, just common sense. Stay away from spicy foods. You're going to get some relief fairly quickly. In all probability you won't even remember you had an ulcer in a few days."

"I don't have one now."

"Vanessa." With a sigh, he brushed back her hair. "Do you want anything?"

"No." Her hand groped for his before he could rise. "Can you—? Do you have to go?"

He kissed her fingers. "Not for a while."

Satisfied, she settled back. "I was never supposed to let you come up here when we were teenagers."

"Nope. Remember the night I climbed in the window?"

"And we sat on the floor and talked until four in the morning. If my father had known, he would have—" She broke off, remembering.

"Now isn't the time to worry about all that."

"It isn't a matter of worry, really, but of wondering. I loved you, Brady. It was innocent, and it was sweet. Why did he have to spoil that?"

"You were meant for big things, Van. He knew it. I was in the way."

"Would you have asked me to stay?" She hadn't thought she would ask, but she had always wanted to know. "If you had known about his plans to take me to Europe, would you have asked me to stay?"

"Yes. I was eighteen and selfish. And if you had stayed, you wouldn't be what you are. And I wouldn't be what I am."

"You haven't asked me if I would have stayed."

"I know you would have."

She sighed. "I guess you only love that intensely once. Maybe it's best to have it over and done with while you're young."

"Maybe."

She closed her eyes, drifting. "I used to dream that you would come and take me away. Especially before a performance, when I stood in the wings, hating it."

His brows drew together. "Hating what?"

"The lights, the people, the stage. I would wish so hard that you would come and we would go away together. Then I knew you wouldn't. And I stopped wishing. I'm so tired."

He kissed her fingers again. "Go to sleep."

"I'm tired of being alone," she murmured before she drifted off.

He sat, watching her, trying to separate his feelings for what had been from what was. And that was the problem, he realized. The longer he was with her, the more the edges between the past and present blurred.

There was one and only one thing that was clear. He had never stopped loving her.

After touching his lips to hers, he turned off the bedside light and left her to sleep.

Chapter 7

Bundled in her ratty blue terry-cloth robe, her hair tousled and her disposition grim, Vanessa trudged downstairs. Because she'd been hounded, she'd been taking the medication Ham Tucker had prescribed for two days. She felt better. It annoyed her to have to admit it, but she was a long way from ready to concede that she'd needed it.

More, she was embarrassed that it was Brady who had supervised her first dose and tucked her into bed. It hadn't been so bad when they'd been sniping at each other, but when she'd weakened and asked him to stay with her, he'd been kind. Doctor to patient, she reminded herself. But she had never been able to resist Brady when he was kind.

The morning suited her mood. Thick gray clouds, thick gray rain. It was, she thought, a perfect day to sit alone in the house and brood. In fact, it was something to look forward to. Rain, depression, and a private pity party. At least solitary sulking would be a change. She'd had little time to be alone since the night of Joanie's dinner party.

Her mother tended to hover, finding excuses to come home two or three times each workday. Dr. Tucker checked in on her twice a day, no matter how much Vanessa protested. Even Joanie had come by, to cluck and fuss, bringing armfuls of lilacs and bowls of chicken soup. Neighbors peeped in from time to time to measure her progress. There were no secrets in Hyattown. Vanessa was certain she'd had good wishes and advice from all two hundred and thirty-three residents of the town.

Except one.

Not that she cared that Brady hadn't found time to come by. She scowled and tugged at the belt of her robe. In fact, she told herself as her fingers trailed over the newel post, she was glad he had been conspicuously absent. The last thing she wanted was Brady Tucker— Hyattown's own Dr. Kildare—looming over her, poking at her and shaking his head in his best I-told-you-so manner. She didn't want to see him. And she certainly didn't need to.

She hated making a fool of herself, she thought as she scuffed barefoot down the hallway to the kitchen. And what other term was there for all but keeling over in Joanie's backyard? Then being carried to bed and having Brady treat her like some whining patient.

An ulcer. That was ridiculous, of course. She was strong, competent and self-sufficient—hardly ulcer material. But she unconsciously pressed a hand to her stomach.

The gnawing ache she'd lived with longer than she could remember was all but gone. Her nights hadn't been disturbed by the slow, insidious burning that had so often kept her awake and miserable. In fact, she'd slept like a baby for two nights running.

A coincidence, Vanessa assured herself. All she'd needed was rest. Rest and a little solitude. The grueling schedule she'd maintained the past few years was bound to wear even the strongest person down a bit.

So she'd give herself another month—maybe two—of Hyattown's version of peace, quiet and restoration before making any firm career decisions.

At the kitchen doorway, she came to an abrupt halt. She hadn't expected to find Loretta there. In fact, she had purposely waited to come down until after she'd heard the front door open and close.

"Good morning." Loretta, dressed in one of her tidy suits, hair and pearls in place, beamed a smile.

"I thought you'd gone."

"No, I ran up to Lester's for a paper." She gestured toward the newspaper folded neatly beside the single place setting. "I thought you might want to see what's happening in the world."

"Thank you." Exasperated, Vanessa stood where she was. She hated the fact that she still fumbled whenever Loretta made a gentle maternal gesture. She was grateful for the consideration, but she realized it was the gratitude of a guest for a hostess's generosity. And so it left her feeling guilty and disheartened. "You didn't have to bother."

"No bother. Why don't you sit down, dear? I'll fix you some tea. Mrs. Hawbaker sent some of her own chamomile over from her herb garden."

"Really, you don't have to—" Vanessa broke off at the sound of a knock on the back door. "I'll get it."

She opened the door, telling herself she didn't want it to be Brady. She didn't care if it was Brady. Then she told herself she wasn't the least bit disappointed when the visitor turned out to be female.

"Vanessa." A brunette who huddled under a dripping umbrella was smiling at her. "You probably don't remember me. I'm Nancy Snooks—used to be Nancy McKenna, Josh McKenna's sister."

"Well, I—"

"Nancy, come in." Loretta hurried to the door. "Lord, it's really coming down, isn't it?"

"Doesn't look like we'll have to worry about a drought this year. I can't stay." She remained on the stoop, shifting from foot to foot. "It's just that I heard Vanessa was back and giving piano lessons. My boy Scott's eight now."

Vanessa saw the blow coming and braced herself. "Oh, well, I'm not really—"

"Annie Crampton's just crazy about you," Nancy said quickly. "Her mama's my second cousin, you know. And when I was talking it over with Bill—Bill's my husband—we agreed that piano lessons would be real good for Scott. Mondays right after school would work out best for us—if you don't have another student then."

"No, I don't, because—"

"Great. Aunt Violet said ten dollars is what you're charging for Annie. Right?"

"Yes, but—"

"We can swing that. I'm working part-time over to the feed and grain. Scott'll be here sharp at four. Sure is nice to have you back, Vanessa. I gotta go. I'll be late for work."

"You be careful driving in this rain," Loretta put in.

"I will. Oh, and congratulations, Mrs. Sexton. Doc Tucker's the best."

"Yes, he is." Loretta managed to smile without laughing out loud as she shut the door on a whoosh of rain. "Nice girl," she commented. "Takes after her aunt Violet."

"Apparently."

"I should warn you." Loretta walked over to set a cup of tea on the table. "Scott Snooks is a terror."

"It figures." It was too early in the morning to think, Vanessa decided. She sat, dropped her heavy head in her hands. "She wouldn't have trapped me if I'd been awake."

"Of course not. How about some nice French toast?"

"You don't have to fix me breakfast." Vanessa's voice was muffled by her hands.

"No trouble at all." Loretta was humming as she poured milk into a bowl. She'd been cheated out of being a mother for twelve years. There was nothing she'd rather do than pamper her daughter with a hot breakfast.

Vanessa scowled down at her tea. "I don't want to keep you. Don't you have to open the shop?"

Still humming, Loretta broke an egg into the bowl. "The beauty of having your own place is calling your own hours." She added touches of cinnamon, sugar and vanilla. "And you need a good breakfast. Ham says you're on the mend, but he wants you to put on ten pounds."

"Ten?" Vanessa nearly choked on her tea. "I don't need—" She bit off an oath as another knock sounded.

"I'll get it this time," Loretta announced. "If it's another hopeful parent, I'll shoo them away."

But it was Brady who stood dripping on the back stoop this time. Without the shelter of an umbrella, he grinned at Vanessa while rain streamed from his dark hair. Instant pleasure turned to instant annoyance the moment he opened his mouth.

"Morning, Loretta." He winked at Vanessa. "Hi, gorgeous."

With something close to a snarl, Vanessa huddled over her steaming tea.

"Brady, what a nice surprise." After accepting his kiss on the cheek, Loretta closed the door on the rain. "Have you had breakfast?" she asked as she went back to the stove to soak the bread.

"No, ma'am." He took an appreciative sniff and hoped he was about to. "Is that French toast?"

"It will be in just a minute. You sit down and I'll fix you a plate."

He didn't have to be asked twice. After dragging his hands through his dripping hair and scattering rain all over creation, he joined Vanessa at the table. He flashed her a smile, a cheerful, friendly look that neatly disguised the fact that he was studying her color. The lack of shadows under her eyes gratified him as much as the mutinous expression in them.

"Beautiful day," he said.

Vanessa lifted her gaze to the rain-lashed windows. "Right."

Undaunted by her grudging response, he shifted in his chair to chat with Loretta as she flipped the browning bread in the skillet.

Not a peep from him in two days, Vanessa thought,

and now he pops up on the doorstep, big as life and twice as irritating. He hadn't even asked her how she was feeling—not that she wanted to be fussed over, she reminded herself. But he was a doctor—and he was the one who'd come up with that ridiculous diagnosis.

"Ah, Loretta." Brady all but drooled when she set a heaping plate of fragrant bread in front of him. "My father's a lucky man."

"I suppose cooking's the first priority when a Tucker goes looking for a wife," Vanessa said, feeling nasty.

Brady only smiled as he glopped on maple syrup. "It couldn't hurt."

Vanessa felt her temper rise. Not because she couldn't cook. Certainly not. It was the narrow-minded, sexist idea that infuriated her. Before she could think of a suitably withering reply, Loretta set a plate in front of her.

"I can't eat all of this."

"I can," Brady said as he started on his own meal. "I'll finish up what you don't."

"If you two are set, I'd best go open the shop. Van, there's plenty of that chicken soup left that Joanie brought over yesterday. It'll heat up fine in the microwave for lunch. If this rain keeps up, I'll probably be home early. Good luck with Scott."

"Thanks."

"Scott?" Brady asked, as Loretta went out.

Vanessa merely propped her elbows on the table. "Don't ask."

Brady waited until Loretta had left them alone before rising to help himself to more coffee. "I wanted to talk to you about the wedding."

"The wedding?" She looked over. "Oh, the wedding. Yes, what about it?"

"Dad's been applying a little Tucker pressure. He thinks he's got Loretta convinced to take the plunge over the Memorial Day weekend."

"Memorial Day? But that's next week."

"Why wait?" Brady said after a sip, echoing his father's sentiments. "That way they can use the annual picnic as a kind of town wedding reception."

"I see." But it was so soon, Vanessa thought frantically. She hadn't even adjusted to being with her mother again, to living in the same house with her, and now... But it wasn't her decision, she reminded herself. "I suppose they'll move into your father's house."

"I think that's the plan." He sat again. "They've been kicking around the idea of renting this one eventually. Does that bother you?"

She concentrated on cutting a neat slice of the bread. How could she know? She hadn't had time to find out if it was home or not. "No, I suppose not. They can hardly live in two houses at once."

Brady thought he understood. "I can't see Loretta selling this place. It's been in your family for years."

"I often wondered why she kept it."

"She grew up here, just as you did." He picked up his coffee again. "Why don't you ask her what she plans to do about it?"

"I might." She moved her shoulders restlessly. "There's no hurry."

Because he knew her, he let it go at that. "What I really wanted to talk to you about was a wedding present. Obviously they won't need a toaster or a set of china."

"No." Vanessa frowned down at her plate. "I suppose not."

"I was thinking—I ran it by Joanie and she likes the idea. Why don't we pool our resources and give them a honeymoon? A couple weeks in Cancún. You know, a suite overlooking the Caribbean, tropical nights, the works. Neither one of them has ever been to Mexico. I think they'd get a charge out of it."

Vanessa looked up at him again. It was a lovely idea, she decided. And it was typical of him to have thought of it. "As a surprise?"

"I think we can pull it off. Dad's been trying to juggle his schedule to get a week free. I can sabotage that so he'll think he can only manage a couple of days. Getting the tickets, making some reservations, that's the easy part. Then we have to pack their bags without getting caught."

Warming to the idea, she smiled. "If your father has the same stars in his eyes my mother does, I think we can manage that. We could give them the tickets at the picnic, then bundle them into a limo. Is there a limo service around here?"

"There's one in Frederick. I hadn't thought of that." He pulled out a pad to make a note.

"Get them the bridal suite," Vanessa said. When he looked up and grinned, she shrugged. "If we're going to do it, let's do it right."

"I like it. One limo, one bridal suite, two first-class tickets. Anything else?"

"Champagne. A bottle in the limo, and another in the room when they arrive. And flowers. Mom likes gardenias." She stopped abruptly as Brady continued to write. She'd called Loretta "Mom." It had come out naturally. It sounded natural. "She—she used to like gardenias."

"Terrific." He slipped the pad back in his jacket pocket. "You didn't leave me any."

Baffled, she followed his gaze to her own empty plate. "I...I guess I was hungrier than I thought."

"That's a good sign. Any burning?"

"No." Off balance, she rose to take her plate to the sink.

"Any pain?"

"No. I told you before, you're not my doctor."

"Um-hmm." He was standing behind her when she turned. "We'll just figure I'm taking Doc Tucker's appointments today. Let's have a little vertical examination." Before she could move aside, he pressed gentle fingers to her abdomen. "Hurt?"

"No, I told you I—"

He pressed firmly under her breastbone. She winced. "Still tender?"

"A little."

He nodded. When he'd touched that spot two days before, she'd nearly gone through the roof. "You're coming along nicely. Another few days and you can even indulge in a burrito."

"Why is it that everyone who comes in here is obsessed with what I eat?"

"Because you haven't been eating enough. Understandable, with an ulcer."

"I don't have an ulcer." But she was aching from his touch—for an entirely different reason. "And would you move?"

"Right after you pay your bill." Before she could object or respond, he pressed his lips to hers, firmly, possessively. Murmuring her name, he took her deeper, until she was clinging to him for balance. The floor seemed to drop away from her feet so that he, and only he, was touching her. His thighs against hers, his fingers knotted in her hair, his mouth, hungry and impatient, roaming her face.

She smelled of the morning, of the rain. He wondered what it would be like to love her in the gloomy light, her sigh whispering against his cheek. And he wondered how much longer he would have to wait.

He lifted his head, keeping his hands in her hair so that her face was tilted toward his. In the misty green of her eyes, he saw himself. Lost in her. Gently now, and with an infinite care that stilled her wildly beating heart, he touched his lips to hers again.

Her arms tightened around him, strengthening, even as every bone in her body seemed to melt. She tilted her head so that their lips met in perfect alignment, with equal demand.

"Vanessa—"

"Don't say anything, not yet." She pressed her mouth to his throat and just held on. She knew she would have to think, but for now, for just a moment, she wanted only to feel.

His pulse throbbed, strong and fast, against her lips. His body was firm and solid. Gradually his hands relaxed their desperate grip and stroked through her hair. She became aware of the hiss and patter of rain, of the cool tiles under her bare feet, of the morning scents of coffee and cinnamon.

But the driving need would not abate, nor would the confusion and fear that blossomed inside her.

"I don't know what to do," she said at length. "I haven't been able to think straight since I saw you again."

Her murmured statement set off dozens of new fires. His hands moved up to her shoulders and gripped harder than he had meant them to. "I want you, Van. You want me. We're not teenagers anymore."

She stepped back as far as his hands would allow. "It's not easy for me."

"No." He studied her as he struggled to examine his own emotions. "I'm not sure I'd want it to be. If you want promises—"

"No," she said quickly. "I don't want anything I can't give back."

He'd been about to make them, hundreds of them. With an effort, he swallowed them all, reminding himself that he'd always moved too fast when it involved Vanessa. "What can you give back?"

"I don't know." She lifted her hands to his and squeezed before she stepped away. "God, Brady, I feel as though I'm slipping in and out of the looking glass."

"This isn't an illusion, Van." It was a struggle to keep from reaching for her again. But he knew that what his father had told him was true. When you held too tight, what you wanted most slipped through your fingers. "This is just you and me."

She studied him, the eyes so blue against the dark lashes, the damp, untidy hair, the stubborn set of his jaw, the impossibly romantic shape of his mouth. It was so easy to remember why she had loved him. And so easy to be afraid she still did.

"I won't pretend I don't want to be with you. At the same time, I want to run the other way, as fast as I can." Her sigh was long and shaky. "And hope like hell you catch up with me. I realize my behavior's been erratic since I've come home, and a big part of that is because I never expected to find you here, or to have all these old feelings revived. And that's part of the problem. I don't know how much of what I feel for you is just an echo and how much is real."

He found himself in the frustrating position of competing with himself. "We're different people now, Van."

"Yes." She looked at him, her eyes level and almost calm. "When I was sixteen, I would have gone anywhere with you, Brady. I imagined us together forever, a house, a family."

"And now?" he said carefully.

"Now we both know things aren't that simple, or that easy. We're different people, Brady, with different lives, different dreams. I had problems before—we both did. I still have them." She lifted her hands, let them fall. "I'm not sure it's wise to begin a relationship with you, a physical relationship, until I resolve them."

"It's more than physical, Vanessa. It's always been more."

She nodded, taking a moment to calm a fresh flood of emotion. "All the more reason to take it slowly. I don't know what I'm going to do with my life, with my music. Having an affair will only make it that much more difficult for both of us when I leave."

Panic. He tasted it. When she left again, it would break his heart. He wasn't sure that particular organ would survive a second time. "If you're asking me to turn off my feelings and walk away, I won't." In one swift movement, he pulled her against him again. The hell with what was right. "And neither will you."

She felt the thrill race up her spine, those twin sprinters—excitement and alarm. The ghost of the boy she had known and loved was in his eyes, reckless, relentless. She'd never been able to resist him.

"I'm asking you to let me sort this through." If he

wanted to use anger, then she would match him blow for blow. "The decision's mine, Brady," she said, jerking away. "I won't be pressured or threatened or seduced. Believe me, it's all been tried before."

It was the wrong switch to pull. His eyes, already hot, turned to blue fire. "I'm not one of your smooth, well-mannered lovers, Van. I won't pressure or threaten or seduce. When the time comes, I'll just take."

Challenged, she tossed her head back. "You won't take anything I don't give. No man does. Oh, I'd like to toss those smooth, well-mannered lovers in your face." She gave him a shove as she walked past him to the stove. "Just to see you squirm. But I'll do better than that." She whirled back, hair flying. "I'll tell you the truth. There haven't been any lovers. Because I haven't wanted there to be." Insolent and mocking, she leaned against the stove. "And if I decide I don't want you, you'll just have to join the ranks of the disappointed."

No one. There had been no one. Almost before he could absorb it, she was hurling her final insult. He bristled, took a step toward her, then managed to stop himself. If he touched her now, one of them would crawl. He didn't want it to be him. He stalked to the back door, and had wrenched it open before he got his temper under control enough to realize that his retreat was exactly what she'd wanted.

So he'd throw her a curve.

"How about going to the movies tonight?"

If he'd suggested a quick trip to the moon, she would have been no less surprised. "What?"

"The movies. Do you want to go to the movies?"

"Why?"

"Because I have a craving for popcorn," he snapped. "Do you want to go or not?"

"I… Yes," she heard herself say.

"Fine." He slammed the door behind him.

Life was a puzzle, Vanessa decided. And she was having a hard time fitting the pieces together. For a week she'd been whirled into wedding and picnic plans. Coleslaw and potato salad, long-stemmed roses and photographers. She was dead sure it was a mistake to try to coordinate a town picnic with an intimate family wedding. It was like trying to juggle bowling balls and feathers.

As the final week passed, she was too busy and too confused to notice that she felt better than she had in years. There was the secret honeymoon, and Joanie's enthusiastic bubbling over every aspect of the upcoming nuptials. There were flowers to be ordered and arranged—and a hundred hamburger patties to make.

She went out with Brady almost every night. To the movies, to dinner. To a concert. He was such an easy and amusing companion that she began to wonder if she had dreamed the passion and anger in the gloomy kitchen.

But each night when he walked her to the door, each night when he kissed her breathless, she realized he was indeed giving her time to think things through. Just as he was making certain she had plenty to think about.

The night before the wedding, she stayed at home. But she thought of him, even as she and Loretta and Joanie bustled around the kitchen putting last-minute touches on a mountain of food.

"I still think the guys should be here helping," Joanie muttered as she slapped a hamburger patty between her hands.

"They'd just be in the way." Loretta molded another

hunk of meat into shape. "Besides, I'm too nervous to deal with Ham tonight."

Joanie laughed. "You're doing fine. Dad's a basket case. When he came by the farm today, he asked me three times for a cup of coffee. He had one in his hand the whole time."

Pleased, Loretta chuckled. "It's nice to know he's suffering, too." She looked at the kitchen clock for the fifth time in five minutes. Eight o'clock, she thought. In fourteen hours she would be married. "I hope it doesn't rain."

Vanessa, who'd been deemed an amateur, looked up from her task of arranging the patties in layers between waxed paper. "The forecast is sunny and high seventies."

"Oh, yes." Loretta managed a smile. "You told me that before, didn't you?"

"Only fifty or sixty times."

Her brows knitted, Loretta looked out the window. "Of course, if it did rain, we could move the wedding indoors. It would be a shame to have the picnic spoiled, though. Ham enjoys it so."

"It wouldn't dare rain," Joanie stated, taking the forgotten patty from the bride-to-be's hands. Unable to resist, she tucked her tongue in her cheek. "It's too bad you had to postpone your honeymoon."

"Oh, well." With a shrug, Loretta went back to work. She didn't want to show her disappointment. "Ham just couldn't manage to clear his schedule. I'll have to get used to that sort of thing, if I'm going to be a doctor's wife." She pressed a hand to her nervous stomach. "Is that rain? Did I hear rain?"

"No," Vanessa and Joanie said in unison.

With a weak laugh, Loretta washed her hands. "I

must be hearing things. I've been so addled this past week. Just this morning I couldn't find my blue silk blouse—and I've misplaced the linen slacks I got on sale just last month. My new sandals, too, and my good black cocktail dress. I can't think where I might have put them."

Vanessa shot Joanie a warning look before her friend could chuckle. "They'll turn up."

"What? Oh, yes…yes, of course they will. Are you sure that's not rain?"

Exasperated, Vanessa put a hand on her hip. "Mom, for heaven's sake, it's not rain. There isn't going to be any rain. Go take a hot bath." When Loretta's eyes filled, Vanessa rolled her eyes. "I'm sorry. I didn't mean to snap at you."

"You called me 'Mom,'" Loretta said, her breath hitching. "I never thought you would again." As tears overflowed, she rushed from the room.

"Damn it." Vanessa leaned her hands on the counter. "I've been working overtime to keep the peace all week, and I blow it the night before the wedding."

"You didn't blow anything." Joanie put a hand on her shoulder and rubbed. "I'm not going to say it's none of my business, because we're friends, and tomorrow we'll be family. I've watched you and Loretta walk around each other ever since you got back. And I've seen the way she looks at you when your back is turned, or when you leave a room."

"I don't know if I can give her what she wants."

"You're wrong," Joanie said quietly. "You can. In a lot of ways you already have. Why don't you go upstairs, make sure she's all right? I'll give Brady a call and have him help me load most of this food up and take it down to Dad's."

"All right."

Vanessa went upstairs quietly, slowly, trying to work out the right things to say. But when she saw Loretta sitting on the bed, nothing seemed right.

"I'm sorry." Loretta dabbed at her eyes with a tissue. "I guess I'm overly emotional tonight."

"You're entitled." Vanessa hesitated in the doorway. "Would you like to be alone?"

"No." Loretta held out a hand. "Would you sit awhile?"

Unable to refuse, Vanessa crossed the room to sit beside her mother.

"For some reason," Loretta began, "I've been thinking about what you were like as a baby. You were so pretty. I know all mothers say that, but you were. So bright and alert, and all that hair." She reached out to touch the tips of Vanessa's hair. "Sometimes I would just sit and watch you as you slept. I couldn't believe you were mine. As long as I can remember, I wanted to have a home and children. Oh, I wanted to fill a house with children. It was my only ambition." She looked down at the tissue she had shredded. "When I had you, it was the happiest day of my life. You'll understand that better when you have a baby of your own."

"I know you loved me." Vanessa chose her words carefully. "That's why the rest was so difficult. But I don't think this is the time for us to talk about it."

"Maybe not." Loretta wasn't sure it would ever be the time for a full explanation. One that might turn her daughter away again, just when she was beginning to open her heart. "I just want you to know that I understand you're trying to forgive, and to forgive without explanations. That means a great deal to me." She took a chance and gripped her daughter's hand. "I love you now even more than I did that first moment, when they put you into my arms. No matter where you go or what you do, I always will."

"I love you, too." Vanessa brought their joined hands to her cheek for a moment. "I always have." And that was what hurt the most. She rose and managed to smile. "I think you should get some sleep. You want to look your best tomorrow."

"Yes. Good night, Van."

"Good night." She closed the door quietly behind her.

Chapter 8

Vanessa heard the hiss at her window and blinked groggily awake. Rain? she thought, trying to remember why it was so important there be no rain that day.

The wedding, she thought with a start, and sat straight up. The sun was up, she realized as she shook herself. It was streaming through her half-opened window like pale gold fingers. But the hiss came again—and a rattle.

Not rain, she decided as she sprang out of bed. Pebbles. Rushing to the window, she threw it all the way up.

And there he was, standing in her backyard, dressed in ripped sweats and battered sneakers, his legs spread and planted, his head back and a fistful of pebbles in his hand.

"It's about time," Brady whispered up at her. "I've been throwing rocks at your window for ten minutes."

Vanessa leaned an elbow on the sill and rested her chin in her palm. "Why?"

"To wake you up."

"Ever hear of a telephone?"

"I didn't want to wake your mother."

She yawned. "What time is it?"

"It's after six." He glanced over to see Kong digging at the marigolds and whistled the dog to him. Now they both stood, looking up at her. "Well, are you coming down?"

She grinned. "I like the view from here."

"You've got ten minutes before I find out if I can still shimmy up a drainpipe."

"Tough choice." With a laugh, she shut the window. In less than ten minutes, she was creeping out the back door in her oldest jeans and baggiest sweater. Thoughts of a romantic assignation were dispelled when she saw Joanie, Jack and Lara.

"What's going on?" she demanded.

"We're decorating." Brady hefted a cardboard box and shoved it at her. "Crepe paper, balloons, wedding bells. The works. We thought we'd shoot for discreet and elegant here for the ceremony, then go all out down at Dad's for the picnic."

"More surprises." The box weighed a ton, and she shifted it. "Where do we start?"

They worked in whispers and muffled laughter, arguing about the proper way to drape crepe paper on a maple tree. Brady's idea of discreet was to hang half a dozen paper wedding bells from the branches and top it off with balloons. But it wasn't until they had carted everything down the block to the Tuckers that he really cut loose.

"It's a reception, not a circus," Vanessa reminded

him. He had climbed into the old sycamore and was gleefully shooting out strips of crepe paper.

"It's a celebration," he replied. "It reminds me of when we'd roll old Mr. Taggert's willow every Halloween. Hand me some more pink."

Despite her better judgment, Vanessa obeyed. "It looks like a five-year-old did it."

"Artistic expression."

With a muttered comment, Vanessa turned. She saw that Jack had climbed on the roof and was busily anchoring a line of balloons along the gutter. While Lara sat on a blanket with a pile of plastic blocks and Kong for company, Joanie tied the last of the wedding bells to the grape arbor. The result of their combined efforts wasn't elegant, and it certainly wasn't artistic. But it was terrific.

"You're all crazy," Vanessa decided when Brady jumped from the tree to land softly beside her. He smelled lightly of soap and sweat. "What's next? A calliope and a snake charmer?"

He reached into a box and drew out another roll of white and a roll of pink. "The mall was out of calliopes, but we've still got some of this left."

Vanessa thought a moment, then grinned. "Give me the tape." With it in her hand, she raced to the house. "Come on," she said, gesturing to Brady. "Give me a boost."

"A what?"

"I need to get up on your shoulders." She got behind him and leaped up nimbly to hook her legs around his waist. "Try to stand still," she muttered as she inched her way upward. He tried not to notice that her thighs were slender and only a thin layer of denim away. "Now I need both rolls."

They juggled the paper and tape between them.

"I like your knees," Brady commented, turning his head to nip at one.

"Just consider yourself a stepladder." She secured the tips of the streamers to the eaves of the house. "Move back, but slowly. I'll twist as you go."

"Go where?"

"To the back of the yard—to that monstrosity that used to be a sycamore tree."

Balancing her and craning his neck behind him to be sure he didn't step on an unwary dog—or his niece—or in a gopher hole, he walked backward. "What are you doing?"

"I'm decorating." She twisted the strips of pink and white together, letting the streamer droop a few inches above Brady's head. "Don't run into the tree." When they reached it, she hooked her feet around Brady's chest and leaned forward. "I just have to reach this branch. Got it."

"Now what?"

"Now we do another from the tree to the other side of the house. Balance," she said, leaning forward to look at him. "That's artistic."

When the deed was done, and the last scrap of colored paper used, she put her hands on her hips and studied the results. "Nice," she decided. "Very nice—except for the mess you made of the sycamore."

"The sycamore is a work of art," he told her. "It's riddled with symbolism."

"It looks like Mr. Taggert's willow on Halloween," Joanie chimed in as she plucked up Lara and settled her on her hip. "One look at that and he's going to know who rolled it in toilet paper every year." She grinned up at Vanessa, who was still perched on Brady's shoulders.

"We'd better run. Only two hours until countdown." She poked a finger in Brady's chest. "You're in charge of Dad until we get back."

"He's not going anywhere."

"I'm not worried about that. He's so nervous he might tie his shoelaces together."

"Or forget to wear shoes at all," Jack put in, taking Joanie's arm to lead her away. "Or he could wear his shoes and forget his pants, all because you were standing here worrying about it so you didn't get home and change and get back in time to nag him."

"I don't nag," she said with a chuckle as he pulled her along. "And Brady, don't forget to check with Mrs. Leary about the cake. Oh, and—" The rest was muffled when Jack clamped a hand over her mouth.

"And I used to put my hands over my ears," Brady murmured. He twisted his head to look up at Vanessa. "Want a ride home?"

"Sure."

He trooped off, still carrying her, through the neighboring yards. "Putting on weight?" He'd noticed she was filling out her jeans very nicely.

"Doctor's orders." She gave his hair an ungentle tug. "So watch your step."

"Purely a professional question. How about I give you an exam?" He turned his head to leer at her.

"Look out for the—" She ducked down so that the clotheslines skimmed over her head. "You might have walked around it."

"Yeah, but now I can smell your hair." He kissed her before she could straighten up again. "Are you going to make me some breakfast?"

"No."

"Coffee?"

She chuckled as she started to squirm down his back. "No."

"Instant?"

"No." She was laughing when her feet hit the ground. "I'm going to take a long, hot shower, then spend an hour primping and admiring myself in the mirror."

He gathered her close, though the dog was trying to wiggle between them. "You look pretty good right now."

"I can look better."

"I'll let you know." He tipped her face up to his. "After the picnic, you want to come by, help me look at paint chips?"

She gave him a quick, impulsive kiss. "I'll let you know," she said before she dashed inside.

Loretta's nerves seemed to have transferred to her daughter. While the bride calmly dressed for her wedding day, Vanessa fussed with the flower arrangements, checked and rechecked the bottle of champagne that had been set aside for the first family toast, and paced from window to window looking for the photographer.

"He should have been here ten minutes ago," she said when she heard Loretta start downstairs. "I knew it was a mistake to hire Mrs. Driscoll's grandson's brother-in-law. I don't understand why—" She turned, breaking off when she saw her mother.

"Oh. You look beautiful."

Loretta had chosen a pale, pale green silk with only a touch of ecru lace along the tea-length hem. It was simple—simply cut, simply beautiful. On an impulse, she'd bought a matching picture hat, and she'd fluffed her hair under the brim.

"You don't think it's too much?" She reached up, her

fingers skimming the hat. "It is just a small, informal wedding."

"It's perfect. Really perfect. I've never seen you look better."

"I feel perfect." She smiled. As a bride should, she was glowing. "I don't know what was wrong with me last night. Today I feel perfect. I'm so happy." She shook her head quickly. "I don't want to cry. I spent forever on my face."

"You're not going to cry," Vanessa said firmly. "The photographer— Oh, thank God, he's just pulling up outside. I'll— Oh, wait. Do you have everything?"

"Everything?"

"You know, something old, something new?"

"I forgot." Struck by bridal superstition, Loretta started a frantic mental search. "The dress is new. And these…" She touched a finger to her pearls. "These were my mother's—and her mother's, so they're old."

"Good start. Blue?"

Color rose in Loretta's cheeks. "Yes, actually, under the dress. I have, ah… My camisole has little blue ribbons down the front. I suppose you think I'm foolish buying fancy lingerie."

"No, I don't." Vanessa touched her mother's arm, and was surprised by the quick impulse she had to hug her. Instead, she stepped back. "That leaves borrowed."

"Well, I—"

"Here." Vanessa unclasped the thin gold braided bracelet she wore. "Take this, and you'll be all set." She peeked out the window again. "Oh, here comes Doc Tucker and the rest of them." With a laugh, she waved. "They look like a parade. Go into the music room until I can hustle them outside."

"Van." Loretta was still standing, holding the bracelet in her hand. "Thank you."

Vanessa waited until her mother was out of sight before opening the door. Mass confusion entered. Joanie was arguing with Brady about the proper way to pin a boutonniere. Jack claimed his wife had tied his tie so tight that he couldn't breathe, much less talk. Ham paced the length of the house and back again before Vanessa could nudge him outside.

"You brought the dog," Vanessa said, staring at Kong, who had a red carnation pinned jauntily to his collar.

"He's family," Brady claimed. "I couldn't hurt his feelings."

"Maybe a leash?" she suggested.

"Don't be insulting."

"He's sniffing at Reverend Taylor's shoes."

"With any luck, that's all he'll do to Reverend Taylor's shoes." He turned back to her as she stifled a giggle. "You were right."

"About what?"

"You can look better."

She was wearing a thin, summery dress with yards of skirt in a bold floral print. Its snug contrasting bodice was a rich teal blue, with a bandeau collar that left the curve of her shoulders bare. The gold rope around her neck, and her braided earrings, matched the bracelet she had given Loretta.

"So can you." In a natural movement, she reached up to straighten the knot in the dark blue tie he was wearing with an oyster-colored suit. "I guess we're all set."

"We're still missing something."

She looked around quickly. The baskets of flowers were in place. Joanie was brushing imaginary dust off her father's sleeve while Reverend Taylor cooed over

Lara and tried to avoid Kong. The wedding bells were twirling slowly in the light breeze.

"What?"

"The bride."

"Oh, Lord. I forgot. I'll go get her." Turning, Vanessa raced into the house. She found Loretta in the music room, sitting on the piano stool taking long, deep breaths. "Are you ready?"

She took one more. "Yes." Rising, she walked through the house. But at the back door she paused and groped for Vanessa's hand. Together they crossed the lawn. With each step, Ham's smile grew wider, her mother's hand steadier. They stopped in front of the minister. Vanessa released her mother's hand, stepped back and took Brady's.

"Dearly beloved…" the minister began.

She watched her mother marry under the shade of the maple with paper wedding bells swaying.

"You may kiss the bride," the minister intoned. A cheer went up from neighboring yards where people had gathered. The camera clicked as Ham brought Loretta close for a long, full-bodied kiss that brought on more whistles and shouts.

"Nice job," Brady said as he embraced his father.

Vanessa put her confused emotions on hold and turned to hug her mother. "Best wishes, Mrs. Tucker."

"Oh, Van."

"No crying yet. We've still got lots of pictures to take."

With a squeal, Joanie launched herself at them both. "Oh, I'm so happy." She plucked Lara from Jack's arms. "Give your grandma a kiss."

"Grandma," Loretta whispered, and with a watery laugh she swung Lara into her arms. "Grandma."

Brady laid an arm over Vanessa's shoulders. "How do you feel, Aunt Van?"

"Amazed." She laughed up at him as Mrs. Driscoll's grandson's brother-in-law scurried around snapping pictures. "Let's go pour the champagne."

Two hours later, she was in the Tucker backyard, hauling a tray of hamburger patties to the grill.

"I thought your father always did the honors," she said to Brady.

"He passed his spatula down to me." He had his suit coat off now, his sleeves rolled up and his tie off. Smoke billowed up from the grill as meat sizzled. He flipped a patty expertly.

"You do that very well."

"You should see me with a scalpel."

"I'll pass, thanks." She shifted to avoid being mowed down by two running boys. "The picnic's just like I remember. Crowded, noisy and chaotic."

People milled around in the yard, in the house, even spilled out along the sidewalks. Some sat at the long picnic tables or on the grass. Babies were passed from hand to hand. The old sat in the shade waving at flies as they gossiped and reminisced. The young ran in the sunshine.

Someone had brought a huge portable stereo. Music poured from the rear corner of the yard, where a group of teenagers had gathered to flirt.

"We'd have been there just a few years back," Brady commented.

"You mean you're too old to hang around a boom box now?"

"No. But they think I am. Now I'm Dr. Tucker—as opposed to my father, who's Doc Tucker—and that automatically labels me an adult." He skewered a hot dog. "It's hell growing up."

"Being dignified," she added as he popped it into a bun and slathered on mustard.

"Setting an example for the younger generation. Say 'ah,'" he told her, then shoved the hot dog in her mouth.

She chewed and swallowed in self-defense. "Maintaining a certain decorum."

"Yeah. You've got mustard on your mouth. Here." He grabbed her hand before she could wipe it off. "I'll take care of it." He leaned down and slid the tip of his tongue over the corner of her mouth. "Very tasty," he decided, then nipped lightly at her bottom lip.

"You're going to burn your burgers," she murmured.

"Quiet. I'm setting an example for the younger generation."

Even as she chuckled, he covered her mouth fully with his, lengthening the kiss, deepening it, drawing it out, until she forgot she was surrounded by people. And so did he.

When he released her, she lifted a hand to her spinning head and tried to find her voice.

"Just like old times," someone shouted.

"Better," Brady said quietly, and would have pulled her close again, but for a tap on his shoulder.

"Let that girl go and behave yourself, Brady Tucker." Violet Driscoll shook her head at the pair of them. "You've got hungry people here. If you want to smooch with your girl, you just wait till later."

"Yes, ma'am."

"Never had a lick of sense." She winked at Vanessa

as she started back to the shade. "But he's a handsome so-and-so."

"She's right." Vanessa tossed back her hair.

"I'm a handsome so-and-so?"

"No, you've never had a lick of sense."

"Hey!" he called after her. "Where are you going?"

Vanessa shot him a long, teasing look over her shoulder and kept walking.

It was like old times, Vanessa thought as she stopped to talk to high school friends and watched children race and shout and gobble down food. Faces had aged, babies had been born, but the mood was the same. There was the smell of good food, the sounds of laughter and of a cranky baby being lulled to sleep. She heard arguments over the Orioles' chances for a pennant this year, talk about summer plans and gardening tips.

She could smell the early roses blooming and see the tangle of morning glories on the trellis next door.

When Brady found her again, she was sitting on the grass with Lara.

"What're you doing?"

"Playing with my niece." They both lifted their heads to smile at him.

Something shifted inside him. Something fast and unexpected. And something inevitable, he realized. Seeing her smiling up at him, a child's head on her shoulder, sunlight pouring over her skin. How could he have known he'd been waiting, almost his entire life, for a moment like this? But the child should be his, he thought. Vanessa and the child should be his.

"Is something wrong?" she asked.

"No." He brought himself back with a long, steadying breath. "Why?"

"The way you were staring at me."

He sat beside her, touched a hand to her hair. "I'm still in love with you, Vanessa. And I don't know what the hell to do about it."

She stared. Even if she could have latched on to the dozens of emotions swirling through her, she couldn't have put any into words. It wasn't a boy she was looking at now. He was a man, and what he had spoken had been said deliberately. Now he was waiting for her to move, toward him or away. But she couldn't move at all.

Lara bounced in her lap and squealed, shattering the silence. "Brady, I—"

"There you are." Joanie dropped down beside them. "Whoops," she said as the tension got through to her. "I'm sorry. I guess it's bad timing."

"Go away, Joanie," Brady told her. "Far away."

"I'd already be gone, since you've asked so nicely, but the limo's here. People are already heading around front to stare at it. I think it's time to see the newlyweds off."

"You're right." Almost using Lara as a shield, Vanessa scrambled to her feet. "We don't want them to miss their plane." She braced herself and looked at Brady again. "You've got the tickets?"

"Yeah, I got them." Before she could skirt around him, he cupped her chin in his hand. "We've still got unfinished business, Van."

"I know." She was grateful her voice could sound so calm when her insides were knotted. "Like Joanie said, it's bad timing." With Lara on her hip, she hurried off to find her mother.

"What's all this about a limo?" Ham demanded as Joanie began unrolling his pushed-up sleeves. "Did somebody die?"

"Nope." Joanie fastened the button on his cuff. "You and your new wife are going on a little trip."

"A trip?" Loretta repeated, as Vanessa handed her her purse.

"When newlyweds take a trip," Brady explained, "it's called a honeymoon."

"But I've got patients all next week."

"No, you don't." With Brady and Jack on either side of Ham, and Vanessa and Joanie flanking Loretta, they led the baffled bride and groom to the front of the house.

"Oh, my" was all Loretta could say as she spotted the gleaming white stretch limo.

"Your plane leaves at six." Brady took an envelope out of his pocket and handed it to his father. *"Vaya con Dios."*

"What is all this?" Ham demanded. Vanessa noted with a chuckle that old shoes and cans were already being tied to the bumper. "My schedule—"

"Is cleared." Brady gave Ham a slap on the back. "See you in a couple weeks."

"A couple weeks?" His eyebrows shot up. "Where the hell are we going?"

"South of the border," Joanie chimed in, and gave her father a hard, smacking kiss. "Don't drink the water."

"Mexico?" Loretta's eyes widened. "Are we going to Mexico? But how can we— The shop. We haven't any luggage."

"The shop's closed," Vanessa told her. "And your luggage is in the trunk." She kissed Loretta on each cheek. "Have a good time."

"In the trunk?" Her baffled smile widened. "My blue silk blouse?"

"Among other things."

"You all did this." Despite the persistent photographer, Loretta began to cry. "All of you."

"Guilty." Brady gave her a huge hug. "Bye, Mom."

"You're a sneaky bunch." Ham had to take out his handkerchief. "Well, Loretta, I guess we've got ourselves a honeymoon."

"Not if you miss your plane." Joanie, always ready to worry, began to push them toward the limo. "Don't sit in the sun too long. It's much more intense down there. Oh, and whatever you buy, make sure you shop around and bargain first. You can change your money at the hotel—there's a phrase book in the carry-on. And if you need—"

"Say goodbye, Joanie," Jack told her.

"Oh, shoot." She rubbed her knuckles under her damp eyes. "Bye. Wave bye-bye, Lara."

"Oh, Ham. Gardenias." Loretta began to weep again.

With shouts and waves from the entire town, the limo began to cruise sedately down Main Street, followed by the clang and thump of cans and shoes, and an escort of running children.

"There they go," Joanie managed, burying her face in Jack's shoulder. He patted her hair.

"It's okay, honey. Kids have to leave home sometime. Come on, I'll get you some potato salad." He grinned at Brady as he led her away.

Vanessa cleared the lump in her throat. "That was quite a send-off."

"I want to talk to you. We can go to your house or mine."

"I think we should wait until—"

"We've already waited too long."

Panicked, she looked around. How was it that they

were alone again so quickly? "The party— You have guests."

"Nobody'll miss us." With a hand on her arm, he turned toward his car.

"Dr. Tucker, Dr. Tucker!" Annie Crampton was racing around the corner of the house. "Come quick! Something's wrong with my grandpa!"

He moved quickly. By the time Vanessa reached the backyard, he was already kneeling beside the old man, loosening his collar.

"Pain," the old man said. "In my chest…can't breathe."

"I got Dad's bag," Joanie said as she passed it to Brady. "Ambulance is coming."

Brady just nodded. "Take it easy, Mr. Benson." He took a small bottle and a syringe out of the bag. "I want you to stay calm." He continued to talk as he worked, calming and soothing with his voice. "Joanie, get his file," he murmured.

Feeling helpless, Vanessa put an arm around Annie's shoulders and drew her back. "Come on, Annie."

"Is Grandpa going to die?"

"Dr. Tucker's taking care of him. He's a very good doctor."

"He takes care of my mom." She sniffled and wiped at her eyes. "He's going to deliver the baby and all, but Grandpa, he's real old. He fell down. He just got all funny-looking and fell down."

"Dr. Tucker was right here." She stroked Annie's flyaway hair. "If he was going to get sick, it was the best place for it. When he's better, you can play your new song for him."

"The Madonna song?"

"That's right." She heard the wail of am ambulance. "They're coming to take him to the hospital."

"Will Dr. Tucker go with him?"

"I'm sure he will." She watched as the attendants hurried out with a stretcher. Brady spoke to them briskly, giving instructions. She saw him put his hands on Annie's mother's shoulders, speaking slowly, calmly, while she looked up at him with trust and tears in her eyes. When Brady started after the stretcher, Vanessa gave Annie a last squeeze.

"Why don't you go sit with your mother for a minute? She'll be scared." How well she knew, Vanessa thought. She remembered the fear and despair she had felt when they had taken her own father. Turning, she rushed after Brady.

"Brady." She knew she couldn't waste his time. When he turned, she saw the concern, the concentration and the impatience in his eyes. "Please let me know how— what happens."

He nodded, then climbed in the rear of the ambulance with his patient.

It was nearly midnight when Brady pulled up in front of his house. There was a sliver of a moon, bone-white against a black sky studded with stars as clear as ice. He sat where he was for a moment, letting his muscles relax one by one. With his windows down he could hear the wind sighing through the trees.

The fatigue of an eighteen-hour-day had finally caught up with him on the drive home. He was grateful Jack had brought his car to the hospital. Without it, he would have been tempted to stretch out in the lounge. Now all he wanted was to ease his tired body into a hot tub, turn on the jets and drink a cold beer.

The lights were on downstairs. He was glad he'd forgotten to turn them off. It was less depressing to come home to an empty house if the lights were on. He'd detoured into town on the way home and driven by Vanessa's. But her lights had been out.

Probably for the best, he thought now. He was tired and edgy. Hardly the mood for patient, sensible talk. Maybe there was an advantage to letting her stew over the fact that he was in love with her.

And maybe there wasn't. He hesitated, his hand on the door. What the hell was wrong with him, he wondered. He'd always been a decisive man. When he'd decided to become a doctor, he'd gone after his degree with a vengeance. When he'd decided to leave his hospital position in New York and come home to practice general medicine, he'd done so without a backward glance or a whisper of regret.

Life-altering decisions, certainly. So why the hell couldn't he decide what to do about Vanessa?

He was going back to town. If she didn't answer her door, he would climb up the damn rainspout and crawl in her bedroom window. One way or the other, they were going to straighten this mess out tonight.

He'd already turned away and started back to his car when the door to the house opened.

"Brady?" Vanessa stood in the doorway, the light at her back. "Aren't you coming in?"

He stopped dead and stared at her. In a gesture of pure frustration, he dragged a hand through his hair. Was it any wonder he couldn't decide what to do about her? She'd never been predictable. Kong raced out of the house, barking, and jumped on him.

"Jack and Joanie dropped us off." Vanessa stood,

twisting the doorknob back and forth. "I hope you don't mind."

"No." With the dog racing in circles around him, he started back to the house. Vanessa stepped back, out of reach.

"I brought some leftovers from the picnic. I didn't know if you'd have a chance to get any dinner."

"No, I didn't."

"Mr. Benson?"

"Stabilized. It was shaky for a while, but he's tough."

"I'm glad. I'm so glad. Annie was frightened." She rubbed her hands on her thighs, linked her fingers together, pulled them apart, then stuck them in the pockets of her skirt. "You must be exhausted—and hungry. There's plenty of food in the fridge. The, ah, kitchen looks wonderful." She gestured vaguely. "The new cabinets, the counters, everything."

"It's coming along." But he made no move toward it. "How long have you been here?"

"Oh, just a couple of hours." Five, to be exact. "You had some books, so I've been reading."

"Why?"

"Well, to pass the time."

"Why are you here, Van?"

She bent to stroke the dog. "That unfinished business you mentioned. It's been a long day, and I've had plenty of time to think."

"And?"

Why didn't he just sweep her away, carry her upstairs? And shut her up. "And I… About what you said this afternoon."

"That I'm in love with you."

She cleared her throat as she straightened. "Yes, that.

I'm not sure what I feel—how I feel. I'm not sure how you feel, either."

"I told you how I feel."

"Yes, but it's very possible that you think you feel that way because you used to—and because falling back into the same routine, the same relationship—with me—is familiar, and comfortable."

"The hell it is. I haven't had a comfortable moment since I saw you sitting at the piano."

"Familiar, then." She began to twist the necklace at her throat. "But I've changed, Brady. I'm not the same person I was when I left here. We'll never be able to pretend those years away. So, no matter how attracted we are to each other, it could be a mistake to take it any further."

He crossed to her, slowly, until they were eye-to-eye. He was ready to make a mistake. More than ready. "Is that what you were waiting here to tell me?"

She moistened his lips. "Partly."

"Then I'll have my say."

"I'd like to finish first." She kept her eyes level. "I came here tonight because I've never been able to get you completely out of my mind. Or my…" Heart. She wanted to say it, but couldn't. "My system," she finished. "I've never stopped caring about you, or wondering. Because of something we had no control over, we were cheated out of growing up enough to make the decision to move apart or to become lovers." She paused, but only for a moment. "I came here tonight because I realized I want what was taken away from us. I want you." She stepped closer and put her arms around him. "Is that clear enough?"

"Yeah." He kissed her gently. "That's clear enough."

She smiled at him. "Make love with me, Brady. I've always wanted you to."

With their hands joined, they walked upstairs together.

Chapter 9

She had already been upstairs while she had waited for him to come home—smoothing and straightening the covers on the bed, fluffing the pillows, standing and looking at the room and wondering what it would be like to walk into it with him.

He turned on the lamp beside the bed. It was a beautiful old rose-tinted globe that sat on a packing crate. The floors were unfinished, the walls spackled with drywall mud. The bed was only a mattress on the floor beneath the windows. It was the most beautiful room she'd ever seen.

He wished he could have given her candles and roses, a huge four-poster with satin sheets. All he could give her was himself.

And suddenly he was as nervous as a boy on his first date.

"The atmosphere's a little thin in here."

"It's perfect," she told him.

He took her hands and raised them to his lips. "I won't hurt you, Van."

"I know." She kissed his hands in turn. "This is going to sound stupid, but I don't know what to do."

He lowered his mouth to hers, testing, tempting. "You'll catch on."

Her lips curved as her hands slid up his back. "I think you're right." With an instinct that was every bit as potent as experience, she let her head fall back, let her hands glide and press and wander.

Her lips parted for his, and she tasted his little groan of pleasure. Then she shivered with pleasure of her own as his strong, clever hands skimmed down her body, his thumb brushing down the side of her breast, his fingers kneading at her waist, his palm cupping her hip, sliding down her thigh, before its upward journey.

She pressed against him, delighting in the shower of sensations. When his teeth scraped lightly down her throat, over her bare shoulder, she murmured his name. Like the wind through the trees, she sighed for him, and swayed. Pliant and willing, she waited to be molded.

Her absolute trust left him shaken. No matter how hot her passion, she was innocent. Her body might be that of a woman, but she was still as untouched as the girl he had once loved and lost. He wouldn't forget it. As the need flamed inside him, he banked it. This time it would be for her. All for her.

Compassion and tenderness were as much a part of his nature as his recklessness. He showed her only the gentle side now, as he eased the snug top down to her hips. He kissed her, soothing her with murmurs even as his hands set off millions of tiny explosions as they tugged her dress to the floor.

She wore a swatch of white lace that seemed to froth over the swell of her breasts before skimming down to nip at her waist. For his own pleasure, he held her at arm's length and just looked.

"You stop my heart," he told her.

With unsteady hands, she reached out to unbutton his shirt. Though her breath was already ragged, she kept her eyes on his as she slid the shirt from his shoulders and let it fall to join her dress on the floor. With her heart pounding wildly in her ears, she linked her arms around his neck.

"Touch me." She tilted her head back, offered her mouth. "Show me."

Though the kiss was hard, demanding, ruthless, he forced his hands to be gentle. Her own were racing over him, bringing a desperate edge to an already driving need. When he lowered her onto the bed, he watched her eyes close on a sigh, then open again, clouded with desire.

He dipped his head to absorb her taste on his tongue as it skimmed along the verge of lace, as it slid beneath to tease her taut nipples. Her hips ached and her fingers dug into his back as the pleasure rocketed through her.

With a flick of the wrist, he unsnapped her garters, then sent her churning as he slowly peeled down her stockings, blazing the newly bared flesh with his lips. It seemed he found every inch of her, every curve, fascinating. His gentle fingers played over her, everywhere, until the music roared in her head.

As patient as he was ruthless, he drove her closer and closer to the edge she'd never seen. Her body was like a furnace, pumping out heat, pulsing with needs as sharp as his. He drove himself mad watching her, seeing the way everything she felt, each new sensation he brought to her, raced over her face, into her eyes.

Desire. Passion. Pleasure. Excitement. They flowed from him to her, then back again. Familiar. Oh, yes. They recognized each other. That brought comfort. Yet it was new, unique, gloriously fresh. That was the adventure.

He reveled in the way her skin flowed through his hands, the way her body tensed and arched at his touch. The way the lamplight slanted over her, over his hands as he peeled the last barrier of lace away.

Naked, she reached for him, tugging frantically at his slacks. Because he knew his own needs were tearing his control to shreds, he cupped her in his hand and sent her flying over the last line.

She cried out, stunned, helpless, her eyes glazing over, as her hand slipped limply from his shoulder. Even as she shuddered, he eased into her, slowly, gently, murmuring her name again and again as the blood roared in his ears and pushed him to take his pleasure quickly. Love demanded gentleness.

She lost her innocence sweetly, painlessly, and with simple joy.

She lay in Brady's bed, tangled in Brady's sheets. A sparrow heralded the dawn. During the night, the dog had crept in to take his rightful place at the foot of the bed. Lazily Vanessa opened her eyes.

Brady's face was barely an inch from hers, and she had to ease back and blink to focus on him. He was deep in sleep, his arm heavy around her waist, his breathing slow and even. Now, completely relaxed and vulnerable, he looked more like the boy she remembered than the man she was beginning to know.

She loved. There was no doubt in her mind that she loved. Her heart nearly burst with it. But did she love the boy or the man?

Very gently, she brushed at the hair on his forehead. All she was really sure of was that she was happy. And, for now, it was enough.

More than enough, she thought as she slowly stretched. During the night he had shown her how beautiful making love could be when two people cared about each other. And how exciting it could be when needs were met and desires reached. Whatever happened tomorrow, or a year from tomorrow, she would never forget what they had shared.

Lightly, not wanting to wake him, she touched her lips to his. Even that quiet contact stirred her. Hesitant, curious, she trailed her fingertips over his shoulders, down the length of his back. The need grew and spread inside her.

As dreams went, Brady thought, this was one of the best. He was under a warm quilt in the first light of day. Vanessa was in bed beside him. Her body was pressed against his, shifting gently, arousing quickly. Those beautiful, talented fingers were stroking along his skin. That soft, sulky mouth was toying with his. When he reached for her, she sighed, arching under his hand.

Everywhere he touched she was warm and smooth. Her arms were around him, strong silken ropes that trapped him gloriously against her. When she said his name, once, then twice, the words slipped under the gauzy curtain of his fantasy. He opened his eyes and saw her.

This was no dream. She was smiling at him. Those misty green eyes were heavy with sleep and passion. Her body was slim and soft and curved against his.

"Good morning," she murmured. "I wasn't sure if you—"

He closed his mouth over hers. Dream and reality melded seductively as he slipped inside her.

The sunlight was stronger when she lay over him, her head on his heart, her body still pulsing.

"You were saying?"

"Hmm." The effort to open her eyes seemed wasted, so she kept them closed. "Was I?"

"You weren't sure if I what?"

She sifted through her thoughts. "Oh. I wasn't sure if you had any morning appointments."

He continued to comb his fingers through her hair. "It's Sunday," he reminded her. "Office is closed. But I have to run into the hospital and check on Mr. Benson and a couple of other patients. How about you?"

"Nothing much. Some lesson plans, now that I have ten students."

"Ten?" There was more snicker than surprise in his voice.

She shifted then, folding her arms over his chest and resting her chin on them. "I was ambushed at the picnic yesterday."

"Ten students." He grinned at her. "That's quite a commitment. Does that mean you're planning to settle in town again?"

"At least for the summer. I haven't decided whether I'll agree to a fall tour."

So he had the summer to convince her, he thought. "How about dinner?"

She narrowed her eyes. "We haven't even had breakfast yet."

"I mean tonight. We could have our own picnic with the leftovers. Just you and me."

Just you and me. "I'd like that."

"Good. Now why don't we start the day off right?"

After a chuckle, she pressed her lips to his chest. "I thought we already had."

"I meant you could wash my back." Grinning, he sat up and dragged her out of bed.

Vanessa discovered she didn't mind being alone in the house. After Brady dropped her off, she changed into jeans and a short-sleeved sweatshirt. She wanted to spend the day at the piano, planning the lessons, practicing and, if her current mood held, composing.

There had never been enough time for composing on tour, she thought as she tied her hair back. But now she had the summer. Even if ten hours a week would be taken up by lessons, and nearly that many again by planning them, she had plenty of time to indulge in her first love.

Her first love, she repeated with a smile. No, that wasn't composing. That was Brady. He had been her first love. Her first lover. And it was more than probable he would be her last.

He loved her. Or believed he did. He would never have used the words unless he believed it. Nor could she, Vanessa reflected. She had to be sure of what was best for herself, for him, for everyone, before she risked her heart with those three words.

Once she said them, he wouldn't let go again. However much he had mellowed over the years, however responsible he had become, there was still enough of that wild and willful boy in him to have him tossing her over his shoulder and carrying her off. While that fantasy might have its appeal, a daydream appeal, she was too sensible a woman to tolerate it in reality.

The past was done, she thought. Mistakes had been made. She wouldn't risk the future.

She didn't want to think about tomorrow. Not yet. She wanted only to think of, and enjoy, today.

As she started toward the music room, the phone rang. She debated just letting it ring—a habit she'd developed in hotel rooms when she hadn't wanted to be disturbed. On the fifth ring, she gave in and answered.

"Hello."

"Vanessa? Is that you?"

"Yes. Frank?" She recognized the voice of her father's nervous and devoted assistant.

"Yes. It's me—I," he corrected.

Vanessa could all but see him running a soothing hand over the wide bald spot on top of his head. "How are you, Frank?"

"Fine. Fine. Oh—how are you?"

"I'm fine, too." She had to smile. Though she knew her father had tolerated Frank Margoni only because the man would work an eighty-hour week without complaint, Vanessa was fond of him. "How's the new protégé?"

"Protégé—? Oh, you mean Francesco. He's brilliant, really brilliant. Temperamental, of course. Throws things. But then, he's an artist. He's going to be playing at the benefit in Cordina."

"Princess Gabriella's benefit? The Aid to Handicapped Children?"

"Yes."

"I'm sure he'll be wonderful."

"Oh, of course. No doubt. Certainly. But, you see, the princess...she's terribly disappointed that you won't perform. She asked me—" there was an audible gulp "—personally, if I would persuade you to reconsider."

"Frank—"

"You'd stay at the palace, of course. Incredible place."

"Yes, I know. Frank, I haven't decided if I'm going to perform again."

"You know you don't mean that, Vanessa. With your gift—"

"Yes, *my* gift," she said impatiently. "Isn't it about time I realized it is mine?"

He was silent a moment. "I know your father was often insensitive to your personal needs, but that was only because he was so aware of the depth of your talent."

"You don't have to explain him to me, Frank."

"No...no, of course I don't."

She let out a long sigh. It wasn't fair to take out her frustrations on the hapless Frank Margoni, as her father always had. "I understand the position you're in, Frank, but I've already sent my regrets, and a donation, to Princess Gabriella."

"I know. That's why she contacted me. She couldn't get ahold of you. Of course, I'm not officially your manager, but the princess knew our connection, so..."

"If I decide to tour again, Frank, I'll depend on you to manage me."

"I appreciate that, Vanessa." His glum voice brightened perceptibly. "And I realize that you've needed some time for yourself. The last few years—grueling, I know. But this benefit is important." He cleared his throat with three distinct clicks. "And the princess is very stubborn."

Reluctantly Vanessa smiled. "Yes, I know."

"It's only one performance," he continued, sensing a weak spot. "Not even a full concert. You'll have carte blanche on the material. They'd like you to play two pieces, but even one would make such a tremendous difference. Your name on the program would add so much." He paused only long enough to suck in a breath. "It's a very worthy cause."

"When is the benefit?"

"Next month."

She cast her eyes to the ceiling. "Next month. It's practically next month already, Frank."

"The third Saturday in June."

"Three weeks." She let out a long breath. "All right, I'll do it. For you, and for Princess Gabriella."

"Vanessa, I can't tell you how much I—"

"Please don't." She softened the order with a laugh. "It's only one night."

"You can stay in Cordina as long as you like."

"One night," she repeated. "Send me the particulars here. And give my best to Her Highness."

"I will, of course. She'll be thrilled. Everyone will be thrilled. Thank you, Vanessa."

"It's all right, Frank. I'll see you in a few weeks."

She hung up and stood silent and still. Odd, but she didn't feel tensed and keyed up at the thought of a performance. And a huge one, she considered. The theater complex in Cordina was exquisite and enormous.

What would happen if she clutched in the wings this time? She would get through it somehow. She always had. Perhaps it was fate that she had been called now, when she was teetering on some invisible line. To go forward, or backward, or to stay.

She would have to make a decision soon, she thought as she walked to the piano. She prayed it would be the right one.

She was playing when Brady returned. He could hear the music, romantic and unfamiliar, flowing through the open windows. There was the hum of bees in the flowers, the purr of a lawn mower, and the music. The magic of it. He saw a woman and a young child standing on the sidewalk, listening.

She had left the door open for him. He had only to push the screen to be inside. He moved quietly. It seemed he was stepping through the liquid notes.

She didn't see him. Her eyes were half-closed. There was a smile on her face, a secret smile. As if whatever images she held in her mind were pouring out through her fingers and onto the keys.

The music was slow, dreamy, enriched by an underlying passion. He felt his throat tighten.

When she finished, she opened her eyes and looked at him. Somehow she had known he would be there when the last note died away.

"Hello."

He wasn't sure he could speak. He crossed to her and lifted her hands. "There's magic here. It astonishes me."

"Musician's hands," she said. "Yours are magic. They heal."

"There was a woman standing on the sidewalk with her little boy. I saw them when I drove up. She was listening to you play, and there were tears on her cheeks."

"There's no higher compliment. Did you like it?"

"Very much. What was it called?"

"I don't know. It's something I've been working on for a while. It never seemed right until today."

"You wrote it?" He looked at the music on the piano and saw the neatly written notes on the staff paper. "I didn't know you composed."

"I'm hoping to do more of it." She drew him down to sit beside her. "Aren't you going to kiss me hello?"

"At least." His lips were warm and firm on hers. "How long have you been writing?"

"For several years—when I've managed to sneak the time. Between traveling, rehearsals, practice and performances, it hasn't been much."

"But you've never recorded anything of your own."

"None of it's really finished. I—" She stopped, tilted her head. "How do you know?"

"I have everything you've ever recorded." At her smug smile, he continued. "Not that I actually play any of them." He gave an exaggerated yelp when her elbow connected with his ribs. "I suppose that's the sign of a temperamental artist."

"That's *artiste* to you, philistine."

"Why don't you tell this philistine about your composing?"

"What's to tell?"

"Do you like it?"

"I love it. It's what I like best."

He was playing with her fingers. "Then why haven't you finished anything?" He felt the tension the moment it entered her.

"I told you. There hasn't been time. Touring isn't all champagne and caviar, you know."

"Come on." Keeping her hands in his, he pulled her to her feet.

"Where are we going?"

"In here, where there's a comfortable couch. Sit." He eased her down, then put his hands on her shoulders. His eyes were dark and searching on her face. "Talk to me."

"About what?"

"I wanted to wait until you were recovered." He felt her stiffen, and shook his head. "Don't do that. As your friend, as a doctor, and as the man who loves you, I want to know what made you ill. I want to make sure it never happens again."

"You've already said I've recovered."

"Ulcers can reoccur."

"I didn't have an ulcer."

"Can it. You can deny it all you want—it won't change the facts. I want you to tell me what's been going on the last few years."

"I've been touring. Performing." Flustered, she shook her head. "How did we move from composing to all this?"

"Because one leads to the other, Van. Ulcers are often caused by emotion. By frustrations, angers, resentments that are bottled up to fester instead of being aired out."

"I'm not frustrated." She set her chin. "And you, of all people, should know I don't bottle things up. Ask around, Brady. My temper is renowned on three continents."

He nodded, slowly. "I don't doubt it. But I never once remember you arguing with your father."

She fell silent at that. It was nothing more than the truth.

"Did you want to compose, or did you want to perform?"

"It's possible to do both. It's simply a matter of discipline and priorities."

"And what was your priority?"

Uncomfortable, she shifted. "I think it's obvious it was performing."

"You said something to me before. You said you hated it."

"Hated what?"

"You tell me."

She pulled away to rise and pace the room. It hardly mattered now, she told herself. But he was sitting here, watching her, waiting. Past experience told her he would dig and dig until he uncovered whatever feelings she wanted to hide.

"All right. I was never happy performing."

"You didn't want to play?"

"No," she corrected. "I didn't want to perform. I have to play, just as I have to breathe, but…" She let her words trail off, feeling like an imbecile. "It's stage fright," she snapped. "It's stupid, it's childish, but I've never been able to overcome it."

"It's not stupid or childish." He rose, and would have gone to her, but she was already backing away. "If you hated performing, why did you keep going on? Of course," he said, before she could answer.

"It was important to him." She sat on the arm of a chair, then stood again, unable to settle. "He didn't understand. He'd put his whole life into my career. The idea that I couldn't perform, that it frightened me—"

"That it made you ill."

"I was never ill. I never missed one performance because of health."

"No, you performed despite your health. Damn it, Van, he had no right."

"He was my father. I know he was a difficult man, but I owed him something."

He was a selfish son of a bitch, Brady thought. But he kept his silence. "Did you ever consider therapy?"

Vanessa lifted her hands. "He opposed it. He was very intolerant of weakness. I suppose that was his weakness." She closed her eyes a moment. "You have to understand him, Brady. He was the kind of man who would refuse to believe what was inconvenient for him. And, as far as he was concerned, it just ceased to exist." Like my mother, she thought with a weary sigh. "I could never find the way to make him accept or even understand the degree of the phobia."

"I'd like to understand."

She cupped her hands over her mouth a moment, then let them fall. "Every time I would go to the theater, I would tell myself that this time, this time, it wouldn't happen. This time I wouldn't be afraid. Then I would stand in the wings, shaking and sick and miserable. My skin would be clammy, and the nausea would make me dizzy. Once I started playing, it would ease off. By the end I'd be fine, so I would tell myself that the next time…" She shrugged.

He understood, too well. And he hated the idea of her, of anyone, suffering time after time, year after year. "Did you ever stop to think that he was living his life through you?"

"Yes." Her voice was dull. "He was all I had left. And, right or wrong, I was all he had. The last year, he was so ill, but he never let me stop, never let me care for him. In the end, because he had refused to listen, refused the treatments, he was in monstrous pain. You're a doctor—you know how horrible terminal cancer is. Those last weeks in the hospital were the worst. There was nothing they could do for him that time. So he died a little every day. I went on performing, because he insisted, then flying back to the hospital in Geneva every chance I had. I wasn't there when he died. I was in Madrid. I got a standing ovation."

"Can you blame yourself for that?"

"No. But I can regret." Her eyes were awash with it.

"What do you intend to do now?"

She looked down at her hands, spread her fingers, curled them into her palms. "When I came back here, I was tired. Just worn out, Brady. I needed time—I still do—to understand what I feel, what I want, where I'm going." She stepped toward him and lifted her hands to his face. "I didn't want to become involved with you, because I knew you'd be one more huge complication." Her lip curved a little. "And I was right. But when I woke up this morning in your bed, I was happy. I don't want to lose that."

He took her wrists. "I love you, Vanessa."

"Then let me work through this." She went easily into his arms. "And just be with me."

He pressed a kiss to her hair. "I'm not going anywhere."

Chapter 10

"That was the last patient, Dr. Tucker."

Distracted, Brady looked up from the file on his desk and focused on his nurse. "What?"

"That was the last patient." She was already swinging her purse over her shoulder and thinking about putting her feet up. "Do you want me to lock up?"

"Yeah. Thanks. See you tomorrow." He listened with half an ear to the clink of locks and the rattle of file drawers. The twelve-hour day was almost at an end. The fourth twelve-hour day of the week. Hyattown was a long way from New York, but as far as time served was concerned, Brady had found practicing general medicine in a small town as demanding as being chief resident in a major hospital. Along with the usual stream of patients, hospital rounds and paperwork, an outbreak of chicken pox and strep throat had kept him tied to his stethoscope for over a week.

Half the town was either scratching or croaking, he thought as he settled down to his paperwork. The waiting room had been packed since the end of the holiday weekend. As the only doctor in residence, he'd been taking office appointments, making house calls, doing rounds. And missing meals, he thought ruefully, wishing they still stocked lollipops, rather than balloons and plastic cars, for their younger patients.

He could get by with frozen microwave meals and coffee for a few days. He could even get by with only patches of sleep. But he couldn't get by without Vanessa. He'd barely seen her since the weekend of the wedding—since the weekend they had spent almost exclusively in bed. He'd been forced to cancel three dates. For some women, he thought, that alone would have been enough to have them stepping nimbly out of a relationship.

Better that she knew up front how bad it could get. Being married to a doctor was being married to inconvenience. Canceled dinners, postponed vacations, interrupted sleep.

Closing the file, he rubbed his tired eyes. She was going to marry him, he determined. He was going to see to that. If he ever wangled an hour free to set the stage and ask her.

He picked up the postcard on the corner of his desk. It had a brilliant view of the sun setting on the water, palm trees and sand—and a quickly scrawled note from his father on the back.

"You'd better be having a good time, Dad," Brady mused as he studied it. "Because when you get back, you're going to pay up."

He wondered if Vanessa would enjoy a tropical honeymoon. Mexico, the Bahamas, Hawaii. Hot, lazy days.

Hot, passionate nights. Moving too fast, he reminded himself. You couldn't have a honeymoon until you had a wedding. And you couldn't have a wedding until you'd convinced your woman she couldn't live without you.

He'd promised himself he would take it slowly with Vanessa. Give her all the romance they'd missed the first time around. Long walks in the moonlight. Champagne dinners. Evening drives and quiet talks. But the old impatience pulled at him. If they were married now, he could drag his weary bones home. She'd be there. Perhaps playing the piano. Or curled up in bed with a book. In the next room, there might be a child sleeping. Or two.

Much too fast, Brady warned himself. But he hadn't known, until he'd seen her again, how much he'd wanted that basic and traditional home. The woman he loved, and the children they made between them. Christmas mornings and Sunday afternoons.

Leaning back, he let his eyes close. He could picture it perfectly. Too perfectly, he admitted. He knew his vision left questions unanswered and problems unresolved. They were no longer children who could live on dreams. But he was too tired to be logical. Too needy to be sensible.

Vanessa stood in the doorway and watched him with a mixture of surprise and awe. This was Brady, she reminded herself. Her Brady. But he looked so different here, so professional, in his white lab coat with the framed diplomas and certificates surrounding him. There were files neatly stacked on his desk, and there was an ophthalmoscope in his pocket.

This wasn't the wild youth hell-bent on giving the world a left jab. This was a settled, responsible man who had hundreds of people depending on him. He had already made his niche.

And where was hers? she wondered. He had made his choices and found his place. She was still floundering. Yet, however much she flailed or stumbled, she was always drawn to him. Always back to him.

With a faint smile on her face, she stepped into the office. "You've got another appointment, Dr. Tucker."

"What?" His eyes snapped open. He stared at her as dream and reality merged. She was standing on the other side of his desk, her hair pulled back, in a breezy cotton blouse and slacks.

"I was going to say code blue, or red alert, one of those things you hear on TV, but I didn't know which would fit." She put the basket she carried on the desk.

"I'd settle for 'Hi.'"

"Hi." With a quick laugh, she looked around the office. "I almost didn't come in," she told him. "When I came to the door, you looked so…intimidating."

"Intimidating?"

"Like a doctor. A real doctor," she said on another laugh. "The kind who uses needles and makes terrifying noncommittal noises and scribbles things on charts."

"Hmm," Brady said. "Ah."

"Exactly."

"I can take off the lab coat."

"No, actually, I think I like it. As long as you promise not to whip out a tongue depressor. I saw your nurse as she was leaving. She said you were through for the day."

"Just." The rest of the paperwork would have to wait. "What's in the basket?"

"Dinner—of sorts. Since you wouldn't make a house

call, I decided to see if you could fit me into your office schedule."

"It's an amazing coincidence, but I've just had a cancellation." The fatigue simply drained away as he looked at her. Her mouth was naked, and there was a dusting of freckles across the bridge of her nose. "Why don't you sit down and tell me what the problem is?"

"Well." Vanessa sat in the chair in front of the desk. "You see, doctor, I've been feeling kind of light-headed. And absentminded. I forget what I'm doing in the middle of doing it and catch myself staring off into space."

"Hmmm."

"Then there have been these aches. Here," she said, and put a hand on her heart.

"Ah."

"Like palpitations. And at night…" She caught her lower lip between her teeth. "I've had these dreams."

"Really?" He came around to sit on the corner of the desk. There was her scent, whispery light, to flirt with him. "What kind of dreams?"

"They're personal," she said primly.

"I'm a doctor."

"So you say." She grinned at him. "You haven't even asked me to take off my clothes."

"Good point." Rising, he took her hand. "Come with me."

"Where?"

"Your case warrants a full examination."

"Brady—"

"That's Dr. Brady to you." He hit the lights in examining room 1. "Now about that ache."

She gave him a slow, measured look. "Obviously you've been dipping into the rubbing alcohol."

He merely took her by the hips and boosted her onto

the examining table. "Relax, sweetie. They don't call me Dr. Feelgood for nothing." He took out his ophthalmoscope and directed the light into her eyes. "Yes, they're definitely green."

"Well, that's a relief."

"You're telling me." He set the instrument aside. "Okay, lose the blouse and I'll test your reflexes."

"Well…" She ran her tongue over her teeth. "As long as I'm here." She let her fingers wander down the buttons, unfastening slowly. Under it she wore sheer blue silk. "I'm not going to have to wear one of those paper things, am I?"

He had to catch his breath as she peeled off the blouse. "I think we can dispense with that. You look to be in excellent health. In fact, I can say without reservation that you look absolutely perfect."

"But I have this ache." She took his hand and pressed it to her breast. "Right now my heart's racing. Feel it?"

"Yeah." Gently he absorbed the feeling of silk and flesh. Her flesh. "I think it's catching."

"My skin's hot," she murmured. "And my legs are weak."

"Definitely catching." With a fingertip he slid a thin silk strap from her shoulder. "You may just have to be quarantined."

"With you, I hope."

He unhooked her slacks. "That's the idea."

When she toed off her sandals, the other strap slithered down her shoulders. Her voice was husky now, and growing breathless. "Do you have a diagnosis?"

He eased the slacks down her hips. "Sounds like the rocking pneumonia and the boogie-woogie flu."

She'd arched up to help him remove her slacks, and now she just stared. "What?"

"Too much Mozart."

"Oh." She twined her arms around his shoulders. It seemed like years since she'd been able to hold him against her. When his lips found the little hollow near her collarbone, she smiled. "Can you help me, Doctor?"

"I'm about to do my damnedest."

His mouth slid over hers. It was like coming home. Her little sigh merged with his as she leaned into him. Dreamily she changed the angle of the kiss and let his taste pour into her. Whatever illness she had, he was exactly the right medicine.

"I feel better already." She nibbled on his lip. "More."

"Van?"

Her heavy eyes opened. While her fingers combed through his hair, she smiled. The light glowed in her eyes. Again he could see himself there, trapped in the misty green. Not lost this time. Found.

Everything he'd ever wanted, ever needed, ever dreamed of, was right here. He felt the teasing pleasure turn to grinding ache in the flash of an instant. With an oath, he dragged her mouth back to his and feasted.

No patience this time. Though the change surprised her, it didn't frighten her. He was her friend, her lover. Her only. There was a desperation and a fervency that thrilled, that demanded, that possessed. As the twin of his emotions rose in her, she pulled him closer.

More, she thought again, but frantically now. She could never get enough of being wanted this wildly. She dragged at his lab coat, even as her teeth scraped over his lip. Desire pumped through her like a drug and had her yanking at his T-shirt before the coat hit the floor.

She wanted the feel of his flesh, the heat of it, under her hands. She wanted the taste of that flesh, the succulence of it, under her lips.

The loving he had shown her until now had been calm and sweet and lovely. This time she craved the fire, the dark, the madness.

Control broken, he pushed her back on the narrow padded table, tearing at the wisp of silk. He could tolerate nothing between them now—only flesh against flesh and heart against heart. She was a wonder of slender limbs and subtle curves, of pale skin and delicate bones. He wanted to taste, to touch, to savor every inch.

But her demands were as great as his. She pulled him to her, sliding agilely over him so that her lips could race from his to his throat, his chest, beyond. Rough and greedy, his hands streaked over her, exploiting everywhere, as her questing mouth drove him mad.

His taste. Hot and dark and male, it made her giddy. His form. Firm and hard and muscled, it made her weak. Already damp, his skin slid under her seeking fingers. And she played him deftly, as she would her most passionate concerto.

She feared her heart would burst from its pounding rhythm. Her head spun with it. Her body trembled. Yet there was a power here. Even through the dizziness she felt it swelling in her. How could she have known she could give so much—and take so much?

His pulse thundered under her fingertips. Between his frenzied murmurs, his breath was ragged. She saw the echo of her own passion in his eyes, tasted it when she crushed her mouth to his. For her, she thought as she let herself drown in the kiss. Only for her.

He grasped her hips, fingers digging in. With each breath he took, her scent slammed into his system, potent as any narcotic. Her hair curtained his face, blocking the light and letting him see only her. The faint smile of knowledge was in her eyes. With her every movement, she enticed.

"For God's sake, Van." Her name was part oath, part prayer. If he didn't have her now, he knew he would die from the need.

She shifted, arching back, as she took him into her. For an instant, time stopped, and with it his breath, his thoughts, his life. He saw only her, her hair streaming back like a wild red river, her body pale and gleaming in the harsh light, her face glowing with the power she had only just discovered.

Then it was all speed and sound as she drove them both.

This was glory. She gave herself to it, her arms reaching up before she lost her hands in her own hair. This was wonder. And delight. No symphony had ever been so rousing. No prelude so passionate. Even as sensation shuddered through her, she begged for more.

There was freedom in the greed. Ecstasy in the knowledge that she could take as much as she wanted. Excitement in understanding that she could give just as generously.

Her heart was roaring in her ears. When she groped for his hands, his fingers clamped on to hers. They held tight as they burst over the peak together.

She slid down to him, boneless, her head spinning and her heart racing still. His skin was damp, as hers was, his body as limp. When she pressed her lips to his throat, she could feel the frantic beating of his pulse.

She had done that, Vanessa realized, still dazed. She

had taken control and given them both pleasure and passion. She hadn't even had to think, only to act, only to feel. Sailing on this new self-awareness, she propped herself up on an elbow and smiled down at him.

His eyes were closed, his face so completely relaxed that she knew he was next to sleep. His heartbeat, was settling down to a purr, as was hers. Through the contentment, she felt need bloom anew.

"Doctor," she murmured, nibbling at his ear.

"Hmm."

"I feel a lot better."

"Good." He drew in a deep breath, let it out. He figured that was the most exercise he would be able to handle for days. "Remember, your health is my business."

"I'm glad to hear that." She ran a fingertip down his chest experimentally. And felt muscles jump. "Because I think I'm going to need more treatments." She trailed the tip of her tongue down his throat. "I still have this ache."

"Take two aspirin and call me in an hour."

She laughed, a low, husky sound that had his blood humming again. "I thought you were dedicated." Slowly, seductively, she roamed his face with kisses. "God, you taste good." She lowered her mouth to his and sunk in.

"Vanessa." He could easily have floated off to sleep with her gentle stroking. But when her hand slid downward, contentment turned into something more demanding. He opened his eyes and saw that she was smiling at him. She was amused, he noted. And—pun intended—completely on top of things. "You're asking for trouble," he told her.

"Yeah." She lowered her head again to nip at his lip. "But am I going to get it?"

He answered the question to their mutual satisfaction.

"Good God," he said when he could breathe again. "I'm going to have this table bronzed."

"I think I'm cured." She pushed the hair from her face as she slid to the floor. "For now."

Groaning a little, he swung his legs off the table. "Wait till you get my bill."

"I'm looking forward to it." She handed him his pants, then slithered into her teddy. She didn't know about him, but she'd never think the same way about examining room 1 again. "And to think I came by to offer you some ham sandwiches."

"Ham?" His fingers paused on the snap of his jeans. "As in food? Like meat and bread?"

"And potato chips."

His mouth was already watering. "Consider yourself paid in full."

She shook back her hair, certain that if she felt any better she'd be breaking the law. "I take it to mean you're hungry."

"I haven't eaten since breakfast. Chicken pox," he explained as she pulled on her blouse. "If someone was to offer me a ham sandwich, I'd kiss her feet."

She wiggled her toes. "I like the sound of that. I'll go get the basket."

"Hold it." He took her arm. "If we stay in this room, my nurse is going to get a shock when she opens up tomorrow."

"Okay." She picked up his T-shirt. "Why don't we take it back to my house?" She rubbed the soft cotton against her cheek before handing it to him. "And eat in bed."

"Good thinking."

An hour later, they were sprawled across Vanessa's bed as Brady poured the last drop from a bottle of chardonnay. Vanessa had scoured the house for candles. Now they were set throughout the room, flickering while Chopin played quietly on the bedside radio.

"That was the best picnic I've had since I was thirteen and raided the Girl Scout overnight jamboree."

She scrounged for the last potato chip, then broke it judiciously in half. "I heard about that." There hadn't been time for Girl Scouts with her training. "You were always rotten."

"Hey, I got to see Betty Jean Baumgartner naked. Well, almost naked," he corrected. "She had on a training bra and panties, but at thirteen that's pretty erotic stuff."

"A rotten creep."

"It was hormones." He sipped his wine. "Lucky for you, I've still got plenty." With a satisfied sigh, he leaned back against the pillow. "Even if they're aging."

Feeling foolish and romantic, she bent over to kiss his knee. "I've missed you, Brady."

He opened his eyes again. "I've missed you, too. I'm sorry this week's been so messed up."

"I understand."

He reached out to twine a lock of her hair around his finger. "I hope you do. Office hours alone doubled this week."

"I know. Chicken pox. Two of my students are down with it. And I heard you delivered a baby—boy, seven pounds six ounces—took out a pair of tonsils... Is it pair or set?" she wondered. "Sewed up a gash in Jack's arm, and splinted a broken finger. All that being above and beyond the day-to-day sniffles, sneezes, aches and exams."

"How do you know?"

"I have my sources." She touched his cheek. "You must be tired."

"I was before I saw you. Anyway, it'll ease off when Dad gets back. Did you get a postcard?"

"Yes, just today." She settled back with her wine. "Palm trees and sand, mariachi players and sunsets. It sounds like they're having a wonderful time."

"I hope so, because I intend to switch places with them when they get back."

"Switch places?"

"I want to go away with you somewhere, Van." He took her hand, kissed it. "Anywhere you want."

"Away?" Her nerves began to jump. "Why?"

"Because I want to be alone with you, completely alone, as we've never had the chance to be."

She had to swallow. "We're alone now."

He set his wine aside, then hers. "Van, I want you to marry me."

She couldn't claim surprise. She had known, once he had used the word *love*, that marriage would follow. Neither did she feel fear, as she'd been certain she would. But she did feel confusion.

They had talked of marriage before, when they'd been so young and marriage had seemed like such a beautiful dream. She knew better now. She knew marriage was work and commitment and a shared vision.

"Brady, I—"

"This isn't the way I planned it," he interrupted. "I'd wanted it to be very traditional—to have the ring and a nicely poetic speech. I don't have a ring, and all I can tell you is that I love you. I always have, I always will."

"Brady." She pressed his hand to her cheek. Nothing he could have said would have been more poetic. "I want to be able to say yes. I didn't realize until just this moment how much I want that."

"Then say it."

Her eyes were wide and wet when they lifted to his. "I can't. It's too soon. No," she said, before he could explode. "I know what you're going to say. We've known each other almost our whole lives. It's true. But in some ways it's just as true that we only met a few weeks ago."

"There was never anyone but you," he said slowly. "Every other woman I got close to was only a substitute. You were a ghost who haunted me everywhere I went, who faded away every time I tried to reach out and touch."

Nothing could have moved her or unnerved her more. "My life's turned upside down since I came back here. I never thought I would see you again—and I thought that if I did it wouldn't matter, that I wouldn't feel. But it does matter, and I do feel, and that only makes it more difficult."

She was saying almost what he wanted to hear. Almost. "Shouldn't that make it easier?"

"No. I wish it did. I can't marry you, Brady, until I look into the mirror and recognize myself."

"I don't know what the hell you're talking about."

"No, you can't." She dragged her hands through her hair. "I barely do myself. All I know is that I can't give you what you want. I may never be able to."

"We're good together, Van." He had to fight to keep from holding too tight. "Damn it, you know that."

"Yes." She was hurting him. She could hardly bear it. "Brady, there are too many things I don't understand about myself. Too many questions I don't have the answers to. Please, I can't talk about marriage, about lifetimes, until I do."

"My feelings aren't going to change."

"I hope not."

He reeled himself back, slowly. "You're not going to get away from me this time, Van. If you cut and run, I'll come after you. If you try to sneak off, I'll be right there."

Pride rose instantly to wage war with regret. "You make that sound like a threat."

"It is."

"I don't like threats, Brady." She tossed her hair back in a gesture as much challenge as annoyance. "You should remember I don't tolerate them."

"And you should remember I make good on them." Very deliberately, he took her by the shoulders and pulled her against him. "You belong to me, Vanessa. Sooner or later you're going to get that through your head."

The thrill raced up her spine, as it always did when she saw that dangerous light in his eyes. But her chin came up. "I belong to myself first, Brady. Or I intend to. You'll have to get that through your head. Then, maybe, we'll have something."

"We have something now." When his mouth came to hers, she tasted the anger, the frustration, and the need. "You can't deny it."

"Then let it be enough." Her eyes were as dark and intent as his. "I'm here, with you. While I am, there's nothing and no one else." Her arms went around him, enfolding. "Let it be enough."

But it wasn't enough. Even as he rolled onto her, as his mouth fastened hungrily on hers, as his blood fired, he knew it wasn't enough.

In the morning, when she woke—alone, with his scent on sheets that were already growing cold—she was afraid it would never be.

Chapter 11

Nice, very nice, Vanessa thought as Annie worked her way through one of her beloved Madonna's compositions. She had to admit it was a catchy tune, bold and sly by turns. She'd had to simplify it a bit for Annie's inexperienced fingers, but the heart was still there. And that was what counted.

Perhaps the improvement in Annie's technique wasn't radical, but there was improvement. And, as far as enthusiasm went, Annie Crampton was her prize student.

Her own attitude had changed, as well, Vanessa admitted. She hadn't known she would enjoy quite so much influencing young hearts and minds with music. She was making a difference here—perhaps only a small one so far, but a difference.

Then there was the added benefit of the lessons helping her keep her mind off Brady. At least for an hour or two every day.

"Well done, Annie."

"I played it all the way through." The wonder on Annie's face was worth the few sour notes she had hit. "I can do it again."

"Next week." Vanessa picked up Annie's book just as she heard the front screen slam. "I want you to work on this next lesson. Hi, Joanie."

"I heard the music." She shifted Lara to her other hip. "Annie Crampton, was that you playing?"

Braces flashed. "I played it all the way through. Miss Sexton said I did a good job."

"And you did. I'm impressed—especially because she could never teach me anything beyond 'Heart and Soul.'"

Vanessa placed a hand on Annie's head. "Mrs. Knight didn't practice."

"I do. And my mom says I've learned more in three weeks than I did in three months up at the music store." She flashed a final grin as she gathered up her books. "And it's more fun, too. See you next week, Miss Sexton."

"I really was impressed," Joanie said as Annie slammed out the front door.

"She has good hands." She held out her own for the baby. "Hello, Lara."

"Maybe you could give her lessons one day."

"Maybe." She cuddled the baby.

"So, other than Annie, how are the lessons going? You're up to, what—?"

"Twelve students. And that's my absolute limit." She pressed her nose against Lara's and had the baby giggling. "Absolutely. But, all in all, they're going fairly well. I've learned to check students' hands before they sit at the piano. I never did figure out what Scott Snooks smeared on the keys."

"What did it look like?"

"Green." She laughed and bounced Lara. "Now we have an inspection before each lesson."

"If you can teach Scott Snooks anything other than murder and mayhem, you're a miracle worker."

"That's the challenge." And she was beginning to enjoy it. "If you've got time, I can defrost a can of lemonade."

"Miss Domesticity." Joanie grinned. "No, really, I only have a couple of minutes. Don't you have another student coming?"

"Saved by the chicken pox." With Lara in tow, Vanessa moved to the living room. "What's your hurry?"

"I just stopped by to see if you needed anything in town. Dad and Loretta will be back in a few hours, and I want to see them. Meanwhile, I've got three dozen errands to run. Hardware store, grocery store, the lumber place. I still can't believe Jack sweet-talked me into that one." She plopped into a chair. "I've spent most of the morning picking up behind Lara the Wrecking Crew as she single-handedly totaled the house. And to think I was thrilled when she took her first step."

"I could use some sheet music." Vanessa gently removed Lara's grasping fingers from her necklace. "I tell you what, I'll write down the titles for you, and in exchange I'll baby-sit."

Joanie shook her head and rubbed a hand over her ear. "Excuse me, did you say baby-sit?"

"Yes. As in you-can-leave-Lara-with-me-for-a-couple-of-hours."

"A couple of hours," she repeated slowly. "Do you mean I can go to the mall, alone, by myself?"

"Well, if you'd rather not—"

Joanie let out a whoop as she jumped up to kiss Vanessa and Lara in turn. "Lara, baby, I love you. Goodbye."

"Joanie, wait." Laughing, Vanessa sprang up to grab her arm. "I haven't written down the titles for the sheet music."

"Oh, yeah. Right. I guess I got a little too excited." She blew her hair out of her eyes. "I haven't been shopping by myself in…I forget." Her smile faded to a look of dismay. "I'm a terrible mother. I was happy about leaving her behind. No, not happy. Thrilled. Ecstatic. Delirious. I'm a terrible mother."

"No, you're a crazy person, but you're a wonderful mother."

Joanie steadied herself. "You're right, it was just the thrill of going to the hardware store without a stroller and a diaper bag that went to my head. Are you sure you can handle it?"

"We'll have a great time."

"Of course you will." Keen-eyed, she surveyed the living room. "Maybe you should move anything important up a couple of feet. And nail it down."

"We'll be fine." She set Lara on the floor and handed her a fashion magazine to peruse—and tear up. "See?"

"Okay…I nursed her before I left home, and there's an emergency bottle of apple juice in her diaper bag. Can you change a diaper?"

"I've seen it done before. How hard can it be?"

"Well, if you're sure you don't have anything you have to do."

"My evening is free. When the newlyweds get home, I only have to walk a half a block to see them."

"I guess Brady will be coming by."

"I don't know."

Joanie kept her eye on Lara as the baby pushed herself up and toddled to the coffee table. "Then it hasn't been my imagination."

"What?"

"That there's been a lot of tension between you two the last week or so."

"You're stalling, Joanie."

"Maybe—but I am interested. The couple of times I've seen Brady recently, he's been either snarling or distracted. I don't want you to tell me it was wishful thinking when I hoped you two would get back together."

"He asked me to marry him."

"He— Wow! Oh, that's wonderful! That's terrific!" As Joanie launched herself into Vanessa's arms, Lara began to bang on the table and squeal. "See, even Lara's excited."

"I said no."

"What?" Slowly, Joanie stepped back. "You said no?"

She turned away from the stunned disappointment in Joanie's face. "It's too soon for all of this, Joanie. I've only been back a few weeks, and so much has happened. My mother, your father…" She walked over to move a vase out of Lara's reach. "When I got here, I wasn't even sure how long I would stay, a couple of weeks, maybe a month. I've been considering a tour next spring."

"But that doesn't mean you can't have a personal life. If you want one."

"I don't know what I want." Feeling helpless, she looked back at Joanie. "Marriage is… I don't even know what it means, so how can I consider marrying Brady?"

"But you love him."

"Yes, I think I do." She lifted her hands, fingers spread. "I don't want to make the same mistake my parents did. I need to be sure we both want the same things."

"What do you want?"

"I'm still figuring it out."

"You'd better figure fast. If I know my brother, he won't give you a lot of time."

"I'll take what I need this time." Before Joanie could argue, she shook her head. "You'd better go if you want to get back before my mother and Ham come home."

"Oh, you're right. I'll go get the diaper bag." She paused at the door. "I know we're already stepsisters, but I'm still holding out for sisters-in-law."

Brady knew he was asking for more grief when he started up the walk to Vanessa's house. During the past week, he had tried to keep his distance. When the woman you loved refused to marry you, it didn't do much for your ego.

He wanted to believe she was just being stubborn, and that backing off and playing it light would bring her around. But he was afraid it went much deeper than that. She'd taken a stand. He could walk away, or he could pound down her door. It wouldn't make any difference.

Either way, he needed to see her.

He knocked on the wooden frame of the screen but got no answer. Hardly surprising, he thought, as the banging and crashing from inside would have drowned out any other sound. Maybe she was in a temper, he thought hopefully. Enraged with herself for turning her back on her chance at happiness.

The image appealed to him. He was almost whistling when he opened the screen and walked down the hall.

Whatever he'd been expecting, it hadn't been his niece gleefully banging pots and pans together on the floor while Vanessa, dusted with flour, stood at the counter. Spotting him, Lara hoisted a stainless steel lid and brought it down with a satisfied bang.

"Hi."

With a hand full of celery, Vanessa turned. She expected her heart to do a quick flip-flop when she saw him. It always did. But she didn't smile. Neither did he.

"Oh. I didn't hear you come in."

"I'm not surprised." He reached down to pick up Lara and give her a quick swing. "What are you doing?"

"Baby-sitting." She rubbed more flour on her nose. "Joanie had to go into town, so I volunteered to watch Lara for a couple of hours."

"She's a handful, isn't she?"

Vanessa blew out a weary breath. She couldn't bear to think about the mess they had left in the living room. "She likes it in here."

He set the baby down, gave her padded bottom a light pat and sent her off to play with a small tower of canned goods. "Wait until she figures out how to rip the labels off. Got anything to drink?"

"Lara's got a bottle of apple juice."

"I wouldn't want to deprive her."

"There's a can of lemonade in the freezer." She went back to chopping celery. "If you want it, you'll have to make it yourself. My hands are full."

"So I see." He opened the freezer. "What are you making?"

"A mess." She brought the knife down with a thunk.

"I thought since my mother and Ham were due back soon it would be nice to have a casserole or something. Joanie's already done so much, I wanted to try to—" She set the knife down in disgust. "I'm no good at this. I'm just no good at it. I've never cooked a meal in my life." She whirled as Brady came to the sink to run cold water into a pitcher. "I'm a grown woman, and if it wasn't for room service and prepackaged meals I'd starve to death."

"You make a great ham sandwich."

"I'm not joking, Brady."

With a wooden spoon, he began to stir the lemonade. "Maybe you should be."

"I came in here thinking I'd try to put myself into this little fantasy. What if I were a doctor's wife?"

He stopped stirring to look at her. "What if you were?"

"What if he were coming home after taking appointments and doing hospital rounds all day? Wouldn't I want to fix him a meal, something we could sit down to together, something we could talk over? Isn't that something he would want? Expect?"

"Why don't you ask him?"

"Damn it, Brady, don't you see? I couldn't make it work."

"All I see is that you're having trouble putting—" He leaned forward to look at the disarray on the counter. "What is this?"

Her mouth moved into a pout. "It's supposed to be a tuna casserole."

"You're having trouble putting a tuna casserole together. And, personally, I hope you never learn how to do it."

"That's not the point."

Struck by tenderness, he brushed at a streak of flour on her cheek. "What is the point?"

"It's a little thing, maybe even a stupid thing. But if I can't even do this—" she shoved and sent an onion scampering down the counter "—how can I work out the bigger ones?"

"Do you think I want to marry you so that I can have a hot meal every night?"

"No. Do you think I want to marry you and feel inept and useless?"

Truly exasperated, he gestured toward the counter. "Because you don't know what to do with a can of tuna?"

"Because I don't know how to be a wife." When her voice rose, she struggled to calm it. Perhaps Lara was too young, and too interested in her pans and cans, to detect an argument, but Vanessa had lived through too many of her own. "And, as much as I care for you, I don't know if I want to be. There's one thing I do well, Brady, and that's my music."

"No one's asking you to give that up, Van."

"And when I go on tour? When I'm gone weeks at a time, when I have to devote endless hours to rehearsals and practicing? What kind of marriage would we have, Brady, in between performances?"

"I don't know." He looked down at his niece, who was contentedly placing cans inside of pots. "I didn't know you were seriously considering going on tour again."

"I have to consider it. It's been a part of my life for too long not to." Calmer now, she went back to dicing vegetables. "I'm a musician, Brady, the same way you're a doctor. What I do doesn't save lives, but it does enrich them."

He pushed an impatient hand through his dark hair.

He was in the business of soothing doubts and fears, as much as he was in the business of healing bodies. Why couldn't he soothe Vanessa's?

"I know what you do is important, Van. I admire it. I admire you. What I don't see is why your talent would have to be an obstacle to our being together."

"It's just one of them," she murmured.

He took her arm, slowly turning her to face him. "I want to marry you. I want to have children with you and make a home for them. We can do that here, where we both belong, if you just trust me."

"I need to trust myself first." She took a bracing breath. "I leave for Cordina next week."

His hand slid away from her arm. "Cordina?"

"Princess Gabriella's annual benefit."

"I've heard of it."

"I've agreed to give a performance."

"I see." Because he needed to do something, he opened a cupboard and took out a glass. "And when did you agree?"

"I signed almost two weeks ago."

His fingers tensed on the glass. "And didn't mention it."

"No, I didn't mention it." She wiped her hands on her thighs. "With everything that was happening between us, I wasn't sure how you would react."

"Were you going to wait until you were leaving for the airport, or were you just going to send me a postcard when you got there? Damn it, Van." He barely controlled the urge to smash the glass against the wall. "What the hell kind of games have you been playing with me? Was all this just killing time, lighting up an old flame?"

She went pale, but her voice was strong. "You know better."

"All I know is that you're leaving."

"It's only a single performance, a few days."

"And then?"

She turned to look out the window. "I don't know. Frank, my manager, is anxious to put a tour together. That's in addition to some special performances I've been asked to do."

"In addition," he repeated. "You came here with an ulcer because you could barely make yourself go out on stage, because you pushed yourself too far too often. And you're already talking about going back and doing it again."

"It's something I have to work out for myself."

"Your father—"

"Is dead," she cut in. "He can't influence me to perform. I hope you won't try to influence me not to." She took a calming breath, but it didn't help. "I don't believe I pushed myself too far. I did what I needed to do. All I want is the chance to decide what that is."

As the war inside him continued, Brady wondered if there could be a victor. Or if there would only be victims. "You've been thinking about going back, starting with Cordina, but you never talked to me about it."

"No. However selfish it sounds, Brady, this is something I needed to decide for myself. I realize it's unfair for me to ask you to wait. So I won't." She closed her eyes tight, then opened them again. "Whatever happens, I want you to know that the last few weeks, with you, have meant everything to me."

"The hell with that." It was too much like a goodbye. He yanked her against him. "You can go to Cordina, you can go anywhere, but you won't forget me. You won't forget this."

There was fury in the kiss. And desperation. She

fought neither. How could she when their mirror images raged within her? She thought that if her life was to end that instant, she would have known nothing but this wild wanting.

"Brady." She brought her hands to his face. When her brow rested against his, she drew a deep breath. "There has to be more than this. For both of us."

"There is more." With his thumbs under her jaw, he tilted her head back. "You know there is."

"I made a promise to myself today. That I would take the time to think over my life, every year of it, every moment that I remembered that seemed important. And when I had done that, I would make the right decision. No more hesitations or excuses or doubts. But for now you have to let me go."

"I let you go once before." Before she could shake her head, he tightened his grip. "You listen to me. If you leave, like this, I won't spend the rest of my life wishing for you. I'll be damned if you'll break my heart a second time."

As they stood close, their eyes locked on each other's, Joanie strolled into the room.

"Well, some baby-sitters." With a laugh, she plucked Lara up and hugged her. "I can't believe I actually missed this monster. Sorry it took so long." She smiled at Lara and kept babbling as she fought her way through the layers of tension. "There was a line a mile long at the grocery." She glanced down at the scattered pots and canned goods. "It looks like she kept you busy."

"She was fine," Vanessa managed. "She ate about half a box of crackers."

"I thought she'd gained a couple pounds. Hi, Brady. Good timing." His one-word comment had her rolling her eyes. "I meant I'm glad you're here. Look who I ran into outside." She turned just as Ham and Loretta walked in, arm in arm. "Don't they look great?" Joanie wanted to know. "So tanned. I know tans aren't supposed to be healthy, but they look so good."

"Welcome back." Vanessa smiled, but stayed where she was. "Did you have a good time?"

"It was wonderful." Loretta set a huge straw bag down on the table. There was warm color on her cheeks, on her bare arms. And, Vanessa noted, that same quiet happiness in her eyes. "It has to be the most beautiful place on earth, all that white sand and clear water. We even went snorkeling."

"Never seen so many fish," Ham said as he dropped yet another straw bag on the table.

"Ha!" Loretta gave him a telling look. "He was looking at all those pretty legs under water. Some of those women down there wear next to nothing." Then she grinned. "The men, too. I stopped looking the other way after the first day or two."

"Hour or two," Ham corrected.

She only laughed and dug into her bag. "Look here, Lara. We brought you a puppet." She dangled the colorful dancer from its strings.

"Among a few dozen other things," Ham put in. "Wait until you see the pictures. I even rented one of those underwater cameras and got shots of the, ah, fish."

"It's going to take us weeks to unpack it all. I can't even think about it." With a sigh, Loretta sat down at the table. "Oh, and the silver jewelry. I suppose I went a little wild with it."

"Very wild," Ham added with a wink.

"I want you both to pick out the pieces you like best," she said to Vanessa and Joanie. "Once we find them. Brady, is that lemonade?"

"Right the first time." He poured her a glass. "Welcome home."

"Wait until you see your sombrero."

"My sombrero?"

"It's red and silver—about ten feet across." She grinned over at Ham. "I couldn't talk him out of it. Oh, it's good to be home." She glanced at the counter. "What's all this?"

"I was…" Vanessa sent a helpless look at the mess she'd made. "I was going to try to fix some dinner. I…I thought you might not want to fuss with cooking your first night back."

"Good old American food." Ham took the puppet to dangle it for the giggling Lara. "Nothing would hit the spot better right now."

"I haven't exactly—"

Catching her drift, Joanie moved over to the counter. "Looks like you were just getting started. Why don't I give you a hand?"

Vanessa stepped back, bumped into Brady, then moved away again. "I'll be back in a minute."

She hurried out and took the stairs at a dash. In her room, she sat on the bed and wondered if she was losing her mind. Surely it was a close thing when a tuna casserole nearly brought her to tears.

"Van." Loretta stood with her hand on the knob. "May I come in a minute?"

"I was coming back down. I just—" She started to rise, then sat again. "I'm sorry. I don't want to spoil your homecoming."

"You haven't. You couldn't." After a moment, she took a chance. Closing the door, she walked over to sit on the bed beside her daughter. "I could tell you were

upset when we came in. I thought it was just because...
well, because of me."

"No. No, not entirely."

"Would you like to talk about it?"

She hesitated so long that Loretta was afraid she
wouldn't speak at all.

"It's Brady. No, it's me," Vanessa corrected, impatient with herself. "He wants me to marry him, and I
can't. There are so many reasons, and he can't understand. *Won't* understand. I can't cook a meal or do laundry or any of the things that Joanie just breezes right
through."

"Joanie's a wonderful woman," Loretta said carefully.
"But she's different from you."

"I'm the one who's different, from Joanie, from you,
from everyone."

Lightly, afraid to go too far, Loretta touched her hair.
"It's not a crime or an abnormality not to know how to
cook."

"I know." But that only made her feel more foolish. "It's simply that I wanted to feel self-sufficient and
ended up feeling inadequate."

"I never taught you how to cook, or how to run a
household. Part of that was because you were so involved with your music, and there wasn't really time.
But another reason, maybe the true one, is that I didn't
want to. I wanted to have that all to myself. The house,
the running of it, was all I really had to fulfill me." She
gave a little sigh as she touched Vanessa's rigid arm.
"But we're not really talking about casseroles and laundry, are we?"

"No. I feel pressured, by what Brady wants. Maybe by
who he wants. Marriage, it sounds so lovely. But—"

"But you grew up in a household where it wasn't."

With a nod, Loretta took Vanessa's hand. "It's funny how blind we can be. All the time you were growing up, I never thought what was going on between your father and me affected you. And of course it did."

"It was your life."

"It was our lives," Loretta told her. "Van, while we were away, Ham and I talked about all of this. He wanted me to explain everything to you. I didn't agree with him until right now."

"Everyone's downstairs."

"There have been enough excuses." She couldn't sit, so she walked over to the window. The marigolds were blooming, a brilliant orange and yellow against the smug-faced pansies.

"I was very young when I married your father. Eighteen." She gave a little shake of her head. "Lord, it seems like a lifetime ago. And certainly like I was another person. How he swept me off my feet! He was almost thirty then, and had just come back after being in Paris, London, New York, all those exciting places."

"His career had floundered," Vanessa said quietly. "He'd never talk about it, but I've read—and, of course, there were others who loved to talk about his failures."

"He was a brilliant musician. No one could take that away from him." Loretta turned. There was a sadness in her eyes now, lingering. "But he took it away from himself. When his career didn't reach the potential he expected, he turned his back on it. When he came back home, he was troubled, moody, impatient."

She took a moment to gather her courage, hoping she was doing the right thing. "I was a very simple girl, Van. I had led a very simple life. Perhaps that was what appealed to him at first. His sophistication—his, well, worldliness—appealed to me. Dazzled me. We made a mistake—as much mine as his. I was overwhelmed by him, flattered, infatuated. And I got pregnant."

Shock robbed Vanessa of speech as she stared at her mother. With an effort, she rose. "Me? You married because of me?"

"We married because we looked at each other and saw only what we wanted to see. You were the result of that. I want you to know that when you were conceived, you were conceived in what we both desperately believed was love. Maybe, because we did believe it, it was love. It was certainly affection and caring and need."

"You were pregnant," Vanessa said quietly. "You didn't have a choice."

"There is always a choice." Loretta stepped forward, drawing Vanessa's gaze to hers. "You were not a mistake or an inconvenience or an excuse. You were the best parts of us, and we both knew it. There were no scenes or recriminations. I was thrilled to be carrying his child, and he was just as happy. The first year we were married, it was good. In many ways, it was even beautiful."

"I don't know what to say. I don't know what to feel."

"You were the best thing that ever happened to me, or to your father. The tragedy was that we were the worst thing that ever happened to each other. You weren't responsible for that. We were. Whatever happened afterward, having you made all the difference."

"What did happen?"

"My parents died, and we moved into this house. The house I had grown up in, the house that belonged to me. I didn't understand then how bitterly he resented that. I'm not sure he did, either. You were three then. Your father was restless. He resented being here, and couldn't bring himself to face the possibility of failure if he tried to pick up his career again. He began to teach you, and almost overnight it seemed that all of the passion, all of the energy he had had, went into making you into the musician, the performer, the star he felt he would never be again."

Blindly she turned to the window again. "I never stopped him. I never tried. You seemed so happy at the piano. The more promise you showed the more bitter he became. Not toward you, never toward you. But toward the situation, and, of course, toward me. And I toward him. You were the one good thing we had ever done together, the one thing we could both love completely. But it wasn't enough to make us love each other. Can you understand that?"

"Why did you stay together?"

"I'm not really sure. Habit. Fear. The small hope that somehow we would find out we really did love each other. There were too many fights. Oh, I know how they used to upset you. When you were older, a teenager, you used to run from the house just to get away from the arguing. We failed you, Van. Both of us. And, though I know he did things that were selfish, even unforgivable, I failed you more, because I closed my eyes to them. Instead of making things right, I looked for an escape. And I found it with another man."

She found the courage to face her daughter again. "There is no excuse. Your father and I were no longer intimate, were barely even civil, but there were other alternatives open to me. I had thought about divorce, but that takes courage, and I was a coward. Suddenly there was someone who was kind to me, someone who found me attractive and desirable. Because it was forbidden, because it was wrong, it was exciting."

Vanessa felt the tears burn the back of her eyes. She had to know, to understand. "You were lonely."

"Oh, God, yes." Loretta's voice was choked. She pressed her lips together. "It's no excuse—"

"I don't want excuses. I want to know how you felt."

"Lost," she whispered. "Empty. I felt as though my life were over. I wanted someone to need me again, to hold me. To say pretty things to me, even if they were lies." She shook her head, and when she spoke again her voice was stronger. "It was wrong, Vanessa, as wrong as it was for your father and I to rush together without looking closely." She came back to the bed, took Vanessa's hand. "I want it to be different for you. It will be different. Holding back from something that's right for you is just as foolish as rushing into something that's wrong."

"And how do I know the difference?"

"You will." She smiled a little. "It's taken me most of my life to understand that. With Ham, I knew."

"It wasn't." She was afraid to ask. "It wasn't Ham that you… He wasn't the one."

"All those years ago? Oh, no. He would never have betrayed Emily. He loved her. It was someone else. He wasn't in town long, only a few months. I suppose that made it easier for me somehow. He was a stranger, someone who didn't know me, didn't care. When I broke it off, he moved on."

"You broke it off? Why?"

Of all the things that had gone before, Loretta knew this would be the most difficult. "It was the night of your prom. I'd been upstairs with you. Remember, you were so upset?"

"He had Brady arrested."

"I know." She tightened her grip on Vanessa's hand. "I swear to you, I didn't know it then. I finally left you alone because, well, you needed to be alone. I was thinking about how I was going to give Brady Tucker a piece of my mind when I got ahold of him. I was still upset when your father came home. But he was livid, absolutely livid. That's when it all came out. He was furious because the sheriff had let Brady go, because Ham had come in and raised holy hell."

She let Vanessa's hands go to press her fingers to her eyes. "I was appalled. He'd never approved of Brady—I knew that. But he wouldn't have approved of anyone who interfered with his plans for you. Yet this—this was so far beyond anything I could imagine. The Tuckers were our friends, and anyone with eyes could see that you and Brady were in love. I admit I had worried about whether you would make love, but we'd talked about it, and you'd seemed very sensible. In any case, your father was raging, and I was so angry, so incensed by his insensitivity, that I lost control. I told him what I had been trying to hide for several weeks. I was pregnant."

"Pregnant," Vanessa repeated. "You— Oh, God."

Loretta sprang up to pace the room. "I thought he would go wild, but instead he was calm. Deadly calm." There was no use telling her daughter what names he had called her in that soft, controlled voice. "He said that there was no question about our remaining together. He would file for divorce. And would take you. The more I shouted, begged, threatened, the calmer he became. He would take you because he was the one who would give you the proper care. I was—well, it was obvious what I was. He already had tickets for Paris. Two tickets. I hadn't known about it, but he had been planning to take you away in any case. I was to say nothing, do nothing to stop him, or he would drag me through a custody suit that he would win when it came out that I was carrying another man's bastard." She began to weep then, silently. "If I didn't agree, he would wait until the child was born and file charges against me as an unfit mother. He swore he would make it his life's work to take that child, as well. And I would have nothing."

"But you…he couldn't…"

"I had barely been out of this county, much less the state. I didn't know what he could do. All I knew was that I was going to lose one child, and perhaps two. You were going to go to Paris, see all those wonderful things, play on all those fabulous stages. You would be someone, have something." Her cheeks drenched, she turned back. "As God is my witness, Vanessa, I don't know if I agreed because I thought it was what you would want, or because I was afraid to do anything else."

"It doesn't matter." She rose and went to her mother. "It doesn't matter anymore."

"I knew you would hate me—"

"No, I don't." She put her arms around Loretta and brought her close. "I couldn't. The baby," she murmured. "Will you tell me what you did?"

Grief, fresh and vital, swam through her. "I miscarried, just shy of three months. I lost both of you, you see. I never had all those babies I'd once dreamed of."

"Oh, Mom." Vanessa rocked as she let her own tears fall. "I'm sorry. I'm so sorry. It must have been terrible for you. Terribly hard."

With her cheek against Vanessa's, she held tight.

"There wasn't a day that went by that I didn't think of you, that I didn't miss you. If I had it to do over—"

But Vanessa shook her head. "No, we can't take the past back. We'll start right now."

Chapter 12

She sat in her dressing room, surrounded by flowers, the scent and the color of them. She barely noticed them. She'd hoped, perhaps foolishly, that one of the luscious bouquets, one of the elegant arrangements, had been sent by Brady.

But she had known better.

He had not come to see her off at the airport. He had not called to wish her luck, or to tell her he would miss her while she was gone. Not his style, Vanessa thought as she studied her reflection in the mirror. It never had been. When Brady Tucker was angry, he was angry. He made no polite, civilized overtures. He just stayed mad.

He had the right, she admitted. The perfect right.

She had left him, after all. She had gone to him, given herself to him, made love to him with all the passion and promise a woman could bring to a man. But she had held back the words. And, by doing so, she had held back herself.

Because she was afraid, she thought now. Of making that dreadful, life-consuming mistake. He would never understand that her caution was as much for him as it was for herself.

She understood now, after listening to her mother. Mistakes could be made for the best of reasons, or the worst of them. It was too late to ask her father, to try to understand his feelings, his reasons.

She only hoped it wasn't too late for herself.

Where were they now, those children who had loved so fiercely and so unwisely? Brady had his life, his skill, and his answers. His family, his friends, his home. From the rash, angry boy he had been had grown a man of integrity and purpose.

And she? Vanessa stared down at her hands, the long, gifted fingers spread. She had her music. It was all she had ever really had that belonged only to her.

Yes, she understood now, perhaps more than she wanted to, her mother's failings, her father's mistakes. They had, in their separate ways, loved her. But that love hadn't made them a family. Nor had it made any of the three of them happy.

So while Brady was setting down his roots in the fertile soil of the town where they had both been young, she was alone in a dressing room filled with flowers, waiting to step onto another stage.

At the knock on her door, she watched the reflection in the dressing room mirror smile. The show started long before the key light clicked on.

"Entrez."

"Vanessa." The Princess Gabriella, stunning in blue silk, swept inside.

"Your Highness." Before she could rise and make her curtsy, Gabriella was waving her to her seat in a gesture that was somehow imperious and friendly all at once.

"Please, don't get up. I hope I'm not disturbing you."

"Of course not. May I get you some wine?"

"If you're having some." Though her feet ached after a backbreaking day on her feet, she only sighed a little as she took a chair. She had been born royal, and royalty was taught not to complain. "It's been so hectic today, I haven't had a chance to see you, make certain you've been comfortable."

"No one could be uncomfortable in the palace, Your Highness."

"Gabriella, please." She accepted the glass of wine. "We're alone." She gave brief consideration to slipping out of her shoes, but thought better of it. "I wanted to thank you again for agreeing to play tonight. It's so important."

"It's always a pleasure to play in Cordina." The lights around the mirror sent the dozens of bugle beads on Vanessa's white dress dancing. "I'm honored that you wanted to include me."

Gabriella gave a quick laugh before she sipped. "You're annoyed that I bothered you while you were on vacation." She tossed back her fall of red-gold hair. "And I don't blame you. But for this, I've learned to be rude—and ruthless."

Vanessa had to smile. Royalty or not, the Princess Gabriella was easy to be with. "Honored and annoyed, then. I hope tonight's benefit is a tremendous success."

"It will be." She refused to accept less. "Eve— You know my sister-in-law?"

"Yes, I've met Her Highness several times."

"She's American—and therefore pushy. She's been a tremendous help to me."

"Your husband, he is also American?"

Gabriella's topaz eyes lit. "Yes. Reeve is also pushy. This year we involved our children quite a bit, so it's been even more of a circus than usual. My brother, Alexander, was away for a few weeks, but he returned in time to be put to use."

"You are ruthless with your family, Gabriella."

"It's best to be ruthless with those you love." She saw something, some cloud, come and go in Vanessa's eyes. She would get to that. "Hannah apologizes for not coming backstage before your performance. Bennett is fussing over her."

"Your younger brother is entitled to fuss when his wife is on the verge of delivering their child."

"Hannah was interested in you, Vanessa." Gabriella couldn't resist a smile. "As your name was linked with Bennett's before his marriage."

Along with half the female population of the free world, Vanessa thought, but she kept her smile bland. "His Highness was the most charming of escorts."

"He was a scoundrel."

"Tamed by the lovely Lady Hannah."

"Not tamed, but perhaps restrained." The princess set her glass aside. "I was sorry when your manager informed us that you wouldn't spend more than another day in Cordina. It's been so long since you visited us."

"There is no place I've felt more welcome." She toyed with the petals of a pure white rose. "I remember the last time I was here, the lovely day I spent at your farm, with your family."

"We would love to have you to ourselves again, whenever your schedule permits." Compassionate by nature, she reached out a hand. "You are well?"

"Yes, thank you. I'm quite well."

"You look lovely, Vanessa, perhaps more so because there's such sadness in your eyes. I understand the look. It faced me in the mirror once, not so many years ago. Men put it there. It's one of their finest skills." Her fingers linked with Vanessa's. "Can I help you?"

"I don't know." She looked down at their joined hands, then up into Gabriella's soft, patient eyes. "Gabriella, may I ask you, what's the most important thing in your life?"

"My family."

"Yes." She smiled. "You had such a romantic story. How you met and fell in love with your husband."

"It becomes more romantic as time passes, and less traumatic."

"He's an American, a former policeman?"

"Of sorts."

"If you had had to give up your position, your, well, birthright, to have married him, would you have done so?"

"Yes. But with great pain. Does this man ask you to give up something that's so much a part of you?"

"No, he doesn't ask me to give up anything. And yet he asks for everything."

Gabriella smiled again. "It is another skill they have."

"I've learned things about myself, about my background, my family, that are very difficult to accept. I'm not sure if I give this man what he wants, for now, that I won't be cheating him and myself in the bargain."

Gabriella was silent a moment. "You know my story, it has been well documented. After I had been kidnapped, and my memory was gone, I looked into my father's face and didn't know him. Into my brothers' eyes and saw the eyes of strangers. However much this hurt me, it hurt them only more. But I had to find myself, discover myself in the most basic of ways. It's very frightening, very frustrating. I'm not a patient or a temperate person."

Vanessa managed another smile. "I've heard rumors."

With a laugh, Gabriella picked up her wine and sipped again. "At last I recognized myself. At last I looked at my family and knew them. But differently," she said, gesturing. "It's not easy to explain. But when I knew them again, when I loved them again, it was with a different heart. Whatever flaws they had, whatever mistakes they had made, however they had wounded me in the past, or I them, didn't matter any longer."

"You're saying you forgot the past."

She gave a quick shake of her head, and her diamonds sizzled. "The past wasn't forgotten. It can't be. But I could see it through different eyes. Falling in love was not so difficult after being reborn."

"Your husband is a fortunate man."

"Yes. I remind him often." She rose. "I'd better leave you to prepare."

"Thank you."

Gabriella paused at the door. "Perhaps on my next trip to America you will invite me to spend a day in your home."

"With the greatest pleasure."

"And I'll meet this man."

"Yes." Vanessa's laugh was quick and easy. "I think you will."

When the door closed, she sat again. Very slowly

she turned her head, until she faced herself in the mirror, ringed by bright lights. She saw dark green eyes, a mouth that had been carefully painted a deep rose. A mane of chestnut hair. Pale skin over delicate features. She saw a musician. And a woman.

"Vanessa Sexton," she murmured, and smiled a little.

Suddenly she knew why she was there, why she would walk out onstage. And why, when she was done, she would go home.

Home.

It was too damn hot for a thirty-year-old fool to be out in the afternoon sun playing basketball. That was what Brady told himself as he jumped up and jammed another basket.

Even though the kids were out of school for the summer, he had the court, and the park, to himself. Apparently children had more sense than a lovesick doctor.

The temperature might have taken an unseasonable hike into the nineties, and the humidity might have decided to join it degree for degree, but Brady figured sweating on the court was a hell of a lot better than brooding alone at home.

Why the hell had he taken the day off?

He needed his work. He needed his hours filled.

He needed Vanessa.

That was something he was going to have to get over. He dribbled into a fast layup. The ball rolled around the rim, then dropped through.

He'd seen the pictures of Vanessa. They'd been all over the damn television, all over the newspaper. People in town hadn't been able to shut up about it—about her—for two days.

He wished he'd never seen her in that glittery white dress, her hair flaming down her back, those gorgeous hands racing over the keys, caressing them, drawing impossible music from them. Her music, he thought now. The same composition she'd been playing that day he'd walked into her house to find her waiting for him.

Her composition. She'd finished it.

Just as she'd finished with him.

He scraped his surgeon's fingers on the hoop.

How could he expect her to come back to a one-horse town, her high school sweetheart? She had royalty cheering her. She could move from palace to palace for the price of a song. All he had to offer her was a house in the woods, an ill-mannered dog and the occasional baked good in lieu of fee.

That was bull, he thought viciously as the ball rammed onto the backboard and careened off. No one would ever love her the way he did, the way he had all of his damn life. And if he ever got his hands on her again, she'd hear about it. She'd need an otolaryngologist by the time her ears stopped ringing.

"Stuff it," he snapped at Kong as the dog began to bark in short, happy yips. He was out of breath, Brady thought as he puffed toward the foul line. Out of shape. And—as the ball nipped the rim and bounced off—out of luck.

He pivoted, grabbed the rebound, and stopped dead in his tracks.

There she was, wearing those damn skimpy shorts, an excuse for a blouse that skimmed just under her breasts, carrying a bottle of grape soda and sporting a bratty smile on her face.

He wiped the sweat out of his eyes. The heat, his mood—and the fact that he hadn't slept in two days—

might be enough to bring on a hallucination. But he didn't like it. Not a bit.

"Hi, Brady." Though her heart was jolting against her ribs, she schooled her voice. She wanted it cool and low and just a little snotty. "You look awful hot." With her eyes on his, Vanessa took a long sip from the bottle, ran her tongue over her upper lip and sauntered the rest of the way to him. "Want a sip?"

He had to be going crazy. He wasn't eighteen anymore. But he could smell her. That floaty, flirty scent. He could feel the hard rubber of the ball in his bare hands, and the sweat dripping down his bare chest and back. As he watched, she leaned over to pet the dog. Still bent, she tossed her hair over her shoulder and sent him one of those taunting sidelong smiles.

"Nice dog."

"What the hell are you doing?"

"I was taking a walk." She straightened, then tipped the bottle to her lips again, draining it before she tossed the empty container into the nearby trash bin. "Your hook shot needs work." Her mouth moved into a pout. "Aren't you going to grab me?"

"No." If he did, he wasn't sure if he would kiss her or strangle her.

"Oh." She felt the confidence that had built up all during the flight, all during the interminable drive home, dry up. "Does that mean you don't want me?"

"Damn you, Vanessa."

Battling tears, she turned away. This wasn't the time for tears. Or for pride. Her little ploy to appeal to his sentiment had been an obvious mistake. "You have every right to be angry."

"Angry?" He heaved the ball away. Delighted, the

dog raced after it. "That doesn't begin to describe what I'm feeling. What kind of game are you playing?"

"It's not a game." Eyes brilliant, she turned back to him. "It's never been a game. I love you, Brady."

He didn't know if her words slashed his heart or healed it. "You took your damn time telling me."

"I took what I had to take. I'm sorry I hurt you." Any moment now, her breath would begin to hitch, mortifying her. "If you decide you want to talk to me, I'll be at home."

He grabbed her arm. "Don't you walk away from me. Don't you walk away from me ever again."

"I don't want to fight with you."

"Tough. You come back here, stir me up. You expect me to let things go on as they have been. To put aside what I want, what I need. To watch you leave time and time again, with never a promise, never a future. I won't do it. It's all or nothing, Van, starting now."

"You listen to me."

"The hell with you." He grabbed her then, but there was no fumbling in this kiss. It was hot and hungry. There was as much pain as pleasure here. Just as he wanted there to be.

She struggled, outraged that he would use force. But his muscles were like iron, sleeked with the sweat that heat and exercise had brought to his skin. The violence that flamed inside him was more potent than any she had known before, the need that vibrated from him more furious.

She was breathless when she finally tore away. And would have struck him if she hadn't seen the dark misery in his eyes.

"Go away, Van," he said tightly. "Leave me alone."

"Brady."

"Go away." He rounded on her again, the violence still darkening his eyes. "I haven't changed that much."

"And neither have I." She planted her feet. "If you've finished playing the macho idiot, I want you to listen to me."

"Fine. I'm going to move to the shade." He turned away from her, snatching up a towel from the court and rubbing it over his head as he walked onto the grass.

She stormed off after him. "You're just as impossible as you ever were."

After a quick, insolent look, he dropped down under the shade of an oak. To distract the dog, he picked up a handy stick and heaved it. "So?"

"So I wonder how the hell I ever fell in love with you. Twice." She took a deep, cleansing breath. This was not going as she had hoped. So she would try again. "I'm sorry I wasn't able to explain myself adequately before I left."

"You explained well enough. You don't want to be a wife."

She gritted her teeth. "I believe I said I didn't know how to be one—and that I didn't know if I wanted to be one. My closest example of one was my mother, and she was miserably unhappy as a wife. And I felt inadequate and insecure."

"Because of the tuna casserole."

"No, damn it, not because of the tuna casserole, because I didn't know if I could handle being a wife and a woman, a mother and a musician. I hadn't worked out my own definition of any of those terms." She frowned down at him. "I hadn't really had the chance to be any of them."

"You were a woman and a musician."

"I was my father's daughter. Before I came back here,

I'd never been anything else." Impassioned, she dropped down beside him. "I performed on demand, Brady. I played the music he chose, went where he directed. And I felt what he wanted me to feel."

She let out a long breath and looked away, to those distant Blue Mountains. "I can't blame him for that. I certainly don't want to—not now. You were right when you said I'd never argued with him. That was my fault. If I had, things might have changed. I'll never know."

"Van—"

"No, let me finish. Please. I've spent so much time working all this out." She could still feel his anger, but she took heart from the fact that he didn't pull his hand away when she touched it. "My coming back here was the first thing I'd done completely on my own in twelve years. And even that wasn't really a choice. I had to come back. Unfinished business." She looked back at him then, and smiled. "You weren't supposed to be a part of that. And when you were, I was even more confused."

She paused to pluck at the grass, to feel its softness between her fingers. "Oh, I wanted you. Even when I was angry, even when I still hurt, I wanted you. Maybe that was part of the problem. I couldn't think clearly around you. I guess I never have been able to. Things got out of control so quickly. I realized, when you talked about marriage, that it wasn't enough just to want. Just to take."

"You weren't just taking."

"I hope not. I didn't want to hurt you. I never did. Maybe, in some ways, I tried too hard not to. I knew you would be upset that I was going to Cordina to perform."

He was calm again. After the roller-coaster ride she'd

taken his emotions on, his anger had burned itself out. "I wouldn't ask you to give up your music, Van. Or your career."

"No, you wouldn't." She rose to walk out of the shade into the sun and he followed her. "But I was afraid I would give up everything, anything, to please you. And if I did, I wouldn't be. I wouldn't be, Brady."

"I love what you are, Van." His hands closed lightly over her shoulder. "The rest is just details."

"No." She turned back. Her eyes were passionate, and her grip was tight. "It wasn't until I was away again that I began to see what I was pulling away from, what I was moving toward. All my life I did what I was told. Decisions were made for me. The choice was always out of my hands. This time *I* decided. I chose to go to Cordina. I chose to perform. And when I stood in the wings, I waited for the fear to come. I waited for my stomach to clutch and the sweat to break out, and the dizziness. But it didn't come." There were tears in her eyes again, glinting in the sunlight. "It felt wonderful. I felt wonderful. I wanted to step out on the stage, into those lights. I wanted to play and have thousands of people listen. *I* wanted. And it changed everything."

"I'm glad for you." He ran his hands up and down her arms before he stepped back. "I am. I was worried."

"It was glorious." Hugging her arms, she spun away. "And in my heart I know I never played better. There was such…freedom. I know I could go back to all the stages, all the halls, and play like that again." She turned back, magnificent in the streaming sunlight. "I know it."

"I am glad for you," he repeated. "I hated thinking about you performing under stress. I'd never be able to allow you to make yourself ill again, Van, but I meant it when I said I wouldn't ask you to give up your career."

"That's good to hear."

"Damn it, Van, I want to know you'll be coming back to me. I know a house in the woods doesn't compare with Paris or London, but I want you to tell me you'll come back at the end of your tours. That when you're here we'll have a life together, and a family. I want you to ask me to go with you whenever I can."

"I would," she said. "I would promise that, but—"

Rage flickered again. "No buts this time."

"But," she repeated, eyes challenging, "I'm not going to tour again."

"You just said—"

"I said I could perform, and I will. Now and then, if a particular engagement appeals, and if I can fit it comfortably into the rest of my life." With a laugh, she grabbed his hands. "Knowing I can perform, when I want, when I choose. That's important to me. Oh, it's not just important, Brady. It's like suddenly realizing I'm a real person. The person I haven't had a chance to be since I was sixteen. Before I went on stage this last time, I looked in the mirror. I knew who I was, I liked who I was. So instead of there being fear when I stepped into the light, there was only joy."

He could see it in her eyes. And more. "But you came back."

"I chose to come back." She squeezed his fingers. "I needed to come back. There may be other concerts, Brady, but I want to compose, to record. And as much as it continues to amaze me, I want to teach. I can do all of those things here. Especially if someone was willing to add a recording studio onto the house he's building."

Closing his eyes, he brought her hands to his lips. "I think we can manage that."

"I want to get to know my mother again—and learn how to cook. But not well enough so you'd depend on it." She waited until he looked at her again. "I chose to come back here, to come back to you. About the only thing I didn't choose to do was love you." Smiling, she framed his face in her hands. "That just happened, but I think I can live with it. And I do love you, Brady, more than yesterday."

She brought her lips to his. Yes, more than yesterday, she realized. For this was richer, deeper, but with all the energy and hope of youth.

"Ask me again," she whispered. "Please."

He was having trouble letting her go, even far enough that he could look down into her eyes. "Ask you what?"

"Damn you, Brady."

His lips were curved as they brushed through her hair. "A few minutes ago, I was mad at you."

"I know." Her sigh vibrated with satisfaction. "I could always wrap you around my little finger."

"Yeah." He hoped she'd keep doing it for the next fifty or sixty years. "I love you, Van."

"I love you, too. Now ask me."

With his hands on her shoulders, he drew her back. "I want to do it right this time. There's no dim light, no music."

"We'll stand in the shade, and I'll hum."

"Anxious, aren't you?" He laughed and gave her another bruising kiss. "I still don't have a ring."

"Yes, you do." She'd come, armed and ready. Reaching into her pocket, she pulled out a ring with a tiny emerald. She watched Brady's face change when he saw it, recognized it.

"You kept it," he murmured before he lifted his gaze to hers. Every emotion he was feeling had suddenly doubled.

"Always." She set it in the palm of his hand. "It worked before. Why don't you try it again?"

His hand wasn't steady. It hadn't been before. He looked at her. There was a promise in her eyes that spanned more than a decade. And that was absolutely new.

"Will you marry me, Van?"

"Yes." She laughed and blinked away tears. "Oh, yes."

He slipped the ring on her finger. It still fit.

* * * * *

LOCAL HERO

For Dan, with thanks for the idea
and the tons of research material.
And for Jason, for keeping me in tune
with the ten-year-old mind.

Chapter 1

Zark drew a painful breath, knowing it could be his last. The ship was nearly out of oxygen, and he was nearly out of time. A life span could pass in front of the eyes in a matter of seconds. He was grateful that he was alone so no one else could witness his joys and mistakes.

Leilah, it was always Leilah. With each ragged breath he could see her, the clear blue eyes and golden hair of his one and only beloved. As the warning siren inside the cockpit wailed, he could hear Leilah's laughter. Tender, sweet. Then mocking.

"By the red sun, how happy we were together!" The words shuddered out between gasps as he dragged himself over the floor toward the command console. "Lovers, partners, friends."

The pain in his lungs grew worse. It seared through him like dozens of hot knives tipped with poison from the pits of Argenham. He couldn't waste air on useless words. But his thoughts…his thoughts even now were on Leilah.

That she, the only woman he had ever loved, should be the cause of his ultimate destruction! His destruction, and the world's as they knew it. What fiendish twist of fate had caused the freak accident that had turned her from a devoted scientist to a force of evil and hate?

She was his enemy now, the woman who had once been his wife. Who was still his wife, Zark told himself as he painfully pulled himself up to the console. If he lived, and stopped her latest scheme to obliterate civilization on Perth, he would have to go after her. He would have to destroy her. If he had the strength.

Commander Zark, Defender of the Universe, Leader of Perth, hero and husband, pressed a trembling finger to the button.

CONTINUED IN THE NEXT EXCITING ISSUE!

"Damn!" Radley Wallace mumbled the oath, then looked around quickly to be sure his mother hadn't heard. He'd started to swear, mostly in whispers, about six months ago, and wasn't anxious for her to find out. She'd get that look on her face.

But she was busy going through the first boxes the movers had delivered. He was supposed to be putting his books away, but had decided it was time to take a break. He liked breaks best when they included Universal Comics and Commander Zark. His mother liked him to read real books, but they didn't have many pictures. As far as Radley was concerned, Zark had it all over Long John Silver or Huck Finn.

Rolling over on his back, Radley stared at the freshly painted ceiling of his new room. The new apartment was okay. Mostly he liked the view of the park, and having an elevator was cool. But he wasn't looking forward to starting in a new school on Monday.

Mom had told him it would be fine, that he would make new friends and still be able to visit with some of the old ones. She was real good about it, stroking his hair and smiling in that way that made him feel everything was really okay. But she wouldn't be there when all the kids gave him the once-over. He wasn't going to wear that new sweater, either, even if Mom said the color matched his eyes. He wanted to wear one of his old sweatshirts so at least something would be familiar. He figured she'd understand, because Mom always did.

She still looked sad sometimes, though. Radley squirmed up to the pillow with the comic clutched in his hand. He wished she wouldn't feel bad because his father had gone away. It had been a long time now, and he had to think hard to bring a picture of his father to his mind. He never visited, and only phoned a couple of times a year. That was okay. Radley wished he could tell his mother it was okay, but he was afraid she'd get upset and start crying.

He didn't really need a dad when he had her. He'd told her that once, and she'd hugged him so hard he hadn't been able to breathe. Then he'd heard her crying in her room that night. So he hadn't told her that again.

Big people were funny, Radley thought with the wisdom of his almost ten years. But his mom was the best. She hardly ever yelled at him, and was always sorry when she did. And she was pretty. Radley smiled as he began to sleep. He guessed his mom was just about as pretty as Princess Leilah. Even though her hair was brown instead of golden and her eyes were gray instead of cobalt blue.

She'd promised they could have pizza for dinner, too,

to celebrate their new apartment. He liked pizza best, next to Commander Zark.

He drifted off to sleep so he, with the help of Zark, could save the universe.

When Hester looked in a short time later, she saw her son, her universe, dreaming with an issue of Universal Comics in his hand. Most of his books, some of which he paged through from time to time, were still in the packing boxes. Another time she would have given him a mild lecture on responsibility when he woke, but she didn't have the heart for it now. He was taking the move so well. Another upheaval in his life.

"This one's going to be good for you, sweetie." Forgetting the mountain of her own unpacking, she sat on the edge of the bed to watch him.

He looked so much like his father. The dark blond hair, the dark eyes and sturdy chin. It was a rare thing now for her to look at her son and think of the man who had been her husband. But today was different. Today was another beginning for them, and beginnings made her think of endings.

Over six years now, she thought, a bit amazed at the passage of time. Radley had been just a toddler when Allan had walked out on them, tired of bills, tired of family, tired of her in particular. That pain had passed, though it had been a long, slow process. But she had never forgiven, and would never forgive, the man for leaving his son without a second glance.

Sometimes she worried that it seemed to mean so little to Radley. Selfishly she was relieved that he had never formed a strong, enduring bond with the man who would leave them behind, yet she often wondered, late at night when everything was quiet, if her little boy held something inside.

When she looked at him, it didn't seem possible. Hester stroked his hair now and turned to look at his view of Central Park. Radley was outgoing, happy and good-natured. She'd worked hard to help him be those things. She never spoke ill of his father, though there had been times, especially in the early years, when the bitterness and anger had simmered very close to the surface. She'd tried to be both mother and father, and most of the time thought she'd succeeded.

She'd read books on baseball so she would know how to coach him. She'd raced beside him, clinging to the back of the seat of his first two-wheeler. When it had been time to let go, she'd forced back the urge to hang on and had cheered as he'd made his wobbly way down the bike path.

She even knew about Commander Zark. With a smile, Hester eased the wrinkled comic book from his fist. Poor, heroic Zark and his misguided wife Leilah. Yes, Hester knew all about Perth's politics and tribulations. Trying to wean Radley from Zark to Dickens or Twain wasn't easy, but neither was raising a child on your own.

"There's time enough," she murmured as she stretched out beside her son. Time enough for real books and for real life. "Oh, Rad, I hope I've done the right thing." She closed her eyes, wishing, as she'd learned to wish rarely, that she had someone to talk to, someone who could advise her or make decisions, right or wrong.

Then, with her arm hooked around her son's waist, she, too, slept.

The room was dim with dusk when she awoke, groggy and disoriented. The first thing Hester realized was that Radley was no longer curled beside her. Grogginess disappeared in a quick flash of panic she knew was foolish. Radley could be trusted not to leave the apartment without permission. He wasn't a blindly obedient child, but her top ten rules were respected. Rising, she went to find him.

"Hi, Mom." He was in the kitchen, where her homing instinct had taken her first. He held a dripping peanut butter and jelly sandwich in his hands.

"I thought you wanted pizza," she said, noting the good-sized glop of jelly on the counter and the yet-to-be-resealed loaf of bread.

"I do." He took a healthy bite, then grinned. "But I needed something now."

"Don't talk with your mouth full, Rad," she said automatically, even as she bent to kiss him. "You could have woken me if you were hungry."

"That's okay, but I couldn't find the glasses."

She glanced around, seeing that he'd emptied two boxes in his quest. Hester reminded herself that she should have made the kitchen arrangements her first priority. "Well, we can take care of that."

"It was snowing when I woke up."

"Was it?" Hester pushed the hair out of her eyes and straightened to see for herself. "Still is."

"Maybe it'll snow ten feet and there won't be any school on Monday." Radley climbed onto a stool to sit at the kitchen counter.

Along with no first day on the new job, Hester thought, indulging in some wishful thinking of her own for a moment. No new pressures, new responsibilities. "I don't think there's much chance of that." As she washed out glasses, she looked over her shoulder. "Are you really worried about it, Rad?"

"Sort of." He shrugged his shoulders. Monday was

still a day away. A lot could happen. Earthquakes, blizzards, an attack from outer space. He concentrated on the last.

He, Captain Radley Wallace of Earth's Special Forces, would protect and shield, would fight to the death, would—

"I could go in with you if you'd like."

"Aw, Mom, the kids would make fun of me." He bit into his sandwich. Grape jelly oozed out the sides. "It won't be so bad. At least that dumb Angela Wiseberry won't be at this school."

She didn't have the heart to tell him there was a dumb Angela Wiseberry at every school. "Tell you what. We'll both go to our new jobs Monday, then convene back here at 1600 for a full report."

His face brightened instantly. There was nothing Radley liked better than a military operation. "Aye, aye, sir."

"Good. Now I'll order the pizza, and while we're waiting we'll put the rest of the dishes away."

"Let the prisoners do it."

"Escaped. All of them."

"Heads will roll," Radley mumbled as he stuffed the last of the sandwich into his mouth.

Mitchell Dempsey II sat at his drawing board without an idea in his head. He sipped cold coffee, hoping it would stimulate his imagination, but his mind remained as blank as the paper in front of him. Blocks happened, he knew, but they rarely happened to him. And not on deadline. Of course, he was going about it backward. Mitch cracked another peanut, then tossed the shell in the direction of the bowl. It hit the side and fell on the floor to join several others. Normally the story line would have come first, then the illustrations. Since he'd been having no luck that way, Mitch had switched in the hope that the change in routine would jog something loose.

It wasn't working, and neither was he.

Closing his eyes, Mitch tried for an out-of-body experience. The old Slim Whitman song on the radio cruised on, but he didn't hear it. He was traveling light-years away; a century was passing. The second millennium, he thought with a smile. He'd been born too soon. Though he didn't think he could blame his parents for having him a hundred years too early.

Nothing came. No solutions, no inspiration. Mitch opened his eyes again and stared at the blank white paper. With an editor like Rich Skinner, he couldn't afford to claim artistic temperament. Famine or plague would barely get you by. Disgusted, Mitch reached for another peanut.

What he needed was a change of scene, a distraction. His life was becoming too settled, too ordinary and, despite the temporary block, too easy. He needed challenge. Pitching the shells, he rose to pace.

He had a long, limber body made solid by the hours he spent each week with weights. As a boy he'd been preposterously skinny, though he'd always eaten like a horse. He hadn't minded the teasing too much until he'd discovered girls. Then, with the quiet determination he'd been born with, Mitch had changed what could be changed. It had taken him a couple of years and a lot of sweat to build himself, but he had. He still didn't take his body for granted, and exercised it as regularly as he did his mind.

His office was littered with books, all read and re-read. He was tempted to pull one out now and bury himself in it. But he was on deadline. The big brown mutt on the floor rolled over on his stomach and watched.

Mitch had named him Taz, after the Tasmanian Devil from the old Warner Brothers cartoons, but Taz was hardly a whirlwind of energy. He yawned now and rubbed his back lazily on the rug. He liked Mitch. Mitch never expected him to do anything that he didn't care to, and hardly ever complained about dog hair on the furniture or an occasional forage into the trash. Mitch had a nice voice, too, low and patient. Taz liked it best when Mitch sat on the floor with him and stroked his heavy brown fur, talking out one of his ideas. Taz could look up into the lean face as if he understood every word.

Taz liked Mitch's face, too. It was kind and strong, and the mouth rarely firmed into a disapproving line. His eyes were pale and dreamy. Mitch's wide, strong hands knew the right places to scratch. Taz was a very contented dog. He yawned and went back to sleep.

When the knock came to the door, the dog stirred enough to thump his tail and make a series of low noises in his throat.

"No, I'm not expecting anyone. You?" Mitch responded. "I'll go see." He stepped on peanut shells in his bare feet and swore, but didn't bother to stoop and pick them up. There was a pile of newspapers to be skirted around, and a bag of clothes that hadn't made it to the laundry. Taz had left one of his bones on the Aubusson. Mitch simply kicked it into a corner before he opened the door.

"Pizza delivery."

A scrawny kid of about eighteen was holding a box that smelled like heaven. Mitch took one long, avaricious sniff. "I didn't order any."

"This 406?"

"Yeah, but I didn't order any pizza." He sniffed again. "Wish I had."

"Wallace?"

"Dempsey."

"Shoot."

Wallace, Mitch thought as the kid shifted from foot to foot. Wallace was taking over the Henley apartment, 604. He rubbed a hand over his chin and considered. If Wallace was that leggy brunette he'd seen hauling in boxes that morning, it might be worth investigating.

"I know the Wallaces," he said, and pulled crumpled bills out of his pocket. "I'll take it on up to them."

"I don't know, I shouldn't—"

"Worry about a thing," Mitch finished, and added another bill. Pizza and the new neighbor might be just the distraction he needed.

The boy counted his tip. "Okay, thanks." For all he knew, the Wallaces wouldn't be half as generous.

With the box balanced in his hand, Mitch started out. Then he remembered his keys. He took a moment to search through his worn jeans before he remembered he'd tossed them at the gateleg table when he'd come in the night before. He found them under it, stuck them in one pocket, found the hole in it and stuck them in the other. He hoped the pizza had some pepperoni.

"That should be the pizza," Hester announced, but caught Radley before he could dash to the door. "Let me open it. Remember the rules?"

"Don't open the door unless you know who it is," Radley recited, rolling his eyes behind his mother's back.

Hester put a hand on the knob, but checked the peephole. She frowned a little at the face. She'd have sworn the man was looking straight back at her with amused and very clear blue eyes. His hair was dark and shaggy, as if it hadn't seen a barber or a comb in a little too long. But the face was fascinating, lean and bony and unshaven.

"Mom, are you going to open it?"

"What?" Hester stepped back when she realized she'd been staring at the delivery boy for a good deal longer than necessary.

"I'm starving," Radley reminded her.

"Sorry." Hester opened the door and discovered the fascinating face went with a long, athletic body. And bare feet.

"Did you order pizza?"

"Yes." But it was snowing outside. What was he doing barefoot?

"Good." Before Hester realized his intention, Mitch strolled inside.

"I'll take that," Hester said quickly. "Take this into the kitchen, Radley." She shielded her son with her body and wondered if she'd need a weapon.

"Nice place." Mitch looked casually around at crates and open boxes.

"I'll get your money."

"It's on the house." Mitch smiled at her. Hester wondered if the self-defense course she'd taken two years before would come back to her.

"Radley, take that into the kitchen while I pay the delivery man."

"Neighbor," Mitch corrected. "I'm in 406—you know, two floors down. The pizza got delivered to my place by mistake."

"I see." But for some reason it didn't make her any less nervous. "I'm sorry for the trouble." Hester reached for her purse.

"I took care of it." He wasn't sure whether she looked more likely to lunge or to flee, but he'd been right about her being worth investigating. She was a tall one, he thought, model height, with that same kind of understated body. Her rich, warm brown hair was pulled back from a diamond-shaped face dominated by big gray eyes and a mouth just one size too large.

"Why don't you consider the pizza my version of the welcoming committee?"

"That's really very kind, but I couldn't—"

"Refuse such a neighborly offer?"

Because she was a bit too cool and reserved for his taste, Mitch looked past her to the boy. "Hi, I'm Mitch." This time his smile was answered.

"I'm Rad. We just moved in."

"So I see. From out of town?"

"Uh-uh. We just changed apartments because Mom got a new job and the other was too small. I can see the park from my window."

"Me, too."

"Excuse me, Mr.—?"

"It's Mitch," he repeated with a glance at Hester.

"Yes, well, it's very kind of you to bring this up." As well as being very odd, she thought. "But I don't want to impose on your time."

"You can have a piece," Radley invited. "We never finish it all."

"Rad, I'm sure Mr.—Mitch has things to do."

"Not a thing." He knew his manners, had been taught them painstakingly. Another time, he might even have put them to use and bowed out, but something about the woman's reserve and the child's warmth made him obstinate. "Got a beer?"

"No, I'm sorry, I—"

"We've got soda," Radley piped up. "Mom lets me have one sometimes." There was nothing Radley liked more than company. He gave Mitch a totally ingenuous smile. "Want to see the kitchen?"

"Love to." With something close to a smirk for Hester, Mitch followed the boy.

She stood in the center of the room for a moment, hands on her hips, unsure whether to be exasperated or furious. The last thing she wanted after a day of lugging boxes was company. Especially a stranger's. The only thing to do now was to give him a piece of the damn pizza and blot out her obligation to him.

"We've got a garbage disposal. It makes great noises."

"I bet." Obligingly Mitch leaned over the sink while Radley flipped the switch.

"Rad, don't run that with nothing in it. As you can see, we're a bit disorganized yet." Hester went to the freshly lined cupboard for plates.

"I've been here for five years, and I'm still disorganized."

"We're going to get a kitten." Radley climbed up on a stool, then reached for the napkins his mother had already put in one of her little wicker baskets. "The other place wouldn't allow pets, but we can have one here, can't we, Mom?"

"As soon as we're settled, Rad. Diet or regular?" she asked Mitch.

"Regular's fine. Looks like you've gotten a lot accomplished in one day." The kitchen was neat as a pin. A thriving asparagus fern hung in a macrame holder in the single window. She had less space than he did, which he thought was too bad. She would probably make better use of the kitchen than he. He took another glance around before settling at the counter. Stuck to the refrigerator was a large crayon drawing of a spaceship. "You do that?" Mitch asked Rad.

"Yeah." He picked up the pizza his mother had set on his plate and bit in eagerly—peanut butter and jelly long since forgotten.

"It's good."

"It's supposed to be the Second Millennium, that's Commander Zark's ship."

"I know." Mitch took a healthy bite of his own slice. "You did a good job."

As he plowed through his pizza, Radley took it for granted that Mitch would recognize Zark's name and mode of transportation. As far as he was concerned, everybody did. "I've been trying to do the Defiance, Leilah's ship, but it's harder. Anyway, I think Commander Zark might blow it up in the next issue."

"Think so?" Mitch gave Hester an easy smile as she joined them at the counter.

"I don't know, he's in a pretty tough spot right now."

"He'll get out okay."

"Do you read comic books?" Hester asked. It wasn't until she sat down that she noticed how large his hands were. He might have been dressed with disregard, but his hands were clean and had the look of easy competence.

"All the time."

"I've got the biggest collection of all my friends. Mom got me the very first issue with Commander Zark in it for Christmas. It's ten years old. He was only a captain then. Want to see?"

The boy was a gem, Mitch thought, sweet, bright

and unaffected. He'd have to reserve judgment on the mother. "Yeah, I'd like that."

Before Hester could tell him to finish his dinner, Radley was off and running. She sat in silence a moment, wondering what sort of man actually read comic books. Oh, she paged through them from time to time to keep a handle on what her son was consuming, but to actually read them? An adult?

"Terrific kid."

"Yes, he is. It's nice of you to…listen to him talk about his comics."

"Comics are my life," Mitch said, straight-faced.

Her reserve broke down long enough for her to stare at him. Clearing her throat, Hester went back to her meal. "I see."

Mitch put his tongue in his cheek. She was some piece of work, all right, he decided. First meeting or not, he saw no reason to resist egging her on. "I take it you don't."

"Don't what?"

"Read comic books."

"No, I, ah, don't have a lot of time for light reading." She rolled her eyes, unaware that that was where Radley had picked up the habit. "Would you like another piece?"

"Yeah." He helped himself before she could serve him. "You ought to take some time, you know. Comics can be very educational. What's the new job?"

"Oh, I'm in banking. I'm the loan officer for National Trust."

Mitch gave an appreciative whistle. "Big job for someone your age."

Hester stiffened automatically. "I've been in banking since I was sixteen."

Touchy, too, he mused as he licked sauce from his thumb. "That was supposed to be a compliment. I have a feeling you don't take them well." Tough lady, he decided, then thought perhaps she'd had to be. There was no ring on her finger, not even the faintest white mark to show there had been one recently. "I've done some business with banks myself. You know, deposits, withdrawals, returned checks."

She shifted uncomfortably, wondering what was taking Radley so long. There was something unnerving about being alone with this man. Though she had always felt comfortable with eye contact, she was having a difficult time with Mitch. He never looked away for very long.

"I didn't mean to be abrupt."

"No, I don't suppose you did. If I wanted a loan at National Trust, who would I ask for?"

"Mrs. Wallace."

Definitely a tough one. "Mrs. is your first name?"

"Hester," she said, not understanding why she resented giving him that much.

"Hester, then." Mitch offered a hand. "Nice to meet you."

Her lips curved a bit. It was a cautious smile, Mitch thought, but better than none at all. "I'm sorry if I've been rude, but it's been a long day. A long week, really."

"I hate moving." He waited until she'd unbent enough to put her hand in his. Hers was cool and as slender as the rest of her. "Got anyone to help you?"

"No." She removed her hand, because his was as overwhelming as it looked. "We're doing fine."

"I can see that." *No Help Wanted.* The sign was up and posted in big letters. He'd known a few women like her, so fiercely independent, so suspicious of men in general that they had not only a defensive shield but an arsenal of poisonous darts behind it. A sensible man gave them a wide berth. Too bad, because she was a looker, and the kid was definitely a kick.

"I forgot where I'd packed it." Radley came back in, flushed with the effort. "It's a classic, the dealer even told Mom."

He'd also charged her an arm and a leg for it, Hester thought. But it had meant more to Radley than any of his other presents.

"Mint condition, too." Mitch turned the first page with the care of a jeweler cutting a diamond.

"I always make sure my hands are clean before I read it."

"Good idea." It was amazing that after all this time the pride would still be there. An enormous feeling it was, too, a huge burst of satisfaction.

It was there on the first page. Story and drawings by Mitch Dempsey. Commander Zark was his baby, and in ten years they'd become very close friends.

"It's a great story. It really explains why Commander Zark devoted his life to defending the universe against evil and corruption."

"Because his family had been wiped out by the evil Red Arrow in his search for power."

"Yeah." Radley's face lit up. "But he got even with Red Arrow."

"In issue 73."

Hester put her chin in her hand and stared at the two of them. The man was serious, she realized, not just humoring the child. He was as obsessed by comic books as her nine-year-old son.

Strange, he looked fairly normal; he even spoke

well. In fact, sitting next to him had been uncomfortable largely because he was so blatantly masculine, with that tough body, angular face and large hands. Hester shook off her thoughts quickly. She certainly didn't want to lean in that direction toward a neighbor, particularly not one whose mental level seemed to have gotten stuck in adolescence.

Mitch turned a couple of pages. His drawing had improved over a decade. It helped to remind himself of that. But he'd managed to maintain the same purity, the same straightforward images that had come to him ten years ago when he'd been struggling unhappily in commercial art.

"Is he your favorite?" Mitch pointed a blunt fingertip toward a drawing of Zark.

"Oh, sure. I like Three Faces, and the Black Diamond's pretty neat, but Commander Zark's my favorite."

"Mine, too." Mitch ruffled the boy's hair. He hadn't realized when he'd delivered a pizza that he would find the inspiration he'd been struggling for all afternoon.

"You can read this sometime. I'd lend it to you, but—"

"I understand." He closed the book carefully and handed it back. "You can't lend out a collector's item."

"I'd better put it away."

"Before you know it, you and Rad will be trading issues." Hester stood up to clear the plates.

"That amuses the hell out of you, doesn't it?"

His tone had her glancing over quickly. There wasn't precisely an edge to it, and his eyes were still clear and mild, but…something warned her to take care.

"I didn't mean to insult you. I just find it unusual for a grown man to read comic books as a habit." She stacked the plates in the dishwasher. "I've always thought it was something boys grew out of at a certain age, but I suppose one could consider it, what, a hobby?"

His brow lifted. She was facing him again, that half smile on her lips. Obviously she was trying to make amends. He didn't think she should get off quite that easily. "Comic books are anything but a hobby with me, Mrs. Hester Wallace. I not only read them, I write them."

"Holy cow, really?" Radley stood staring at Mitch as though he'd just been crowned king. "Do you really? Honest? Oh, boy, are you Mitch Dempsey? The real Mitch Dempsey?"

"In the flesh." He tugged on Radley's ear while Hester looked at him as though he'd stepped in from another planet.

"Oh, boy, Mitch Dempsey right here! Mom, this is Commander Zark. None of the kids are going to believe it. Do you believe it, Mom, Commander Zark right here in our kitchen!"

"No," Hester murmured as she continued to stare. "I can't believe it."

Chapter 2

Hester wished she could afford to be a coward. It would be so easy to go back home, pull the covers over her head and hide out until Radley came home from school. No one who saw her would suspect that her stomach was in knots or that her palms were sweaty despite the frigid wind that whipped down the stairs as she emerged from the subway with a crowd of Manhattan's workforce.

If anyone had bothered to look, they would have seen a composed, slightly preoccupied woman in a long red wool coat and white scarf. Fortunately for Hester, the wind tunnel created by the skyscrapers whipped color into cheeks that would have been deadly pale. She had to concentrate on not chewing off her lipstick as she walked the half block to National Trust. And to her first day on the job.

It would only take her ten minutes to get back home, lock herself in and phone the office with some excuse.

She was sick, there'd been a death in the family—preferably hers. She'd been robbed.

Hester clutched her briefcase tighter and kept walking. Big talk, she berated herself. She'd walked Radley to school that morning spouting off cheerful nonsense about how exciting new beginnings were, how much fun it was to start something new. Baloney, she thought, and hoped the little guy wasn't half as scared as she was.

She'd earned the position, Hester reminded herself. She was qualified and competent, with twelve years of experience under her belt. And she was scared right out of her shoes. Taking a deep breath, she walked into National Trust.

Laurence Rosen, the bank manager, checked his watch, gave a nod of approval and strode over to greet her. His dark blue suit was trim and conservative. A woman could have powdered her nose in the reflection from his shiny black shoes. "Right on time, Mrs. Wallace, an excellent beginning. I pride myself on having a staff that makes optimum use of time." He gestured toward the back of the bank, and her office.

"I'm looking forward to getting started, Mr. Rosen," she said, and felt a wave of relief that it was true. She'd always liked the feel of a bank before the doors opened to the public. The cathedral-like quiet, the pregame anticipation.

"Good, good, we'll do our best to keep you busy." He noted with a slight frown that two secretaries were not yet at their desks. In a habitual gesture, he passed a hand over his hair. "Your assistant will be in momentarily. Once you're settled, Mrs. Wallace, I'll expect you to keep close tabs on her comings and goings. Your efficiency depends largely on hers."

"Of course."

Her office was small and dull. She tried not to wish for something airier—or to notice that Rosen was as stuffy as they came. The increase this job would bring to her income would make things better for Radley. That, as always, was the bottom line. She'd make it work, Hester told herself as she took off her coat. She'd make it work well.

Rosen obviously approved of her trim black suit and understated jewelry. There was no room for flashy clothes or behavior in banking. "I trust you looked over the files I gave you."

"I familiarized myself with them over the weekend." She moved behind the desk, knowing it would establish her position. "I believe I understand National Trust's policy and procedure."

"Excellent, excellent. I'll leave you to get organized then. Your first appointment's at—" he turned pages over on her desk calendar "—9:15. If you have any problems, contact me. I'm always around somewhere."

She would have bet on it. "I'm sure everything will be fine, Mr. Rosen. Thank you."

With a final nod, Rosen strode out. The door closed behind him with a quiet click. Alone, Hester let herself slide bonelessly into her chair. She'd gotten past the first hurdle, she told herself. Rosen thought she was competent and suitable. Now all she had to do was be those things. She would be, because too much was riding on it. Not the least of those things was her pride. She hated making a fool of herself. She'd certainly done a good job of that the night before with the new neighbor.

Even hours later, remembering it, her cheeks warmed. She hadn't meant to insult the man's—even now she couldn't bring herself to call it a profession—his work, then, Hester decided. She certainly hadn't meant to make any personal observations. The problem had been that she hadn't been as much on her guard as usual. The man had thrown her off by inviting himself in and joining them for dinner and charming Radley, all in a matter of minutes. She wasn't used to people popping into her life. And she didn't like it.

Radley loved it. Hester picked up a sharpened pencil with the bank's logo on the side. He'd practically glowed with excitement, and hadn't been able to speak of anything else even after Mitch Dempsey had left.

She could be grateful for one thing. The visit had taken Radley's mind off the new school. Radley had always made friends easily, and if this Mitch was willing to give her son some pleasure, she shouldn't criticize. In any case, the man seemed harmless enough. Hester refused to admit to the uncomfortable thrill she'd experienced when his hand had closed over hers. What possible trouble could come from a man who wrote comic books for a living? She caught herself chewing at her lipstick at the question.

The knock on the door was brief and cheerful. Before she could call out, it was pushed open.

"Good morning, Mrs. Wallace. I'm Kay Lorimar, your assistant. Remember, we met for a few minutes a couple of weeks ago."

"Yes, good morning, Kay." Her assistant was everything Hester had always wanted to be herself: petite, well-rounded, blond, with small delicate features. She folded her hands on the fresh blotter and tried to look authoritative.

"Sorry I'm late." Kay smiled and didn't look the least bit sorry. "Everything takes longer than you think it does on Monday. Even if I pretend it's Tuesday it doesn't seem to help. I don't know why. Would you like some coffee?"

"No, thank you, I've an appointment in a few minutes."

"Just ring if you change your mind." Kay paused at the door. "This place could sure use some cheering up, it's dark as a dungeon. Mr. Blowfield, that's who you're replacing, he liked things dull—matched him, you know." Her smile was ingenuous, but Hester hesitated to answer it. It would hardly do for her to get a reputation as a gossip the first day on the job. "Anyway, if you decide to do any redecorating, let me know. My roommate's into interior design. He's a real artist."

"Thank you." How was she supposed to run an office with a pert little cheerleader in tow? Hester wondered. One day at a time. "Just send Mr. and Mrs. Browning in when they arrive, Kay."

"Yes, ma'am." She sure was more pleasant to look at than old Blowfield, Kay thought. But it looked as if she had the same soul. "Loan application forms are in the bottom left drawer of the desk, arranged according to type. Legal pads in the right. Bank stationery, top right. The list of current interest rates are in the middle drawer. The Brownings are looking for a loan to remodel their loft as they're expecting a child. He's in electronics, she works part-time at Bloomingdale's. They've been advised what papers to bring with them. I can make copies while they're here."

Hester lifted her brow. "Thank you, Kay," she said, not certain whether to be amused or impressed.

When the door closed again, Hester sat back and smiled. The office might be dull, but if the morning was any indication, nothing else at National Trust was going to be.

* * *

Mitch liked having a window that faced the front of the building. That way, whenever he took a break, he could watch the comings and goings. After five years, he figured he knew every tenant by sight and half of them by name. When things were slow or, better, when he was ahead of the game, he whiled away time by sketching the more interesting of them. If his time stretched further, he made a story line to go with the faces.

He considered it the best of practice because it amused him. Occasionally there was a face interesting enough to warrant special attention. Sometimes it was a cabdriver or a delivery boy. Mitch had learned to look close and quick, then sketch from lingering impressions. Years before, he had sketched faces for a living, if a pitiful one. Now he sketched them for entertainment and was a great deal more satisfied.

He spotted Hester and her son when they were still half a block away. The red coat she wore stood out like a beacon. It certainly made a statement, Mitch mused as he picked up his pencil. He wondered if the coolly distant Mrs. Wallace realized what signals she was sending out. He doubted it.

He didn't need to see her face to draw it. Already there were a half a dozen rough sketches of her tossed on the table in his workroom. Interesting features, he told himself as his pencil began to fly across the pad. Any artist would be compelled to capture them.

The boy was walking along beside her, his face all but obscured by a woolen scarf and hat. Even from this distance, Mitch could see the boy was chattering earnestly. His head was angled up toward his mother. Every now and again she would glance down as if to comment; then the boy would take over again. A few steps away from the building, she stopped. Mitch saw the wind catch at her hair as she tossed her head back and laughed. His fingers went limp on the pencil as he leaned closer to the window. He wanted to be nearer, near enough to hear the laugh, to see if her eyes lit up with it. He imagined they did, but how? Would that subtle, calm gray go silvery or smoky?

She continued to walk, and in seconds was in the building and out of sight.

Mitch stared down at his sketch pad. He had no more than a few lines and contours. He couldn't finish it, he thought as he set the pencil down. He could only see her laughing now, and to capture that on paper he'd need a closer look.

Picking up his keys, he jangled them in his hand. He'd given her the better part of a week. The aloof Mrs. Wallace might consider another neighborly visit out of line, but he didn't. Besides, he liked the kid. Mitch would have gone upstairs to see him before, but he'd been busy fleshing out his story. He owed the kid for that, too, Mitch considered. The little weekend visit had not only crumbled the block, but had given Mitch enough fuel for three issues. Yeah, he owed the kid.

He pushed the keys into his pocket and walked into his workroom. Taz was there, a bone clamped between his paws as he snoozed. "Don't get up," Mitch said mildly. "I'm going out for a while." As he spoke, he ruffled through papers. Taz opened his eyes to half-mast and grumbled. "I don't know how long I'll be." After wracking through his excuse for a filing system, Mitch found the sketch. Commander Zark in full military regalia, sober-faced, sad-eyed, his gleaming ship at his back. Beneath it was the caption: THE MISSION: Capture Princess Leilah—or DESTROY her!!

Mitch wished briefly that he had the time to ink and color it, but figured the kid would like it as is. With a careless stroke he signed it, then rolled it into a tube.

"Don't wait dinner for me," he instructed Taz.

"I'll get it!" Radley danced to the door. It was Friday, and school was light-years away.

"Ask who it is."

Radley put his hand on the knob and shook his head. He'd been going to ask. Probably. "Who is it?"

"It's Mitch."

"It's Mitch!" Radley shouted, delighted. In the bedroom, Hester scowled and pulled the sweatshirt over her head.

"Hi." Breathless with excitement, Radley opened the door to his latest hero.

"Hi, Rad, how's it going?"

"Fine. I don't have any homework all weekend." He reached out a hand to draw Mitch inside. "I wanted to come down and see you, but Mom said no 'cause you'd be working or something."

"Or something," Mitch muttered. "Look, it's okay with me if you come over. Anytime."

"Really?"

"Really." The kid was irresistible, Mitch thought as he ruffled the boy's hair. Too bad his mother wasn't as friendly. "I thought you might like this." Mitch handed him the rolled sketch.

"Oh, wow." Awestruck, reverent, Radley stared at the drawing. "Jeez, Commander Zark and the Second Millennium. Can I have it, really? To keep?"

"Yeah."

"I gotta show Mom." Radley turned and dashed toward the bedroom as Hester came out. "Look what

Mitch gave me. Isn't it great? He said I could keep it and everything."

"It's terrific." She put a hand on Radley's shoulder as she studied the sketch. The man was certainly talented, Hester decided. Even if he had chosen such an odd way to show it. Her hand remained on Radley's shoulder as she looked over at Mitch. "That was very nice of you."

He liked the way she looked in the pastel sweats, casual, approachable, if not completely relaxed. Her hair was down, too, with the ends just sweeping short of her shoulders. Parted softly on the side and unpinned, it gave her a completely different look.

"I wanted to thank Rad." Mitch forced himself to look away from her face, then smiled at the boy. "You helped me through a block last weekend."

"I did?" Radley's eyes widened. "Honest?"

"Honest. I was stuck, spinning wheels. After I talked to you that night, I went down and everything fell into place. I appreciate it."

"Wow, you're welcome. You could stay for dinner again. We're just having Chinese chicken, and maybe I could help you some more. It's okay, isn't it, Mom? Isn't it?"

Trapped again. And again she caught the gleam of amusement in Mitch's eyes. "Of course."

"Great. I want to go hang this up right away. Can I call Josh, too, and tell him about it? He won't believe it."

"Sure." She barely had time to run a hand over his hair before he was off and running.

"Thanks, Mitch." Radley paused at the turn of the hallway. "Thanks a lot."

Hester found the deep side pockets in her sweats and slipped her hands inside. There was absolutely no reason for the man to make her nervous. So why did he? "That was really very kind of you."

"Maybe, but I haven't done anything that's made me feel that good in a long time." He wasn't completely at ease himself, Mitch discovered, and he tucked his thumbs into the back pockets of his jeans. "You work fast," he commented as he glanced around the living room.

The boxes were gone. Bright, vivid prints hung on the walls and a vase of flowers, fresh as morning, sat near the window, where sheer curtains filtered the light. Pillows were plumped, furniture gleamed. The only signs of confusion were a miniature car wreck and a few plastic men scattered on the carpet. He was glad to see them. It meant she wasn't the type who expected the boy to play only in his room.

"Dali?" He walked over to a lithograph hung over the sofa.

She caught her bottom lip between her teeth as Mitch studied one of her rare extravagances. "I bought that in a little shop on Fifth that's always going out of business."

"Yeah, I know the one. It didn't take you long to put things together here."

"I wanted everything back to normal as soon as possible. The move wasn't easy for Radley."

"And you?" He turned then, catching her off guard with the sudden sharp look.

"Me? I—ah…"

"You know," he began as he crossed over to her, attracted by her simple bafflement. "You're a lot more articulate when you talk about Rad than you are when you talk about Hester."

She stepped back quickly, aware that he would have

touched her and totally unsure what her reaction might
have been. "I should start dinner."

"Want some help?"

"With what?"

This time she didn't move quickly enough. He cupped
her chin in his hand and smiled. "With dinner."

It had been a long time since a man had touched her
that way. He had a strong hand with gentle fingers. That
had to be the reason her heart leaped up to her throat
and pounded there. "Can you cook?"

What incredible eyes she had. So clear, so pale a gray
they were almost translucent. For the first time in years
he felt the urge to paint, just to see if he could bring
those eyes to life on canvas. "I make a hell of a peanut
butter sandwich."

She lifted a hand to his wrist, to move his away, she
thought. But her fingers lay there lightly a moment, ex-
perimenting. "How are you at chopping vegetables?"

"I think I can handle it."

"All right, then." She backed up, amazed that she had
allowed the contact to go for so long. "I still don't have
any beer, but I do have some wine this time."

"Fine." What the hell were they talking about? Why
were they talking at all, when she had a mouth that was
made to fit on a man's? A little baffled by his own train
of thought, he followed her into the kitchen.

"It's really a simple meal," she began. "But when it's
all mixed up, Radley hardly notices he's eating something
nutritious. A Twinkie's the true way to his heart."

"My kind of kid."

She smiled a little, more relaxed now that she had her
hands full. She set celery and mushrooms on the chopping block. "The trick's in moderation." Hester took the
chicken out, then remembered the wine. "I'm willing

to concede to Rad's sweet tooth in small doses. He's willing to accept broccoli on the same terms."

"Sounds like a wise arrangement." She opened the wine. Inexpensive, he thought with a glance at the label, but palatable. She filled two glasses, then handed him one. It was silly, but her hands were damp again. It had been some time since she'd shared a bottle of wine or fixed a simple dinner with a man. "To neighbors," he said, and thought she relaxed fractionally as he touched his glass to hers.

"Why don't you sit down while I bone the chicken? Then you can deal with the vegetables."

He didn't sit, but did lean back against the counter. He wasn't willing to give her the distance he was sure she wanted. Not when she smelled so good. She handled the knife like an expert, he noted as he sipped his wine. Impressive. Most of the career women he knew were more experienced in takeouts. "So, how's the new job?"

Hester moved her shoulders. "It's working out well. The manager's a stickler for efficiency, and that trickles down. Rad and I have been having conferences all week so we can compare notes."

Was that what they'd been talking about when they'd walked home today? he wondered. Was that why she'd laughed? "How's Radley taking the new school?"

"Amazingly well." Her lips softened and curved again. He was tempted to touch a fingertip to them to feel the movement. "Whatever happens in Rad's life, he rolls with. He's incredible."

There was a shadow there, a slight one, but he could see it in her eyes. "Divorce is tough," he said, and watched Hester freeze up.

"Yes." She put the boned and cubed chicken in a bowl. "You can chop this while I start the rice."

"Sure." No trespassing, he thought, and let it drop. For now. He'd gone with the law of averages when he'd mentioned divorce, and realized he'd been on the mark. But the mark was still raw. Unless he missed his guess, the divorce had been a lot tougher on her than on Radley. He was also sure that if he wanted to draw her out, it would have to be through the boy. "Rad mentioned that he wanted to come down and visit, but you'd put him off."

Hester handed Mitch an onion before she put a pan on the stove. "I didn't want him disturbing your work."

"We both know what you think of my work."

"I had no intention of offending you the other night," she said stiffly. "It was only that—"

"You can't conceive of a grown man making a living writing comic books."

Hester remained silent as she measured out water. "It's none of my business how you make your living."

"That's right." Mitch took a long sip of wine before he attacked the celery. "In any case, I want you to know that Rad can come see me whenever he likes."

"That's very nice of you, but—"

"No buts, Hester. I like him. And since I'm in the position of calling my own hours, he won't bother me. What do I do with the mushrooms?"

"Slice." She put the lid on the rice before crossing over to show him. "Not too thin. Just make sure…" Her words trailed off when he closed his hand over hers on the knife.

"Like this?" The move was easy. He didn't even have to think about it, but simply shifted until she was trapped between his arms, her back pressed against him. Giving in to the urge, he bent down so that his mouth was close to her ear.

"Yes, that's fine." She stared down at their joined

hands and tried to keep her voice even. "It really doesn't matter."

"We aim to please."

"I have to put on the chicken." She turned and found herself in deeper water. It was a mistake to look up at him, to see that slight smile on his lips and that calm, confident look in his eyes. Instinctively she lifted a hand to his chest. Even that was a mistake. She could feel the slow, steady beat of his heart. She couldn't back up, because there was no place to go, and stepping forward was tempting, dangerously so. "Mitch, you're in my way."

He'd seen it. Though it had been free briefly and suppressed quickly, he'd seen the passion come into her eyes. So she could feel and want and wonder. Maybe it was best if they both wondered a little while longer. "I think you're going to find that happening a lot." But he shifted aside and let her pass. "You smell good, Hester, damn good."

That quiet statement did nothing to ease her pulse rate. Humoring Radley or not, she vowed this would be the last time she entertained Mitch Dempsey. Hester turned on the gas under the wok and added peanut oil. "I take it you do your work at home, then. No office?"

He'd let her have it her way for the time being. The minute she'd turned in his arms and looked up at him, he'd known he'd have it his way—have her his way— before too long. "I only have to go a couple of times a week. Some of the writers or artists prefer working in the office. I do better work at home. After I have the story and the sketches, I take them in for editing and inking."

"I see. So you don't do the inking yourself?" she asked, though she'd have been hard-pressed to define what inking was. She'd have to ask Radley.

"Not anymore. We have some real experts in that,

and it gives me more time to work on the story. Believe it or not, we shoot for quality, the kind of vocabulary that challenges a kid and a story that entertains."

After adding chicken to the hot oil, Hester took a deep breath. "I really do apologize for anything I said that offended you. I'm sure your work's very important to you, and I know Radley certainly appreciates it."

"Well said, Mrs. Wallace." He slid the vegetable-laden chopping block toward her.

"Josh doesn't believe it." Radley bounced into the room, delighted with himself. "He wants to come over tomorrow and see. Can he? His mom says okay if it's okay with you? Okay, Mom?"

Hester turned from the chicken long enough to give Radley a hug. "Okay, Rad, but it has to be after noon. We have some shopping to do in the morning."

"Thanks. Just wait till he sees. He's gonna go crazy. I'll tell him."

"Dinner's nearly ready. Hurry up and wash your hands."

Radley rolled his eyes at Mitch as he raced from the room again.

"You're a big hit," Hester commented.

"He's nuts about you."

"The feeling's mutual."

"So I noticed." Mitch topped off his wine. "You know, I was curious. I always thought bankers kept bankers' hours. You and Rad don't get home until five or so." When she turned her head to look at him, he merely smiled. "Some of my windows face the front. I like to watch people going in and out."

It gave her an odd and not entirely comfortable feeling to know he'd watched her walk home. Hester dumped the vegetables in and stirred. "I get off at four, but then I have to pick Rad up from the sitter." She glanced over her shoulder again. "He hates it when I call her a sitter. Anyway, she's over by our old place, so it takes awhile. I have to start looking for someone closer."

"A lot of kids his age and younger come home on their own."

Her eyes did go smoky, he noted. All she needed was a touch of anger. Or passion. "Radley isn't going to be a latchkey child. He isn't coming home to an empty house because I have to work."

Mitch set her glass by her elbow. "Coming home to empty can be depressing," he murmured, remembering his own experiences. "He's lucky to have you."

"I'm luckier to have him." Her tone softened. "If you'd get out the plates, I'll dish this up."

Mitch remembered where she kept her plates, white ones with little violet sprigs along the edges. It was odd to realize they pleased him when he'd become so accustomed to disposable plastic. He took them out, then set them beside her. Most things were best done on impulse, he'd always thought. He went with the feeling now.

"I guess it would be a lot easier on Rad if he could come back here after school."

"Oh, yes. I hate having to drag him across town, though he's awfully good about it. It's just so hard to find someone you can trust, and who Radley really likes."

"How about me?"

Hester reached to turn off the gas, but stopped to stare at him. Vegetables and chicken popped in hot oil. "I'm sorry?"

"Rad could stay with me in the afternoons." Again Mitch put a hand over hers, this time to turn off the heat. "He'd only be a couple floors away from his own place."

"With you? No, I couldn't."

"Why not?" The more he thought of it, the more Mitch

liked the idea. He and Taz could use the company in the afternoons, and as a bonus he'd be seeing a lot more of the very interesting Mrs. Wallace. "You want references? No criminal record, Hester. Well, there was the case of my motorcycle and the prize roses, but I was only eighteen."

"I didn't mean that—exactly." When he grinned, she began to fuss with the rice. "I mean I couldn't impose that way. I'm sure you're busy."

"Come on, you don't think I do anything all day but doodle. Let's be honest."

"We've already agreed it isn't any of my business," she began.

"Exactly. The point is I'm home in the afternoons, I'm available and I'm willing. Besides, I may even be able to use Rad as a consultant. He's good, you know." Mitch indicated the drawing on the refrigerator. "The kid could use some art lessons."

"I know. I was hoping I'd be able to swing it this summer, but I don't—"

"Want to look a gift horse in the mouth," Mitch finished. "Look, the kid likes me, I like him. And I'll swear to no more than one Twinkie an afternoon."

She laughed then, as he'd seen her laugh a few hours before from his window. It wasn't easy to hold himself back, but something told him if he made a move now, the door would slam in his face and the bolt would slide shut. "I don't know, Mitch. I do appreciate the offer, God knows it would make things easier, but I'm not sure you understand what you're asking for."

"I hasten to point out that I was once a small boy." He wanted to do it, he discovered. It was more than a gesture or impulse; he really wanted to have the kid around. "Look, why don't we put this to a vote and ask Rad?"

"Ask me what?" Radley had run some water over his

hands after he'd finished talking to Josh, and figured his mother was too busy to give them a close look.

Mitch picked up his wine, then lifted a brow. My ball, Hester thought. She could have put the child off, but she'd always prided herself on being honest with him. "Mitch was just suggesting that you might like to stay with him after school in the afternoons instead of going over to Mrs. Cohen's."

"Really?" Astonishment and excitement warred until he was bouncing with both. "Really, can I?"

"Well, I wanted to think about it and talk to you before—"

"I'll behave." Radley rushed over to wrap his arms around his mother's waist. "I promise. Mitch is much better than Mrs. Cohen. Lots better. She smells like mothballs and pats me on the head."

"I rest my case," Mitch murmured.

Hester sent Mitch a smoldering look. She wasn't accustomed to being outnumbered or to making a decision without careful thought and consideration. "Now, Radley, you know Mrs. Cohen's very nice. You've been staying with her for over two years."

Radley squeezed harder and played his ace. "If I stayed with Mitch I could come right home. And I'd do my homework first." It was a rash promise, but it was a desperate situation. "You'd get home sooner, too, and everything. Please, Mom, say yes."

She hated to deny him anything, because there were too many things she'd already had to. He was looking up at her now with his cheeks rosy with pleasure. Bending, she kissed him. "All right, Rad, we'll try it and see how it works out."

"It's going to be great." He locked his arms around her neck before he turned to Mitch. "It's going to be just great."

Chapter 3

Mitch liked to sleep late on weekends—whenever he thought of them as weekends. Because he worked in his own home, at his own pace, he often forgot that to the vast majority there was a big difference between Monday mornings and Saturday mornings. This particular Saturday, however, he was spending in bed, largely dead to the world.

He'd been restless the evening before after he'd left Hester's apartment. Too restless to go back to his own alone. On the spur of the moment he'd gone out to the little lounge where the staff of Universal Comics often got together. He'd run into his inker, another artist and one of the staff writers for *The Great Beyond,* Universal's bid for the supernatural market. The music had been loud and none too good, which had been exactly what his mood had called for.

From there he'd been persuaded to attend an all-night

horror film festival in Times Square. It had been past six when he'd come home, a little drunk and with only enough energy left to strip and tumble into bed—where he'd promised himself he'd stay for the next twenty-four hours. When the phone rang eight hours later, he answered it mostly because it annoyed him.

"Yeah?"

"Mitch?" Hester hesitated. It sounded as though he'd been asleep. Since it was after two in the afternoon, she dismissed the thought. "It's Hester Wallace. I'm sorry to bother you."

"What? No, it's all right." He rubbed a hand over his face, then pushed at the dog, who had shifted to the middle of the bed. "Damn it, Taz, shove over. You're breathing all over me."

Taz? Hester thought as both brows lifted. She hadn't thought that Mitch would have a roommate. She caught her bottom lip between her teeth. That was something she should have checked out. For Radley's sake.

"I really am sorry," she continued in a voice that had cooled dramatically. "Apparently I've caught you at a bad time."

"No." Give the stupid mutt an inch and he took a mile, Mitch thought as he hefted the phone and climbed to the other side of the bed. "What's up?"

"Are you?"

It was the mild disdain in her voice that had him bristling. That and the fact that it felt as though he'd eaten a sandbox. "Yeah, I'm up. I'm talking to you, aren't I?"

"I only called to give you all the numbers and information you need if you watch Radley next week."

"Oh." He pushed the hair out of his eyes and glanced around, hoping he'd left a glass of watered-down soda or something close at hand. No luck. "Okay. You want to wait until I get a pencil?"

"Well, I..." He heard her put her hand over the receiver and speak to someone—Radley, he imagined from the quick intensity of the voice. "Actually, if it wouldn't put you out, Radley was hoping we could come by for a minute. He wants to introduce you to his friend. If you're busy, I can just drop the information by later."

Mitch started to tell her to do just that. Not only could he go back to sleep, but he might just be able to wrangle five minutes alone with her. Then he thought of Radley standing beside his mother, looking up at her with those big dark eyes. "Give me ten minutes," he muttered, and hung up before Hester could say a word.

Mitch pulled on jeans, then went into the bath to fill the sink with cold water. He took a deep breath and stuck his face in it. He came up swearing but awake. Five minutes later he was pulling on a sweatshirt and wondering if he'd remembered to wash any socks. All the clothes that had come back from the laundry neatly folded had been dumped on the chair in the corner of the bedroom. He briefly considered pushing his way through them, then let it go when he heard the knock. Taz's tail thumped on the mattress.

"Why don't you pick up this place?" Mitch asked him. "It's a pigsty."

Taz grinned, showing a set of big white teeth, then made a series of growls and groans.

"Excuses. Always excuses. And get out of bed. Don't you know it's after two?" Mitch rubbed a hand over his unshaven chin, then went to open the door.

She looked great, just plain great, with a hand on a shoulder of each boy and a half smile on her face. Shy?

he thought, a little surprised as he realized it. He had thought her cool and aloof, but now he believed she used that to hide an innate shyness, which he found amazingly sweet.

"Hiya, Rad."

"Hi, Mitch," Radley returned, almost bursting with importance. "This is my friend Josh Miller. He doesn't believe you're Commander Zark."

"Is that so?" Mitch looked down at the doubting Thomas, a skinny towhead about two inches taller than Rad. "Come on in."

"It's nice of you to put up with this," Hester began. "We weren't going to have any peace until Rad and Josh had it settled." The living room looked as though it had exploded. That was Hester's first thought as Mitch closed the door behind them. Papers and clothes and wrappers were everywhere. She imagined there was furniture, too, but she couldn't have described it.

"Tell Josh you're Commander Zark," Radley insisted.

"I guess you could say that." The notion pleased him. "I created him, anyway." He looked down again at Josh, whose pout had gone beyond doubt to true suspicion. "You two go to school together?"

"Used to." Josh stood close to Hester as he studied Mitch. "You don't look like Commander Zark."

Mitch rubbed a hand over his chin again. "Rough night."

"He is too Zark. Hey, look, Mom. Mitch has a VCR." Radley easily overlooked the clutter and homed in on the entertainment center. "I'm saving up my allowance to buy one. I've got seventeen dollars."

"It adds up," Mitch murmured, and flicked a finger

down his nose. "Why don't we go into the office? I'll show you what's cooking in the spring issue."

"Wow."

Taking this as an assent, Mitch led the way.

The office, Hester noted, was big and bright and every bit as chaotic as the living room. She was a creature of order, and it was beyond her how anyone could produce under these conditions. Yet there was a drawing board set up, and tacked to it were sketches and captions.

"You can see Zark's going to have his hands full when Leilah teams up with the Black Moth."

"The Black Moth. Holy cow." Faced with the facts, Josh was duly impressed. Then he remembered his comic book history, and suspicion reared again. "I thought he destroyed the Moth five issues ago."

"The Moth only went into hibernation after Zark bombarded the Zenith with experimental ZT-5. Leilah used her scientific genius to bring him out again."

"Wow." This came from Josh as he stared at the over-sized words and drawings. "How come you make this so big? It can't fit in a comic book."

"It has to be reduced."

"I read all about that stuff." Radley gave Josh a superior glance. "I got this book out of the library that gave the history of comic books, all the way back to the 1930s."

"The Stone Age." Mitch smiled as the boys continued to admire his work. Hester was doing some admiring of her own. Beneath the clutter, she was certain there was a genuine, French rococo cupboard. And books. Hundreds of them. Mitch watched her wander the room. And would have gone on watching if Josh hadn't tugged on his arm.

"Please, can I have your autograph?"

Mitch felt foolishly delighted as he stared down at the earnest face. "Sure." Shuffling through papers, he found a blank one and signed it. Then, with a flourish, he added a quick sketch of Zark.

"Neat." Josh folded the paper reverently and slipped it in his back pocket. "My brother's always bragging because he's got an autographed baseball, but this is better."

"Told ya." With a grin, Radley moved closer to Mitch. "And I'm going to be staying with Mitch after school until Mom gets home from work."

"No kidding?"

"All right, guys, we've taken up enough of Mr. Dempsey's time." Hester started to shoo the boys along when Taz strolled into the room.

"Gee whiz, he's really big." Radley started forward, hand out, when Hester caught him.

"Radley, you know better than to go up to a strange dog."

"Your mom's right," Mitch put in. "But in this case it's okay. Taz is harmless."

And enormous, Hester thought, keeping a firm grip on both boys.

Taz, who had a healthy respect for little people, sat in the doorway and eyed them both. Small boys had a tendency to want to play rough and pull ears, which Taz suffered heroically but could do without. Waiting to see which way the wind blew, he sat and thumped his tail.

"He's anything but an aggressive dog," Mitch reassured Hester. He stepped around her and put a hand on Taz's head. Without, Hester noted, having to bend over.

"Does he do tricks?" Radley wanted to know. It was one of his most secret wishes to own a dog. A big one.

But he never asked, because he knew they couldn't keep one shut in an apartment all day alone.

"No, all Taz does is talk."

"Talk?" Josh went into a fit of laughter. "Dogs can't talk."

"He means bark," Hester said, relaxing a little.

"No, I mean talk." Mitch gave Taz a couple of friendly pats. "How's it going, Taz?"

In answer, the dog pushed his head hard against Mitch's leg and began to groan and grumble. Eyes wide and sincere, he looked up at his master and howled and hooted until both boys were nearly rolling with laughter.

"He *does* talk." Radley stepped forward, palm up. "He really does." Taz decided Radley didn't look like an ear puller and nuzzled his long snout in the boy's hand. "He likes me. Look, Mom." It was love at first sight as Radley threw his arms around the dog's neck. Automatically Hester started forward.

"He's as gentle as they come, I promise you." Mitch put a hand on Hester's arm. Even though the dog was already grumbling out his woes in Radley's ear and allowing Josh to pet him, Hester wasn't convinced.

"I don't imagine he's used to children."

"He fools around with kids in the park all the time." As if to prove it, Taz rolled over to expose his belly for stroking. "Added to that is the fact that he's bone lazy. He wouldn't work up the energy to bite anything that hadn't been put in a bowl for him. You aren't afraid of dogs, are you?"

"No, of course not." Not really, she added to herself. Because she hated to show a weakness, Hester crouched down to pet the huge head. Unknowingly she hit the perfect spot, and Taz recognized a patsy when he saw one. He shifted to lay a paw on her thigh and, with his dark, sad eyes on hers, began to moan. Laughing, Hester rubbed behind his ears. "You're just a big baby, aren't you?"

"An operator's more like it," Mitch murmured, wondering what sort of trick he'd have to do to get Hester to touch him with such feeling.

"I can play with him every day, can't I, Mitch?"

"Sure." Mitch smiled down at Radley. "Taz loves attention. You guys want to take him for a walk?"

The response was immediate and affirmative. Hester straightened up, looking doubtfully at Taz. "I don't know, Rad."

"Please, Mom, we'll be careful. You already said me and Josh could play in the park for a little while."

"Yes, I know, but Taz is awfully big. I wouldn't want him to get away from you."

"Taz is a firm believer in conserving energy. Why run if strolling gets you to the same place?" Mitch went back into his office, rooted around and came up with Taz's leash. "He doesn't chase cars, other dogs or park police. He will, however, stop at every tree."

With a giggle, Radley took the leash. "Okay, Mom?"

She hesitated, knowing there was a part of her that wanted to keep Radley with her, within arm's reach. And, for his sake, it was something she had to fight. "A half hour." The words were barely out when he and Josh let out a whoop. "You have to get your coats—and gloves."

"We will. Come on, Taz."

The dog gave a huge sigh before gathering himself up. Grumbling only a little, he stationed himself between the two boys as they headed out.

"Why is it every time I see that kid I feel good?"

"You're very kind to him. Well, I should go upstairs and make sure they bundle up."

"I think they can handle it. Why don't you sit down?" He took advantage of her brief hesitation by taking her arm. "Come over by the window. You can watch them go out."

She gave in because she knew how Radley hated to be hovered over. "Oh, I have my office number for you, and the name and number of his doctor and the school." Mitch took the paper and stuck it in his pocket. "If there's any trouble at all, call me. I can be home in ten minutes."

"Relax, Hester. We'll get along fine."

"I want to thank you again. It's the first time since he started school, that Rad's looked forward to a Monday."

"I'm looking forward to it myself."

She looked down, waiting to see the familiar blue cap and coat. "We haven't discussed terms."

"What terms?"

"How much you want for watching him. Mrs. Cohen—"

"Good God, Hester, I don't want you to pay me."

"Don't be ridiculous. Of course I'll pay you."

He put a hand on her shoulder until she'd turned to face him. "I don't need the money, I don't want the money. I made the offer because Rad's a nice kid and I enjoy his company."

"That's very kind of you, but—"

His exasperated sigh cut her off. "Here come the buts again."

"I couldn't possibly let you do it for nothing."

Mitch studied her face. He'd thought her tough at

their first meeting, and tough she was—at least on the outside. "Can't you accept a neighborly gesture?"

Her lips curved a bit, but her eyes remained solemn. "I guess not."

"Five bucks a day."

This time the smile reached her eyes. "Thank you."

He caught the ends of her hair between his thumb and forefinger. "You drive a hard bargain, lady."

"So I've been told." Cautiously she took a step away. "Here they come." He hadn't forgotten his gloves, she noted as she leaned closer to the window. Nor had he forgotten that he'd been taught to walk to the corner and cross at the light. "He's in heaven, you know. Rad's always wanted a dog." She touched a hand to the window and continued to watch. "He doesn't mention it because he knows we can't keep one in the apartment when no one's home all day. So he's settled for the promise of a kitten."

Mitch put a hand on her shoulder again, but gently this time. "He doesn't strike me as a deprived child, Hester. There's nothing for you to feel guilty about."

She looked at him then, her eyes wide and just a little sad. Mitch discovered he was just as drawn to that as he had been to her laughter. Without planning to, without knowing he'd needed to, he lifted a hand to her cheek. The pale gray of her irises deepened. Her skin warmed. Hester backed away quickly.

"I'd better go. I'm sure they'll want hot chocolate when they get back in."

"They have to bring Taz back here first," Mitch reminded her. "Take a break, Hester. Want some coffee?"

"Well, I—"

"Good. Sit down and I'll get it."

Hester stood in the center of the room a moment, a bit amazed at how smoothly he ran things—his way. She was much too used to setting her own rules to accept anyone else's. Still, she told herself it would be rude to leave, that her son would be back soon and that the least she could do after Mitch had been so good to the boy was bear his company for a little while.

She would have been lying if she'd denied that he interested her. In a casual way, of course. There was something about the way he looked at her, so deep and penetrating, while at the same time he appeared to take most of life as a joke. Yet there was nothing funny about the way he touched her.

Hester lifted fingertips to her cheek, where his had been. She would have to take care to avoid too much of that sort of contact. Perhaps, with effort, she could think of Mitch as a friend, as Radley did already. It might not sit well with her to be obliged to him, but she could swallow that. She'd swallowed worse.

He was kind. She let out a little breath as she tried to relax. Experience had given her a very sensitive antenna. She could recognize the kind of man who tried to ingratiate himself with the child to get to the mother. If she was sure of anything, it was that Mitch genuinely liked Radley. That, if nothing else, was a point in his favor.

But she wished he hadn't touched her that way, looked at her that way, made her feel that way.

"It's hot. Probably lousy, but hot." Mitch walked in with two mugs. "Don't you want to sit down?"

Hester smiled at him. "Where?"

Mitch set the mugs down on a stack of papers, then pushed magazines from the sofa. "Here."

"You know…" She stepped over a stack of old newspapers. "Radley's very good at tidying. He'd be glad to help you."

"I function best in controlled confusion."

Hester joined him on the sofa. "I can see the confusion, but not the controlled."

"It's here, believe me. I didn't ask if you wanted anything in the coffee, so I brought it black."

"Black's fine. This table—it's Queen Anne, isn't it?"

"Yeah." Mitch set his bare feet on it, then crossed them at the ankles. "You've got a good eye."

"One would have to under the circumstances." Because he laughed, she smiled as she took her first sip. "I've always loved antiques. I suppose it's the endurance. Not many things last."

"Sure they do. I once had a cold that lasted six weeks." He settled back as she laughed. "When you do that, you get a dimple at the corner of your mouth. Cute."

Hester was immediately self-conscious again. "You have a very natural way with children. Did you come from a large family?"

"No. Only child." He continued to study her, curious about her reaction to the most casual of compliments.

"Really? I wouldn't have guessed it."

"Don't tell me you're of the school who believes only a woman can relate to children?"

"No, not really," she hedged, because that had been her experience thus far. "It's just that you're particularly good with them. No children of your own?" The question came out quickly, amazing and embarrassing her.

"No. I guess I've been too busy being a kid myself to think about raising any."

"That hardly makes you unusual," she said coolly.

He tilted his head as he studied her. "Tossing me in with Rad's father, Hester?"

Something flashed in her eyes. Mitch shook his head as he sipped again. "Damn, Hester, what did the bastard do to you?" She froze instantly. Mitch was quicker. Even as she started to rise, he put a restraining hand on her arm. "Okay, hands off that one until you're ready. I apologize if I hit a sore spot, but I'm curious. I've spent a couple of evenings with Rad now, and he's never mentioned his father."

"I'd appreciate it if you wouldn't ask him any questions."

"Fine." Mitch was capable of being just as snotty. "I didn't intend to grill the kid."

Hester was tempted to get up and excuse herself. That would be the easiest way. But the fact was that she was trusting her son to this man every afternoon. She supposed it would be best if he had some background.

"Rad hasn't seen his father in almost seven years."

"At all?" He couldn't help his surprise. His own family had been undemonstrative and distant, but he never went more than a year without seeing his parents. "Must be rough on the kid."

"They were never close. I think Radley's adjusted very well."

"Hold on. I wasn't criticizing you." He'd placed his hand over hers again, too firmly to be shaken off. "I know a happy, well-loved boy when I see one. You'd walk through fire for him. Maybe you don't think it shows, but it does."

"There's nothing that's more important to me than Radley." She wanted to relax again, but he was sitting too close, and his hand was still on hers. "I only told you this so that you wouldn't ask him questions that might upset him."

"Does that sort of thing happen often?"

"Sometimes." His fingers were linked with hers now. She couldn't quite figure out how he'd managed it. "A new friend, a new teacher. I really should go."

"How about you?" He touched her cheek gently and turned her face toward him. "How have you adjusted?"

"Just fine. I have Rad, and my work."

"And no relationships?"

She wasn't sure if it was embarrassment or anger, but the sensation was very strong. "That's none of your business."

"If people only talked about what was their business, they wouldn't get very far. You don't strike me as a man-hater, Hester."

She lifted a brow. When pushed, she could play the game by someone else's rules. And she could play it well. "I went through a period of time when I despised men on principle. Actually, it was a very rewarding time of my life. Then, gradually, I came to the opinion that some members of your species weren't lower forms of life."

"Sounds promising."

She smiled again, because he made it easy. "The point is, I don't blame all men for the faults of one."

"You're just cautious."

"If you like."

"The one thing I'm sure I like is your eyes. No, don't look away." Patiently, he turned her face back to his. "They're fabulous—take it from an artist's standpoint."

She had to stop being so jumpy, Hester ordered herself. With an effort, she remained still. "Does that mean they're going to appear in an upcoming issue?"

"They just might." He smiled, appreciating the thought and the fact that though tense, she was able to hold her own. "Poor old Zark deserves to meet someone who understands him. These eyes would."

"I'll take that as a compliment." And run. "The boys will be back in a minute."

"We've got some time yet. Hester, do you ever have fun?"

"What a stupid question. Of course I do."

"Not as Rad's mother, but as Hester." He ran a hand through her hair, captivated.

"I *am* Rad's mother." Though she managed to rise, he stood with her.

"You're also a woman. A gorgeous one." He saw the look in her eyes and ran his thumb along her jawline. "Take my word for it. I'm an honest man. You're one gorgeous bundle of nerves."

"That's silly. I don't have anything to be nervous about." Other than the fact that he was touching her, and his voice was quiet, and the apartment was empty.

"I'll take the shaft out of my heart later," he murmured. He bent to kiss her, then had to catch her when she nearly stumbled over the newspapers. "Take it easy. I'm not going to bite you. This time."

"I have to go." She was as close to panic as she ever allowed herself to come. "I have a dozen things to do."

"In a minute." He framed her face. She was trembling, he realized. It didn't surprise him. What did was that he wasn't steady himself. "What we have here, Mrs. Wallace, is called attraction, chemistry, lust. It doesn't really matter what label you put on it."

"Maybe not to you."

"Then we'll let you pick the label later." He stroked his thumbs over her cheekbones, gently, soothingly. "I already told you I'm not a maniac. I'll have to remember to get those references."

"Mitch, I told you I appreciate what you're doing for Rad, but I wish you'd—"

"Here and now doesn't concern Rad. This is you and me, Hester. When was the last time you let yourself be alone with a man who wanted you?" He casually brushed his thumb over her lips. Her eyes went to smoke. "When was the last time you let anyone do this?"

His mouth covered hers quickly, with a force that came as a shock. She hadn't been prepared for violence. His hands had been so gentle, his voice so soothing. She hadn't expected this edgy passion. But God, how she'd wanted it. With the same reckless need, she threw her arms around his neck and answered demand for demand.

"Too long," Mitch managed breathlessly when he tore his mouth from hers. "Thank God." Before she could utter more than a moan, he took her mouth again.

He hadn't been sure what he'd find in her—ice, anger, fear. The unrestrained heat came as much of a shock to his system as to hers. Her wide, generous mouth was warm and willing, with all traces of shyness swallowed by passion. She gave more than he would have asked for, and more than he'd been prepared to take.

His head spun, a fascinating and novel sensation he couldn't fully appreciate as he struggled to touch and taste. He dragged his hands through her hair, scattering the two thin silver pins she'd used to pull it back from her face. He wanted it free and wild in his hands, just as he wanted her free and wild in his bed. His plans to go slowly, to test the waters, evaporated in an overwhelming desire to dive in headfirst. Thinking only of this, he slipped his hands under her sweater. The skin there was tender and warm. The silky little concoction she wore was cool and soft. He slid his hands around her waist and up to cup her breasts.

She stiffened, then shuddered. She hadn't known how much she'd wanted to be touched like this. Needed like this. His taste was so dark, so tempting. She'd forgotten what it was like to hunger for such things. It was madness, the sweet release of madness. She heard him murmur her name as he moved his mouth down her throat and back again.

Madness. She understood it. She'd been there before, or thought she had. Though it seemed sweeter now, richer now, she knew she could never go there again.

"Mitch, please." It wasn't easy to resist what he was offering. It surprised Hester how difficult it was to draw away, to put the boundaries back. "We can't do this."

"We are," he pointed out, and drew the flavor from her lips again. "And very well."

"*I* can't." With the small sliver of willpower she had left, she struggled away. "I'm sorry. I should never have let this happen." Her cheeks were hot. Hester put her hands to them, then dragged them up through her hair.

His knees were weak. That was something to think about. But for the moment he concentrated on her. "You're taking a lot on yourself, Hester. It seems to be a habit of yours. I kissed you, and you just happened to kiss me back. Since we both enjoyed it, I don't see where apologies are necessary on either side."

"I should have made myself clear." She stepped back,

hit the newspapers again, then skirted around them. "I do appreciate what you're doing for Rad—"

"Leave him out of this, for God's sake."

"I can't." Her voice rose, surprising her again. She knew better than to lose control. "I don't expect you to understand, but I can't leave him out of it." She took a deep breath, amazed that it did nothing to calm her pulse rate. "I'm not interested in casual sex. I have Rad to think about, and myself."

"Fair enough." He wanted to sit down until he'd recovered, but figured the situation called for an eye-to-eye discussion. "I wasn't feeling too casual about it myself."

That was what worried her. "Let's just drop it."

Anger was an amazing stimulant. Mitch stepped forward, and caught her chin in his hand. "Fat chance."

"I don't want to argue with you. I just think that—" The knock came as a blessed reprieve. "That's the boys."

"I know." But he didn't release her. "Whatever you're interested in, have time for, room for, might just have to be adjusted." He was angry, really angry, Mitch realized. It wasn't like him to lose his temper so quickly. "Life's full of adjustments, Hester." Letting her go, he opened the door.

"It was great." Rosy-cheeked and bright-eyed, Radley tumbled in ahead of Josh and the dog. "We even got Taz to run once, for a minute."

"Amazing." Mitch bent to unclip the leash. Grumbling with exhaustion, Taz walked to a spot by the window, then collapsed.

"You guys must be freezing." Hester kissed Radley's forehead. "It must be time for hot chocolate."

"Yeah!" Radley turned his beaming face to Mitch. "Want some? Mom makes real good hot chocolate."

It was tempting to put her on the spot. Perhaps it was a good thing for both of them that his temper was already fading. "Maybe next time." He pulled Radley's cap over his eyes. "I've got some things to do."

"Thanks a lot for letting us take Taz out. It was really neat, wasn't it, Josh?"

"Yeah. Thanks, Mr. Dempsey."

"Anytime. See you Monday, Rad."

"Okay." The boys fled, laughing and shoving. Mitch looked, but Hester was already gone.

Chapter 4

Mitchell Dempsey II had been born rich, privileged and, according to his parents, with an incorrigible imagination. Maybe that was why he'd taken to Radley so quickly. The boy was far from rich, not even privileged enough to have a set of parents, but his imagination was first-class.

Mitch had always liked crowds as much as one-on-one social situations. He was certainly no stranger to parties, given his mother's affection for entertaining and his own gregarious nature, and no one who knew him would ever have classed him as a loner. In his work, however, he had always preferred the solitary. He worked at home not because he didn't like distractions—he was really fond of them—but because he didn't care to have anyone looking over his shoulder or timing his progress. He'd never considered working any way other than alone. Until Radley.

They made a pact the first day. If Radley finished his homework, with or without Mitch's dubious help, he could then choose to either play with Taz or give his input into Mitch's latest story line. If Mitch had decided to call it quits for the day, they could entertain themselves with his extensive collection of videotapes or with Radley's growing army of plastic figures.

To Mitch, it was natural—to Radley, fantastic. For the first time in his young life he had a man who was part of his daily routine, one who talked to him and listened to him. He had someone who was not only as willing to spend time to set up a battle or wage a war as his mother was, but someone who understood his military strategy.

By the end of their first week, Mitch was not only a hero, creator of Zark and owner of Taz, but the most solid and dependable person in his life other than his mother. Radley loved, without guards or restrictions.

Mitch saw it, wondered at it and found himself just as captivated. He had told Hester no less than the truth when he'd said that he'd never thought about having children. He'd run his life on his own clock for so long that he'd never considered doing things differently. If he'd known what it was to love a small boy, to find pieces of himself in one, he might have done things differently.

Perhaps it was because of his discoveries that he thought of Radley's father. What kind of man could create something that special and then walk away from it? His own father had been stern and anything but understanding, but he'd been there. Mitch had never questioned the love.

A man didn't get to be thirty-five without knowing several contemporaries who'd been through divorces—

many of them bitter. But he also was acquainted with several who'd managed to call a moratorium with their ex-wives in order to remain fathers. It was difficult enough to understand how Radley's father not only could have walked out, but could have walked away. After a week in Radley's company, it was all but impossible.

And what of Hester? What kind of man left a woman to struggle alone to raise a child they had brought into the world together? How much had she loved him? That was a thought that dug into his brain too often for comfort. The results of the experience were obvious. She was tense and overly cautious around men. Around him, certainly, Mitch thought with a grimace as he watched Radley sketch. So cautious that she'd stayed out of his path throughout the week.

Every day between 4:15 and 4:25, he received a polite call. Hester would ask him if everything had gone well, thank him for watching Radley, then ask him to send her son upstairs. That afternoon, Radley had handed him a neatly written check for twenty-five dollars drawn on the account of Hester Gentry Wallace. It was still crumpled in Mitch's pocket.

Did she really think he was going to quietly step aside after she'd knocked the wind out of him? He hadn't forgotten what she'd felt like pressed against him, inhibitions and caution stripped away for one brief, stunning moment. He intended to live that moment again, as well as the others his incorrigible imagination had conjured up.

If she did think he'd bow out gracefully, Mrs. Hester Wallace was in for a big surprise.

"I can't get the retro rockets right," Radley complained. "They never look right."

Mitch set aside his own work, which had stopped humming along the moment he'd started to think of Hester. "Let's have a look." He took the spare sketch pad he'd lent to Radley. "Hey, not bad." He grinned, foolishly pleased with Radley's attempt at the Defiance. It seemed the few pointers he'd given the kid had taken root. "You're a real natural, Rad."

The boy blushed with pleasure, then frowned again. "But see, the boosters and retros are all wrong. They look stupid."

"Only because you're trying to detail too soon. Look, light strokes, impressions first." He put a hand over the boy's to guide it. "Don't be afraid to make mistakes. That's why they make those big gum erasers."

"You don't make mistakes." Radley caught his tongue between his teeth as he struggled to make his hand move as expertly as Mitch's.

"Sure I do. This is my fifteenth eraser this year."

"You're the best artist in the whole world," Radley said, looking up, his heart in his eyes.

Moved and strangely humbled, Mitch ruffled the boy's hair. "Maybe one of the top twenty, but thanks." When the phone rang, Mitch felt a strange stab of disappointment. The weekend meant something different now—no Radley. For a man who had lived his entire adult life without responsibilities, it was a sobering thought to realize he would miss one. "That should be your mother."

"She said we could go out to the movies tonight 'cause it's Friday and all. You could come with us."

Giving a noncommittal grunt, Mitch answered the phone. "Hi, Hester."

"Mitch, I—everything okay?"

Something in her tone had his brows drawing together. "Just dandy."

"Did Radley give you the check?"

"Yeah. Sorry, I haven't had a chance to cash it yet."

If there was one thing she wasn't in the mood for at the moment, it was sarcasm. "Well, thanks. If you'd send Radley upstairs, I'd appreciate it."

"No problem." He hesitated. "Rough day, Hester?"

She pressed a hand to her throbbing temple. "A bit. Thank you, Mitch."

"Sure." He hung up, still frowning. Turning to Radley, he made the effort to smile. "Time to transfer your equipment, Corporal."

"Sir, yes, sir!" Radley gave a smart salute. The intergalactic army he'd left at Mitch's through the week was tossed into his backpack. After a brief search, both of his gloves were located and pushed in on top of the plastic figures. Radley stuffed his coat and hat in before kneeling down to hug Taz. "Bye, Taz. See ya." The dog rumbled a goodbye as he rubbed his snout into Radley's shoulder. "Bye, Mitch." He went to the door, then hesitated. "I guess I'll see you Monday."

"Sure. Hey, maybe I'll just walk up with you. Give your mom a full report."

"Okay!" Radley brightened instantly. "You left your keys in the kitchen. I'll get them." Mitch watched the tornado pass, then swirl back. "I got an A in spelling. When I tell Mom, she'll be in a real good mood. We'll probably get sodas."

"Sounds like a good deal to me," Mitch said, and let himself be dragged along.

Hester heard Radley's key in the lock and set down the ice pack. Leaning closer, she checked her face in the bathroom mirror, saw a bruise was already forming, and swore. She'd hoped to be able to tell Radley about the mishap, gloss over it and make it a joke before any battle scars showed. Hester downed two aspirin and prayed the headache would pass.

"Mom! Hey, Mom!"

"Right here, Radley." She winced at her own raised voice, then put on a smile as she walked out to greet him. The smile faded when she saw her son had brought company.

"Mitch came up to report," Radley began as he shrugged out of his backpack.

"What the hell happened to you?" Mitch crossed over to her in two strides. He had her face in his hands and fury in his eyes. "Are you all right?"

"Of course I am." She shot him a quick warning look, then turned to Radley. "I'm fine."

Radley stared up at her, his eyes widening, then his bottom lip trembling as he saw the black-and-blue mark under her eye. "Did you fall down?"

She wanted to lie and say yes, but she'd never lied to him. "Not exactly." She forced a smile, annoyed to have a witness to her explanation. "It seems that there was a man at the subway station who wanted my purse. I wanted it, too."

"You were mugged?" Mitch wasn't sure whether to swear at her or gather her close and check for injuries. Hester's long, withering look didn't give him the chance to do either.

"Sort of." She moved her shoulders to show Radley it was of little consequence. "It wasn't all that exciting, I'm afraid. The subway was crowded. Someone saw what was going on and called security, so the man changed his mind about my purse and ran away."

Radley looked closer. He'd seen a black eye before. Joey Phelps had had a really neat one once. But he'd never seen one on his mother. "Did he hit you?"

"Not really. That part was sort of an accident." An accident that hurt like the devil. "We were having this tug-of-war over my purse, and his elbow shot up. I didn't duck quick enough, that's all."

"Stupid," Mitch muttered loud enough to be heard.

"Did you hit him?"

"Of course not," Hester answered, and thought longingly of her ice pack. "Go put your things away now, Radley."

"But I want to know about—"

"Now," his mother interrupted in a tone she used rarely and to great effect.

"Yes, ma'am," Radley mumbled, and lugged the backpack off the couch.

Hester waited until he'd turned the corner into his room. "I want you to know I don't appreciate your interference."

"You haven't begun to see interference. What the hell's wrong with you? You know better than to fight with a mugger over a purse. What if he'd had a knife?" Even the thought of it had his reliable imagination working overtime.

"He didn't have a knife." Hester felt her knees begin to tremble. The damnedest thing was that the reaction had chosen the most inopportune moment to set in. "And he doesn't have my purse, either."

"Or a black eye. For God's sake, Hester, you could have been seriously hurt, and I doubt there's anything in your purse that would warrant it. Credit cards can be canceled, a compact or a lipstick replaced."

"I suppose if someone had tried to lift your wallet you'd have given him your blessing."

"That's different."

"The hell it is."

He stopped pacing long enough to give her a long study. Her chin was thrust out, in the same way he'd seen Radley's go a few times. He'd expected the stubbornness, but he had to admit he hadn't expected the ready temper, or his admiration for it. But that was beside the point, he reminded himself as his gaze swept over her bruised cheekbone again.

"Let's just back up a minute. In the first place, you've got no business taking the subway alone."

She let out what might have been a laugh. "You've got to be kidding."

The funny thing was, he couldn't remember ever having said anything quite that stupid. It brought his own temper bubbling over. "Take a cab, damn it."

"I have no intention of taking a cab."

"Why?"

"In the first place it would be stupid, and in the second I can't afford it."

Mitch dragged the check out of his pocket and pushed it into her hand. "Now you can afford it, along with a reasonable tip."

"I have no intention of taking this." She shoved the crumpled check back at him. "Or of taking a taxi when the subway is both inexpensive and convenient. And I have less intention of allowing you to take a small incident and blow it into a major calamity. I don't want Radley upset."

"Fine, then take a cab. For the kid's sake, if not your own. Think how it would have been for him if you'd really been hurt."

The bruise stood out darkly as her cheeks paled. "I don't need you or anyone to lecture me on the welfare of my son."

"No, you do just fine by him. It's when it comes to Hester that you've got a few loose screws." He jammed his hands into his pockets. "Okay, you won't take a cab. At least promise you won't play Sally Courageous the next time some lowlife decides he likes the color of your purse."

Hester brushed at the sleeve of her jacket. "Is that the name of one of your characters?"

"It might be." He told himself to calm down. He didn't have much of a temper as a rule, but when it started to perk, it could come to a boil in seconds. "Look, Hester, did you have your life savings in your bag?"

"Of course not."

"Family heirlooms?"

"No."

"Any microchips vital to national security?"

She let out an exasperated sigh and dropped onto the arm of a chair. "I left them at the office." She pouted as she looked up at him. "Don't give me that disgusting smile now."

"Sorry." He changed it to a grin.

"I just had such a rotten day." Without realizing it, she slipped off her shoe and began to massage her instep. "The first thing this morning, Mr. Rosen went on an efficiency campaign. Then there was the staff meeting, then the idiot settlement clerk, who made a pass at me."

"What idiot settlement clerk?"

"Never mind." Tired, she rubbed her temple. "Just take it that things went from bad to worse until I was ready to bite someone's head off. Then that jerk grabbed my purse, and I just exploded. At least I have the satisfaction of knowing he'll be walking with a limp for a few days."

"Got in a few licks, did you?"

Hester continued to pout as she gingerly touched her eye with her fingertips. "Yeah."

Mitch walked over, then bent down to her level. With a look more of curiosity than sympathy, he examined the damage. "You're going to have a hell of a shiner."

"Really?" Hester touched the bruise again. "I was hoping this was as bad as it would get."

"Not a chance. It's going to be a beaut."

She thought of the stares and the explanations that would be necessary the following week. "Terrific."

"Hurt?"

"Yes."

Mitch touched his lips to the bruise before she could evade him. "Try some ice."

"I've already thought of that."

"I put my things away." Radley stood in the hallway looking down at his shoes. "I had homework, but I already did it."

"That's good. Come here." Radley continued to look at his shoes as he walked to her. Hester put her arms around his neck and squeezed. "Sorry."

"'S okay. I didn't mean to make you mad."

"You didn't make me mad. Mr. Rosen made me mad. That man who wanted my purse made me mad, but not you, baby."

"I could get you a wet cloth the way you do when my head hurts."

"Thanks, but I think I need a hot bath and an ice pack." She gave him another squeeze, then remembered.

"Oh, we had a date didn't we? Cheeseburgers and a movie."

"We can watch TV instead."

"Well, why don't we see how I feel in a little while?"

"I got an *A* on my spelling test."

"My hero," Hester said, laughing.

"You know, that hot bath's a good idea. Ice, too." Mitch was already making plans. "Why don't you get started on that while I borrow Rad for a little while."

"But he just got home."

"It'll only take a little while." Mitch took her arm and started to lead her toward the hall. "Put some bubbles in the tub. They're great for the morale. We'll be back in half an hour."

"But where are you going?"

"Just an errand I need to run. Rad can keep me company, can't you, Rad?"

"Sure."

The idea of a thirty-minute soak was too tempting. "No candy, it's too close to dinner."

"Okay, I won't eat any," Mitch promised, and scooted her into the bath. Putting a hand on Radley's shoulder, he marched back into the living room. "Ready to go out on a mission, Corporal?"

Radley's eyes twinkled as he saluted. "Ready and willing, sir."

The combination of ice pack, hot bath and aspirin proved successful. By the time the water had cooled in the tub, Hester's headache was down to dull and manageable. She supposed she owed Mitch for giving her a few minutes to herself, Hester admitted as she pulled on jeans. Along with most of the pain, the shakiness had drained away in the hot water. In fact, when she took the time to examine her bruised eye, she felt downright proud of herself. Mitch had been right, bubbles had been good for the morale.

She pulled a brush through her hair and wondered how disappointed Radley would be if they postponed their trip to the movies. Hot bath or no, the last thing she felt like doing at the moment was braving the cold to sit in a crowded theater. She thought a matinee the next day might satisfy him. It would mean adjusting her schedule a bit, but the idea of a quiet evening at home after the week she'd put in made doing the laundry after dinner a lot more acceptable.

And what a week, Hester thought as she pulled on slippers. Rosen was a tyrant and the settlement clerk was a pest. She'd spent almost as much time during the last five days placating one and discouraging the other as she had processing loans. She wasn't afraid of work, but she did resent having to account for every minute of her time. It was nothing personal; Hester had discovered that within the first eight-hour stretch. Rosen was equally overbearing and fussy with everyone on his staff.

And that fool Cummings. Hester pushed the thought of the overamorous clerk out of her mind and sat on the edge of the bed. She'd gotten through the first two weeks, hadn't she? She touched her cheekbone gingerly. With the scars to prove it. It would be easier now. She wouldn't have the strain of meeting all those new people. The biggest relief of all was that she didn't have to worry about Radley.

She'd never admit it to anyone, but she'd waited for Mitch to call every day that week to tell her Radley was too much trouble, he'd changed his mind, he was tired of spending his afternoons with a nine-year-old. But the fact was that every afternoon when Radley had come upstairs the boy had been full of stories about Mitch and Taz and what they'd done.

Mitch had showed him a series of sketches for the big anniversary issue. They'd taken Taz to the park. They'd watched the original, uncut, absolutely classic *King Kong* on the VCR. Mitch had showed him his comic book collection, which included the first issues of *Superman* and *Tales From the Crypt,* which everyone knew, she'd been informed, were practically priceless. And did she know that Mitch had an original, honest-to-God *Captain Midnight* decoder ring? Wow.

Hester rolled her eyes, then winced when the movement reminded her of the bruise. The man might be odd, she decided, but he was certainly making Radley happy. Things would be fine as long as she continued to think of him as Radley's friend and forgot about that unexpected and unexplainable connection they'd made last weekend.

Hester preferred to think about it as a connection rather than any of the terms Mitch had used. Attraction, chemistry, lust. No, she didn't care for any of those words, or for her immediate and unrestrained reaction to him. She knew what she'd felt. Hester was too honest to deny that for one crazed moment she'd welcomed the sensation of being held and kissed and desired. It wasn't something to be ashamed of. A woman who'd been alone as long as she had was bound to feel certain stirrings around an attractive man.

Then why didn't she feel any of those stirrings around Cummings?

Don't answer that, she warned herself. Sometimes it was best not to dig too deeply when you really didn't want to know.

Think about dinner, she decided. Poor Radley was

going to have to make do with soup and a sandwich instead of his beloved cheeseburger tonight. With a sigh, she rose as she heard the front door open.

"Mom! Mom, come see the surprise."

Hester made sure she was smiling, though she wasn't sure she could take any more surprises that day. "Rad, did you thank Mitch for…oh." He was back, Hester saw, automatically adjusting her sweater. The two of them stood just inside the doorway with identical grins on their faces. Radley carried two paper bags, and Mitch hefted what looked suspiciously like a tape machine with cables dangling.

"What's all this?"

"Dinner and a double feature," Mitch informed her. "Rad said you like chocolate shakes."

"Yes, I do." The aroma finally carried to her. Sniffing, she eyed Radley's bags. "Cheeseburgers?"

"Yeah, and fries. Mitch said we could have double orders. We took Taz for a walk. He's eating his downstairs."

"He's got lousy table manners." Mitch carried the unit over to Hester's television.

"And I helped Mitch unhook the VCR. We got *Raiders of the Lost Ark*. Mitch has millions of movies."

"Rad said you like musical junk."

"Well, yes, I—"

"We got one of them, too." Rad set the bags down to go over and sit with Mitch on the floor. "Mitch said it's pretty funny, so I guess it'll be okay." He put a hand on Mitch's leg and leaned closer to watch the hookup.

"Singin' in the Rain." Handing Radley a cable, Mitch sat back to let him connect it.

"Really?"

He had to smile. There were times she sounded just like the kid. "Yeah. How's the eye?"

"Oh, it's better." Unable to resist, Hester walked over to watch. How odd it seemed to see her son's small hands working with those of a man.

"It's a tight squeeze, but the VCR just about fits under your television stand." Mitch gave Radley's shoulder a quick squeeze before he rose. "Colorful." With a finger under her chin, he turned Hester's face to the side to examine her eye. "Rad and I thought you looked a little beat, so we figured we'd bring the movie to you."

"I was." She touched her hand to his wrist a moment. "Thanks."

"Anytime." He wondered what her reaction, and Radley's, would be if he kissed her right now. Hester must have seen the question in his eyes, because she backed up quickly.

"Well, I guess I'd better get some plates so the food doesn't get cold."

"We've got plenty of napkins." He gestured toward the couch. "Sit down while my assistant and I finish up."

"I did it." Flushed with success, Radley scrambled back on all fours. "It's all hooked up."

Mitch bent to check the connections. "You're a regular mechanic, Corporal."

"We get to watch *Raiders* first, right?"

"That was the deal." Mitch handed him the tape. "You're in charge."

"It looks like I have to thank you again," Hester said when Mitch joined her on the couch.

"What for? I figured to wangle myself in on your date with Rad tonight." He pulled a burger out of the bag. "This is cheaper."

"Most men wouldn't choose to spend a Friday night with a small boy."

"Why not?" He took a healthy bite, and after swallowing continued, "I figure he won't eat half his fries, and I'll get the rest."

Radley took a running leap and plopped onto the couch between them. He gave a contented and very adult sigh as he snuggled down. "This is better than going out. Lots better."

He was right, Hester thought as she relaxed and let herself become caught up in Indiana Jones's adventures. There had been a time when she'd believed life could be that thrilling, romantic, heart-stopping. Circumstances had forced her to set those things aside, but she'd never lost her love of the fantasy of films. For a couple of hours it was possible to close off reality and the pressures that went with it and be innocent again.

Radley was bright-eyed and full of energy as he switched tapes. Hester had no doubt his dreams that night would revolve around lost treasures and heroic deeds. Snuggling against her, he giggled at Donald O'Connor's mugging and pratfalls, but began to nod off soon after Gene Kelly's marvelous dance through the rain.

"Fabulous, isn't it?" Mitch murmured. Radley had shifted so that his head rested against Mitch's chest.

"Absolutely. I never get tired of this movie. When I was a little girl, we'd watch it whenever it came on TV. My father's a big movie buff. You can name almost any film, and he'll tell you who was in it. But his first love was always the musical."

Mitch fell silent again. It took very little to learn how one person felt about another—a mere inflection in their voice, a softening of their expression. Hester's family had been close, as he'd always regretted his hadn't been. His father had never shared Mitch's love of fantasy or film, as he had never shared his father's devotion to business. Though he would never have considered himself a lonely child—his imagination had been company enough—he'd always missed the warmth and affection he'd heard so clearly in Hester's voice when she'd spoken of her father.

When the credits rolled, he turned to her again. "Your parents live in the city?"

"Here? Oh, no." She had to laugh as she tried to picture either of her parents coping with life in New York. "No, I grew up in Rochester, but my parents moved to the Sunbelt almost ten years ago—Fort Worth. Dad's still in banking and my mother has a part-time job in a bookstore. We were all amazed when she went to work. I guess all of us thought she didn't know how to do anything but bake cookies and fold sheets."

"How many's we?"

Hester sighed a little as the screen went blank. She couldn't honestly remember when she'd enjoyed an evening more. "I have a brother and a sister. I'm the oldest. Luke's settled in Rochester with a wife and a new baby on the way, and Julia's in Atlanta. She's a disc jockey."

"No kidding?"

"Wake up, Atlanta, it's 6:00 a.m., time for three hits in a row." She laughed a little as she thought of her sister. "I'd give anything to take Rad down for a visit."

"Miss them?"

"It's just hard thinking how spread out we all are. I know how nice it would be for Rad to have more family close by."

"What about Hester?"

She looked over at him, a bit surprised to see how natural Radley looked dozing in the crook of his arm. "I have Rad."

"And that's enough?"

"More than." She smiled; then, uncurling her legs, she rose. "And speaking of Rad, I'd better take him in to bed."

Mitch picked the boy up and settled him over his shoulder. "I'll carry him."

"Oh, that's all right. I do it all the time."

"I've got him." Radley turned his face into Mitch's neck. What an amazing feeling, he thought, a little shaken by it. "Just show me where."

Telling herself it was silly to feel odd, Hester led him into Radley's bedroom. The bed had been made à la Rad, which meant the *Star Wars* spread was pulled up over rumpled sheets. Mitch narrowly missed stepping on a pint-size robot and a worn rag dog. There was a night-light burning by the dresser, because for all Radley's bravado he was still a bit leery about what might or might not be in the closet.

Mitch laid him down on the bed, then began to help Hester take off the boy's sneakers. "You don't have to bother." Hester untangled a knot in the laces with the ease of experience.

"It's not a bother. Does he use pajamas?" Mitch was already tugging off Radley's jeans. In silence, Hester moved over to Radley's dresser and took out his favorites. Mitch studied the bold imprint of Commander Zark. "Good taste. It always ticked me off they didn't come in my size."

The laugh relaxed her again. Hester bundled the top over Radley's head while Mitch pulled the bottoms over his legs.

"Kid sleeps like a rock."

"I know. He always has. He rarely woke up during the night even as a baby." As a matter of habit, she picked up the rag dog and tucked it in beside him before kissing his cheek. "Don't mention Fido," she murmured. "Radley's a bit sensitive about still sleeping with him."

"I never saw a thing." Then, giving in to the need, he brushed a hand over Radley's hair. "Pretty special, isn't he?"

"Yes, he is."

"So are you." Mitch turned and touched her hair in turn. "Don't close up on me, Hester," he said as she shifted her gaze away from his. "The best way to accept a compliment is to say thank you. Give it a shot."

Embarrassed more by her reaction to him than by his words, she made herself look at him. "Thank you."

"That's a good start. Now let's try it again." He slipped his arms around her. "I've been thinking about kissing you again for almost a week."

"Mitch, I—"

"Did you forget your line?" She'd lifted her hands to his shoulders to hold him off. But her eyes... He much preferred the message he read in them. "That was another compliment. I don't make a habit of thinking about a woman who goes out of her way to avoid me."

"I haven't been. Exactly."

"That's okay, because I figured it was because you couldn't trust yourself around me."

That had her eyes locking on his again, strong and steady. "You have an amazing ego."

"Thanks. Let's try another angle, then." As he spoke, he moved his hand up and down her spine, lighting little fingers of heat. "Kiss me again, and if the bombs don't go off this time I'll figure I was wrong."

"No." But despite herself she couldn't dredge up the will to push him away. "Radley's—"

"Sleeping like a rock, remember?" He touched his lips, very gently, to the swelling under her eye. "And even if he woke up, I don't think the sight of me kissing his mother would give him nightmares."

She started to speak again, but the words were only a sigh as his mouth met hers. He was patient this time, even…tender. Yet the bombs went off. She would have sworn they shook the floor beneath her as she dug her fingers hard into his shoulders.

It was incredible. Impossible. But the need was there, instant, incendiary. It had never been so strong before, not for anyone. Once, when she'd been very young, she'd had a hint of what true, ripe passion could be. And then it had been over. She had come to believe that, like so many other things, such passions were only temporary. But this—this felt like forever.

He'd thought he knew all there was to know about women. Hester was proving him wrong. Even as he felt himself sliding down that warm, soft tunnel of desire, he warned himself not to move too quickly or take too much. There was a hurricane in her, one he had already realized had been channeled and repressed for a long, long time. The first time he'd held her he'd known he had to be the one to free it. But slowly. Carefully. Whether she knew it or not, she was as vulnerable as the child sleeping beside them.

Then her hands were in his hair, pulling him closer. For one mad moment, he dragged her hard against him and let them both taste of what might be.

"Bombs, Hester." She shuddered as he traced his tongue over her ear. "The city's in shambles."

She believed him. With his mouth hot on hers, she believed him. "I have to think."

"Yeah, maybe you do." But he kissed her again. "Maybe we both do." He ran his hands down her body in one long, possessive stroke. "But I have a feeling we're going to come up with the same answer."

Shaken, she backed away. And stumbled over the robot. The crash didn't penetrate Radley's dreams.

"You know, you run into things every time I kiss you." He was going to have to go now or not at all. "I'll pick up the VCR later."

There was a little breath of relief as she nodded. She'd been afraid he'd ask her to sleep with him, and she wasn't at all sure what her answer would have been. "Thank you for everything."

"Good, you're learning." He stroked a finger down her cheek. "Take care of the eye."

Cowardly or not, Hester stayed by Radley's bed until she heard the front door shut. Then, easing down, she put a hand on her sleeping son's shoulder. "Oh, Rad, what have I gotten into?"

Chapter 5

When the phone rang at 7:25, Mitch had his head buried under a pillow. He would have ignored it, but Taz rolled over, stuck his snout against Mitch's cheek and began to grumble in his ear. Mitch swore and shoved at the dog, then snatched up the receiver and dragged it under the pillow.

"What?"

On the other end of the line, Hester bit her lip. "Mitch, it's Hester."

"So?"

"I guess I woke you up."

"Right."

It was painfully obvious that Mitch Dempsey wasn't a morning person. "I'm sorry. I know it's early."

"Is that what you called to tell me?"

"No...I guess you haven't looked out the window yet."

"Honey, I haven't even looked past my eyelids yet."

"It's snowing. We've got about eight inches, and it's not expected to let up until around midday. They're calling for twelve to fifteen inches."

"Who are they?"

Hester switched the phone to her other hand. Her hair was still wet from the shower, and she'd only had a chance to gulp down one cup of coffee. "The National Weather Service."

"Well, thanks for the bulletin."

"Mitch! Don't hang up."

He let out a long sigh, then shifted away from Taz's wet nose. "Is there more news?"

"The schools are closed."

"Whoopee."

She was tempted, very tempted to hang up the phone in his ear. The trouble was, she needed him. "I hate to ask, but I'm not sure I can get Radley all the way over to Mrs. Cohen's. I'd take the day off, but I have back-to-back appointments most of the day. I'm going to try to shift things around and get off early, but—"

"Send him down."

There was the briefest of hesitations. "Are you sure?"

"Did you want me to say no?"

"I don't want to interfere with any plans you had."

"Got any hot coffee?"

"Well, yes, I—"

"Send that, too."

Hester stared at the phone after it clicked in her ear, and tried to remind herself to be grateful.

Radley couldn't have been more pleased. He took Taz for his morning walk, threw snowballs—which the dog, on principle, refused to chase—and rolled in the thick blanket of snow until he was satisfactorily covered.

Since Mitch's supplies didn't run to hot chocolate, Radley raided his mother's supply, then spent the rest of the morning happily involved with Mitch's comic books and his own sketches.

As for Mitch, he found the company appealing rather than distracting. The boy lay sprawled on the floor of his office and, between his reading or sketching, rambled on about whatever struck his fancy. Because he spoke to either Mitch or Taz, and seemed to be content to be answered or not, it suited everyone nicely.

By noon the snow had thinned to occasional flurries, dashing Radley's fantasy about another holiday. In tacit agreement, Mitch pushed away from his drawing board.

"You like tacos?"

"Yeah." Radley turned away from the window. "You know how to make them?"

"Nope. But I know how to buy them. Get your coat, Corporal, we've got places to go."

Radley was struggling into his boots when Mitch walked out with a trio of cardboard tubes. "I've got to stop by the office and drop these off."

Radley's mouth dropped down to his toes. "You mean the place where they make the comics?"

"Yeah." Mitch shrugged into his coat. "I guess I could do it tomorrow if you don't want to bother."

"No, I want to." The boy was up and dragging Mitch's sleeve. "Can we go today? I won't touch anything, I promise. I'll be real quiet, too."

"How can you ask questions if you're quiet?" He pulled the boy's collar up. "Get Taz, will you?"

It was always a bit of a trick, and usually an expensive one, to find a cabdriver who didn't object to a hundred-and-fifty pound dog as a passenger. Once inside, however, Taz sat by the window and morosely watched New York pass by.

"It's a mess out here, isn't it?" The cabbie shot a grin in the rearview mirror, pleased with the tip Mitch had given him in advance. "Don't like the snow myself, but my kids do." He gave a tuneless whistle to accompany the big-band music on his radio. "I guess your boy there wasn't doing any complaining about not going to school. No, sir," the driver continued, without any need for an answer. "Nothing a kid likes better than a day off from school, is there? Even going to the office with your dad's better than school, isn't it, kid?" The cabbie let out a chuckle as he pulled to the curb. The snow there had already turned gray. "Here you go. That's a right nice dog you got there, boy." He gave Mitch his change and continued to whistle as they got out. He had another fare when he pulled away.

"He thought you were my dad," Radley murmured as they walked down the sidewalk.

"Yeah." He started to put a hand on Radley's shoulder, then waited. "Does that bother you?"

The boy looked up, wide-eyed and, for the first time, shy. "No. Does it bother you?"

Mitch bent down so they were at eye level. "Well, maybe it wouldn't if you weren't so ugly."

Radley grinned. As they continued to walk, he slipped his hand into Mitch's. He'd already begun to fantasize about Mitch as his father. He'd done it once before with his second grade teacher, but Mr. Stratham hadn't been nearly as neat as Mitch.

"Is this it?" He stopped as Mitch walked toward a tall, scarred brownstone.

"This is it."

Radley struggled with disappointment. It looked so— ordinary. He'd thought they would at least have the flag of Perth or Ragamond flying. Understanding perfectly, Mitch led him inside.

There was a guard in the lobby who lifted a hand to Mitch and continued to eat his pastrami sandwich. Acknowledging the greeting, Mitch took Radley to an elevator and drew open the iron gate.

"This is pretty neat," Radley decided.

"It's neater when it works." Mitch pushed the button for the fifth floor, which housed the editorial department. "Let's hope for the best."

"Has it ever crashed?" The question was half wary, half hopeful.

"No, but it has been known to go on strike." The car shuddered to a stop on 5. Mitch swung the gate open again. He put a hand on Radley's head. "Welcome to bedlam."

It was precisely that. Radley forgot his disappointment with the exterior in his awe at the fifth floor. There was a reception area of sorts. In any case, there was a desk and a bank of phones manned by a harassed-looking black woman in a Princess Leilah sweatshirt. The walls around her were crammed with posters depicting Universal's most enduring characters: the Human Scorpion, the Velvet Saber, the deadly Black Moth and, of course, Commander Zark.

"How's it going, Lou?"

"Don't ask." She pushed a button on a phone. "I ask you, is it my fault the deli won't deliver his corned beef?"

"If I put him in a good mood, will you dig up some samples for me?"

"Universal Comics, please hold." The receptionist pushed another button. "You put him in a good mood, you've got my firstborn."

"Just the samples, Lou. Put on your helmet, Corporal. This could be messy." He led Radley down a short hall into the big, brightly lit hub of activity. It was a series of cubicles with a high noise level and a look of chaos. Pinned to the corkboard walls were sketches, rude messages and an occasional photograph. In a corner was a pyramid made of empty soda cans. Someone was tossing wadded-up balls of paper at it.

"Scorpion's never been a joiner. What's his motivation for hooking up with Worldwide Law and Justice?"

A woman with pencils poking out of her wild red hair at dangerous angles shifted in her swivel chair. Her eyes, already huge, were accented by layers of liner and mascara. "Look, let's be real. He can't save the world's water supply on his own. He needs someone like Atlantis."

A man sat across from her, eating an enormous pickle. "They hate each other. Ever since they bumped heads over the Triangular Affair."

"That's the point, dummy. They'll have to put personal feelings aside for the sake of mankind. It's a moral." Glancing over, she caught sight of Mitch. "Hey, Dr. Deadly's poisoned the world's water supply. Scorpion's found an antidote. How's he going to distribute it?"

"Sounds like he'd better mend fences with Atlantis," Mitch replied. "What do you think, Radley?"

For a moment, Rad was so tongue-tied he could only stare. Then, taking a deep breath, he let the words blurt out. "I think they'd make a neat team, 'cause they'd always be fighting and trying to show each other up."

"I'm with you, kid." The redhead held out her hand. "I'm M. J. Jones."

"Wow, really?" He wasn't sure whether he was more impressed with meeting M. J. Jones or with discovering she was a woman. Mitch didn't see the point in mentioning that she was one of the few in the business.

"And this grouch over here is Rob Myers. You bring him as a shield, Mitch?" she asked without giving Rob time to swallow his pickle. They'd been married for six years, and she obviously enjoyed frustrating him.

"Do I need one?"

"If you don't have something terrific in those tubes, I'd advise you to slip back out again." She shoved aside a stack of preliminary sketches. "Maloney just quit, defected to Five Star."

"No kidding?"

"Skinner's been muttering about traitors all morning. And the snow didn't help his mood. So if I were you... Oops, too late." Respecting rats who deserted tyrannically captained ships, M.J. turned away and fell into deep discussion with her husband.

"Dempsey, you were supposed to be in two hours ago."

Mitch gave his editor an ingratiating smile. "My alarm didn't go off. This is Radley Wallace, a friend of mine. Rad, this is Rich Skinner."

Radley stared. Skinner looked exactly like Hank Wheeler, the tanklike and overbearing boss of Joe David, alias the Fly. Later, Mitch would tell him that the resemblance was no accident. Radley switched Taz's leash to his other hand.

"Hello, Mr. Skinner. I really like your comics. They're lots better than Five Star. I hardly ever buy Five Star, because the stories aren't as good."

"Right." Skinner dragged a hand through his thinning hair. "Right," he repeated with more conviction. "Don't waste your allowance on Five Star, kid."

"No, sir."

"Mitch, you know you're not supposed to bring that mutt in here."

"You know how Taz loves you." On cue, Taz lifted his head and howled.

Skinner started to swear, then remembered the boy. "You got something in those tubes, or did you just come by to brighten up my dull day?"

"Why don't you take a look for yourself?"

Grumbling, Skinner took the tubes and marched off. As Mitch started to follow, Radley grabbed at his hand. "Is he really mad?"

"Sure. He likes being mad best."

"Is he going to yell at you like Hank Wheeler yells at the Fly?"

"Maybe."

Radley swallowed and buried his hand in Mitch's. "Okay."

Amused, Mitch led Radley into Skinner's office, where the venetian blinds had been drawn to shut off any view of the snow. Skinner unrolled the contents of the first tube and spread them over his already cluttered desk. He didn't sit, but loomed over them while Taz plopped down on the linoleum and went to sleep.

"Not bad," Skinner announced after he had studied the series of sketches and captions. "Not too bad. This new character, Mirium, you have plans to expand her?"

"I'd like to. I think Zark's ready to have his heart tugged from a different direction. Adds more emotional conflict. He loves his wife, but she's his biggest enemy.

Now he runs into this empath and finds himself torn up all over again because he has feelings for her, as well."

"Zark never gets much of a break."

"I think he's the best," Radley piped in, forgetting himself.

Skinner lifted his bushy brows and studied Radley carefully. "You don't think he gets carried away with this honor and duty stuff?"

"Uh-uh." He wasn't sure if he was relieved or disappointed that Skinner wasn't going to yell. "You always know Zark's going to do the right thing. He doesn't have any super powers and stuff, but he's real smart."

Skinner nodded, accepting the opinion. "We'll give your Mirium a shot, Mitch, and see what the reader response is like." He let the papers roll into themselves again. "This is the first time I can remember you being this far ahead of deadline."

"That's because I have an assistant now." Mitch laid a hand on Radley's shoulder.

"Good work, kid. Why don't you take your assistant on a tour?"

It would take Radley weeks to stop talking about his hour at Universal Comics. When they left, he carried a shopping bag full of pencils with Universal's logo, a Mad Matilda mug that had been unearthed from someone's storage locker, a half dozen rejected sketches and a batch of comics fresh off the presses.

"This was the best day in my whole life," Radley said, dancing down the snow-choked sidewalk. "Wait until I show Mom. She won't believe it."

Oddly enough, Mitch had been thinking of Hester himself. He lengthened his stride to keep up with Radley's skipping pace. "Why don't we go by and pay her a visit?"

"Okay." He slipped his hand into Mitch's again. "The bank's not nearly as neat as where you work, though. They don't let anyone play radios or yell at each other, but they have a vault where they keep lots of money— millions of dollars—and they have cameras everywhere so they can see anybody who tries to rob them. Mom's never been in a bank that's been robbed."

Since the statement came out as an apology, Mitch laughed. "We can't all be blessed." He ran a hand over his stomach. He hadn't put anything into it in at least two hours. "Let's grab that taco first."

Inside the staid and unthreatened walls of National Trust, Hester dealt with a stack of paperwork. She enjoyed this part of her job, the organized monotony of it. There was also the challenge of sorting through the facts and figures and translating them into real estate, automobiles, business equipment, stage sets or college funds. Nothing gave her greater pleasure than to be able to stamp a loan with her approval.

She'd had to teach herself not to be softhearted. There were times the facts and figures told you to say no, no matter how earnest the applicant might be. Part of her job was to dictate polite and impersonal letters of refusal. Hester might not have cared for it, but she accepted that responsibility, just as she accepted the occasional irate phone call from the recipient of a loan refusal.

At the moment she was stealing half an hour, with the muffin and coffee that would be her lunch, to put together three loan packages she wanted approved by the board when they met the following day. She had another appointment in fifteen minutes. And, with that and a lack of interruptions, she could just finish. She wasn't particularly pleased when her assistant buzzed through.

"Yes, Kay."

"There's a young man out here to see you, Mrs. Wallace."

"His appointment isn't for fifteen minutes. He'll have to wait."

"No, it isn't Mr. Greenburg. And I don't think he's here for a loan. Are you here for a loan, honey?"

Hester heard the familiar giggle and hurried to the door. "Rad? Is everything all right—oh."

He wasn't alone. Hester realized she'd been foolish to think Radley would have made the trip by himself. Mitch was with him, along with the huge, mild-eyed dog.

"We just ate tacos."

Hester eyed the faint smudge of salsa on Radley's chin. "So I see." She bent to hug him, then glanced up at Mitch. "Is everything okay?"

"Sure. We were just out taking care of a little business and decided to drop by." He took a good long look. She'd covered most of the colorful bruise with makeup. Only a hint of yellow and mauve showed through. "The eye looks better."

"I seem to have passed the crisis."

"That your office?" Without invitation, he strolled over to stick his head inside. "God, how depressing. Maybe you can talk Radley into giving you one of his posters."

"You can have one," Radley agreed immediately. "I got a bunch of them when Mitch took me to Universal. Wow, Mom you should see it. I met M. J. Jones and Rich

Skinner and I saw this room where they keep zillions of comics. See what I got." He held up his shopping bag. "For free. They said I could."

Her first feeling was one of discomfort. It seemed her obligation to Mitch grew with each day. Then she looked down at Radley's eager, glowing face. "Sounds like a pretty great morning."

"It was the best ever."

"Yellow alert," Kay murmured. "Rosen at three o'clock."

It didn't take words to show Mitch that Rosen was a force to be reckoned with. He saw Hester's face poker up instantly as she smoothed a hand over her hair to be sure it was in place.

"Good afternoon, Mrs. Wallace." He glanced meaningfully at the dog, who sniffed the toe of his shoe. "Perhaps you've forgotten that pets are not permitted inside the bank."

"No, sir. My son was just—"

"Your son?" Rosen gave Radley a brief nod. "How do you do, young man. Mrs. Wallace, I'm sure you remember that bank policy frowns on personal visits during working hours."

"Mrs. Wallace, I'll just put these papers on your desk for your signature—when your lunch break is over." Kay shuffled some forms importantly, then winked at Radley.

"Thank you, Kay."

Rosen harrumphed. He couldn't argue with a lunch break, but it was his duty to deal with other infractions of policy. "About this animal—"

Finding Rosen's tone upsetting, Taz pushed his nose against Radley's knee and moaned. "He's mine." Mitch stepped forward, his smile charming, his hand outstretched. Hester had time to think that with that look he could sell Florida swampland. "Mitchell Dempsey II. Hester and I are good friends, very good friends. She's told me so much about you and your bank." He gave Rosen's hand a hearty political shake. "My family has several holdings in New York. Hester's convinced me I should use my influence to have them transfer to National Trust. You might be familiar with some of the family companies. Trioptic, D and H Chemicals, Dempsey Paperworks?"

"Well, of course, of course." Rosen's limp grip on Mitch's hand tightened. "It's a pleasure to meet you, a real pleasure."

"Hester persuaded me to come by and see for myself how efficiently National Trust ticked." He definitely had the man's number, Mitch thought. Dollar signs were already flitting through the pudgy little brain. "I am impressed. Of course, I could have taken Hester's word for it." He gave her stiff shoulder an intimate little squeeze. "She's just a whiz at financial matters. I can tell you, my father would snatch her up as a corporate adviser in a minute. You're lucky to have her."

"Mrs. Wallace is one of our most valued employees."

"I'm glad to hear it. I'll have to bring up National Trust's advantages when I speak with my father."

"I'll be happy to take you on a tour personally. I'm sure you'd like to see the executive offices."

"Nothing I'd like better, but I am a bit pressed for time." If he'd had days stretching out before him, he wouldn't have spent a minute of them touring the stuffy corners of a bank. "Why don't you work up a package I can present at the next board meeting?"

"Delighted." Rosen's face beamed with pleasure.

Bringing an account as large and diversified as Dempsey's to National Trust would be quite a coup for the stuffy bank manager.

"Just send it through Hester. You don't mind playing messenger, do you, darling?" Mitch said cheerfully.

"No," she managed.

"Excellent," Rosen said, the excitement evident in his voice. "I'm sure you'll find we can serve all your family's needs. We are the bank to grow with, after all." He patted Taz's head. "Lovely dog," he said and strode off with a new briskness in his step.

"What a fusty old snob," Mitch decided. "How do you stand it?"

"Would you come into my office a moment?" Hester's voice was as stiff as her shoulders. Recognizing the tone, Radley rolled his eyes at Mitch. "Kay, if Mr. Greenburg comes in, please have him wait."

"Yes, ma'am."

Hester led the way into her office, then closed the door and leaned against it. There was a part of her that wanted to laugh, to throw her arms around Mitch and howl with delight over the way he'd handled Rosen. There was another part, the part that needed a job, a regular salary and employee benefits, that cringed.

"How could you do that?"

"Do what?" Mitch took a look around the office. "The brown carpet has to go. And this paint. What do you call this?"

"Yuk," Radley ventured as he settled in a chair with Taz's head in his lap.

"Yeah, that's it. You know, your work area has a lot to do with your work production. Try that on Rosen."

"I won't be trying anything with Rosen once he finds out what you did. I'll be fired."

"Don't be silly. I never promised my family would move their interests to National Trust. Besides, if he puts together an intriguing enough package, they just might." He shrugged, indicating it made little difference to him. "If it'll make you happier, I can move my personal accounts here. A bank's a bank as far as I'm concerned."

"Damn it." It was very rare for her to swear out loud and with heat. Radley found the fur on Taz's neck of primary interest. "Rosen's got corporate dynasty on his mind, thanks to you. He's going to be furious with me when he finds out you made all that up."

Mitch tapped a hand on a tidy stack of papers. "You're obsessively neat, did you know that? And I didn't make anything up. I could have," he said thoughtfully. "I'm good at it, but there didn't seem to be any reason to."

"Would you stop?" Frustrated, she moved to him to slap his hands away from her work. "All that business about Trioptic and D and H Chemicals." Letting out a long sigh, she dropped down on the edge of the desk. "I know you did it to try to help me, and I appreciate the thought, but—"

"You do?" With a smile, he fingered the lapel of her suit jacket.

"You mean well, I suppose," Hester murmured.

"Sometimes." He leaned a little closer. "You smell much too good for this office."

"Mitch." She put a hand on his chest and glanced nervously at Radley. The boy had an arm hooked around Taz and was already deeply involved in one of his new comic books.

"Do you really think it would be a traumatic experience if the kid saw me kiss you?"

"No." At his slight movement, she pressed harder. "But that's beside the point."

"What *is* the point?" He took his hand from her jacket to fiddle with the gold triangle at her ear.

"The point is I'm going to have to see Rosen and explain to him that you were just…" What was the word she wanted? "Fantasizing."

"I've done a lot of that," he admitted as he moved his thumb down her jawline. "But I'm damned if I think it's any of his business. Want me to tell you the one about you and me in the life raft on the Indian Ocean?"

"No." This time she had to laugh, though the reaction in her stomach had more to do with heat than humor. Curiosity pricked at her so that she met his eyes, then looked quickly away again. "Why don't you and Rad go home? I have another appointment, then I'll go and explain things to Mr. Rosen."

"You're not mad anymore?"

She shook her head and gave in to the urge to touch his face. "You were just trying to help. It was sweet of you."

He imagined she'd have taken the same attitude with Radley if he'd tried to wash the dishes and had smashed her violet-edged china on the floor. Telling himself it was a kind of test, he pressed his lips firmly to hers. He felt each layer of reaction—the shock, the tension, the need. When he drew back, he saw more than indulgence in her eyes. The fire flickered briefly, but with intensity.

"Come on, Rad, your mom has to get back to work. If we're not in the apartment when you get home, we're in the park."

"Fine." Unconsciously she pressed her lips together to seal in the warmth. "Thanks."

"Anytime."

"Bye, Rad, I'll be home soon."

"Okay." He lifted his arms to squeeze her neck. "You're not mad at Mitch anymore?"

"No," she answered in the same carrying whisper. "I'm not mad at anyone."

She was smiling when she straightened, but Mitch saw the worried look in her eye. He paused with his hand on the knob. "You're really going to go up to Rosen and tell him I made that business up?"

"I have to." Then, because she felt guilty about launching her earlier attack, she smiled. "Don't worry. I'm sure I can handle him."

"What if I told you I didn't make it up, that my family founded Trioptic forty-seven years ago?"

Hester lifted a brow. "I'd say don't forget your gloves. It's cold out there."

"Okay, but do yourself a favor before you bare your soul to Rosen. Look it up in *Who's Who.*"

With her hands in her pockets, Hester walked to her office door. From there she saw Radley reach up to put a gloved hand into Mitch's bare one.

"Your son's adorable," Kay said, offering Hester a file. The little skirmish with Rosen had completely changed her opinion of the reserved Mrs. Wallace.

"Thanks." When Hester smiled, Kay's new opinion was cemented. "And I do appreciate you covering for me that way."

"That's no big deal. I don't see what's wrong with your son dropping by for a minute."

"Bank policy," Hester murmured under her breath, and Kay let out a snort.

"Rosen policy, you mean. Beneath that gruff exterior is a gruff interior. But don't worry about him. I happen to know he considers your work production far superior to your predecessor's. As far as he's concerned, that's the bottom line."

Kay hesitated a moment as Hester nodded and flipped through the file. "It's tough raising a kid on your own. My sister has a little girl, she's just five. I know some nights Annie's just knocked out from wearing all the badges, you know."

"Yes, I do."

"My parents want her to move back home so Mom can watch Sarah while Annie works, but Annie's not sure it's the best thing."

"Sometimes it's hard to know if accepting help's right," Hester murmured, thinking of Mitch. "And sometimes we forget to be grateful that someone's there to offer it." She shook herself and tucked the file under her arm. "Is Mr. Greenburg here?"

"Just came in."

"Fine, send him in, Kay." She started for her office, then stopped. "Oh, and Kay, dig me up a copy of *Who's Who.*"

Chapter 6

He was loaded.

Hester was still dazed when she let herself into her apartment. Her downstairs neighbor with the bare feet and the holes in his jeans was an heir to one of the biggest fortunes in the country.

Hester took off her coat and, out of habit, went to the closet to hang it up. The man who spent his days writing the further adventures of Commander Zark came from a family who owned polo ponies and summer houses. Yet he lived on the fourth floor of a very ordinary apartment building in Manhattan.

He was attracted to her. She'd have had to be blind and deaf not to be certain of that, and yet she'd known him for weeks and he hadn't once mentioned his family or his position in an effort to impress her.

Who was he? she wondered. She'd begun to think she had a handle on him, but now he was a stranger all over again.

She had to call him, tell him she was home and to send Radley up. Hester looked at the phone with a feeling of acute embarrassment. She'd lectured him about spinning a tale to Mr. Rosen; then, in her soft-hearted and probably condescending way, she'd forgiven him. It all added up to her doing what she hated most. Making a fool of herself.

Swearing, Hester snatched up the phone. She would have felt much better if she could have rapped Mitchell Dempsey II over the head with it.

She'd dialed half the numbers when she heard Radley's howl of laughter and the sound of stomping feet in the hall outside. She opened the door just as Radley was digging his key out of his pocket.

Both of them were covered with snow. Some that was beginning to melt dripped from Radley's ski cap and boot tops. They looked unmistakably as if they'd been rolling in it.

"Hi, Mom. We've been in the park. We stopped by Mitch's to get my bag, then came on up because we thought you'd be home. Come on out with us."

"I don't think I'm dressed for snow wars."

She smiled and peeled off her son's snow-crusted cap but, Mitch noted, she didn't look up. "So change." He leaned against the doorjamb, ignoring the snow that fell at his feet.

"I built a fort. Please come out and see. I already started a snow warrior, but Mitch said we should check in so you wouldn't worry."

His consideration forced her to look up. "I appreciate that."

He was watching her thoughtfully—too thoughtfully, Hester decided. "Rad says you build a pretty good snow warrior yourself."

"Please, Mom. What if we got a freak heat wave and the snow was all gone tomorrow? It's like the greenhouse effect, you know. I read all about it."

She was trapped and knew it. "All right, I'll change. Why don't you fix Mitch some hot chocolate and warm up?"

"All right!" Radley dropped down on the floor just inside the door. "You have to take off your boots," he told Mitch. "She gets mad if you track up the carpet."

Mitch unbuttoned his coat as Hester walked away. "We wouldn't want to make her mad."

Within fifteen minutes, Hester had changed into corduroys, a bulky sweater and old boots. In place of her red coat was a blue parka that showed some wear. Mitch kept one hand on Taz's leash and the other in his pocket as they walked across to the park. He couldn't say why he enjoyed seeing her dressed casually with Radley's hand joined tight with hers. He couldn't say for certain why he'd wanted to spend this time with her, but it had been he who'd planted the idea of another outing in Radley's head, and he who'd suggested that they go up together to persuade her to come outside.

He liked the winter. Mitch took a deep gulp of cold air as they walked through the soft, deep snow of Central Park. Snow and stinging air had always appealed to him, particularly when the trees were draped in white and there were snow castles to be built.

When he'd been a boy, his family had often wintered in the Caribbean, away from what his mother had termed the "mess and inconvenience." He'd picked up an affection for scuba and white sand, but had never felt that a palm tree replaced a pine at Christmas.

The winters he'd liked best had been spent in his uncle's country home in New Hampshire, where there'd been woods to walk in and hills to sled. Oddly enough, he'd been thinking of going back there for a few weeks— until the Wallaces popped up two floors above, that is. He hadn't realized until today that he'd shuffled those plans to the back of his mind as soon as he'd seen Hester and her son.

Now she was embarrassed, annoyed and uncomfortable. Mitch turned to study her profile. Her cheeks were already rosy with cold, and she'd made certain that Radley walked between them. He wondered if she realized how obvious her strategies were. She didn't use the boy, not in the way some parents used their offspring for their own ambitions or purposes. He respected her for that more than he could have explained. But she had, by putting Radley in the center, relegated Mitch to the level of her son's friend.

And so he was, Mitch thought with a smile. But he'd be damned if he was going to let it stop there.

"There's the fort. See?" Radley tugged on Hester's hand, then let it go to run, too impatient to wait any longer.

"Pretty impressive, huh?" Before she could avoid it, Mitch draped a casual arm over her shoulder. "He's really got a knack."

Hester tried to ignore the warmth and pressure of his arm as she looked at her son's handiwork. The walls of the fort were about two feet high, smooth as stone, with one end sloping nearly a foot higher in the shape of a round tower. They'd made an arched doorway high enough for Radley to crawl through. When Hester reached the fort, she saw him pass through on his hands and knees and pop up inside, his arms held high.

"It's terrific, Rad. I imagine you had a great deal to do with it," she said quietly to Mitch.

"Here and there." Then he smiled, as though he was laughing at himself. "Rad's a better architect than I'll ever be."

"I'm going to finish my snow warrior." Belly down, Rad crawled through the opening again. "Build one, Mom, on the other side of the fort. They'll be the sentries." Rad began to pack and smooth snow on his already half-formed figure. "You help her, Mitch, 'cause I've got a head start."

"Fair's fair." Mitch scooped up a handful of snow. "Any objections to teamwork?"

"No, of course not." Still avoiding giving him a straight look, Hester knelt in the snow. Mitch dropped the handful of snow on her head.

"I figured that was the quickest way to get you to look at me." She glared, then began to push the snow into a mound. "Problem, Mrs. Wallace?"

Seconds ticked by as she pushed at the snow. "I got a copy of *Who's Who*."

"Oh?" Mitch knelt down beside her.

"You were telling the truth."

"I've been known to from time to time." He shoved some more snow on the mound she was forming. "So?"

Hester frowned and punched the snow into shape. "I feel like an idiot."

"I told the truth, and you feel like an idiot." Patiently Mitch smoothed over the base she was making. "Want to explain the correlation?"

"You let me lecture you."

"It's kinda hard to stop you when you get rolling."

Hester began to dig out snow with both hands to form the legs. "You let me think you were some poor, eccentric Good Samaritan. I was even going to offer to put patches on your jeans."

"No kidding." Incredibly touched, Mitch caught her chin in his snow-covered glove. "That's sweet."

There was no way she was going to let his charm brush away the discomfort of her embarrassment. "The fact is, you're a rich, eccentric Good Samaritan." She shoved his hand away and began to gather snow for the torso.

"Does this mean you won't patch my jeans?"

Hester's long-suffering breath came out in a white plume. "I don't want to talk about it."

"Yes, you do." Always helpful, Mitch packed on more snow and succeeded in burying her up to the elbows. "Money shouldn't bother you, Hester. You're a banker."

"Money doesn't bother me." She yanked her arms free and tossed two good-sized hunks of snow into his face. Because she had to fight back a giggle, she turned her back. "I just wish the situation had been made clear earlier, that's all."

Mitch wiped the snow from his face, then scooped up more, running his tongue along the inside of his lip. He'd had a lot of experience in forming what he considered the ultimate snowball. "What's the situation, Mrs. Wallace?"

"I wish you'd stop calling me that in that tone of voice." She turned, just in time to get the snowball right between the eyes.

"Sorry." Mitch smiled, then began to brush off her coat. "Must've slipped. About this situation…"

"There is no situation between us." Before she realized it, she'd shoved him hard enough to send him sprawling in the snow. "Excuse me." Her laughter came out in hitches that were difficult to swallow. "I didn't mean to do that. I don't know what it is about you that makes me do things like that." He sat up and continued to stare at her. "I *am* sorry," she repeated. "I think it's best if we just let this other business drop. Now, if I help you up, will you promise not to retaliate?"

"Sure." Mitch held out a gloved hand. The moment he closed it over hers, he yanked her forward. Hester went down, face first. "I don't *always* tell the truth, by the way." Before she could respond, he wrapped his arms around her and began to roll.

"Hey, you're supposed to be building another sentry."

"In a minute," Mitch called to Rad, while Hester tried to catch her breath. "I'm teaching your mom a new game. Like it?" he asked her as he rolled her underneath him again.

"Get off me. I've got snow down my sweater, down my jeans—"

"No use trying to seduce me here. I'm stronger than that."

"You're crazy." She tried to sit up, but he pinned her beneath him.

"Maybe." He licked a trace of snow from her cheek and felt her go utterly still. "But I'm not stupid." His voice had changed. It wasn't the easy, carefree voice of her neighbor now, but the slow, soft tones of a lover. "You feel something for me. You may not like it, but you feel it."

It wasn't the unexpected exercise that had stolen her breath, and she knew it. His eyes were so blue in the lowering sunlight, and his hair glistened with a dusting of snow. And his face was close, temptingly close. Yes, she felt something, she felt something almost from the first minute she saw him, but she wasn't stupid, either.

"If you let go of my arms I'll show you just how I feel."

"Why do I think I wouldn't like it? Never mind." He brushed his lips over hers before she could answer. "Hester, the situation is this. You have feelings for me that have nothing to do with my money, because you didn't know until a few hours ago that I had any to speak of. Some of those feelings don't have anything to do with the fact that I'm fond of your son. They're very personal, as in you and me."

He was right, absolutely and completely right. She could have murdered him for it. "Don't tell me how I feel."

"All right." After he spoke, he surprised her by rising and helping her to her feet. Then he took her in his arms again. "I'll tell you how *I* feel then. I care for you—more than I'd counted on."

She paled beneath her cold-tinted cheeks. There was more than a hint of desperation in her eyes as she shook her head and tried to back away. "Don't say that to me."

"Why not?" He struggled against impatience as he lowered his brow to hers. "You'll have to get used to it. I did."

"I don't want this. I don't want to feel this way."

He tipped her head back, and his eyes were very serious. "We'll have to talk about that."

"No. There's nothing to talk about. This is just getting out of hand."

"It's not out of hand yet." He tangled his fingers in the tips of her hair, but his eyes never left hers. "I'm almost certain it will be before long, but it isn't yet. You're too smart and too strong for that."

She'd be able to breathe easier in a moment. She was sure of it. She'd be able to breathe easier as soon as she was away from him. "No, I'm not afraid of you." Oddly, she discovered that much was true.

"Then kiss me." His voice was coaxing now, gentle. "It's nearly twilight. Kiss me, once, before the sun goes down."

She found herself leaning into him, lifting her lips up and letting her lashes fall without questioning why it should seem so right, so natural to do as he asked. There would be questions later, though she was certain the answers wouldn't come as easily. For now, she touched her lips to his and found them cool, cool and patient.

The world was all ice and snow, forts and fairylands, but his lips were real. They fit on hers firmly, warming her soft, sensitive skin while the racing of her heart heated her body. There was the rushing whoosh of traffic in the distance, but closer, more intimate, was the whisper of her coat sliding against his as they pressed tighter together.

He wanted to coax, to persuade, and just once to see her lips curve into a smile as he left them. He knew there were times when a man who preferred action and impulse had to go step by step. Especially when the prize at the top was precious.

He hadn't been prepared for her, but he knew he could accept what was happening between them with more ease than she. There were still secrets tucked inside her, hurts that had only partially healed. He knew better than to wish for the power to wipe all that aside. How she'd lived and what had happened to her were all part of the woman she was. The woman he was very, very close to falling in love with.

So he would take it step by step, Mitch told himself as he placed her away from him. And he would wait.

"That might have cleared up a few points, but I think we still have to talk." He took her hand to keep her close another moment. "Soon."

"I don't know." Had she ever been this confused before? She'd thought she'd left these feelings, these doubts behind her long ago.

"I'll come up or you can come down, but we'll talk."

He was jockeying her into a corner, one she knew she'd be backed into sooner or later. "Not tonight," she said, despising herself for being a coward. "Rad and I have a lot to do."

"Procrastination's not your style."

"It is this time," she murmured, and turned away quickly. "Radley, we have to go in."

"Look, Mom, I just finished, isn't it great?" He stood back to show off his warrior. "You hardly started yours."

"Maybe we'll finish it tomorrow." She walked to him quickly and took him by the hand. "We have to go in and fix dinner now."

"But can't we just—"

"No, it's nearly dark."

"Can Mitch come?"

"No, he can't." She shot a glance over her shoulder as they walked. He was hardly more than a shadow now, standing beside her son's fort. "Not tonight."

Mitch put a hand on his dog's head as Taz whined and started forward. "Nope. Not this time."

* * *

There didn't seem any way of avoiding him, Hester thought as she started down to Mitch's apartment at her son's request. She had to admit it had been foolish of her to try. On the surface, anyone would think that Mitch Dempsey was the solution to many of her problems. He was genuinely fond of Radley, and gave her son both a companion and a safe and convenient place to stay while she worked. His time was flexible, and he was very generous with it.

The truth was, he'd complicated her life. No matter how much she tried to look at him as Radley's friend or her slightly odd neighbor, he brought back feelings she hadn't experienced in almost ten years. Fluttery pulses and warm surges were things Hester had attributed to the very young or the very optimistic. She'd stopped being either when Radley's father had left them.

In all the years that had followed that moment, she'd devoted herself to her son—to making the best possible home for him, to make his life as normal and well balanced as possible. If Hester the woman had gotten lost somewhere in the shuffle, Radley's mother figured it was a fair exchange. Now Mitch Dempsey had come along and made her feel and, worse, had made her wish.

Taking a deep breath, Hester knocked on Mitch's door. Radley's friend's door, she told herself firmly. The only reason she was here was because Radley had been so excited about showing her something. She wasn't here to see Mitch; she wasn't hoping he would reach out and run his fingertips along her cheek as he sometimes did. Hester's skin warmed at the thought of it.

Hester linked her hands together and concentrated on Radley. She would see whatever it was he was so anxious for her to see, and then she would get them both back upstairs to their own apartment—and safety.

Mitch answered the door. He wore a sweatshirt sporting a decal of a rival super hero across the chest, and sweatpants with a gaping hole in one knee. There was a towel slung over his shoulders. He used one end of it to dry the sweat off his face.

"You haven't been out running in this weather?" she asked before she'd allowed herself to think, immediately regretting the question and the obvious concern in her voice.

"No." He took her hand to draw her inside. She smelled like the springtime that was still weeks and weeks away. Her dark blue suit gave her a look of uncreased professionalism he found ridiculously sexy. "Weights," he told her. The fact was, he'd been lifting weights a great deal since he'd met Hester Wallace. Mitch considered it the second best way to decrease tension and rid the body of excess energy.

"Oh." So that explained the strength she'd felt in his arms. "I didn't realize you went in for that sort of thing."

"The Mr. Macho routine?" he said, laughing. "No, I don't, actually. The thing is, if I don't work out regularly, my body turns into a toothpick. It's not a pretty sight." Because she looked nervous enough to jump out of her skin, Mitch couldn't resist. He leered and flexed his arm. "Want to feel my pecs?"

"I'll pass, thanks." Hester kept her hands by her sides. "Mr. Rosen sent this package." She slipped the fat bank portfolio out from where she'd held it at her side. "Just remember, you asked for it."

"So I did." Mitch accepted it, then tossed it on a pile

of magazines on the coffee table. "Tell him I'll pass it along."

"And will you?"

He lifted a brow. "I usually keep my word."

She was certain of that. It reminded her that he'd said they would talk, and soon. "Radley called and said there was something he had to show me."

"He's in the office. Want some coffee?"

It was such a casual offer, so easy and friendly, that she nearly agreed. "Thanks, but we really can't stay. I had to bring some paperwork home with me."

"Fine. Just go on in. I need a drink."

"Mom!" The minute she stepped into the office, Radley jumped up and grabbed her hands. "Isn't it great? It's the neatest present I ever got in my life." With his hands still locked on hers, Radley dragged her over to a scaled-down drawing board.

It wasn't a toy. Hester could see immediately that it was top-of-the-line equipment, if child-sized. The small swivel stool was worn, but the seat was leather. Radley already had graph paper tacked to the board, and with compass and ruler had begun what appeared to be a set of blueprints.

"Is this Mitch's?"

"It was, but he said I could use it now, for as long as I wanted. See, I'm making the plans for a space station. This is the engine room. And over here and here are the living quarters. It's going to have a greenhouse, sort of like the one they had in this movie Mitch let me watch. Mitch showed me how to draw things to scale with these squares."

"I see." Pride in her son overshadowed any tension as she crouched down for a better look. "You catch on fast, Rad. This is wonderful. I wonder if NASA has an opening."

He chuckled, facedown, as he did when he was both pleased and embarrassed. "Maybe I could be an engineer."

"You can be anything you want." She pressed a kiss to his temple. "If you keep drawing like this, I'm going to need an interpreter to know what you're doing. All these tools." She picked up a square. "I guess you know what they're for."

"Mitch told me. He uses them sometimes when he draws."

"Oh?" She turned the square over in her hand. It looked so—professional.

"Even comic art needs a certain discipline," Mitch said from the doorway. He held a large glass of orange juice, which was already half-gone. Hester rose. He looked—virile, she realized.

There was a faint vee of dampness down the center of his shirt. His hair had been combed through with no more than his fingers and, not for the first time, he hadn't bothered to shave off the night's growth of beard. Beside her, her son was happily remodeling his blueprint.

Virile, dangerous, nerve-wracking he might be, but a kinder man she'd never met. Concentrating on that, Hester stepped forward. "I don't know how to thank you."

"Rad already has."

She nodded, then laid a hand on Radley's shoulder. "You finish that up, Rad. I'll be in the other room with Mitch."

Hester walked into the living room. It was, as she'd come to expect, cluttered and chaotic. Taz nosed around the carpet looking for cookie crumbs. "I thought I knew

Rad inside and out," Hester began. "But I didn't know a drawing board would mean so much to him. I guess I would have thought him too young to appreciate it."

"I told you once he had a natural talent."

"I know." She gnawed on her lip. She wished she had accepted the offer of coffee so that she'd have something to do with her hands. "Rad told me that you were giving him some art lessons. You've done more for him than I ever could have expected. Certainly much more than you're obligated to."

He gave her a long, searching look. "It hasn't got anything to do with obligation. Why don't you sit down?"

"No." She linked her hands together, then pulled them apart again. "No, that's all right."

"Would you rather pace?"

It was the ease of his smile that had her unbending another notch. "Maybe later. I just wanted to tell you how grateful I am. Rad's never had..." A father. The words had nearly come out before Hester had swallowed them in a kind of horror. She hadn't meant that, she assured herself. "He's never had anyone to give him so much attention—besides me." She let out a little breath. That was what she'd meant to say. Of course it was. "The drawing board was very generous. Rad said it was yours."

"My father had it made for me when I was about Rad's age. He'd hoped I'd stop sketching monsters and start doing something productive." He said it without bitterness, but with a trace of amusement. Mitch had long since stopped resenting his parents' lack of understanding.

"It must mean a great deal to you for you to have kept it all this time. I know Rad loves it, but shouldn't you keep it for your own children?"

Mitch took a sip of juice and glanced around the apartment. "I don't seem to have any around at the moment."

"But still—"

"Hester, I wouldn't have given it to him if I hadn't wanted him to have it. It's been in storage for years, gathering dust. It gives me a kick to see Rad putting it to use." He finished off the juice, then set the glass down before he crossed to her. "The present's for Rad, with no strings attached to his mother."

"I know that, I didn't mean—"

"No, I don't think you did, exactly." He was watching her now, unsmiling, with that quiet intensity he drew out at unexpected moments. "I doubt if it was even in the front of your mind, but it was milling around in there somewhere."

"I don't think you're using Radley to get to me, if that's what you mean."

"Good." He did as she'd imagined he might, and ran a finger along her jawline. "Because the fact is, Mrs. Wallace, I'd like the kid without you, or you without the kid. It just so happens that in this case, you came as a set."

"That's just it. Radley and I are a unit. What affects him affects me."

Mitch tilted his head as a new thought began to dawn. "I think I'm getting a signal here. You don't think I'm playing pals and buddies with Rad to get Rad's mother between the sheets?"

"Of course not." She drew back sharply, looking toward the office. "If I had thought that, Radley wouldn't be within ten feet of you."

"But…" He laid his arms on her shoulders, linking his hands loosely behind her neck. "You're wondering if your feelings for me might be residual of Radley's feelings."

"I never said I had feelings for you."

"Yes, you did. And you say it again every time I manage to get this close. No, don't pull away, Hester." He tightened his hands. "Let's be upfront. I want to sleep with you. It has nothing to do with Rad, and less than I figured to do with the primal urge I felt the first time I saw your legs." Her eyes lifted warily to his, but held. "It has to do with the fact that I find you attractive in a lot of ways. You're smart, you're strong and you're stable. It might not sound very romantic, but the fact is, your stability is very alluring. I've never had a lot of it myself."

He brushed his linked hands up the back of her neck. "Now, maybe you're not ready to take a step like this at the moment. But I'd appreciate it if you'd take a straight look at what you want, at what you feel."

"I'm not sure I can. You only have yourself. I have Rad. Whatever I do, whatever decisions I make, ripple down to affect him. I promised myself years ago that he would never be hurt by another one of his parents. I'm going to keep that promise."

He wanted to demand that she tell him about Radley's father then and there, but the boy was just in the next room. "Let me tell you what I believe. You could never make a decision that could hurt Rad. But I do think you could make one that could hurt yourself. I want to be with you, Hester, and I don't think our being together is going to hurt Radley."

"It's all done." Radley streamed out of the office, the graph paper in both hands. Hester immediately started to move away. To prove a point to both of them, Mitch held her where she was. "I want to take it and show Josh tomorrow. Okay?"

Knowing a struggle would be worse than submission, Hester stayed still with Mitch's arms on her shoulders. "Sure you can."

Radley studied them a moment. He'd never seen a man with his arms around his mother, except his grandpa or his uncle. He wondered if this made Mitch like family. "I'm going over to Josh's tomorrow afternoon and I'm staying for a sleepover. We're going to stay up all night."

"Then I'll just have to look after your mom, won't I?"

"I guess." Radley began to roll the graph paper into a tube as Mitch had shown him.

"Radley knows I don't have to be looked after."

Ignoring her, Mitch continued to speak to Radley. "How about if I took your mom on a date?"

"You mean get dressed up and go to a restaurant and stuff?"

"Something like that."

"That'd be okay."

"Good. I'll pick her up at seven."

"I really don't think—"

"Seven's not good?" Mitch interrupted Hester. "All right, seven-thirty, but that's as late as it gets. If I don't eat by eight I get nasty." He gave Hester a quick kiss on the temple before releasing her. "Have a good time at Josh's."

"I will." Radley gathered up his coat and backpack. Then he walked to Mitch and hugged him. The words that had been on the tip of Hester's tongue dried up. "Thanks for the drawing board and everything. It's really neat."

"You're welcome. See you Monday." He waited until Hester was at the door. "Seven-thirty."

She nodded and closed the door quietly behind her.

Chapter 7

She could have made excuses, but the fact was, Hester didn't want to. She knew Mitch had hustled her into this dinner date, but as she crossed the wide leather belt at her waist and secured it, she discovered she didn't mind. In fact, she was relieved that he'd made the decision for her—almost.

The nerves were there. She stood in front of the bureau mirror and took a few long, deep breaths. Yes, there were nerves, but they weren't the stomach-roiling sort she experienced when she went on job interviews. Though she wasn't quite sure where her feelings lay when it came to Mitch Dempsey, she was glad to be certain she wasn't afraid.

Picking up her brush, she studied her reflection as she smoothed her hair. She didn't look nervous, Hester decided. That was another point in her favor. The black wool dress was flattering with its deep cowl neck and nipped-in waist. The red slash of belt accented the line before the skirt flared out. For some reason, red gave her confidence. She considered the bold color another kind of defense for a far-from-bold person.

She fixed oversized scarlet swirls at her ears. Like most of her wardrobe, the dress was practical. It could go to the office, to a PTA meeting or a business lunch. Tonight, she thought with a half smile, it was going on a date.

Hester tried not to dwell on how long it had been since she'd been on a date, but comforted herself with the fact that she knew Mitch well enough to keep up an easy conversation through an evening. An adult evening. As much as she adored Radley, she couldn't help but look forward to it.

When she heard the knock, she gave herself a last quick check, then went to answer. The moment she opened the door, her confidence vanished.

He didn't look like Mitch. Gone were the scruffy jeans and baggy sweatshirts. This man wore a dark suit with a pale blue shirt. And a tie. The top button of the shirt was open, and the tie of dark blue silk was knotted loose and low, but it was still a tie. He was clean-shaven, and though some might have thought he still needed a trim, his hair waved dark and glossy over his ears and the collar of his shirt.

Hester was suddenly and painfully shy.

She looked terrific. Mitch felt a moment's awkwardness himself as he looked at her. Her evening shoes put her to within an inch of his height so that they were eye to eye. It was the wariness in hers that had him relaxing with a smile.

"Looks like I picked the right color." He offered her an armful of red roses.

She knew it was foolish for a woman of her age to be flustered by something as simple as flowers. But her heart rushed up to her throat as she gathered them to her.

"Did you forget your line again?" he murmured.

"My line?"

"Thank you."

The scent of the roses flowed around her, soft and sweet. "Thank you."

He touched one of the petals. He already knew her skin felt much the same. "Now you're supposed to put them in water."

Feeling a great deal more than foolish, Hester stepped back. "Of course. Come in."

"The apartment feels different without Rad," he commented when Hester went to get a vase.

"I know. Whenever he goes to a sleepover, it takes me hours to get used to the quiet." He'd followed her into the kitchen. Hester busied herself with arranging the roses. I am a grown woman, she reminded herself, and just because I haven't been on a date since high school doesn't mean I don't remember how.

"What do you usually do when you have a free evening?"

"Oh, I read, watch a late movie." She turned with the vase and nearly collided with him. Water sloshed dangerously close to the top of the vase.

"The eye's barely noticeable now." He lifted a fingertip to where the bruise had faded to a shadow.

"It wasn't such a calamity." Her throat had tightened. Grown woman or not, she found herself enormously glad that the vase of roses was between them. "I'll get my coat."

After carrying the roses to the table beside the sofa,

Hester went to the closet. She slipped one arm into the sleeve before Mitch came up behind her to help her finish. He made such an ordinary task sensual, she thought as she stared straight ahead. He brushed his hands over her shoulders, lingered, then trailed them down her arms before bringing them up again to gently release her hair from the coat collar.

Hester's hands were balled into fists as she turned her head. "Thank you."

"You're welcome." With his hands on her shoulders, Mitch turned her to face him. "Maybe you'll feel better if we get this out of the way now." He kept his hands where they were and touched his lips, firm and warm, to hers. Hester's rigid hands went lax. There was nothing demanding or passionate in the kiss. It moved her unbearably with its understanding.

"Feel better?" Mitch murmured.

"I'm not sure."

With a laugh, he touched his lips to hers again. "Well, I do." Linking his hand with hers, he walked to the door.

The restaurant was French, subdued and very exclusive. The pale flowered walls glowed in the quiet light and the flicker of candles. Diners murmured their private conversations over linen cloths and crystal stemware. The hustle and bustle of the streets were shut out by beveled glass doors.

"Ah, Monsieur Dempsey, we haven't seen you in some time." The maitre d' stepped forward to greet him.

"You know I always come back for your snails."

With a laugh, the maitre d' waved a waiter aside.

"Good evening, *mademoiselle*. I'll take you to your table."

The little booth was candlelit and secluded, a place for hand-holding and intimate secrets. Hester's leg brushed Mitch's as they settled.

"The sommelier will be right with you. Enjoy your evening."

"No need to ask if you've been here before."

"From time to time I get tired of frozen pizza. Would you like champagne?"

"I'd love it."

He ordered a bottle, pleasing the wine steward with the vintage. Hester opened her menu and sighed over the elegant foods. "I'm going to remember this the next time I'm biting into half a tuna sandwich between appointments."

"You like your job?"

"Very much." She wondered if *soufflé de crabe* was what it sounded like. "Rosen can be a pain, but he does push you to be efficient."

"And you like being efficient."

"It's important to me."

"What else is, other than Rad?"

"Security." She looked over at him with a half smile. "I suppose that has to do with Rad. The truth is, anything that's been important to me over the last few years has to do with Rad."

She glanced up as the steward brought the wine and began his routine for Mitch's approval. Hester watched the wine rise in her fluted glass, pale gold and frothy. "To Rad, then," Mitch said as he lifted his glass to touch hers. "And his fascinating mother."

Hester sipped, a bit stunned that anything could taste so good. She'd had champagne before, but like everything that had to do with Mitch, it hadn't been quite like this. "I've never considered myself fascinating."

"A beautiful woman raising a boy on her own in one of the toughest cities in the world fascinates me." He sipped and grinned. "Added to that, you do have terrific legs, Hester."

She laughed, and even when he slipped his hand over hers, felt no embarrassment. "So you said before. They're long, anyway. I was taller than my brother until he was out of high school. It infuriated him, and I had to live down the name Stretch."

"Mine was String."

"String?"

"You know those pictures of the eighty-pound weakling? That was me."

Over the rim of her glass, Hester studied the way he filled out the suit jacket. "I don't believe it."

"One day, if I'm drunk enough, I'll show you pictures."

Mitch ordered in flawless French that had Hester staring. This was the comic-book writer, she thought, who built snow forts and talked to his dog. Catching the look, Mitch lifted a brow. "I spent a couple of summers in Paris during high school."

"Oh." It reminded her forcefully where he'd come from. "You said you didn't have any brothers or sisters. Do your parents live in New York?"

"No." He broke off a hunk of crusty French bread. "My mother zips in from time to time to shop or go to the theater, and my father might come in occasionally on business, but New York isn't their style. They still live most of the year in Newport, where I grew up."

"Oh, Newport. We drove through once when I was a kid. We'd always take these rambling car vacations in the summer." She tucked her hair behind her ear in an unconscious gesture that gave him a tantalizing view of her throat. "I remember the houses, the enormous mansions with the pillars and flowers and ornamental trees. We even took pictures. It was hard to believe anyone really lived there." Then she caught herself up abruptly and glanced over at Mitch's amused face. "You did."

"It's funny. I spent some time with binoculars watching the tourists in the summer. I might have homed in on your family."

"We were the ones in the station wagon with the suitcases strapped to the roof."

"Sure, I remember you." He offered her a piece of bread. "I envied you a great deal."

"Really?" She paused with her butter knife in midair. "Why?"

"Because you were going on vacation and eating hot dogs. You were staying in motels with soda machines outside the door and playing car bingo between cities."

"Yes," she murmured. "I suppose that sums it up."

"I'm not pulling poor-little-rich boy," he added when he saw the change in her eyes. "I'm just saying that having a big house isn't necessarily better than having a station wagon." He added more wine to her glass. "In any case, I finished my rebellious money-is-beneath-me stage a long time ago."

"I don't know if I can believe that from someone who lets dust collect on his Louis Quinze."

"That's not rebellion, that's laziness."

"Not to mention sinful," she put in. "It makes me itch for a polishing cloth and lemon oil."

"Any time you want to rub my mahogany, feel free."

She lifted a brow when he smiled at her. "So what did you do during your rebellious stage?"

Her fingertips grazed his. It was one of the few times she'd touched him without coaxing. Mitch lifted his gaze from their hands to her face. "You really want to know?"

"Yes."

"Then we'll make a deal. One slightly abridged life story for another."

It wasn't the wine that was making her reckless, Hester knew, but him. "All right. Yours first."

"We'll start off by saying my parents wanted me to be an architect. It was the only practical and acceptable profession they could see me using my drawing abilities for. The stories I made up didn't really appall them, they merely baffled them—so they were easily ignored. Straight out of high school, I decided to sacrifice my life to art."

Their appetizers were served. Mitch sighed approvingly over his escargots.

"So you came to New York?"

"No, New Orleans. At that time my money was still in trusts, though I doubt I would have used it, in any case. Since I refused to use my parents' financial backing, New Orleans was as close to Paris as I could afford to get. God, I loved it. I starved, but I loved the city. Those dripping, steamy afternoons, the smell of the river. It was my first great adventure. Want one of these? They're incredible."

"No, I—"

"Come on, you'll thank me." He lifted his fork to her lips. Reluctantly, Hester parted them and accepted.

"Oh." The flavor streamed, warm and exotic, over her tongue. "It's not what I expected."

"The best things usually aren't."

She lifted her glass and wondered what Radley's reaction would be when she told him she'd eaten a snail. "So what did you do in New Orleans?"

"I set up an easel in Jackson Square and made my living sketching tourists and selling watercolors. For three years I lived in one room where I baked in the summer and froze in the winter and considered myself one lucky guy."

"What happened?"

"There was a woman. I thought I was crazy about her and vice versa. She modeled for me when I was going through my Matisse period. You should have seen me then. My hair was about your length, and I wore it pulled back and fastened with a leather thong. I even had a gold earring in my left ear."

"You wore an earring?"

"Don't smirk, they're very fashionable now. I was ahead of my time." Appetizers were cleared away to make room for green salads. "Anyway, we were going to play house in my miserable little room. One night, when I'd had a little too much wine, I told her about my parents and how they'd never understood my artistic drive. She got absolutely furious."

"She was angry with your parents?"

"You are sweet," he said unexpectedly, and kissed her hand. "No, she was angry with me. I was rich and hadn't told her. I had piles of money and expected her to be satisfied with one filthy little room in the Quarter where she had to cook red beans and rice on a hot plate. The funny thing was she really cared for me when she'd thought I was poor, but when she found out I wasn't, and that I didn't intend to use what was available to me—and, by association, to her—she was infuriated.

We had one hell of a fight, where she let me know what she really thought of me and my work."

Hester could picture him, young, idealistic and struggling. "People say things they don't mean when they're angry."

He lifted her hand and kissed her fingers. "Yes, very sweet." His hand remained on hers as he continued. "Anyway, she left and gave me the opportunity to take stock of myself. For three years I'd been living day to day, telling myself I was a great artist whose time was coming. The truth was I wasn't a great artist. I was a clever one, but I'd never be a great one. So I left New Orleans for New York and commercial art. I was good. I worked fast tucked in my little cubicle and generally made the client happy—and I was miserable. But my credentials there got me a spot at Universal, originally as an inker, then as an artist. And then—" he lifted his glass in salute "—there was Zark. The rest is history."

"You're happy." She turned her hand under his so their palms met. "It shows. Not everyone is as content with themselves as you are, as at ease with himself and what he does."

"It took me awhile."

"And your parents? Have you reconciled with them?"

"We came to the mutual understanding that we'd never understand each other. But we're family. I have my stock portfolio, so they can tell their friends the comic-book business is something that amuses me. Which is true enough."

Mitch ordered another bottle of champagne with the main course. "Now it's your turn."

She smiled and let the delicate soufflé melt on her tongue. "Oh, I don't have anything so exotic as an artist's garret in New Orleans. I had a very average childhood with a very average family. Board games on Saturday nights, pot roast on Sundays. Dad had a good job, Mom stayed home and kept the house. We loved each other very much, but didn't always get along. My sister was very outgoing, head cheerleader, that sort of thing. I was miserably shy."

"You're still shy," Mitch murmured as he wound his fingers around hers.

"I didn't think it showed."

"In a very appealing way. What about Rad's father?" He felt her hand stiffen in his. "I've wanted to ask, Hester, but we don't have to talk about it now if it upsets you."

She drew her hand from his to reach for her glass. The champagne was cold and crisp. "It was a long time ago. We met in high school. Radley looks a great deal like his father, so you can understand that he was very attractive. He was also just a little wild, and I found that magnetic."

She moved her shoulders a little, restlessly, but was determined to finish what she'd started. "I really was painfully shy and a bit withdrawn, so he seemed like something exciting to me, even a little larger than life. I fell desperately in love with him the first time he noticed me. It was as simple as that. In any case, we went together for two years and were married a few weeks after graduation. I wasn't quite eighteen and was absolutely sure that marriage was going to be one adventure after another."

"And it wasn't?" he asked when she paused.

"For a while it was. We were young, so it never seemed terribly important that Allan moved from one job to another, or quit altogether for weeks at a time. Once he sold the living room set that my parents had given us as a wedding present so that we could take a trip to Jamaica. It seemed impetuous and romantic, and at that time we didn't have any responsibilities except to ourselves. Then I got pregnant."

She paused again and, looking back, remembered her own excitement and wonder and fear at the idea of carrying a child. "I was thrilled. Allan got a tremendous kick out of it and started buying strollers and high chairs on credit. Money was tight, but we were optimistic, even when I had to cut down to part-time work toward the end of my pregnancy and then take maternity leave after Radley was born. He was beautiful." She laughed a little. "I know all mothers say that about their babies, but he was honestly the most beautiful, the most precious thing I'd ever seen. He changed my life. He didn't change Allan's."

She toyed with the stem of her glass and tried to work out in her mind what she hadn't allowed herself to think about for a very long time. "I couldn't understand it at the time, but Allan resented having the burden of responsibility. He hated it that we couldn't just stroll out of the apartment and go to the movies or go dancing whenever we chose. He was still unbelievably reckless with money, and because of Rad I had to compensate."

"In other words," Mitch said quietly, "you grew up."

"Yes." It surprised her that he saw that so quickly, and it relieved her that he seemed to understand. "Allan wanted to go back to the way things were, but we weren't children anymore. As I look back, I can see that he was jealous of Radley, but at the time I just wanted him to grow up, to be a father, to take charge. At twenty he was still the sixteen-year-old boy I'd known in high school, but I wasn't the same girl. I was a mother. I'd gone back to work because I'd thought the extra income would ease some of the strain. One day I'd come home after picking Radley up at the sitter's, and Allan was gone. He'd left a note saying he just couldn't handle being tied down any longer."

"Did you know he was leaving?"

"No, I honestly didn't. In all probability it was done on impulse, the way Allan did most things. It would never have occurred to him that it was desertion, to him it would've meant moving on. He thought he was being fair by taking only half the money, but he left all the bills. I had to get another part-time job in the evenings. I hated that, leaving Rad with a sitter and not seeing him. That six months was the worst time of my life."

Her eyes darkened a moment; then she shook her head and pushed it all back into the past. "After a while I'd straightened things out enough to quit the second job. About that time, Allan called. It was the first I'd heard from him since he'd left. He was very amiable, as if we'd been nothing more than passing acquaintances. He told me he was heading up to Alaska to work. After he hung up, I called a lawyer and got a very simple divorce."

"It must have been difficult for you." Difficult? he thought—he couldn't even imagine what kind of hell it had been. "You could have gone home to your parents."

"No. I was angry for a long, long time. The anger made me determined to stay right here in New York and make it work for me and Radley. By the time the anger had died down, I was making it work."

"He's never come back to see Rad?"

"No, never."

"His loss." He cupped her chin, then leaned over to kiss her lightly. "His very great loss."

She found it easy to lift a hand to his cheek. "The same can be said about that woman in New Orleans."

"Thanks." He nibbled her lips again, enjoying the faint hint of champagne. "Dessert?"

"Hmmm?"

He felt a wild thrill of triumph at her soft, distracted sigh. "Let's skip it." Moving back only slightly, he signaled the waiter for the check, then handed Hester the last of the champagne. "I think we should walk awhile."

The air was biting, almost as exhilarating as the wine. Yet the wine warmed her, making her feel as though she could walk for miles without feeling the wind. She didn't object to Mitch's arm around her shoulders or to the fact that he set the direction. She didn't care where they walked as long as the feelings that stirred inside her didn't fade.

She knew what it was like to fall in love—to be in love. Time slowed down. Everything around you went quickly, but not in a blur. Colors were brighter, sounds sharper, and even in midwinter you could smell flowers. She had been there once before, had felt this intensely once before, but had thought she would never find that place again. Even as a part of her mind struggled to remind her that this couldn't be love—or certainly shouldn't be—she simply ignored it. Tonight she was just a woman.

There were skaters at Rockefeller Center, swirling around and around the ice as the music flowed. Hester watched them, tucked in the warmth of Mitch's arms. His cheek rested on her hair, and she could feel the strong, steady rhythm of his heart.

"Sometimes I bring Rad here on Sundays to skate or just to watch like this. It seems different tonight." She turned her head, and her lips were barely a whisper from his. "Everything seems different tonight."

If she looked at him like that again, Mitch knew he'd break his vow to give her enough time to clear her head and would bundle her into the nearest cab so that he could have her home and in bed before the look broke. Calling on willpower, he shifted her so he could brush his lips over her temple. "Things look different at night, especially after champagne." He relaxed again, her head against his shoulder. "It's a nice difference. Not necessarily steeped in reality, but nice. You can get enough reality from nine to five."

"Not you." Unaware of the tug-of-war she was causing inside him, she turned in his arms. "You make fantasies from nine to five, or whatever hours you choose."

"You should hear the one I'm making up now." He drew another deep breath. "Let's walk some more, and you can tell me about one of yours."

"A fantasy?" Her stride matched his easily. "Mine isn't nearly as earth-shaking as yours, I imagine. It's just a house."

"A house." He walked toward the Park, hoping they'd both be a little steadier on their feet by the time they reached home. "What kind of house?"

"A country house, one of those big old farmhouses with shutters at the windows and porches all around. Lots of windows so you could look at the woods—there would have to be woods. Inside there would be high ceilings and big fireplaces. Outside would be a garden with wisteria climbing on a trellis." She felt the sting of winter on her cheeks, but could almost smell the summer.

"You'd be able to hear the bees hum in it all summer long. There'd be a big yard for Radley, and he could have a dog. I'd have a swing on the porch so I could sit outside in the evening and watch him catch lightning bugs in a jar." She laughed and let her head rest on his shoulder. "I told you it wasn't earth-shaking."

"I like it." He liked it so well he could picture it, white shuttered and hip roofed, with a barn off in the distance. "But you need a stream so Rad could fish."

She closed her eyes a moment, then shook her head. "As much as I love him, I don't think I could bait a hook. Build a tree house maybe, or throw a curveball, but no worms."

"You throw a curveball?"

She tilted her head and smiled. "Right in the strike zone. I helped coach Little League last year."

"The woman's full of surprises. You wear shorts in the dugout?"

"You're obsessed with my legs."

"For a start."

He steered her into their building and toward the elevators. "I haven't had an evening like this in a very long time."

"Neither have I."

She drew back far enough to study him as they began the ride to her floor. "I've wondered about that, about the fact that you don't seem to be involved with anyone."

He touched her chin with his fingertip. "Aren't I?"

She heard the warning signal, but wasn't quite sure what to do about it. "I mean, I haven't noticed you dating or spending any time with women."

Amused, he flicked the finger down her throat. "Do I look like a monk?"

"No." Embarrassed and more than a little unsettled, she looked away. "No, of course not."

"The fact is, Hester, after you've had your share of

wild oats, you lose your taste for them. Spending time with a woman just because you don't want to be alone isn't very satisfying."

"From the stories I hear around the office from the single women, there are plenty of men who disagree with you."

He shrugged as they stepped off the elevator. "It's obvious you haven't played the singles scene." Her brows drew together as she dug for her key. "That was a compliment, but my point is it gets to be a strain or a bore—"

"And this is the age of the meaningful relationship."

"You say that like a cynic. Terribly uncharacteristic, Hester." He leaned against the jamb as she opened the door. "In any case, I'm not big on catchphrases. Are you going to ask me in?"

She hesitated. The walk had cleared her head enough for the doubts to seep through. But along with the doubts was the echo of the way she'd felt when they'd stood together in the cold. The echo was stronger. "All right. Would you like some coffee?"

"No." He shrugged out of his coat as he watched her.

"It's no trouble. It'll only take a minute."

He caught her hands. "I don't want coffee, Hester. I want you." He slipped her coat from her shoulders. "And I want you so bad it makes me jumpy."

She didn't back away, but stood, waiting. "I don't know what to say. I'm out of practice."

"I know." For the first time his own nerves were evident as he dragged a hand through his hair. "That's given me some bad moments. I don't want to seduce you." Then he laughed and walked a few paces away. "The hell I don't."

"I knew—I tried to tell myself I didn't, but I knew when I went out with you tonight that we'd come back here like this." She pressed a hand to her stomach, surprised that it was tied in knots. "I think I was hoping you'd just sort of sweep me away so I wouldn't have to make a decision."

He turned to her. "That's a cop-out, Hester."

"I know." She couldn't look at him then, wasn't certain she dared. "I've never been with anyone but Rad's father. The truth is, I've never wanted to be."

"And now?" He only wanted a word, one word.

She pressed her lips together. "It's been so long, Mitch. I'm frightened."

"Would it help if I told you I am, too?"

"I don't know."

"Hester." He crossed to her to lay his hands on her shoulders. "Look at me." When she did, her eyes were wide and achingly clear. "I want you to be sure, because I don't want regrets in the morning. Tell me what you want."

It seemed her life was a series of decisions. There was no one to tell her which was right or which was wrong. As always, she reminded herself that once the decision was made, she alone would deal with the consequences and accept the responsibility.

"Stay with me tonight," she whispered. "I want you."

Chapter 8

He cupped her face in his hands and felt her tremble. He touched his lips to hers and heard her sigh. It was a moment he knew he would always remember. Her acceptance, her desire, her vulnerability.

The apartment was silent. He would have given her music. The scent of the roses she'd put in a vase was pale next to the fragrance of the garden he imagined for her. The lamp burned brightly. He wouldn't have chosen the secrets of the dark, but rather the mystery of candlelight.

How could he explain to her that there was nothing ordinary, nothing casual in what they were about to give each other? How could he make her understand that he had been waiting all his life for a moment like this? He wasn't certain he could choose the right words, or that the words he did choose would reach her.

So he would show her.

With his lips still lingering on hers, he swept her up into his arms. Though he heard her quick intake of breath, she wrapped her arms around him.

"Mitch—"

"I'm not much of a white knight." He looked at her, half smiling, half questioning. "But for tonight we can pretend."

He looked heroic and strong and incredibly, impossibly sweet. Whatever doubts had remained slipped quietly away. "I don't need a white knight."

"Tonight I need to give you one." He kissed her once more before he carried her into the bedroom.

There was a part of him that needed, ached with that need, so much so that he wanted to lay her down on the bed and cover her with his body. There were times that love ran swiftly, even violently. He understood that and knew that she would, too. But he set her down on the floor beside the bed and touched only her hand.

He drew away just a little. "The light."

"But—"

"I want to see you, Hester."

It was foolish to be shy. It was wrong, she knew, to want to have this moment pass in the dark, anonymously. She reached for the bedside lamp and turned the switch.

The light bathed them, capturing them both standing hand in hand and eye to eye. The quick panic returned, pounding in her head and her heart. Then he touched her and quieted it. He drew off her earrings and set them on the bedside table so that the metal clicked quietly against the wood. She felt a rush of heat, as though with that one simple, intimate move he had already undressed her.

He reached for her belt, then paused when her hands fluttered nervously to his. "I won't hurt you."

"No." She believed him and let her hands drop away. He unhooked her belt to let it slide to the floor. When he lowered his lips to hers again, she slipped her arms around his waist and let the power guide her.

This was what she wanted. She couldn't lie to herself or make excuses. For tonight, she wanted to think only as a woman, to be thought of only as a woman. To be desired, enjoyed, wondered over. When their lips parted, their eyes met. And she smiled.

"I've been waiting for that." He touched a finger to her lips, overcome with a pleasure that was so purely emotional even he couldn't describe it.

"For what?"

"For you to smile at me when I kiss you." He brought his hand to her face. "Let's try it again."

This time the kiss went deeper, edging closer to those uncharted territories. She lifted her hands to his shoulders, then slid them around to encircle his neck. He felt her fingers touch the skin there, shyly at first, then with more confidence.

"Still afraid?"

"No." Then she smiled again. "Yes, a little. I'm not—" she looked away, and he once more brought her face back to his.

"What?"

"I'm not sure what to do. What you like."

He wasn't stunned by her words so much as humbled. He'd said he'd cared for her, and that was true. But now his heart, which had been teetering on the edge, fell over into love.

"Hester, you leave me speechless." He drew her against him, hard, and just held her there. "Tonight, just do what seems right. I think we'll be fine."

He began by kissing her hair, drawing in the scent

that had so appealed to him. The mood was already set, seduction on either side unnecessary. He felt her heart begin to race against his; then she turned her head and found his lips with her own.

His hands weren't steady as he drew down the long zipper at her back. He knew it was an imperfect world, but needed badly to give her one perfect night. No one would ever have called him a selfish man, but it was a fact that he'd never before put someone else's needs so entirely before his own.

He drew the wool from her shoulders, down her arms. She wore a simple chemise beneath it, plain white without frills or lace. No fantasy of silk or satin could have excited him more.

"You're lovely." He pressed a kiss to one shoulder, then the other. "Absolutely lovely."

She wanted to be. It had been so long since she'd felt the need to be any more than presentable. When she saw his eyes, she felt lovely. Gathering her courage together, she began to undress him in turn.

He knew it wasn't easy for her. She drew his jacket off, then began to unknot his tie before she was able to lift her gaze to his again. He could feel her fingers tremble lightly against him as she unbuttoned his shirt.

"You're lovely, too," she murmured. The last, the only man she had ever touched this way had been little more than a boy. Mitch's muscles were subtle but hard, and though his chest was smooth, it was that of a man. Her movements were slow, from shyness rather than a knowledge of arousal. His stomach muscles quivered as she reached for the hook of his slacks.

"You're driving me crazy."

She drew her hands back automatically. "I'm sorry."

"No." He tried to laugh, but it sounded like a groan. "I like it."

Her fingers trembled all the more as she slid his slacks over his hips. Lean hips, with the muscles long and hard. She felt a surge that was both fascination and delight as she brought her hands to them. Then she was against him, and the shock of flesh against flesh vibrated through her.

He was fighting every instinct that pushed him to move quickly, to take quickly. Her shy hands and wondering eyes had taken him to the brink and he had to claw his way back. She sensed a war going on inside him, felt the rigidity of his muscles and heard the raggedness of his breathing.

"Mitch?"

"Just a minute." He buried his face in her hair. The battle for control was hard won. He felt weakened by it, weakened and stunned. When he found the soft, sensitive skin of her neck, he concentrated on that alone.

She strained against him, turning her head instinctively to give him freer access. It seemed as though a veil had floated down over her eyes so that the room, which had become so familiar to her, was hazy. She could feel her blood begin to pound where his lips rubbed and nibbled; then it was throbbing hot, close to the skin, softening it, sensitizing it. Her moan sounded primitive in her own ears. Then it was she who was drawing him down to the bed.

He'd wanted another minute before he let his body spread over hers. There were explosions bombarding his system, from head to heart to loins. He knew he had to calm them before they shattered his senses. But her hands were moving over him, her hips straining upward. With an effort, Mitch rolled so that they were side by side.

He brought his lips down on her, and for a moment all the needs, the fantasies, the darker desires centered there. Her mouth was moist and hot, pounding into his brain how she would be when he filled her. He was already dragging the thin barrier of her chemise aside so that she gasped when her breasts met him unencumbered. As his lips closed over the first firm point, he heard her cry out his name.

This was abandonment. She'd been sure she'd never wanted it, but now, as her body went fluid in her movements against his, she thought she might never want anything else. The feelings of flesh against flesh, growing hot and damp, were new and exhilarating. As were the avid seeking of mouths and the tastes they found and drew in. His murmurs to her were hot and incoherent, but she responded. The light played over his hands as he showed her how a touch could make the soul soar.

She was naked, but the shyness was gone. She wanted him to touch and taste and look his fill, just as she was driven to. His body was a fascination of muscle and taut skin. She hadn't known until now that to touch another, to please another, could bring on such wild waves of passion. He cupped a hand over her, and the passion contracted into a ball of flame in her center that abruptly, almost violently, burst. Gasping for breath, she reached for him.

He'd never had a woman respond so utterly. Watching her rise and peak had given him a delirious thrust of pleasure. He wanted badly to take her up and over again and again, until she was limp and mindless. But his control was slipping, and she was calling for him.

His body covered hers, and he filled her.

He couldn't have said how long they moved together—minutes, hours. But he would never forget how her eyes had opened and stared into his.

He was a little shaken as he lay with her on top of the crumpled spread with drops of freezing rain striking the windows. He turned his head toward the hiss and wondered idly how long it had been going on. As far as he could remember, he'd never been so involved with a woman that the outside world, and all its sights and sounds, had simply ceased to exist.

He turned away again and drew Hester against him. His body was cooling rapidly, but he had no desire to move. "You're quiet," he murmured.

Her eyes were closed. She wasn't ready to open them again. "I don't know what to say."

"How about 'Wow'?"

She was surprised she could laugh after such intensity. "Okay. Wow."

"Try for more enthusiasm. How about 'Fantastic, incredible, earth-shattering?'"

She opened her eyes now and looked into his. "How about beautiful?"

He caught her hand in his and kissed it. "Yeah, that'll do." When he propped himself up on his elbow to look down at her, she shifted. "Too late to be shy now," he told her. Then he ran a hand, light and possessively, down her body. "You know, I was right about your legs. I don't suppose I could talk you into putting on a pair of shorts and those little socks that stop at the ankles."

"I beg your pardon?"

Her tone had him gathering her to him and covering her face with kisses. "I have a thing about long legs in shorts and socks. I drive myself crazy watching women jog in the park in the summer. When they color-coordinate them, I'm finished."

"You're crazy."

"Come on, Hester, don't you have some secret turn-on? Men in muscle shirts, in tuxedos with black tie and studs undone?"

"Don't be silly."

"Why not?"

Why not, indeed, she thought, catching her bottom lip between her teeth. "Well, there is something about jeans riding low on the hips with the snap undone."

"I'll never snap my jeans again as long as I live."

She laughed again. "That doesn't mean I'm going to start wearing shorts and socks."

"That's okay. I get excited when I see you in a business suit."

"You do not."

"Oh, yes, I do." He rolled her on top of him and began to play with her hair. "Those slim lapels and high-collar blouses. And you always wear your hair up." With it caught in his hands, he lifted it on top of her head. It wasn't the same look at all, but one that still succeeded in making his mouth dry. "The efficient and dependable Mrs. Wallace. Every time I see you dressed that way I imagine how fascinating it would be to peel off those professional clothes and take out those tidy little pins." He let her hair slide down through his fingers.

Thoughtful, Hester rested her cheek against his cheek. "You're a strange man, Mitch."

"More than likely."

"You depend so much on your imagination, on what it might be, on fantasies and make-believe. With me it's facts and figures, profit and loss, what is or what isn't."

"Are you talking about our jobs or our personalities?"

"Isn't one really the same as the other?"

"No. I'm not Commander Zark, Hester."

She shifted, lulled by the rhythm of his heart. "I suppose what I mean is that the artist in you, the writer in you, thrives on imagination or possibilities. I guess the banker in me looks for checks and balances."

He was silent for a moment, stroking her hair. Didn't she realize how much more there was to her? This was the woman who fantasized about a home in the country, the one who threw a curveball, the one who had just taken a man of flesh and blood and turned him into a puddle of need.

"I don't want to get overly philosophical, but why do you think you chose to deal with loans? Do you get the same feeling when you turn down an application as you do when you approve one?"

"No, of course not."

"Of course not," he repeated. "Because when you approve one, you've had a hand in the possibilities. I have no doubt that you play by the book, that's part of your charm, but I'd wager you get a great deal of personal satisfaction by being able to say, 'Okay, buy your home, start your business, expand.'"

She lifted her head. "You seem to understand me very well." No one else had, she realized with a jolt. Ever.

"I've been giving you a great deal of thought." He drew her to him, wondering if she could feel how well their bodies fit. "A very great deal. In fact, I haven't thought about another woman since I delivered your pizza."

She smiled at that, and would have settled against him again, but he held her back. "Hester..." It was one of the few times in his life he'd ever felt self-conscious. She was looking at him expectantly, even patiently, while he struggled for the right words. "The thing is, I don't want to think about another woman, or be with another woman—this way." He struggled again, then swore. "Damn, I feel like I'm back in high school."

Her smile was cautious. "Are you going to ask me to go steady?"

It wasn't exactly what he'd had in mind, but he could see by the look in her eyes that he'd better go slowly. "I could probably find my class ring if you want."

She looked down at her hand, which was resting so naturally on his heart. Was it foolish to be so moved? If not, it was certainly dangerous. "Maybe we can just leave it that there's no one else I want to be with this way, either."

He started to speak, then stopped himself. She needed time to be sure that was true, didn't she? There had only been one other man in her life, and she'd been no more than a girl then. To be fair, he had to give her room to be certain. But he didn't want to be fair. No, Mitch Dempsey was no self-sacrificing Commander Zark.

"All right." He'd devised and won enough wars to know how to plan strategy. He'd win Hester before she realized there'd been a battle.

Drawing her down to him, he closed his mouth over hers and began the first siege.

It was an odd and rather wonderful feeling to wake up in the morning beside a lover—even one who nudged you over to the edge of the mattress. Hester opened her eyes and, lying very still, savored it.

His face was buried against the back of her neck, and his arm was wrapped tightly around her waist—which was fortunate, as without it she would have rolled onto the floor. Hester shifted slightly and experienced the arousing sensation of having her sleep-warmed skin rub cozily against his.

She'd never had a lover. A husband, yes, but her wedding night, her first initiation into womanhood, had been nothing like the night she'd just shared with Mitch. Was it fair to compare them? she wondered. Would she be human if she didn't?

That first night so long ago had been frenzied, complicated by her nerves and her husband's hurry. Last night the passion had built layer by layer, as though there'd been all the time in the world to enjoy it. She'd never known that making love could be so liberating. In truth, she hadn't known a man could sincerely want to give pleasure as much as he desired to take it.

She snuggled into the pillow and watched the thin winter light come through the windows. Would things be different this morning? Would there be an awkwardness between them or, worse, a casualness that would diminish the depth of what they'd shared? The simple fact was she didn't know what it was like to have a lover—or to be one.

She was putting too much emphasis on one evening, she told herself, sighing. How could she not, when the evening had been so special?

Hester touched a hand to his, let it linger a moment, then shifted to rise. Mitch's arm clamped down.

"Going somewhere?"

She tried to turn over, but discovered his legs had pinned her. "It's almost nine."

"So?" His fingers spread out lazily to stroke.

"I have to get up. I need to pick Rad up in a couple of hours."

"Hmmm." He watched his little dream bubble of a morning in bed with her deflate, then reconstructed it to fit two hours. "You feel so good." He released his hold, but only so he could turn her around so they were face-to-face. "Look good, too," he decided as he studied her face through half-closed eyes. "And taste—" he touched his lips to hers, and there was nothing awkward, nothing casual "—wonderful. Imagine this." He ran a hand down her flank. "We're on an island—the South Seas, let's say. The ship was wrecked a week ago, and we're the only survivors." His eyes closed as he pressed a kiss to her forehead. "We've been living on fruit and the fish I cleverly catch with my pointed stick."

"Who cleans them?"

"This is a fantasy, you don't worry about details like that. Last night there was a storm—a big, busting tropical storm—and we had to huddle together for warmth and safety under the lean-to I built."

"You built?" Her lips curved against his. "Do I do anything useful?"

"You can do all you want in your own fantasy. Now shut up." He snuggled closer and could almost smell the salt air. "It's morning, and the storm washed everything clean. There are gulls swooping down near the surf. We're lying together on an old blanket."

"Which you heroically salvaged from the wreck."

"Now you're catching on. When we wake up, we discover we'd tangled together during the night, drawn together despite ourselves. The sun's hot—it's already warmed our half-naked bodies. Still dazed with sleep, already aroused, we come together. And then…" His lips hovered a breath away from hers. Hester let her eyes close as she found herself caught up in the picture he painted. "And then a wild boar attacks, and I have to wrestle him."

"Half-naked and unarmed?"

"That's right. I'm badly bitten, but I kill him with my bare hands."

Hester opened her eyes again to narrow slits. "And while you're doing that, I put the blanket over my head and whimper."

"Okay." Mitch kissed the tip of her nose. "But afterward you're very, very grateful that I saved your life."

"Poor, defenseless female that I am."

"That's the ticket. You're so grateful you tear the rags of your skirt to make bandages for my wounds, and then…" He paused for impact. "You make me coffee."

Hester drew back, not certain whether to be amazed or amused. "You went through that whole scenario so I'd offer to make you coffee?"

"Not just coffee, morning coffee, the first cup of coffee. Life's blood."

"I'd have made it even without the story."

"Yeah, but did you like the story?"

She combed the hair away from her face as she considered. "Next time I get to catch the fish."

"Deal."

She rose and, though she knew it was foolish, wished that she'd had her robe within arm's reach. Going to the closet, she slipped it on with her back still to him. "Do you want some breakfast?"

He was sitting up, rubbing his hands over his face when she turned. "Breakfast? You mean likes eggs or something? Hot food?" The only time he managed a hot breakfast was when he had the energy to drag himself to the corner diner. "Mrs. Wallace, for a hot breakfast you can have the crown jewels of Perth."

"All that for bacon and eggs?"

"Bacon, too? God, what a woman."

She laughed, sure he was joking. "Go ahead and get a shower if you want. It won't take long."

He hadn't been joking. Mitch watched her walk from the room and shook his head. He didn't expect a woman to offer to cook for him, or for one to offer as though he had a right to expect it. But this, he remembered, was the woman who would have sewed patches on his jeans because she'd thought he couldn't afford new ones.

Mitch climbed out of bed, then slowly, thoughtfully ran a hand through his hair. The aloof and professional Hester Wallace was a very warm and special woman, and he had no intention of letting her get away.

She was stirring eggs in a skillet when he came into the kitchen. Bacon was draining on a rack, and coffee was already hot. He stood in the doorway a moment, more than a little surprised that such a simple domestic scene would affect him so strongly. Her robe was flannel and covered her from neck to ankle, but to him Hester had never looked more alluring. He hadn't realized he'd been looking for this—the morning smells, the morning sounds of the Sunday news on the radio on the counter, the morning sights of the woman who'd shared his night moving competently in the kitchen.

As a child, Sunday mornings had been almost formal affairs—brunch at eleven, served by a uniformed member of the staff. Orange juice in Waterford, shirred eggs on Wedgwood. He'd been taught to spread the Irish linen on his lap and make polite conversation. In later years, Sunday mornings had meant a bleary-eyed search through the cupboards or a dash down to the nearest diner.

He felt foolish, but he wanted to tell Hester that the simple meal at her kitchen counter meant as much to him as the long night in her bed. Crossing to her, he wrapped his arms around her waist and pressed a kiss to her neck.

Strange how a touch could speed up the heart rate and warm the blood. Absorbing the sensation, she leaned back against him. "It's almost done. You didn't say how you liked your eggs, so you've got them scrambled with a little dill and cheese."

She could have offered him cardboard and told him to eat it with a plastic fork. Mitch turned her to face him and kissed her long and hard. "Thanks."

He'd flustered her again. Hester turned to the eggs in time to prevent them from burning. "Why don't you sit down?" She poured coffee into a mug and handed it to him. "With your life's blood."

He finished half the mug before he sat. "Hester, you know what I said about your legs?"

She glanced over as she heaped eggs on a plate. "Yes?"

"Your coffee's almost as good as they are. Tremendous qualities in a woman."

"Thanks." She set the plate in front of him before moving to the toaster.

"Aren't you eating any of this?"

"No, just toast."

Mitch looked down at the pile of golden eggs and crisp bacon. "Hester, I didn't expect you to fix me all this when you aren't eating."

"It's all right." She arranged a stack of toast on a plate. "I do it for Rad all the time."

He covered her hand with his as she sat beside him. "I appreciate it."

"It's only a couple of eggs," she said, embarrassed. "You should eat them before they get cold."

"The woman's a marvel," Mitch commented as he obliged her. "She raises an interesting and well-balanced son, holds down a demanding job, and cooks." Mitch bit into a piece of bacon. "Want to get married?"

She laughed and added more coffee to both mugs. "If it only takes scrambled eggs to get you to propose, I'm surprised you don't have three or four wives hidden in the closet."

He hadn't been joking. She would have seen it in his eyes if she'd looked at him, but she was busy spreading butter on toast. Mitch watched her competent, ringless hands a moment. It had been a stupid way to propose and a useless way to make her see he was serious. It was also too soon, he admitted as he scooped up another forkful of eggs.

The trick would be first to get her used to having him around, then to have her trust him enough to believe he would stay around. Then there was the big one, he mused as he lifted his cup. She had to need him. She wouldn't ever need him for the roof over her head or the food in her cupboards. She was much too self-sufficient for that, and he admired it. In time, she might come to need him for emotional support and companionship. It would be a start.

The courting of Hester would have to be both complex and subtle. He wasn't certain he knew exactly how to go about it, but he was more than ready to start. Today was as good a time as any.

"Got any plans for later?"

"I've got to pick up Rad around noon." She lingered over her toast, realizing it had been years since she had shared adult company over breakfast and that it had an appeal all its own. "Then I promised that I'd take him and Josh to a matinee. *The Moon of Andromeda.*"

"Yeah? Terrific movie. The special effects are tremendous."

"You've seen it?" She felt a twinge of disappointment. She'd been wondering if he might be willing to come along.

"Twice. There's a scene between the mad scientist and the sane scientist that'll knock you out. And there's this mutant that looks like a carp. Fantastic."

"A carp." Hester sipped her coffee. "Sounds wonderful."

"A cinematic treat for the eyes. Can I tag along?"

"You just said you've seen it twice already."

"So? The only movies I see once are dogs. Besides, I'd like to see Rad's reaction to the laser battle in deep space."

"Is it gory?"

"Nothing Rad can't handle."

"I wasn't asking for him."

With a laugh, Mitch took her hand. "I'll be there to protect you. How about it? I'll spring for the popcorn." He brought her hand up to his lips. "Buttered."

"How could I pass up a deal like that?"

"Good. Look, I'll give you a hand with the dishes, then I've got to go down and take Taz out before his bladder causes us both embarrassment."

"Go on ahead. There isn't that much, and Taz is probably moaning at the door by this time."

"Okay." He stood with her. "But next time I cook."

Hester gathered up the plates. "Peanut butter and jelly?"

"I can do better than that if it impresses you."

She smiled and reached for his empty mug. "You don't have to impress me."

He caught her face in his hands while she stood with her hands full of dishes. "Yes, I do." He nibbled at her lips, then abruptly deepened the kiss until they were both breathless. She was forced to swallow when he released her.

"That's a good start."

He was smiling as he brushed his lips over her forehead. "I'll be up in an hour."

Hester stood where she was until she heard the door close, then quietly set the dishes down again. How in the world had it happened? she wondered. She'd fallen in love with the man. He'd be gone only an hour, yet she wanted him back already.

Taking a deep breath, she sat down again. She had to keep herself from overreacting, from taking this, as she took too many other things, too seriously. He was fun, he was kind, but he wasn't permanent. There was nothing permanent but her and Radley. She'd promised herself years ago that she would never forget that again. Now, more than ever, she had to remember it.

Chapter 9

"Rich, you know I hate business discussions before noon."

Mitch sat in Skinner's office with Taz snoozing at his feet. Though it was after ten and he'd been up working for a couple of hours, he hadn't been ready to venture out and talk shop. He'd had to leave his characters on the drawing board in a hell of a predicament, and Mitch imagined they resented being left dangling as much as he resented leaving them.

"If you're going to give me a raise, that's fine by me, but you could've waited until after lunch."

"You're not getting a raise." Skinner ignored the phone that rang on his desk. "You're already overpaid."

"Well, if I'm fired, you could definitely have waited a couple of hours."

"You're not fired." Skinner drew his brows together until they met above his nose. "But if you keep bringing that hound in here, I could change my mind."

"I made Taz my agent. Anything you say to me you can say in front of him."

Skinner sat back in his chair and folded hands that were swollen at the knuckles from years of nervous cracking. "You know, Dempsey, someone who didn't know you so well would think you were joking. The problem is, I happen to know you're crazy."

"That's why we get along so well, right? Listen, Rich, I've got Mirium trapped in a roomful of wounded rebels from Zirial. Being an empath, she's not feeling too good herself. Why don't we wrap this up so I can get back and take her to the crisis point?"

"Rebels from Zirial," Skinner mused. "You aren't thinking of bringing back Nimrod the Sorceror?"

"It's crossed my mind, and I could get back and figure out what he's got up his invisible sleeve if you'd tell me why you dragged me in here."

"You work here," Skinner pointed out.

"That's no excuse."

Skinner puffed out his cheeks and let the subject drop. "You know Two Moon Pictures has been negotiating with Universal for the rights to product Zark as a full-length film?"

"Sure. That's been going on a year, a year and a half now." Since the wheeling and dealing didn't interest him, Mitch stretched out a leg and began to massage Taz's flank with his foot. "The last thing you told me was that the alfalfa sprouts from L.A. couldn't get out of their hot tubs long enough to close the deal." Mitch grinned. "You've got a real way with words, Rich."

"The deal closed yesterday," Rich said flatly. "Two Moon wants to go with Zark."

Mitch's grin faded. "You're serious?"

"I'm always serious," Rich said, studying Mitch's

reaction. "I thought you'd be a little more enthusiastic. Your baby's going to be a movie star."

"To tell you the truth, I don't know how I feel." Pushing himself out of the chair, Mitch began to pace Rich's cramped office. As he passed the window, he pulled open the blinds to let in slants of hard winter light. "Zark's always been personal. I don't know how I feel about him going Hollywood."

"You got a kick out of when B.C. Toys made the dolls."

"Action figures," Mitch corrected automatically. "I guess that's because they stayed pretty true to the theme." It was silly, he knew. Zark didn't belong to him. He'd created him, true, but Zark belonged to Universal, just like all the other heroes and villains of the staff's fertile imaginations. If, like Maloney, Mitch decided to move on, Zark would stay behind, the responsibility of someone else's imagination. "Did we retain any creative leeway?"

"Afraid they're going to exploit your firstborn?"

"Maybe."

"Listen, Two Moon bought the rights to Zark because he has potential at the box office—the way he is. It wouldn't be smart businesswise to change him. Let's look at the bottom line—comics are big business. A hundred and thirty million a year isn't something to shrug off. The business is thriving now the way it hasn't since the forties, and even though it's bound to level off, it's going to stay hot. Those jokers on the coast might dress funny, but they know a winner when they see one. Still, if you're worried, you could take their offer."

"What offer?"

"They want you to write the screenplay."

Mitch stopped where he was. "Me? I don't write movies."

"You write Zark—apparently that's enough for the producers. Our publishers aren't stupid, either. Stingy," he added with a glance at his worn linoleum, "but not stupid. They wanted the script to come from in-house, and there's a clause in the contract that says we have a shot. Two Moon agreed to accept a treatment from you first. If it doesn't pan out, they still want you on the project as a creative consultant."

"Creative consultant." Mitch rolled the title around on his tongue.

"If I were you, Dempsey, I'd get myself a two-legged agent."

"I just might. Look, I'm going to have to think about it. How long are they giving me?"

"Nobody mentioned a time frame. I don't think the possibility of your saying no occurred to them. But then, they don't know you like I do."

"I need a couple of days. There's someone I have to talk to."

Skinner waited until he'd started out. "Mitch, opportunity doesn't often kick down your door this way."

"Just let me make sure I'm at home first. I'll be in touch."

When it rains it pours, Mitch thought as he and Taz walked. It had started off as a fairly normal, even ordinary new year. He'd planned to dig his heels in a bit and get ahead of schedule so that he could take three or four weeks off to ski, drink brandy and kick up some snow on his uncle's farm. He'd figured on meeting one or two attractive women on the slopes to make the evenings interesting. He'd thought to sketch a little, sleep a lot and cruise the lodges. Very simple.

Then, within weeks, everything had changed. In Hester he'd found everything he'd ever wanted in his personal life, but he'd only begun to convince her that he was everything she'd ever wanted in hers. Now he was being offered one of the biggest opportunities of his professional life, but he couldn't think of one without considering the other.

In truth, he'd never been able to draw a hard line of demarcation between his professional and personal lives. He was the same man whether he was having a couple of drinks with friends or burning the midnight oil with Zark. If he'd changed at all, it had been Hester and Radley who had caused it. Since he'd fallen for them, he wanted the strings he'd always avoided, the responsibilities he'd always blithely shrugged off.

So he went to her first.

Mitch strolled into the bank with his ears tingling from the cold. The long walk had given him time to think through everything Skinner had told him, and to feel the first twinges of excitement. Zark, in Technicolor, in stereophonic sound, in Panavision.

Mitch stopped at Kay's desk. "She had lunch yet?"

Kay rolled back from her terminal. "Nope."

"Anybody with her now?"

"Not a soul."

"Good. When's her next appointment?"

Kay ran her finger down the appointment book. "Two-fifteen."

"She'll be back. If Rosen stops by, tell him I took Mrs. Wallace to lunch to discuss some refinancing."

"Yes, sir."

She was working on a long column of figures when Mitch opened the door. She moved her fingers quickly over the adding machine, which clicked as it spewed out a stream of tape. "Kay, I'm going to need Lorimar's construction estimate. And would you mind ordering me a sandwich? Anything as long as it's quick. I'd like to have these figures upstairs by the end of the day. Oh, and I'll need the barter exchange transactions on the Duberry account. Look up the 1099."

Mitch shut the door at his back. "God, all this bank talk excites me."

"Mitch." Hester glanced up with the last of the figures still rolling through her head. "What are you doing here?"

"Breaking you out, and we have to move fast. Taz'll distract the guards." He was already taking her coat from the rack behind the door. "Let's go. Just keep your head down and look natural."

"Mitch, I've got—"

"To eat Chinese take-out and make love with me. In whatever order you like. Here, button up."

"I've only half-finished with these figures."

"They won't run away." He buttoned her coat, then closed his hands over her collar. "Hester, do you know how long it's been since we had an hour alone? Four days."

"I know. I'm sorry, things have been busy."

"Busy." He nodded toward her desk. "No one's going to argue with you there, but you've also been holding me off."

"No, I haven't." The truth was she'd been holding herself off, trying to prove to herself that she didn't need him as badly as it seemed. It hadn't been working as well as she'd hoped. There was tangible proof of that now as she stood facing him with her heart beating fast. "Mitch, I explained how I felt about…being with you with Radley in the apartment."

"And I'm not arguing that point, either." Though he would have liked to. "But Rad's in school and you have a constitutional right to a lunch hour. Come with me, Hester." He let his brow rest on hers. "I need you."

She couldn't resist or refuse or pretend she didn't want to be with him. Knowing she might regret it later, she turned her back on her work. "I'd settle for a peanut butter and jelly. I'm not very hungry."

"You got it."

Fifteen minutes later, they were walking into Mitch's apartment. As usual, his curtains were open wide so that the sun poured through. It was warm, Hester thought as she slipped out of her coat. She imagined he kept the thermostat up so that he could be comfortable in his bare feet and short-sleeved sweatshirts. Hester stood with her coat in her hands and wondered what to do next.

"Here, let me take that." Mitch tossed her coat carelessly over a chair. "Nice suit, Mrs. Wallace," he murmured, fingering the lapel of the dark blue pin-stripe.

She put a hand over his, once again afraid that things were moving too fast. "I feel…"

"Decadent?"

Once again, it was the humor in his eyes that relaxed her. "More like I've just climbed out my bedroom window at midnight."

"Did you ever?"

"No. I thought about it a lot, but I could never figure out what I was supposed to do once I climbed down."

"That's why I'm nuts about you." He kissed her cautious smile and felt her lips soften and give under his. "Climb out the bedroom window to me, Hester. I'll show you what to do." Then his hands were in her hair, and her control scattered as quickly as the pins.

She wanted him. Perhaps it had a great deal to do

with madness, but oh, how she wanted him. In the long nights since they'd been together like this, she'd thought of him, of how he touched her, where he touched her, and now his hands were there, just as she remembered. This time she moved faster than he, pulling his sweater up over his head to feast on the warm, taut flesh beneath. Her teeth nipped into his lip, insisting, inciting, until he was dragging the jacket from her and fumbling with the buttons that ranged down the back of her blouse.

His touch wasn't as gentle when he found her, nor was he as patient. But she had long since thrown caution aside. Now, pressed hard against him, she gripped passion with both hands. Whether it was day or night no longer mattered. She was where she wanted to be, where, no matter how she struggled to pretend otherwise, she needed to be.

Madness, yes, it was madness. She wondered how she'd lived so long without it.

He unfastened her skirt so that it flowed over her hips and onto the floor. With a groan of satisfaction he pressed his mouth to her throat. Four days? Had it only been four days? It seemed like years since he had had her close and alone. She was as hot and as desperate against him as he'd dreamed she would be. He could savor the feel of her even as desire clamped inside his gut and swam in his head. He wanted to spend hours touching, being touched, but the intensity of the moment, the lack of time and her urgent murmurs made it impossible.

"The bedroom," she managed as he pulled the thin straps of her lingerie over her shoulders.

"No, here. Right here." He fastened his mouth on hers and pulled her to the floor.

He would have given her more. Even though his

own system was straining toward the breaking point, he would have given her more, but she was wrapped around him. Before he could catch his breath, her hands were on his hips, guiding her to him. She dug her fingers into his flesh as she murmured his name, and whole galaxies seemed to explode inside his head.

When she could think again, Hester stared at the dust motes that danced in a beam of sunlight. She was lying on a priceless Aubusson with Mitch's head pillowed between her breasts. It was the middle of the day, she had a pile of paperwork on her desk, and she'd just spent the better part of her lunch making love on the floor. She couldn't remember ever being more content.

She hadn't known life could be like this—an adventure, a carnival. For years she hadn't believed there was room for the madness of love and lovemaking in a world that revolved around responsibilities. Now, just now, she was beginning to realize she could have both. For how long, she couldn't be sure. Perhaps one day would be enough. She combed her fingers through his hair.

"I'm glad you came to take me to lunch."

"If this is any indication, we're going to have to make it a habit. Still want that sandwich?"

"Uh-uh. I don't need anything." But you. Hester sighed, realizing she was going to have to accept that. "I'm going to have to get back."

"You don't have an appointment until after two. I checked. Your barter exchange transactions can wait a few more minutes, can't they?"

"I suppose."

"Come on." He was up and pulling her to her feet.

"Where?"

"We'll have a quick shower, then I need to talk to you."

Hester accepted his offer of a robe and tried not to

worry about what he had to say. She understood Mitch well enough to know he was full of surprises. The trouble was, she wasn't certain she was ready for another. Shoulders tense, she sat beside him on the couch and waited.

"You look like you're waiting for the blindfold and your last cigarette."

Hester shook back her still damp hair and tried to smile. "No, it's just that you sounded so serious."

"I've told you before, I have my serious moments." He shoved magazines off the table with his foot. "I had some news today, and I haven't decided how I feel about it. I wanted to see what you thought."

"Your family?" she began, instantly concerned.

"No." He took her hand. "I guess I'm making it sound like bad news, and it's not. At least I don't think it is. A production company in Hollywood just cut a deal with Universal to make a movie out of Zark."

Hester stared at him a moment, then blinked. "A movie. Well, that's wonderful. Isn't it? I mean, I know he's very popular in comics, but a movie would be even bigger. You should be thrilled, and very proud that your work can translate that way."

"I just don't know if they can pull it off, if they can bring him to the screen with the right tone, the right emotion. Don't look at me that way."

"Mitch, I know how you feel about Zark. At least I think I do. He's your creation, and he's important to you."

"He's real to me," Mitch corrected. "Up here," he said, tapping his temple. "And, as corny as it might sound, in here." He touched a hand to his heart. "He made a difference in my life, made a difference in how I looked at myself and my work. I don't want to see them screw him up and make him into some cardboard hero or, worse, into something infallible and perfect."

Hester was silent a moment. She began to understand that giving birth to an idea might be as life-altering as giving birth to a child. "Let me ask you something: why did you create him?"

"I wanted to make a hero—a very human one—with flaws and vulnerabilities, and I guess with high standards. Someone kids could relate to because he was just flesh and blood, but powerful enough inside to fight back. Kids don't have a hell of a lot of choices, you know. I remember when I was young I wanted to be able to say 'no, I don't want to, I don't like that.' When I read, I could see there were possibilities, ways out. That's what I wanted Zark to be."

"Do you think you succeeded?"

"Yeah. On a personal level, I succeeded when I came up with the first issue. Professionally, Zark has pushed Universal to the top. He translates into millions of dollars a year for the business."

"Do you resent that?"

"No, why should I?"

"Then you shouldn't resent seeing him take the next step."

Mitch fell silent, thinking. He might have known Hester would see things more clearly and be able to cut through everything to the most practical level. Wasn't that just one more reason he needed her?

"They offered to let me do the screenplay."

"What?" She was sitting straight up now, eyes wide. "Oh, Mitch, that's wonderful. I'm so proud of you."

He continued to play with her fingers. "I haven't done it yet."

"Don't you think you can?"

"I'm not sure."

She started to speak, then caught herself. After a

moment, she spoke carefully. "Strange, if anyone had asked, I would have said you were the most self-confident man I'd ever met. Added to that, I'd have said that you'd be much too selfish with Zark to let anyone else write him."

"There's a difference between writing a story line for a comic series and writing a screenplay for a major motion picture."

"So?"

He had to laugh. "Tossing my own words back at me, aren't you?"

"You can write, I'd be the first to say that you have a very fluid imagination, and you know your character better than anyone else. I don't see the problem."

"Screwing up is the problem. Anyway, if I don't do the script, they want me as creative consultant."

"I can't tell you what to do, Mitch."

"But?"

She leaned forward, putting her hands on his shoulders. "Write the script, Mitch. You'll hate yourself if you don't try. There aren't any guarantees, but if you don't take the risk, there's no reward either."

He lifted a hand to hers and held it firmly as he watched her. "Do you really feel that way?"

"Yes, I do. I also believe in you." She leaned closer and touched her mouth to his.

"Marry me, Hester."

With her lips still on his, she froze. Slowly, very slowly, she drew away. "What?"

"Marry me." He took her hands in his to hold them still. "I love you."

"Don't. Please don't do this."

"Don't what? Don't love you?" He tightened his grip as she struggled to pull away. "It's a great deal too late for that, and I think you know it. I'm not lying when I tell you that I've never felt about anyone the way I feel about you. I want to spend my life with you."

"I can't." Her voice was breathless. It seemed each word she pushed out seared the back of her throat. "I can't marry you. I don't want to marry anyone. You don't understand what you're asking."

"Just because I haven't been there doesn't mean I don't know." He'd expected surprise, even some resistance. But he could see now he'd totally miscalculated. There was out-and-out fear in her eyes and full panic in her voice. "Hester, I'm not Allan and we both know you're not the same woman you were when you were married to him."

"It doesn't matter. I'm not going through that again, and I won't put Radley through it." She pulled away and started to dress. "You're not being reasonable."

"*I'm* not?" Struggling for calm, he walked behind her and began to do up her buttons. Her back went rigid. "You're the one who's basing her feelings now on something that happened years ago."

"I don't want to talk about it."

"Maybe not, and maybe now's not the best time, but you're going to have to." Though she resisted, he turned her around. "We're going to have to."

She wanted to get away, far enough that she could bury everything that had been said. But for the moment she had to face it. "Mitch, we've known each other for a matter of weeks, and we've just begun to be able to accept what's happening between us."

"What *is* happening?" he demanded. "Aren't you the one who said at the beginning that you weren't interested in casual sex?"

She paled a bit, then turned away to pick up her suit jacket. "There wasn't anything casual about it."

"No, there wasn't, not for either of us. You understand that?"

"Yes, but—"

"Hester, I said I loved you. Now I want to know how you feel about me."

"I don't know." She let out a gasp when he grabbed her shoulders again. "I tell you I don't know. I think I love you. Today. You're asking me to risk everything I've done, the life I've built for myself and Rad, over an emotion I already know can change overnight."

"Love doesn't change overnight," he corrected. "It can be killed or it can be nurtured. That's up to the people involved. I want a commitment from you, a family, and I want to give those things back to you."

"Mitch, this is all happening too fast, much too fast for both of us."

"Damn it, Hester, I'm thirty-five years old, not some kid with hot pants and no brains. I don't want to marry you so I can have convenient sex and a hot breakfast, but because I know we could have something together, something real, something important."

"You don't know what marriage is like, you're only imagining."

"And you're only remembering a bad one. Hester, look at me. Look at me," he demanded again. "When the hell are you going to stop using Radley's father as a yardstick?"

"He's the only one I've got." She shook him off again and tried to catch her breath. "Mitch, I'm flattered that you want me."

"The hell with that."

"Please." She dragged a hand through her hair. "I do

care about you, and the only thing I'm really sure of is that I don't want to lose you."

"Marriage isn't the end of a relationship, Hester."

"I can't think about marriage. I'm sorry." The panic flowed in and out of her voice until she was forced to stop and calm it. "If you don't want to see me anymore, I'll try to understand. But I'd rather…I hope we can just let things go on the way they are."

He dug his hands into his pockets. He had a habit of pushing too far too fast, and knew it. But he hated to waste the time he could already imagine them having together. "For how long, Hester?"

"For as long as it lasts." She closed her eyes. "That sounds hard. I don't mean it to. You mean a great deal to me, more than I thought anyone ever would again."

Mitch brushed a finger over her cheek and brought it away wet. "A low blow," he murmured, studying the tear.

"I'm sorry. I don't mean to do this. I had no idea that you were thinking along these lines."

"I can see that." He gave a self-deprecating laugh. "In three dimensions."

"I've hurt you. I can't tell you how much I regret that."

"Don't. I asked for it. The truth is, I hadn't planned on asking you to marry me for at least a week."

She started to touch his hand, then stopped. "Mitch, can we just forget all this, go on as we were?"

He reached out and straightened the collar of her jacket. "I'm afraid not. I've made up my mind, Hester. That's something I try to do only once or twice a year. Once I've done it, there's no turning back." His gaze came up to hers with that rush of intensity she felt to the bone. "I'm going to marry you, sooner or later. If it has to be later, that's fine. I'll just give you some time to get used to it."

"Mitch, I won't change my mind. It wouldn't be fair if I let you think I would. It isn't a matter of a whim, but of a promise I made to myself."

"Some promises are best broken."

She shook her head. "I don't know what else to say. I just wish—"

He pressed his finger to her lips. "We'll talk about it later. I'll take you back to work."

"No, don't bother. Really," she said when he started to argue. "I'd like some time to think, anyway. Being with you makes that difficult."

"That's a good start." He took her chin in his hand and studied her face. "You look fine, but next time don't cry when I ask you to marry me. It's hell on the ego." He kissed her before she could speak. "See you later, Mrs. Wallace. Thanks for lunch."

A little dazed, she walked out into the hall. "I'll call you later."

"Do that. I'll be around."

He closed the door, then turned to lean back against it. Hurt? He rubbed a spot just under his heart. Damn right it hurt. If anyone had told him that being in love could cause the heart to twist, he'd have continued to avoid it. He'd had a twinge when his long-ago love in New Orleans had deserted him. It hadn't prepared him for this sledgehammer blow. What could possibly have?

But he wasn't giving up. What he had to do was figure out a plan of attack—subtle, clever and irresistible. Mitch glanced down at Taz consideringly.

"Where do you think Hester would like to go on our honeymoon?"

The dog grumbled, then rolled over on his back.

"No," Mitch decided. "Bermuda's overdone. Never mind, I'll come up with something."

Chapter 10

"Radley, you and your friends have to tone down the volume on the war, please." Hester took the measuring tape from around her neck and stretched it out over the wall space. Perfect, she thought with a satisfied nod. Then she took the pencil from behind her ear to mark two *X*s where the nails would go.

The little glass shelves she would hang were a present to herself, one that was completely unnecessary and pleased her a great deal. She didn't consider the act of hanging them herself a show of competence or independence, but simply one more of the ordinary chores she'd been doing on her own for years. With a hammer in one hand, she lined up the first nail. She'd given it two good whacks when someone knocked on the door.

"Just a minute." She gave the nail a final smack. From Radley's bedroom came the sounds of antiaircraft and whistling missiles. Hester took the second nail out of her mouth and stuck it in her pocket. "Rad, we're going to be arrested for disturbing the peace." She opened the door to Mitch. "Hi."

The pleasure showed instantly, gratifying him. It had been two days since he'd seen her, since he'd told her he loved her and wanted to marry her. In two days he'd done a lot of hard thinking, and could only hope that, despite herself, Hester had done some thinking, too.

"Doing some remodeling?" he asked with a nod at the hammer.

"Just hanging a shelf." She wrapped both hands around the handle of the hammer, feeling like a teenager. "Come in."

He glanced toward Radley's room as she shut the door. It sounded as though a major air strike was in progress. "You didn't mention you were opening a playground."

"It's been a lifelong dream of mine. Rad, they've just signed a treaty—hold your fire!" With a cautious smile for Mitch, she waved him toward a chair. "Radley has Josh over today, and Ernie—Ernie lives upstairs and goes to school with Rad."

"Sure, the Bitterman kid. I know him. Nice," he commented as he looked at the shelves.

"They're a present for completing a successful month at National Trust." Hester ran a finger along a beveled edge. She really did want this more than a new outfit.

"You're on the reward program?"

"Self-reward."

"The best kind. Want me to finish that for you?"

"Oh?" She glanced down at the hammer. "Oh, no, thanks. I can do it. Why don't you sit down? I'll get you some coffee."

"You hang the shelf, I'll get the coffee." He kissed the tip of her nose. "And relax, will you?"

"Mitch." He'd taken only two steps away when she reached for his arm. "I'm awfully glad to see you. I was afraid, well, that you were angry."

"Angry?" He gave her a baffled look. "About what?"

"About…" She trailed off as he continued to stare at her in a half interested, half curious way that made her wonder if she'd imagined everything he'd said. "Nothing." She dug the nail out of her pocket. "Help yourself to the coffee."

"Thanks." He grinned at the back of her head. He'd done exactly what he'd set out to do—confuse her. Now she'd be thinking about him, about what had been said between them. The more she thought about it, the closer she'd be to seeing reason.

Whistling between his teeth, he strolled into the kitchen while Hester banged in the second nail.

He *had* asked her to marry him. She remembered everything he'd said, everything she'd said in return. And she knew that he'd been angry and hurt. Hadn't she spent two days regretting that she'd had to cause that? Now he strolled in as though nothing had happened.

Hester set down the hammer, then lifted the shelves. Maybe he'd cooled off enough to be relieved that she'd said no. That could be it, she decided, wondering why the idea didn't ease her mind as much as it should have.

"You made cookies." Mitch came in carrying two mugs, with a plate of fresh cookies balanced on top of one.

"This morning." She smiled over her shoulder as she adjusted the shelves.

"You want to bring that up a little on the right." He sat on the arm of a chair, then set her mug down so his hands would be free for the chocolate-chip cookies. "Terrific," he decided after the first bite. "And, if I say so myself, I'm an expert."

"I'm glad they pass." With her mind on her shelves, Hester stepped back to admire them.

"It's important. I don't know if I could marry a woman who made lousy cookies." He picked up a second one and examined it. "Yeah, maybe I could," he said as Hester turned slowly to stare at him. "But it would be tough." He devoured the second one and smiled at her. "Luckily, it won't have to be an issue."

"Mitch." Before she could work out what to say, Radley came barreling in, his two friends behind him.

"Mitch!" Delighted with the company, Radley screeched to a halt beside him so that Mitch's arm went naturally around his shoulders. "We just had the neatest battle. We're the only survivors."

"Hungry work. Have a cookie."

Radley took one and shoved it into his mouth. "We've got to go up to Ernie's and get more weapons." He reached for another cookie, then caught his mother's eye. "You didn't bring Taz up."

"He stayed up late watching a movie. He's sleeping in today."

"Okay." Radley accepted this before turning to his mother. "Is it okay if we go up to Ernie's for a while?"

"Sure. Just don't go outside unless you let me know."

"We won't. You guys go ahead. I gotta get something."

He raced back to the bedroom while his friends trooped to the door.

"I'm glad he's making some new friends," Hester commented as she reached for her mug. "He was worried about it."

"Radley's not the kind of kid who has trouble making friends."

"No, he's not."

"He's also fortunate to have a mother who lets them come around and bakes cookies for them." He took another sip of coffee. His mother's cook had baked little cakes. He thought Hester would understand it wasn't quite the same thing. "Of course, once we're married we'll have to give him some brothers and sisters. What are you going to put on the shelf?"

"Useless things," she murmured, staring at him. "Mitch, I don't want to fight, but I think we should clear this up."

"Clear what up? Oh, I meant to tell you I started on the script. It's going pretty well."

"I'm glad." And confused. "Really, that's wonderful, but I think we should talk about this business first."

"Sure, what business was that?"

She opened her mouth, and was once more interrupted by her son. When Radley came in, Hester walked away to put a small china cat on the bottom shelf.

"I made something for you in school." Embarrassed, Radley held his hands behind his back.

"Yeah?" Mitch set his coffee down. "Do I get to see it?"

"It's Valentine's Day, you know." After a moment's hesitation, he handed Mitch a card fashioned out of construction paper and blue ribbon. "I made Mom this heart with lace stuff, but I thought the ribbon was better for guys." Radley shuffled his feet. "It opens."

Not certain he could trust his voice, Mitch opened the card. Radley had used his very best block printing.

"To my best friend, Mitch. I love you, Radley." He had to clear his throat, and hoped he wouldn't make a fool out of himself. "It's great. I, ah, nobody ever made me a card before."

"Really?" Embarrassment faded with surprise. "I make them for Mom all the time. She says she likes them better than the ones you buy."

"I like this one a lot better," Mitch told him. He wasn't sure boys that were nearly ten tolerated being kissed, but he ran a hand over Radley's hair and kissed him anyway. "Thanks."

"You're welcome. See ya."

"Yeah." Mitch heard the door slam as he stared down at the little folded piece of construction paper.

"I didn't know he'd made it," Hester said quietly. "I guess he wanted to keep it a secret."

"He did a nice job." At the moment, he didn't have the capacity to explain what the paper and ribbon meant to him. Rising, he walked to the window with the card in his hands. "I'm crazy about him."

"I know." She moistened her lips. She did know it. If she'd ever doubted the extent of Mitch's feelings for her son, she'd just seen full proof of it. It only made things more difficult. "In just a few weeks, you've done so much for him. I know neither one of us have the right to expect you to be there, but I want you to know it means a lot that you are."

He had to clamp down on a surge of fury. He didn't want her gratitude, but one hell of a lot more. Keep cool,

Dempsey, he warned himself. "The best advice I can give you is to get used to it, Hester."

"That's exactly what I can't do." Driven, she went to him. "Mitch, I do care for you, but I'm not going to depend on you. I can't afford to expect or anticipate or rely."

"So you've said." He set the card down carefully on the table. "I'm not arguing."

"What were you saying before—"

"What did I say?"

"About when we were married."

"Did I say that?" He smiled at her as he wound her hair around his finger. "I don't know what I could have been thinking of."

"Mitch, I have a feeling you're trying to throw me off guard."

"Is it working?"

Treat it lightly, she told herself. If he wanted to make a game of it, she'd oblige him. "Only to the point that it confirms what I've always thought about you. You're a very strange man."

"In what context?"

"Okay, to begin with, you talk to your dog."

"He talks back, so that doesn't count. Try again." With her hair still wound around his finger, he tugged her a bit closer. Whether she realized it or not, they were talking about their relationship, and she was relaxed.

"You write comic books for a living. And you read them."

"Being a woman with banking experience, you should understand the importance of a good investment. Do you know what the double issue of my *Defenders of Perth* is worth to a collector? Modesty prevents me from naming figures."

"I bet it does."

He acknowledged this with a slight nod. "And, Mrs. Wallace, I'd be happy to debate the value of literature in any form with you. Did I mention that I was captain of the debating team in high school?"

"No." She had her hands on his chest, once again drawn to the tough, disciplined body beneath the tattered sweater. "There's also the fact that you haven't thrown out a newspaper or magazine in five years."

"I'm saving up for the big paper drive of the second millennium. Conservation is my middle name."

"You also have an answer for everything."

"There's only one I want from you. Did I mention that I fell for your eyes right after I fell for your legs?"

"No, you didn't." Her lips curved just a little. "I never told you that the first time I saw you, through the peephole, I stared at you for a long time."

"I know." He grinned back at her. "If you look in those things right, you can see a shadow."

"Oh," she said, and could think of nothing else to say.

"You know, Mrs. Wallace, those kids could come running back in here anytime. Do you mind if we stop talking for a few minutes?"

"No." She slipped her arms around him. "I don't mind at all."

She didn't want to admit even to herself that she felt safe, protected, with his arms around her. But she did. She didn't want to accept that she'd been afraid of losing him, terrified of the hole he would have left in her life. But the fear had been very real. It faded now as she lifted her lips to his.

She couldn't think about tomorrow or the future Mitch sketched so easily with talk of marriage and family. She'd been taught that marriage was forever, but she'd learned that it was a promise easily made and easily broken. There would be no more broken promises in her life, no more broken vows.

Feelings might rush through her, bringing with them longings and silver-dusted dreams. Her heart might be lost to him, but her will was still her own. Even as her hands gripped him tighter, pulled him closer, Hester told herself it was that will that would save them both unhappiness later.

"I love you, Hester." He murmured the words against her mouth, knowing she might not want to hear them but that it was something he had to say. If he said it enough, she might begin to believe the words and, more, the meaning behind them.

He wanted forever from her—forever for her—not just a moment like this, stolen in the sunlight that poured through the window, or other moments, taken in the shadows. Only once before had he wanted anything with something close to this intensity. That had been something abstract, something nebulous called art. The time had eventually come when he'd been forced to admit that dream would never be within reach.

But Hester was here in his arms. He could hold her like this and taste the sweet, warm longings that stirred in her. She wasn't a dream, but a woman he loved and wanted and would have. If keeping her meant playing games until the layers of her resistance were washed away, then he'd play.

He lifted his hands to her face, twining his fingers into her hair. "I guess the kids will be coming back."

"Probably." Her lips sought his again. Had she ever felt this sense of urgency before? "I wish we had more time."

"Do you?"

Her eyes were half-closed as he drew away. "Yes."

"Let me come back tonight."

"Oh, Mitch." She stepped into his arms to rest her head on his shoulder. For the first time in a decade, she found the mother and the woman at war. "I want you. You know that, don't you?"

Her heart was still pumping hard and fast against his. "I think I figured it out."

"I wish we could be together tonight, but there's Rad."

"I know how you feel about me staying here with Rad in the next room. Hester…" He ran his hands up her arms to rest them on her shoulders. "Why not be honest with him, tell him we care about each other and want to be together?"

"Mitch, he's only a baby."

"No, he's not. No, wait," he continued before she could speak again. "I'm not saying we should make it seem casual or careless, but that we should let Radley know how we feel about each other, and when two grown people feel this strongly about each other they need to show it."

It seemed so simple when he said it, so logical, so natural. Gathering her thoughts, she stepped back. "Mitch, Rad loves you, and he loves with the innocence and lack of restriction of a child."

"I love him, too."

She looked into his eyes and nodded. "Yes, I think you do, and if it's true, I hope you'll understand. I'm afraid that if I bring Radley into this at this point he'll come to depend on you even more than he already does. He'd come to look at you as…"

"As a father," Mitch finished. "You don't want a father in his life, do you, Hester?"

"That's not fair." Her eyes, usually so calm and clear, turned to smoke.

"Maybe not, but if I were you I'd give it some hard thought."

"There's no reason to say cruel things because I won't have sex with you when my son's sleeping in the next room."

He caught her by the shirt so fast she could only stare. She'd seen him annoyed, pushed close to the edge, but never furious. "Damn you, do you think that's all I'm talking about? If all I wanted was sex, I could go downstairs and pick up the phone. Sex is easy, Hester. All it takes is two people and a little spare time."

"I'm sorry." She closed her eyes, knowing she'd never said or done anything in her life she'd been more ashamed of. "That was stupid, Mitch, I just keep feeling as though my back's against the wall. I need some time, please."

"So do I. But the time I need is with you." He dropped his hands and stuck them in his pockets. "I'm pressuring you. I know it and I'm not going to stop, because I believe in us."

"I wish I could, also, honestly I do, but there's too much at stake for me."

And for himself, Mitch thought, but was calm enough now to hold off. "We'll let it ride for a while. Are you and Rad up to hitting a few arcades at Times Square tonight?"

"Sure. He'd love it." She stepped toward him again. "So would I."

"You say that now, but you won't after I humiliate you with my superior skill."

"I love you."

He let out a long breath, fighting back the urge to grab her again and refuse to let go. "You going to let me know when you're comfortable with that?"

"You'll be the first."

He picked up the card Radley had made him. "Tell Rad I'll see him later."

"I will." He was halfway to the door when she started after him. "Mitch, why don't you come to dinner tomorrow? I'll fix a pot roast."

He tilted his head. "The kind with the little potatoes and carrots all around?"

"Sure."

"And biscuits?"

She smiled. "If you want."

"Sounds great, but I'm tied up."

'Oh." She struggled with the need to ask how, but reminded herself she didn't have the right.

Mitch smiled, selfishly pleased to see her disappointment. "Can I have a rain check?"

"Sure." She tried to answer the smile. "I guess Radley told you about his birthday next week," she said when Mitch reached the door.

"Only five or six times." He paused, his hand on the knob.

"He's having a party next Saturday afternoon. I know he'd like you to come if you can."

"I'll be there. Look, why don't we take off about seven? I'll bring the quarters."

"We'll be ready." He wasn't going to kiss her goodbye, she thought. "Mitch, I—"

"I almost forgot." Casually he reached in his back pocket and pulled out a small box.

"What is it?"

"It's Valentine's Day, isn't it?" He put it in her hand. "So this is a Valentine's Day present."

"A Valentine's Day present," she repeated dumbly.

"Yeah, tradition, remember? I thought about candy, but I figured you'd spend a whole lot of time making sure Radley didn't eat too much of it. But look, if you'd rather have candy, I'll just take this back and—"

"No." She pulled the box out of his reach, then laughed. "I don't even know what it is."

"You'd probably find out if you open the box."

Flipping the lid, she saw the thin gold chain that held a heart no bigger than her thumbnail. It glittered with the diamonds that formed it. "Oh, Mitch, it's gorgeous."

"Something told me it'd be a bigger hit with you than candy. Candy would have made you think about oral hygiene."

"I'm not that bad," she countered, then lifted the heart out of the box. "Mitch, it's really beautiful, I love it, but it's too—"

"Conventional, I know," he interrupted as he took it from her. "But I'm just that kind of guy."

"You are?"

"Just turn around and let me hook it for you."

She obeyed, lifting one hand up under her hair. "I do love it, but I don't expect you to buy me expensive presents."

"Um-hmm." His brows were drawn together as he worked the clasp. "I didn't expect bacon and eggs, but you seemed to get a kick out of fixing them." The clasp secured, he turned her around to face him. "I get a kick out of seeing you wear my heart around your neck."

"Thank you." She touched a finger to the heart. "I didn't buy you any candy, either, but maybe I can give you something else."

She was smiling when she kissed him, gently, teasingly, with a power that surprised them both. It took only an instant, an instant to be lost, to need, to imagine. His back was to the door as he moved his hands from her face to her hair to her shoulders, then to her hips to mold her even more truly against him. The fire burned, hot and fast, so that even when she drew away he felt singed by it. With his eyes on hers, Mitch let out a very long, very slow breath.

"I guess those kids will be coming back."

"Any minute."

"Uh-huh." He kissed her lightly on the brow before he turned and opened the door. "See you later."

He would go down to get Taz, Mitch thought as he started down the hall. Then he was going for a walk. A long one.

True to his word Mitch's pockets were filled with quarters. The arcades were packed with people and echoed with the pings and whistles and machine-gun sound effects of the games. Hester stood to the side as Mitch and Radley used their combined talents to save the world from intergalactic wars.

"Nice shooting, Corporal." Mitch slapped the boy's shoulder as a Phaser II rocket disintegrated in a flash of colored light.

"It's your turn." Radley relinquished the controls to his superior officer. "Watch out for the sensor missiles."

"Don't worry. I'm a veteran."

"We're going to beat the high score." Radley tore his eyes away from the screen long enough to look at his mother. "Then we can put our initials up. Isn't this a neat place? It's got everything."

Everything, Hester thought, including some seamy-looking characters in leather and tattoos. The machine behind her let out a high-pitched scream. "Just stay close, okay?"

"Okay, Corporal, we're only seven hundred points away from the high score. Keep your eyes peeled for nuclear satellites."

"Aye, aye, sir." Radley clenched his jaw and took the controls.

"Good reflexes," Mitch said to Hester as he watched Radley control his ship with one hand and fire surface-to-air missiles with the other.

"Josh has one of those home video games. Rad loves to go over and play things like this." She caught her bottom lip between her teeth as Radley's ship barely missed annihilation. "I can never figure out how he can tell what's going on. Oh, look, he's passed the high score."

They continued to watch in tense silence as Radley fought bravely to the last man. As a finale, the screen exploded in brilliant fireworks of sound and light.

"A new record." Mitch hoisted Radley in the air. "This calls for a field promotion. Sergeant, inscribe your initials."

"But you got more points than I did."

"Who's counting? Go ahead."

Face flushed with pride, Radley clicked the button that ran through the alphabet. R.A.W. A for Allan, Mitch thought, and said nothing.

"My initials spell raw, and backward they spell war—pretty neat, huh?"

"Pretty neat," Mitch agreed. "Want to give it a shot, Hester?"

"No, thanks. I'll just watch."

"Mom doesn't like to play," Radley confided. "Her palms sweat."

"Your palms sweat?" Mitch repeated with a grin.

Hester sent a telling look in Radley's direction. "It's the pressure. I can't take being responsible for the fate of the world. I know it's a game," she said before Mitch could respond. "But I get, well, caught up."

"You're terrific, Mrs. Wallace." He kissed her as Radley looked on and considered.

It made him feel funny to see Mitch kiss his mother. He wasn't sure if it was a good funny or a bad funny. Then Mitch dropped a hand to his shoulder. It always made Radley feel nice when Mitch put his hand there.

"Okay, what'll it be next, the Amazon jungles, medieval times, a search for the killer shark?"

"I like the one with the ninja. I saw a ninja movie at Josh's once—well, almost did. Josh's mom turned it off because one of the women was taking her clothes off and stuff."

"Oh, yeah?" Mitch stifled a laugh as Hester's mouth dropped open. "What was the name?"

"Never mind." Hester gripped Radley's hand. "I'm sure Josh's parents just made a mistake."

"Josh's father thought it was about throwing stars and kung fu. Josh's mom got mad and made him take it back to the video place and get something else. But I still like ninjas."

"Let's see if we can find a free machine." Mitch fell into step beside Hester. "I don't think he was marked for life."

"I'd still like to know what 'and stuff' means."

"Me, too." He swung an arm around her shoulders to steer her through a clutch of teenagers. "Maybe we could rent it."

"I'll pass, thanks."

"You don't want to see *Naked Ninjas from Nagasaki?*" When she turned around to stare at him, Mitch held out both hands, palms up. "I made it up. I swear."

"Hmmm."

"Here's one. Can I play this one?"

Mitch continued to grin at Hester as he dug out quarters.

The time passed so that Hester almost stopped hearing the noise from both machines and people. To placate Radley she played a few of the less intense games, ones that didn't deal with world domination or universal destruction. But for the most part she watched him, pleased to see him enjoying what was for him a real night on the town.

They must look like a family, she thought as Radley and Mitch bent over the controls in a head-to-head duel. She wished she still believed in such things. But to her, families and lifetime commitments were as fanciful as the machines that spewed out color and light around them.

Day-to-day, Hester thought with a little sigh. That was all she could afford to believe in now. In a few hours she would tuck Radley in bed and go to her room alone. That was the only way to make sure they were both safe. She heard Mitch laugh and shout encouragement to Radley, and looked away. It was the only way, she told herself again. No matter how much she wanted or was tempted to believe again, she couldn't risk it.

"How about the pinball machines?" Mitch suggested.

"They're okay." Though they rang with wild colors and lights, Radley didn't find them terribly exciting. "Mom likes them though."

"Are you any good?"

Hester pushed aside her uneasy thoughts. "Not bad."

"Care to go one-on-one?" He jingled the quarters in his pockets.

Though she'd never considered herself highly competitive, she was swayed by his smug look. "All right."

She'd always had a touch for pinball, a light enough, quick enough touch to have beaten her brother nine times out of ten. Though these machines were electronic and more sophisticated than the ones she'd played in her youth, she didn't doubt she could make a good showing.

"I could give you a handicap," Mitch suggested as he pushed coins into the slot.

"Funny, I was just going to say the same thing to you." With a smile, Hester took the controls.

It had something to do with black magic and white knights. Hester tuned out the sounds and concentrated on keeping the ball in play. Her timing was sharp. Mitch stood behind her with his hands tucked in his back pockets and nodded as she sent the ball spinning.

He liked the way she leaned into the machine, her lips slightly parted, her eyes narrowed and alert. Now and then she would catch her tongue between her teeth and push her body forward as if to follow the ball on its quick, erratic course.

The little silver ball rammed into rubber, sending bells ringing and lights flashing. By the time her first ball dropped, she'd already racked up an impressive score.

"Not bad for an amateur," Mitch commented with a wink at Radley.

"I'm just warming up." With a smile, she stepped back.

Radley watched the progress of the ball as Mitch took

control. But he had to stand on his toes to get the full effect. It was pretty neat when the ball got hung up in the top of the machine where the bumpers sent it vibrating back and forth in a blur. He glanced behind him at the rows of other machines and wished he'd thought to ask for another quarter before they'd started to play. But if he couldn't play, he could watch. He edged away to get a closer look at a nearby game.

"Looks like I'm ahead by a hundred," Mitch said as he stepped aside for Hester.

"I didn't want to blow you away with the first ball. It seemed rude." She pulled back the plunger and let the ball rip.

This time she had the feel and the rhythm down pat. She didn't let the ball rest as she set it right, then left, then up the middle where it streaked through a tunnel and crashed into a lighted dragon. It took her back to her childhood, when her wants had been simple and her dreams still gilt-edged. As the machine rocked with noise, she laughed and threw herself into the competition.

Her score flashed higher and higher with enough fanfare to draw a small crowd. Before her second ball dropped, people were choosing up sides.

Mitch took position. Unlike Hester, he didn't block out the sounds and lights, but used them to pump the adrenaline. He nearly lost the ball, causing indrawn breaths behind him, but caught it on the tip of his flipper to shoot it hard into a corner. This time he finished fifty points behind her.

The third and final turn brought more people. Hester thought she heard someone placing bets before she tuned them out and put all her concentration on the ball and her timing. She was nearly exhausted before she backed away again.

"You're going to need a miracle, Mitch."

"Don't get cocky." He flicked his wrists like a concert pianist and earned a few hoots and cheers from the crowd.

Hester had to admit as she watched his technique that he played brilliantly. He took chances that could have cost him his last ball, but turned them into triumph. He stood spread-legged and relaxed, but she saw in his eyes that kind of deep concentration that she'd come to expect from him, but had yet to become used to. His hair fell over his forehead, as careless as he was. There was a slight smile on his face that struck her as both pleased and reckless.

She found herself watching him rather than the ball as she toyed with the little diamond heart she'd worn over a plain black turtleneck.

This was the kind of man women dreamed about and made heroes of. This was the kind of man a woman could come to lean upon if she wasn't careful. With a man like him, a woman could have years of laughter. The defenses around her heart weakened a bit with her sigh.

The ball was lost in the dragon's cave with a series of roars.

"She got you by ten points," someone in the crowd pointed out. "Ten points, buddy."

"Got yourself a free game," someone else said, giving Hester a friendly slap on the back.

Mitch shook his head as he wiped his hands on the thighs of his jeans. "About that handicap—" he began.

"Too late." Ridiculously pleased with herself, Hester

hooked her thumbs in her belt loops and studied her score. "Superior reflexes. It's all in the wrist."

"How about a rematch?"

"I don't want to humiliate you again." She turned, intending to offer Radley the free game. "Rad, why don't you…Rad?" She nudged her way through the few lingering onlookers. "Radley?" A little splinter of panic shot straight up her spine. "He's not here."

"He was here a minute ago." Mitch put a hand on her arm and scanned what he could see of the room.

"I wasn't paying any attention." She brought a hand up to her throat, where the fear had already lodged, and began to walk quickly. "I know better than to take my eyes off him in a place like this."

"Stop." He kept his voice calm, but her fear had already transferred itself to him. He knew how easy it was to whisk one small boy away in a crowd. You couldn't pour your milk in the morning without being aware of it. "He's just wandering around the machines. We'll find him. I'll go around this way, you go down here."

She nodded and spun away without a word. They were six or seven deep at some of the machines. Hester stopped at each one, searching for a small blond boy in a blue sweater. She called for him over the noise and clatter of machines.

When she passed the big glass doors and looked outside to the lights and crowded sidewalks of Times Square, her heart turned over in her breast. He hadn't gone outside, she told herself. Radley would never do something so expressly forbidden. Unless someone had taken him, or…

Gripping her hands together tightly, she turned away. She wouldn't think like that. But the room was so big, filled with so many people, all strangers. And the noise, the noise was more deafening than she'd remembered. How could she have heard him if he'd called out for her?

She started down the next row, calling. Once she heard a young boy laugh and spun around. But it wasn't Radley. She'd covered half the room, and ten minutes was gone, when she thought she would have to call the police. She quickened her pace and tried to look everywhere at once as she went from row to row.

There was so much noise, and the lights were so bright. Maybe she should double back—she might have missed him. Maybe he was waiting for her now by that damn pinball machine, wondering where she'd gone. He might be afraid. He could be calling for her. He could be...

Then she saw him, hoisted in Mitch's arms. Hester shoved two people aside as she ran for them. "Radley!" She threw her arms around both of them and buried her face in his hair.

"He'd gone over to watch someone play," Mitch began as he stroked a hand up and down her back. "He ran into someone he knew from school."

"It was Ricky Nesbit, Mom. He was with his big brother, and they lent me a quarter. We went to play a game. I didn't know it was so far away."

"Radley." She struggled with the tears and kept her voice firm. "You know the rules about staying with me. This is a big place with a lot of people. I have to be able to trust you not to wander away."

"I didn't mean to. It was just that Ricky said it would just take a minute. I was coming right back."

"Rules have reasons, Radley, and we've been through them."

"But, Mom—"

"Rad." Mitch shifted the boy in his arms. "You scared your mother and me."

"I'm sorry," His eyes clouded up. "I didn't mean to make you scared."

"Don't do it again." Her voice softened as she kissed his cheek. "Next time it's solitary confinement. You're all I've got, Rad." She hugged him again. Her eyes were closed so that she didn't see the change in Mitch's expression. "I can't let anything happen to you."

"I won't do it again."

All she had, Mitch thought as he set the boy down. Was she still so stubborn that she couldn't admit, even to herself, that she had someone else now, too? He jammed his hands into his pockets and tried to force back both anger and hurt. She was going to have to make room in her life soon, very soon, or he'd damn well make it for her.

Chapter 11

He wasn't sure if he was doing more harm than good by staying out of Hester's way for a few days, but Mitch needed time himself. It wasn't his style to dissect and analyze, but to feel and act. However, he'd never felt quite this strongly before or acted quite so rashly.

When possible, he buried himself in work and in the fantasies he could control. When it wasn't, he stayed alone in his rooms, with old movies flickering on the television or music blaring through the stereo. He continued to work on the screenplay he didn't know if he could write, in the hope that the challenge of it would stop him from marching two floors up and demanding that Hester Wallace came to her senses.

She wanted him, yet she didn't want him. She opened to him, yet kept the most precious part of her closed. She trusted him, yet didn't believe in him enough to share her life with him.

You're all I've got, Rad. And all she wanted? Mitch was forced to ask himself the question. How could such a bright, giving woman base the rest of her life on a mistake she'd made over ten years before?

The helplessness of it infuriated him. Even when he'd hit bottom in New Orleans, he hadn't been helpless. He'd faced his limitations, accepted them, and had channeled his talents differently. Had the time come for him to face and accept his limitations with Hester?

He spent hours thinking about it, considering compromises and then rejecting them. Could he do as she asked and leave things as they were? They would be lovers, with no promises between them and no talk of a future. They could have a relationship as long as there was no hint of permanency or bonds. No, he couldn't do as she asked. Now that he had found the only woman he wanted in his life, he couldn't accept her either part-time or partway.

It was something of a shock to discover he was such an advocate of marriage. He couldn't say that he'd seen very many that had been made in heaven. His parents had been well suited—the same tastes, the same class, the same outlook—but he couldn't remember ever witnessing any passion between them. Affection and loyalty, yes, and a united front against their son's ambitions, but they lacked the spark and simmer that added excitement.

He asked himself if it was only passion he felt for Hester, but knew the answer already. Even as he sat alone he could imagine them twenty years in the future, sitting on the porch swing she'd described. He could see them growing older together, filing away memories and traditions.

He wasn't going to lose that. However long it took,

however many walls he had to scale, he wasn't going to lose that.

Mitch dragged a hand through his hair, then gathered up the boxes he needed to lug upstairs.

She was afraid he wasn't coming. There had been some subtle change in Mitch since the night they'd gone to Times Square. He'd been strangely distant on the phone, and though she'd invited him up more than once, he'd always made an excuse.

She was losing him. Hester poured punch into paper cups and reminded herself that she'd known it was only temporary. He had the right to live his own life, to go his own way. She could hardly expect him to tolerate the distance she felt she had to put between them or to understand the lack of time and attention she could give him because of Radley and her job. All she could hope was that he would remain a friend.

Oh, God, she missed him. She missed having him to talk to, to laugh with, even to lean on—though she could only allow herself to lean a little. Hester set the pitcher on the counter and took a deep breath. It couldn't matter, she couldn't *let* it matter now. There were ten excited and noisy boys in the other room. Her responsibility, she reminded herself. She couldn't stand here listing her regrets when she had obligations.

As she carried the tray of drinks into the living room, two boys shot by her. Three more were wrestling on the floor, while the others shouted to be heard over the record player. Hester had already noted that one of Radley's newest friends wore a silver earring and spoke knowledgeably about girls. She set the tray down and glanced quickly at the ceiling.

Give me a few more years of comic books and erector sets. Please, I'm just not ready for the rest of it yet.

"Drink break," she said out loud. "Michael, why don't you let Ernie out of that headlock now and have some punch? Rad, set down the kitten. They get cranky if they're handled too much."

With reluctance, Radley set the little bundle of black-and-white fur in a padded basket. "He's really neat. I like him the best." He snatched a drink off the tray as several other hands reached out. "I really like my watch, too." He held it out, pushing a button that sent it from time mode to the first in a series of miniature video games.

"Just make sure you don't play with it when you should be paying attention in school."

Several boys groaned and elbowed Radley. Hester had just about convinced them to settle down with one of Radley's board games when the knock sounded at the door.

"I'll get it!" Radley hopped up and raced for the door. He had one more birthday wish. When he opened the door, it came true. "Mitch! I knew you'd come. Mom said you'd probably gotten real busy, but I knew you'd come. I got a kitten. I named him Zark. Want to see?"

"As soon as I get rid of some of these boxes." Even arms as well tuned as his were beginning to feel the strain. Mitch set them on the sofa and turned, only to have Zark's namesake shoved into his hands. The kitten purred and arched under a stroking finger. "Cute. We'll have to take him down and introduce him to Taz."

"Won't Taz eat him?"

"You've got to be kidding." Mitch tucked the kitten under his arm and looked at Hester. "Hi."

"Hi." He needed a shave, his sweater had a hole in

the seam, and he looked wonderful. "We were afraid you wouldn't make it."

"I said I'd be here." Lazily he scratched between the kitten's ears. "I keep my promises."

"I got this watch, too." Radley held up his wrist. "It tells the time and the date and stuff, then you can play Dive Bomb and Scrimmage."

"Oh, yeah, Dive Bomb?" Mitch sat on the arm of the couch and watched Radley send the little dots spinning. "Never have to be bored on a long subway ride again, right?"

"Or at the dentist's office. You want to play?"

"Later. I'm sorry I'm late. I got hung up in the store."

"That's okay. We didn't have the cake yet 'cause I wanted to wait. It's chocolate."

"Great. Aren't you going to ask for your present?"

"I'm not supposed to." He sneaked a look at his mother, who was busy keeping some of his friends from wrestling again. "Did you really get me something?"

"Nah." Laughing at Radley's expression, he ruffled his hair. "Sure I did. It's right there on the couch."

"Which one?"

"All of them."

Radley's eyes grew big as saucers. "All of them?"

"They all sort of go together. Why don't you open that one first?"

Because of the lack of time and materials, Mitch hadn't wrapped the boxes. He'd barely had enough forethought to put tape over the name brand and model, but buying presents for young boys was a new experience, and one he'd enjoyed immensely. Radley began to pry open the heavy cardboard with assistance from his more curious friends.

"Wow, a PC." Josh craned his head over Radley's shoulder. "Robert Sawyer's got one just like it. You can play all kinds of things on it."

"A computer." Radley stared in amazement at the open box, then turned to Mitch. "Is it for me, really? To keep?"

"Sure you can keep it—it's a present. I was hoping you'd let me play with it sometime."

"You can play with it anytime, anytime you want." He threw his arms around Mitch's neck, forgetting to be embarrassed because his friends were watching. "Thanks. Can we hook it up right now?"

"I thought you'd never ask."

"Rad, you'll have to clear off the desk in your room. Hold it," Hester added when a flood of young bodies started by. "That doesn't mean shoving everything on the floor, okay? You take care of it properly, and Mitch and I will bring this in."

They streaked away with war whoops that warned her she'd be finding surprises under Radley's bed and under the rug for some time. She'd worry about that later. Now she crossed the room to stand beside Mitch.

"That was a terribly generous thing to do."

"He's bright. A kid that bright deserves one of these."

"Yes." She looked at the boxes yet to be opened. There'd be a monitor, disk drives, software. "I've wanted to get him one, but haven't been able to swing it."

"I didn't mean that as a criticism, Hester."

"I know you didn't." She gnawed at her lip in a gesture that told him her nerves were working at her. "I also know this isn't the time to talk, and that we have to. But before we take this in to Rad, I want to tell you how glad I am that you're here."

"It's where I want to be." He ran a thumb along her jawline. "You're going to have to start believing that."

She took his hand and turned her lips into his palm. "You might not feel the same way after you spend the next hour or so with ten fifth-graders." She smiled as the first minor crash sounded from Radley's bedroom. "'Once more unto the breach'?"

The crash was followed by several young voices raised in passionate argument. "How about, 'Lay on, MacDuff'?"

"Whatever." Drawing a deep breath, Hester lifted the first box.

It was over. The last birthday guest had been dragged away by his parents. A strange and wonderful silence lay over the living room. Hester sat in a chair, her eyes half-closed, while Mitch lay sprawled on the couch with his closed completely. In the silence Hester could hear the occasional click of Radley's new computer, and the mewing of Zark, who sat in his lap. With a contented sigh, she surveyed the living room.

It was in shambles. Paper cups and plates were strewn everywhere. The remains of potato chips and pretzels were in bowls, with a good portion of them crushed into the carpet. Scraps of wrapping paper were scattered among the toys the boys had decided worthy of attention. She didn't want to dwell on what the kitchen looked like.

Mitch opened one eye and looked at her. "Did we win?"

"Absolutely." Reluctantly, Hester dragged herself up. "It was a brilliant victory. Want a pillow?"

"No." Taking her hand, he flipped her down on top of him.

"Mitch, Radley is—"

"Playing with his computer," he finished, then nuzzled her bottom lip. "I'm betting he breaks down and puts some of the educational software in before it's over."

"It was pretty clever of you to mix those in."

"I'm a pretty clever kind of guy." He shifted her until she fit into the curve of his shoulder. "Besides, I figured I'd win you over with the machine's practicality, and Rad and I could play the games."

"I'm surprised you don't have one of your own."

"Actually…it seemed like such a good idea when I went in for Rad's that I picked up two. To balance my household accounts," he said when Hester looked up at him. "And modernize my filing system."

"You don't have a filing system."

"See?" He settled his cheek on her hair. "Hester, do you know what one of the ten greatest boons to civilization is?"

"The microwave oven?"

"The afternoon nap. This is a great sofa you've got here."

"It needs reupholstering."

"You can't see that when you're lying on it." He tucked his arm around her waist. "Sleep with me awhile."

"I really have to clean up." But she found it easy to close her eyes.

"Why? Expecting company?"

"No. But don't you have to go down and take Taz out?"

"I slipped Ernie a couple of bucks to walk him."

Hester snuggled into his shoulder. "You are clever."

"That's what I've been trying to tell you."

"I haven't even thought about dinner," she murmured as her mind began to drift.

"Let 'em eat cake."

With a quiet laugh, she slipped into sleep beside him.

Radley wandered in a few moments later, the kitten curled in his arms. He'd wanted to tell them about his latest score. Standing at the foot of the sofa, he scratched the kitten's ears and studied his mom and Mitch thoughtfully. Sometimes when he had a bad dream or wasn't feeling very good, his mom would sleep with him. It always made him feel better. Maybe sleeping with Mitch made his mom feel better.

He wondered if Mitch loved his mom. It made his stomach feel funny to think about it. He wanted Mitch to stay and be his friend. If they got married, did that mean Mitch would go away? He would have to ask, Radley decided. His mom always told him the truth. Shifting the kitten to one arm, he lifted the bowl of chips and carried it into his room.

It was nearly dark when she awoke. Hester opened her eyes and looked directly into Mitch's. She blinked, trying to orient herself. Then he kissed her, and she remembered everything.

"We must have slept for an hour," she murmured.

"Closer to two. How do you feel?"

"Groggy. I always feel groggy if I sleep during the day." She stretched her shoulders and heard Radley giggling in his room. "He must still be at that computer. I don't think I've ever seen him happier."

"And you?"

"Yes." She traced his lips with her fingertip. "I'm happy."

"If you're groggy and happy, this might be the perfect time for me to ask you to marry me again."

"Mitch."

"No? Okay, I'll wait until I can get you drunk. Any more of that cake left?"

"A little. You're not angry?"

Mitch combed his fingers through his hair as he sat up. "About what?"

Hester put her hands on his shoulders, then rested her cheek on his. "I'm sorry I can't give you what you want."

He tightened his arms around her; then with an effort, he relaxed. "Good. That means you're close to changing your mind. I'd like a double-ring ceremony."

"Mitch!"

"What?"

She drew back and, because she didn't trust his smile, shook her head. "Nothing. I think it's best to say nothing. Go ahead and help yourself to the cake. I'm going to get started in here."

Mitch glanced around the room, which looked to be in pretty good shape by his standards. "You really want to clean this up tonight?"

"You don't expect me to leave this mess until the morning," she began, then stopped herself. "Forget I said that. I forgot who I was talking to."

Mitch narrowed his eyes suspiciously. "Are you accusing me of being sloppy?"

"Not at all. I'm sure there's a lot to be said for living in a 'junkyard' decor with a touch of 'paper drive' thrown in. It's uniquely you." She began to gather up paper plates. "It probably comes from having maids as a child."

"Actually, it comes from never being able to mess up a room. My mother couldn't stand disorder." He'd always been fond of it, Mitch mused, but there was something to be said for watching Hester tidy up. "For my tenth birthday, she hired a magician. We sat in little folding chairs—the boys in suits, the girls in organdy dresses—and watched the performance. Then we were served a light lunch on the terrace. There were enough servants around so that when it was over there wasn't a crumb to be picked up. I guess I'm overcompensating."

"Maybe a little." She kissed both of his cheeks. What an odd man he was, she thought, so calm and easygoing on one hand, so driven by demons on the other. She strongly believed that childhood affected adulthood, even to old age. It was the strength of that belief that made her so fiercely determined to do the best she could by Radley. "You're entitled to your dust and clutter, Mitch. Don't let anyone take it away from you."

He kissed her cheek in return. "I guess you're entitled to your neat and tidy. Where's your vacuum?"

She drew back, brow lifted. "Do you know what one is?"

"Cute. Very cute." He pinched her, hard, just under the ribs. Hester jumped back with a squeal. "Ah, ticklish, huh?"

"Cut it out," she warned, holding out the stack of paper plates like a shield. "I wouldn't want to hurt you."

"Come on." He crouched like a wrestler. "Two falls out of three."

"I'm warning you." Wary of the gleam in his eye, she backed up as he advanced. "I'll get violent."

"Promise?" He lunged, gripping her under the waist. In reflex, Hester lifted her arms. The plates, dripping with cake and ice cream, caught him full in the face. "Oh, God." Her own scream of laughter had her falling backward into a chair. She opened her mouth to speak, but only doubled up again.

Very slowly Mitch wiped a hand over his cheek, then studied the smear of chocolate. Watching, Hester let out another peal of laughter and held her sides helplessly.

"What's going on?" Radley came into the living room staring at his mother, who could do nothing but point. Shifting his gaze, Radley stared in turn at Mitch. "Jeez." Radley rolled his eyes and began to giggle. "Mike's little sister gets food all over her face like that. She's almost two."

The control Hester had been scratching for slipped out of her grip. Choking with laughter, she pulled Radley against her. "It was—it was an accident," she managed, then collapsed again.

"It was a deliberate sneak attack," Mitch corrected. "And it calls for immediate retribution."

"Oh, please." Hester held out a hand, knowing she was too weak to defend herself. "I'm sorry. I swear. It was a reflex, that's all."

"So's this." He came closer, and though she ducked behind Radley, Mitch merely sandwiched the giggling boy between them. And he kissed her, her mouth, her nose, her cheeks, while she squirmed and laughed and struggled. When he was finished, he'd transferred a satisfactory amount of chocolate to her face. Radley took one look at his mother and slipped, cackling, to the floor.

"Maniac," she accused as she wiped chocolate from her chin with the back of her hand.

"You look beautiful in chocolate, Hester."

* * *

It took more than an hour to put everything to rights again. By popular vote, they ended up sharing a pizza as they once had before, then spending the rest of the evening trying out Radley's birthday treasures. When he began to nod over the keyboard, Hester nudged him into bed.

"Quite a day." Hester set the kitten in his basket at the foot of Radley's bed, then stepped out into the hall.

"I'd say it's a birthday he'll remember."

"So will I." She reached up to rub at a slight stiffness at the base of her neck. "Would you like some wine?"

"I'll get it." He turned her toward the living room. "Go sit down."

"Thanks." Hester sat on the couch, stretched out her legs and slipped off her shoes. It was definitely a day she would remember. Sometime during it, she'd come to realize that she could also have a night to remember.

"Here you go." Mitch handed her a glass of wine, then slipped onto the sofa beside her. Holding his own glass up, he shifted her so that she rested against him.

"This is nice." With a sigh, she brought the wine to her lips.

"Very nice." He bent to brush his lips over her neck. "I told you this was a great sofa."

"Sometimes I forget what it's like to relax like this. Everything's done, Radley's happy and tucked into bed, tomorrow's Sunday and there's nothing urgent to think about."

"No restless urge to go out dancing or carousing?"

"No." She stretched her shoulders. "You?"

"I'm happy right here."

"Then stay." She pressed her lips together a moment. "Stay tonight."

He was silent. His hand stopped its easy massage of her neck, then began again, slowly. "Are you sure that's what you want?"

"Yes." She drew a deep breath before she turned to look at him. "I've missed you. I wish I knew what was right and what was wrong, what was best for all of us, but I know I've missed you. Will you stay?"

"I'm not going anywhere."

She settled back against him, content. For a long time they sat just as they were, half dreaming, in silence, with lamplight glowing behind them.

"Are you still working on the script?" she asked at length.

"Mmm-hmm." He could get used to this, he thought, very used to having Hester snuggled beside him in the late evening with the lamplight dim and the scent of her hair teasing his senses. "You were right. I'd have hated myself if I hadn't tried to write it. I guess I had to get past the nerves."

"Nerves?" She smiled over her shoulder. "You?"

"I've been known to have them, when something's either unfamiliar or important. They were stretched pretty thin the first time I made love with you."

Hearing it not only surprised her but made the memory of it all the sweeter. "They didn't show."

"Take my word for it." He stroked the outside of her thigh, lightly and with a casualness that was its own kind of seduction. "I was afraid that I'd make the wrong move and screw up something that was more important than anything else in my life."

"You didn't make any wrong moves, and you make me feel very special."

When she rose, it felt natural to hold out a hand to him, to have his close over hers. She switched off lights as they walked to the bedroom.

Mitch closed the door. Hester turned down the bed. He knew it could be like this every night, for all the years they had left. She was on the edge of believing it. He knew it, he could see it in her eyes when he crossed to her. Her eyes remained on his while she unbuttoned her blouse.

They undressed in silence, but the air had already started to hum. Though nerves had relaxed, anticipation was edgier than ever. Now they knew what they could bring to each other. They slipped into bed together and turned to each other.

It felt so right, just the way his arms slipped around her to bring her close. Just the way their bodies met, merging warmth to warmth. She knew the feel of him now, the firmness, the strength. She knew how easily hers fit against it. She tipped her head back and, with her eyes still on his, offered her mouth.

Kissing him was like sliding down a cool river toward churning white water.

The sound of pleasure came deep in his throat as she pressed against him. The shyness was still there, but without the reserve and hesitation. Now there was only sweetness and an offering.

It was like this each time they came together. Exhilarating, stunning and right. He cupped the back of her head in his hand as she leaned over him. The light zing of the wine hadn't completely faded from her tongue. He tasted it, and her, as she explored his mouth. He sensed a boldness growing in her that hadn't been there before, a new confidence that caused her to come to him with her own demands and needs.

Her heart was open, he thought as her lips raced over his throat. And Hester was free. He'd wanted this for her—for them. With something like a laugh, he rolled over her and began to drive her toward madness.

She couldn't get enough of him. She took her hands, her mouth, over him quickly, almost fiercely, but found it impossible to assuage the greed. How could she have known a man could feel so good, so exciting? How could she have known that the scent of his skin would make her head reel and her desires sharpen? Just her name murmured in his voice aroused her.

Locked together, they tumbled over the sheets, tangling in the blanket, shoving it aside because the need for its warmth was long past. He moved as quickly as she, discovering new secrets to delight and torment her. She heard him gasp out her name as she ranged kisses over his chest. She felt his body tense and arch as she moved her hands lower.

Perhaps the power had always been there inside her, but Hester was certain it had been born in her that night. The power to arouse a man past the civilized, and perhaps past the wise. Wise or not, she gloried in it when he trapped her beneath him and let desire rule.

His mouth was hot and hungry as it raced over her. Demands, promises, pleas swirled through her head, but she couldn't speak. Even her breath was trapped as he drove her up and up. She caught him close, as though he were a lifeline in a sea that raged.

Then they both went under.

Chapter 12

The sky was cloudy and threatening snow. Half dozing, Hester turned away from the window to reach for Mitch. The bed beside her was rumpled but empty.

Had he left her during the night? she wondered as she ran her hand over the sheets where he'd slept. Her first reaction was disappointment. It would have been so sweet to have had him there to turn to in the morning. Then she drew her hand back and cupped it under her cheek.

Perhaps it was best that he'd gone. She couldn't be sure how Radley would feel. If Mitch was there to reach out to, she knew it would only become more difficult to keep herself from doing so again and again. No one knew how hard and painfully she'd worked to stop herself from needing anyone. Now, after all the years of struggling, she'd just begun to see real progress. She'd made a good home for Radley in a good neighborhood and had a strong, well-paying job. Security, stability.

She couldn't risk those things again for the emotional morass that came with depending on someone else. But she was already beginning to depend on him, Hester thought as she pushed back the blankets. No matter how much her head told her it was best that he wasn't here, she was sorry he wasn't. She *was* sorry, sorrier than he could ever know, that she was strong enough to stand apart from him.

Hester slipped on her robe and went to see if Radley wanted breakfast.

She found them together, hunched over the keyboard of Radley's computer while graphics exploded on the screen. "This thing's defective," Mitch insisted. "That was a dead-on shot."

"You missed by a mile."

"I'm going to tell your mother you need glasses. Look, this is definite interference. How am I supposed to concentrate when this stupid cat's chewing on my toes?"

"Poor sportsmanship," Radley said soberly as Mitch's last man was obliterated.

"Poor sportsmanship! I'll show you poor sportsmanship." With that he snatched Radley up and held him upside down. "Now is this machine defective, or what?"

"No." Giggling, Radley braced his hands on the floor. "Maybe *you* need glasses."

"I'm going to have to drop you on your head. You really leave me no choice. Oh, hi, Hester." With his arm hooked around Radley's legs, he smiled at her.

"Hi, Mom!" Though his cheeks were turning pink, Radley was delighted with his upside-down position. "I beat Mitch three times. But he's not really mad."

"Says who?" Mitch flipped the boy upright, then

dropped him lightly on the bed. "I've been humiliated."

"I destroyed him," Radley said with satisfaction.

"I can't believe I slept through it." She offered them both a cautious smile. It didn't seem as though Radley was anything but delighted to find Mitch here. As for herself, she wasn't having an easy time keeping the pleasure down, either. "I suppose after three major battles you'd both like some breakfast."

"We already ate." Radley leaned over the bed to reach for the kitten. "I showed Mitch how to make French toast. He said it was real good."

"That was before you cheated."

"I did not." Radley rolled on his back and let the kitten creep up his stomach. "Mitch washed the pan, and I dried it. We were going to fix you some, but you just kept on sleeping."

The idea of the two men in her life fiddling in the kitchen while she slept left her flustered. "I guess I didn't expect anyone to be up so early."

"Hester." Mitch stepped closer to swing an arm over her shoulders. "I hate to break this to you, but it's after eleven."

"Eleven?"

"Yeah. How about lunch?"

"Well, I…"

"You think about it. I guess I should go down and take care of Taz."

"I'll do it." Radley was up and bouncing. "I can give him his food and take him for a walk and everything. I know how, you showed me."

"It's okay with me. Hester?"

She was having trouble just keeping up. "All right. But you'll have to bundle up."

"I will." He was already reaching for his coat. "Can I bring Taz back with me? He hasn't met Zark yet."

Hester glanced at the tiny ball of fur, thinking of Taz's big white teeth. "I don't know if Taz would care for Zark."

"He loves cats," Mitch assured her as he picked up Radley's ski cap off the floor. "In a purely noncannibalistic way." He reached in his pocket for his keys.

"Be careful," she called as Radley rushed by, jingling Mitch's keys. The front door slammed with a vengeance.

"Good morning," Mitch said, and turned her into his arms.

"Good morning. You could have woken me up."

"It was tempting." He ran his hands up the back of her robe. "Actually, I was going to make some coffee and bring you in a cup. Then Radley came in. Before I knew it, I was up to my wrists in egg batter."

"He, ah, didn't wonder what you were doing here?"

"No." Knowing exactly how her mind was working, he kissed the tip of her nose. Then, shifting her to his side, he began to walk with her to the kitchen. "He came in while I was boiling water and asked if I was fixing breakfast. After a brief consultation, we decided he was the better qualified of the two. There's some coffee left, but I think you'd be better off pouring it out and starting again."

"I'm sure it's fine."

"I love an optimist."

She almost managed a smile as she reached in the refrigerator for the milk. "I thought you'd gone."

"Would you rather I had?"

She shook her head but didn't look at him. "Mitch, it's so hard. It just keeps getting harder."

"What does?"

"Trying not to want you here like this all the time."

"Say the word and I'll move in, bag and dog."

"I wish I could. I really wish I could. Mitch, when I walked into Rad's bedroom this morning and saw the two of you together, something just clicked. I stood there thinking this is the way it could be for us."

"That's the way it *will* be for us, Hester."

"You're so sure." With a small laugh, she turned to lean her palms on the counter. "You're so absolutely sure, and have been almost from the beginning. Maybe that's one of the things that frightens me."

"A light went on for me when I saw you, Hester." He came closer to put his hands on her shoulders. "I haven't gone through my life knowing exactly what I wanted, and I can't claim that everything always goes the way I'd planned, but with you I'm sure." He pressed his lips to her hair. "Do you love me, Hester?"

"Yes." With a long sigh, she shut her eyes. "Yes, I love you."

"Then marry me." Gently he turned her around to face him. "I won't ask you to change anything but your name."

She wanted to believe him, to believe it was possible to start a new life just once more. Her heart was thudding hard against her ribs as she wrapped her arms around him. *Take the chance,* it seemed to be telling her. *Don't throw love away.* Her fingers tensed against him. "Mitch, I—" When the phone rang, Hester let out a pent-up breath. "I'm sorry."

"So am I," he muttered, but released her.

Her legs were still unsteady as she picked up the receiver to the wall phone. "Hello." The giddiness fled, and with it all the blossoming pleasure. "Allan."

Mitch looked around quickly. Her eyes were as flat as her voice. She'd already twisted the phone cord around her hand as if she wanted to anchor herself. "Fine," she said. "We're both fine. Florida? I thought you were in San Diego."

So he'd moved again, Hester thought as she listened to the familiar voice, restless as ever. She listened with the cold patience of experience as he told her how wonderful, how terrific, how incredibly he was doing.

"Rad isn't here at the moment," she told him, though Allan hadn't asked. "If you want to wish him a happy birthday, I can have him call you back." There was a pause, and Mitch saw her eyes change and the anger come. "Yesterday." She set her teeth, then took a long breath through them. "He's ten, Allan. Radley was ten yesterday. Yes, I'm sure it's difficult for you to imagine."

She fell silent again, listening. The dull anger lodged itself in her throat, and when she spoke again, her voice was hollow. "Congratulations. Hard feelings?" She didn't care for the sound of her own laugh. "No, Allan, there are no feelings whatsoever. All right, then, good luck. I'm sorry, that's as enthusiastic as it gets. I'll tell Radley you called."

She hung up, careful to bolt down the need to slam down the receiver. Slowly she unwound the cord which was biting into her hand.

"You okay?"

She nodded and walked to the stove to pour coffee she didn't want. "He called to tell me he's getting married again. He thought I'd be interested."

"Does it matter?"

"No." She sipped it black and welcomed the bitterness. "What he does stopped mattering years ago. He didn't know it was Radley's birthday." The anger came bubbling to the surface no matter how hard she tried to keep it submerged. "He didn't even know how old he was." She slammed the cup down so that coffee sloshed over the sides. "Radley stopped being real for him the minute he walked out the door. All he had to do was shut it behind him."

"What difference does it make now?"

"He's Radley's father."

"No." His own anger sprang out. "That's something you've got to work out of your system, something you've got to start accepting. The only part he played in Rad's life was biological. There's no trick to that, and no automatic bond of loyalty comes with it."

"He has a responsibility."

"He doesn't want it, Hester." Struggling for patience, he took her hands. "He's cut himself off from Rad completely. No one's going to call that admirable, and it's obvious it wasn't done for the boy's sake. But would you rather have him strolling in and out of Radley's life at his own whim, leaving the kid confused and hurting?"

"No, but I—"

"You want him to care, and he doesn't care." Though her hands remained in his, he felt the change. "You're pulling back from me."

It was true. She could regret it, but she couldn't stop it. "I don't want to."

"But you are." This time, it was he who pulled away. "It only took a phone call."

"Mitch, please try to understand."

"I've been trying to understand." There was an edge to his voice now that she hadn't heard before. "The man left you, and it hurt, but it's been over a long time."

"It's not the hurt," she began, then dragged a hand

through her hair. "Or maybe it is, partly. I don't want to go through that ever again, the fear, the emptiness. I loved him. You have to understand that maybe I was young, maybe I was stupid, but I loved him."

"I've always understood that," he said, though he didn't like to hear it. "A woman like you doesn't make promises lightly."

"No, when I make them I mean to keep them. I wanted to keep this one." She picked up the coffee again, wrapping both hands around the cup to keep them warm. "I can't tell you how badly I wanted to keep my marriage together, how hard I tried. I gave up part of myself when I married Allan. He told me we were going to move to New York, we were going to do things in a big way, and I went. Leaving my home, my family and friends was the most terrifying thing I'd ever done, but I went because he wanted it. Almost everything I did during our marriage I did because he wanted it. And because it was easier to go along than to refuse. I built my life around his. Then, at the age of twenty, I discovered I didn't have a life at all."

"So you made one, for yourself and for Radley. That's something to be proud of."

"I am. It's taken me eight years, eight years to feel I'm really on solid ground again. Now there's you."

"Now there's me," he said slowly, watching her. "And you just can't get past the idea that I'll pull the rug out from under you again."

"I don't want to be that woman again." She said the words desperately, searching for the answers even as she struggled to give them to him. "A woman who focuses all her needs and goals around someone else. If I found myself alone this time, I'm not sure I could stand up again."

"Listen to yourself. You'd rather be alone now than risk the fact that things might not work out for the next fifty years? Take a good look at me, Hester, I'm not Allan Wallace. I'm not asking you to bury yourself to make me happy. It's the woman you are today who I love, the woman you are today who I want to spend my life with."

"People change, Mitch."

"And they can change together." He drew a deep breath. "Or they can change separately. Why don't you let me know when you make up your mind what you want to do?"

She opened her mouth, then closed it again when he walked away. She didn't have the right to call him back.

He shouldn't complain, Mitch thought as he sat at his new keyboard and toyed with the next scene in his script. The work was going better than he'd expected—and faster. It was becoming easy for him to bury himself in Zark's problems and let his own stew.

At this point, Zark was waiting by Leilah's bedside, praying that she would survive the freak accident that had left her beauty intact but her brain damaged. Of course, when she awoke she would be a stranger. His wife of two years would become his greatest enemy, her mind as brilliant as ever but warped and evil. All his plans and dreams would be shattered forever. Whole galaxies would be in peril.

"You think you've got problems?" Mitch muttered. "Things aren't exactly bouncing along for me, either."

Eyes narrowed, he studied the screen. The atmosphere was good, he thought as he tipped back. Mitch didn't have any problem imagining a twenty-third-century hospital room. He didn't have any trouble imagining Zark's distress or the madness brewing in Leilah's unconscious brain. What he did have trouble imagining was his life without Hester.

"Stupid." The dog at his feet yawned in agreement. "What I should do is go down to that damn bank and drag her out. She'd love that, wouldn't she?" he said with a laugh as he pushed away from the machine and stretched. "I could beg." Mitch rolled that around in his mind and found it uncomfortable. "I could, but we'd probably both be sorry. There's not much left after reasoning, and I've tried that. What would Zark do?"

Mitch rocked back on his heels and closed his eyes. Would Zark, hero and saint, back off? Would Zark, defender of right and justice, bow out gracefully? Nope, Mitch decided. When it came to love, Zark was a patsy. Leilah kept kicking astrodust in his face, but he was still determined to win her back.

At least Hester hadn't tried to poison him with nerve gas. Leilah had pulled that and more, but Zark was still nuts about her.

Mitch studied the poster of Zark he'd tacked to the wall for inspiration. We're in the same boat, buddy, but I'm not going to pull out the oars and start rowing, either. And Hester's going to find herself in some turbulent waters.

He glanced at the clock on his desk, but remembered it had stopped two days before. He was pretty sure he'd sent his watch to the laundry along with his socks. Because he wanted to see how much time he had before Hester was due home, he walked into the living room. There, on the table, was an old mantel clock that Mitch was fond enough of to remember to wind. Just as he glanced at it, he heard Radley at the door.

"Right on time," Mitch said when he swung the door open. "How cold is it?" He grazed his knuckles down Radley's cheek in a routine they'd developed. "Forty-three degrees."

"It's sunny," Radley said, dragging off his backpack.

"Shooting for the park, are you?" Mitch waited until Radley had folded his coat neatly over the arm of the sofa. "Maybe I can handle it after I fortify myself. Mrs. Jablanski next door made cookies. She feels sorry for me because no one's fixing me hot meals, so I copped a dozen."

"What kind?"

"Peanut butter."

"All right!" Radley was already streaking into the kitchen. He liked the ebony wood and smoked glass table Mitch had set by the wall. Mostly because Mitch didn't mind if the glass got smeared with fingerprints. He settled down, content with milk and cookies and Mitch's company. "We have to do a dumb state project," he said with his mouth full. "I got Rhode Island. It's the smallest state. I wanted Texas."

"Rhode Island." Mitch smiled and munched on a cookie. "Is that so bad?"

"Nobody cares about Rhode Island. I mean, they've got the Alamo and stuff in Texas."

"Well, maybe I can give you a hand with it. I was born there."

"In Rhode Island? Honest?" The tiny state took on a new interest.

"Yeah. How long do you have?"

"Six weeks," Radley said with a shrug as he reached for another cookie. "We've got to do illustrations, which is okay, but we've got to do junk like manufacturing and natural resources, too. How come you moved away?"

He started to make some easy remark, then decided to honor Hester's code of honesty. "I didn't get along with my parents very well. We're better friends now."

"Sometimes people go away and don't come back."

The boy spoke so matter-of-factly that Mitch found himself responding the same way. "I know."

"I used to worry that Mom would go away. She didn't."

"She loves you." Mitch ran a hand along the boy's hair.

"Are you going to marry her?"

Mitch paused in midstroke. "Well, I…" Just how did he handle this one? "I guess I've been thinking about it." Feeling ridiculously nervous, he rose to heat up his coffee. "Actually, I've been thinking about it a lot. How would you feel if I did?"

"Would you live with us all the time?"

"That's the idea." He poured the coffee, then sat down beside Radley again. "Would that bother you?"

Radley looked at him with dark and suddenly inscrutable eyes. "One of my friends' moms got married again. Kevin says since they did his stepfather isn't his friend anymore."

"Do you think if I married your mom I'd stop being your friend?" He caught Radley's chin in his hand. "I'm not your friend because of your mom, but because of you. I can promise that won't change when I'm your stepfather."

"You wouldn't be my stepfather. I don't want one of those." Radley's chin trembled in Mitch's hand. "I want a real one. Real ones don't go away."

Mitch slipped his hands under Radley's arms and

lifted him onto his lap. "You're right. Real ones don't."
Out of the mouth of babes, he thought, and nuzzled
Radley against him. "You know, I haven't had much
practice being a father. Are you going to get mad at me
if I mess up once in a while?"

Radley shook his head and burrowed closer. "Can
we tell Mom?"

Mitch managed a laugh. "Yeah, good idea. Get
your coat, Sergeant, we're going on a very important
mission."

Hester was up to her elbows in numbers. For some
reason, she was having a great deal of trouble adding
two and two. It didn't seem terribly important anymore.
That, she knew, was a sure sign of trouble. She went
through files, calculated and assessed, then closed them
again with no feeling at all.

His fault, she told herself. It was Mitch's fault that
she was only going through the motions, and thinking
about going through the same motions day after day for
the next twenty years. He'd made her question herself.
He'd made her deal with the pain and anger she'd tried
to bury. He'd made her want what she'd once sworn
never to want again.

And now what? She propped her elbows on the stack
of files and stared into space. She was in love, more
deeply and more richly in love than she'd ever been
before. The man she was in love with was exciting, kind
and committed, and he was offering her a new beginning.

That was what she was afraid of, Hester admitted.
That was what she kept heading away from. She hadn't
fully understood before that she had blamed herself, not
Allan, all these years. She had looked on the breakup

of her marriage as a personal mistake, a private failure. Rather than risk another failure, she was turning away her first true hope.

She said it was because of Radley, but that was only partly true. Just as the divorce had been a private failure, making a full commitment to Mitch had been a private fear.

He'd been right, she told herself. He'd been right about so many things all along. She wasn't the same woman who had loved and married Allan Wallace. She wasn't even the same woman who had struggled for a handhold when she'd found herself alone with a small child.

When was she going to stop punishing herself? Now, Hester decided, picking up the phone. Right now. Her hand was steady as she dialed Mitch's number, but her heart wasn't. She caught her bottom lip between her teeth and listened to the phone ring—and ring.

"Oh, Mitch, won't we ever get the timing right?" She hung up the receiver and promised herself she wouldn't lose her courage. In an hour she would go home and tell him she was ready for that new beginning.

At Kay's buzz, Hester picked up the receiver again. "Yes, Kay."

"Mrs. Wallace, there's someone here to see you about a loan."

With a frown, Hester checked her calendar. "I don't have anything scheduled."

"I thought you could fit him in."

"All right, but buzz me in twenty minutes. I've got to clear some things up before I leave."

"Yes, ma'am."

Hester tidied her desk and was preparing to rise when

Mitch walked in. "Mitch? I was just... What are you doing here? Rad?"

"He's waiting with Taz in the lobby."

"Kay said I had someone waiting to see me."

"That's me." He stepped up to the desk and set down a briefcase.

She started to reach for his hand, but his face seemed so set. "Mitch, you didn't have to say you'd come to apply for a loan."

"That's just what I'm doing."

She smiled and settled back. "Don't be silly."

"Mrs. Wallace, you *are* the loan officer at this bank?"

"Mitch, really, this isn't necessary."

"I'd hate to tell Rosen you sent me to a competitor." He flipped open the briefcase. "I've brought the financial information usual in these cases. I assume you have the necessary forms for a mortgage application?"

"Of course, but—"

"Then why don't you get one out?"

"All right, then." If he wanted to play games, she'd oblige him. "So you're interested in securing a mortgage. Are you purchasing the property for investment purposes, for rental or for a business?"

"No, it's purely personal."

"I see. Do you have a contract of sale?"

"Right here." It pleased him to see her mouth drop open.

Taking the papers from him, Hester studied them. "This is real."

"Of course it's real. I put a bid on the place a couple of weeks ago." He scratched at his chin as if thinking back. "Let's see, that would have been the day I had to forgo pot roast. You haven't offered it again."

"You bought a house?" She scanned the papers again. "In Connecticut?"

"They accepted my offer. The papers just came through. I believe the bank will want to get its own appraisal. There is a fee for that, isn't there?"

"What? Oh, yes, I'll fill out the papers."

"Fine. In the meantime, I do have some snapshots and a blueprint." He slipped them out of the briefcase and placed them on her desk. "You might want to look them over."

"I don't understand."

"You might begin to if you look at the pictures."

She lifted them and stared at her fantasy house. It was big and sprawling, with porches all around and tall, wide windows. Snow mantled the evergreens beside the steps and lay stark and white on the roof.

"There are a couple of outbuildings you can't see. A barn, a henhouse—both unoccupied at the moment. The lot is about five acres, with woods and a stream. The real estate agent claims the fishing's good. The roof needs some work and the gutters have to be replaced, and inside it could use some paint or paper and a little help with the plumbing. But it's sound." He watched her as he spoke. She didn't look up at him, but continued to stare, mesmerized by the snapshots. "The house has been standing for a hundred and fifty years. I figure it'll hold up a while longer."

"It's lovely." Tears pricked the back of her eyes, but she blinked them away. "Really lovely."

"Is that from the bank's point of view?"

She shook her head. He wasn't going to make it easy. And he shouldn't, she admitted to herself. She'd already made it difficult enough for both of them. "I didn't know you were thinking of relocating. What about your work?"

"I can set up my drawing board in Connecticut just as easily as I can here. It's a reasonable commute, and I don't exactly spend a lot of time in the office."

"That's true." She picked up a pen, but rather than writing down the necessary information only ran it through her fingers.

"I'm told there's a bank in town. Nothing along the lines of National Trust, but a small independent bank. Seems to me someone with experience could get a good position there."

"I've always preferred small banks." There was a lump in her throat that had to be swallowed. "Small towns."

"They've got a couple of good schools. The elementary school is next to a farm. I'm told sometimes the cows get over the fence and into the playground."

"Looks like you've covered everything."

"I think so."

She stared down at the pictures, wondering how he could have found what she'd always wanted and how she could have been lucky enough that he would have cared. "Are you doing this for me?"

"No." He waited until she looked at him. "I'm doing it for us."

Her eyes filled again. "I don't deserve you."

"I know." Then he took both her hands and lifted her to her feet. "So you'd be pretty stupid to turn down such a good deal."

"I'd hate to think I was stupid." She drew her hands away to come around the desk to him. "I need to tell you something, but I'd like you to kiss me first."

"Is that the way you get loans around here?" Taking

her by the lapels, he dragged her against him. "I'm going to have to report you, Mrs. Wallace. Later."

He closed his mouth over hers and felt the give, the strength and the acceptance. With a quiet sound of pleasure, he slipped his hands up to her face and felt the slow, lovely curve of her lips as she smiled.

"Does this mean I get the loan?"

"We'll talk business in a minute." She held on just a little longer, then drew away. "Before you came in, I'd been sitting here. Actually, I'd been sitting here for the last couple of days, not getting anything done because I was thinking of you."

"Go on, I think I'm going to like this story."

"When I wasn't thinking about you, I was thinking about myself and the last dozen years of my life I've put a lot of energy into *not* thinking about it, so it wasn't easy."

She kept his hand in hers, but took another step away. "I realize that what happened to me and Allan was destined to happen. If I'd been smarter, or stronger, I would have been able to admit a long time ago that what we had could only be temporary. Maybe if he hadn't left the way he did..." She trailed off, shaking her head. "It doesn't matter now. That's the point I had to come to, that it just doesn't matter. Mitch, I don't want to live the rest of my life wondering if you and I could have made it work. I'd rather spend the rest of my life *trying* to make it work. Before you came in today with all of this, I'd decided to ask you if you still wanted to marry me."

"The answer to that is yes, with a couple of stipulations."

She'd already started to move into his arms, but drew back. "Stipulations?"

"Yeah, you're a banker, you know about stipulations, right?"

"Yes, but I don't look at this as a transaction."

"You better hear me out, because it's a big one." He ran his hands up her arms, then dropped them to his side. "I want to be Rad's father."

"If we were married, you would be."

"I believe stepfather's the term used in that case. Rad and I agreed we didn't go for it."

"Agreed?" She spoke carefully, on guard again. "You discussed this with Rad?"

"Yeah, I discussed it with Rad. He brought it up, but I'd have wanted to talk to him, anyway. He asked me this afternoon if I was going to marry you. Did you want me to lie to him?"

"No." She paused a moment, then shook her head. "No, of course not. What did he say?"

"Basically he wanted to know if I'd still be his friend, because he'd heard sometimes stepfathers change a bit once their foot's in the door. Once we'd gotten past that hurdle, he told me he didn't want me as a stepfather."

"Oh, Mitch." She sank down on the edge of the desk.

"He wants a real father, Hester, because real fathers don't go away." Her eyes darkened very slowly before she closed them.

"I see."

"The way I look at it, you've got another decision to make. Are you going to let me adopt him?" Her eyes shot open again with quick surprise. "You've decided to share yourself. I want to know if you're going to share Rad, all the way. I don't see a problem with me being his father emotionally. I just want you to know that I want it legally. I don't think there'd be a problem with your ex-husband."

"No, I'm sure there wouldn't be."

"And I don't think there'd be a problem with Rad. So is there a problem with you?"

Hester rose from the desk to pace a few steps away. "I don't know what to say to you. I can't come up with the right words."

"Pick some."

She turned back with a deep breath. "I guess the best I can come up with is that Radley's going to have a terrific father, in every way. And I love you very, very much."

"Those'll do." He caught her to him with relief. "Those'll do just fine." Then he was kissing her again, fast and desperate. With her arms around him, she laughed. "Does this mean you're going to approve the loan?"

"I'm sorry, I have to turn you down."

"What?"

"I would, however, approve a joint application from you and your wife." She caught his face in her hands. "Our house, our commitment."

"Those are terms I can live with—" he touched her lips with his "—for the next hundred years or so." He swung her around in one quick circle. "Let's go tell Rad." With their hands linked, they started out. "Say, Hester, how do you feel about honeymooning in Disneyland?"

She laughed and walked through the door with him. "I'd love it. I'd absolutely love it."

* * * * *

You are cordially invited to experience…

The WEDDING
of the Century
& other stories

Three critically acclaimed authors deliver
three tantalizing tales of dreams come true!

The Wedding of the Century by MARY JO PUTNEY

Sarah Vangelder wanted more for herself than to be sold into
marriage for the price of a dukedom. But marriage to Justin Aubrey
might be the adventure she's always dreamed of….

Jesse's Wife by KRISTIN JAMES

When a late-night walk destroys her reputation, Amy McCallister
finds herself married off to Jesse, a sinfully handsome farmhand. But
can he convince her to give him her heart?

Seduced by Starlight by CHARLOTTE FEATHERSTONE

Notorious rake Jase Markham has loved his brother's fiancée for as
long as he can remember. When his brother casts Blossom aside, Jase
resolves to make her his—but will she overlook his reputation?

Pick up your copy today!

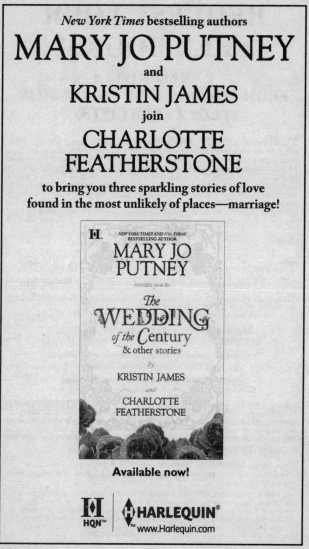

REQUEST YOUR FREE BOOKS!

2 FREE NOVELS
FROM THE ROMANCE COLLECTION
PLUS 2 FREE GIFTS!

YES! Please send me 2 FREE novels from the Romance Collection and my 2 FREE gifts (gifts are worth about $10). After receiving them, if I don't wish to receive any more books, I can return the shipping statement marked "cancel." If I don't cancel, I will receive 4 brand-new novels every month and be billed just $5.74 per book in the U.S. or $6.24 per book in Canada. That's a saving of at least 28% off the cover price. It's quite a bargain! Shipping and handling is just 50¢ per book in the U.S. and 75¢ per book in Canada.* I understand that accepting the 2 free books and gifts places me under no obligation to buy anything. I can always return a shipment and cancel at any time. Even if I never buy another book, the two free books and gifts are mine to keep forever.

194/394 MDN FDC5

Name	(PLEASE PRINT)

Address		Apt. #

City	State/Prov.	Zip/Postal Code

Signature (if under 18, a parent or guardian must sign)

Mail to the **Reader Service:**
IN U.S.A.: P.O. Box 1867, Buffalo, NY 14240-1867
IN CANADA: P.O. Box 609, Fort Erie, Ontario L2A 5X3

Not valid for current subscribers to the Romance Collection or the Romance/Suspense Collection.

Want to try two free books from another line?
Call 1-800-873-8635 or visit www.ReaderService.com.

* Terms and prices subject to change without notice. Prices do not include applicable taxes. Sales tax applicable in N.Y. Canadian residents will be charged applicable taxes. Offer not valid in Quebec. This offer is limited to one order per household. All orders subject to credit approval. Credit or debit balances in a customer's account(s) may be offset by any other outstanding balance owed by or to the customer. Please allow 4 to 6 weeks for delivery. Offer available while quantities last.

Your Privacy—The Reader Service is committed to protecting your privacy. Our Privacy Policy is available online at www.ReaderService.com or upon request from the Reader Service.

We make a portion of our mailing list available to reputable third parties that offer products we believe may interest you. If you prefer that we not exchange your name with third parties, or if you wish to clarify or modify your communication preferences, please visit us at www.ReaderService.com/consumerchoice or write to us at Reader Service Preference Service, P.O. Box 9062, Buffalo, NY 14269. Include your complete name and address.

MROM11

NORA ROBERTS

28594	O'HURLEY'S RETURN	___ $7.99 U.S.	___ $9.99 CAN.
28592	O'HURLEY BORN	___ $7.99 U.S.	___ $9.99 CAN.
28590	SWEET RAINS	___ $7.99 U.S.	___ $9.99 CAN.
28588	NIGHT TALES: NIGHT SHIELD & NIGHT MOVES	___ $7.99 U.S.	___ $9.99 CAN.
28587	NIGHT TALES: NIGHTSHADE & NIGHT SMOKE	___ $7.99 U.S.	___ $9.99 CAN.
28586	NIGHT TALES: NIGHT SHIFT & NIGHT SHADOW	___ $7.99 U.S.	___ $9.99 CAN.
28583	WORTH THE RISK	___ $7.99 U.S.	___ $9.99 CAN.
28595	WINDFALL	___ $7.99 U.S.	___ $8.99 CAN.
28580	THE MacKADE BROTHERS: DEVIN AND SHANE	___ $7.99 U.S.	___ $8.99 CAN.
28578	THE LAW OF LOVE	___ $7.99 U.S.	___ $8.99 CAN.
28575	THE MacKADE BROTHERS: RAFE AND JARED	___ $7.99 U.S.	___ $8.99 CAN.
28574	CHARMED & ENCHANTED	___ $7.99 U.S.	___ $7.99 CAN.
28597	LOVE BY DESIGN	___ $7.99 U.S.	___ $9.99 CAN.
28569	THE MacGREGOR GROOMS	___ $7.99 U.S.	___ $7.99 CAN.
28568	WAITING FOR NICK & CONSIDERING KATE	___ $7.99 U.S.	___ $7.99 CAN.
28565	TREASURES	___ $7.99 U.S.	___ $9.50 CAN.
28134	THE MacGREGORS: ALAN & GRANT	___ $7.99 U.S.	___ $9.99 CAN.
28133	THE MacGREGORS: SERENA & CAINE	___ $7.99 U.S.	___ $9.99 CAN.

(limited quantities available)

TOTAL AMOUNT	$ _____
POSTAGE & HANDLING	$ _____
($1.00 FOR 1 BOOK, 50¢ for each additional)	
APPLICABLE TAXES*	$ _____
TOTAL PAYABLE	$ _____

(check or money order—please do not send cash)

To order, complete this form and send it, along with a check or money order for the total above, payable to Harlequin Books, to: **In the U.S.:** 3010 Walden Avenue, P.O. Box 9077, Buffalo, NY 14269-9077; **In Canada:** P.O. Box 636, Fort Erie, Ontario, L2A 5X3.

Name: _____
Address: _____ City: _____
State/Prov.: _____ Zip/Postal Code: _____
Account Number (if applicable): _____

075 CSAS

*New York residents remit applicable sales taxes.
*Canadian residents remit applicable GST and provincial taxes.

Silhouette®
Where love comes alive™

Visit Silhouette Books at www.Harlequin.com

PSNR0611BL